JUDGMENT PREY

WITHDRAWN

JUDGMENT PREY

JOHN SANDFORD

THORNDIKE PRESS
A part of Gale, a Cengage Company

LIBRARY OF CONGRESS CIP DATA ON FILE.
CATALOGUING IN PUBLICATION FOR THIS BOOK
IS AVAILABLE FROM THE LIBRARY OF CONGRESS.

ISBN-13: 979-8-88579-022-2 (hardcover alk. paper)

Published in 2023 by arrangement with G. P. Putnam's Sons, an imprint of Penguin Publishing Group, a division of Penguin Random House LLC.

Printed in the United States of America
1 2 3 4 5 6 7 27 26 25 24 23

JUDGMENT PREY

1

A sullen wedge of gunmetal-colored clouds rolled in from the west, autumn's jackboot crunching down on the Twin Cities. A cold breeze sent fallen leaves skittering along the darkened October streets as a flash of blackbirds passed above the treetops, heading south.

Alex Sand was in the side yard with his boys, Blaine and Arthur, shooting baskets under a yard light. The storm was coming fast. They could smell it, taste it, they could hear the trees bending at the wind front; the falling temperature prickled their skin.

Arthur, the younger son, rolled behind his father who was throwing a pick at Blaine, but Blaine, instead of challenging the pick, rolled the other way and met Arthur coming around, stole the ball, dribbled it once and laid it into the basket.

He rebounded his own shot, made a face at Art and called, "Hey, piggy, piggy,

piggy . . ."

Arthur, who still carried what the family called "baby fat," shouted, "Shut up, you fuck," and both boys took boxing stances, feigning an intention to duke it out right there, with bare fists.

Alex: "Hey, hey, hey . . . knock it off, both of you. If I hear that word again, Art, I will . . . tell your mother."

They all laughed at the toothless threat. Alex took the ball from his son, looked up at the darkening sky, and said, "We should get in. It's coming."

They hurried around to the front of the house, shoulders hunched against the first fat drops of cold rain, up the steps across the porch and inside.

They were trailed by the killer, who moved unseen from behind a privet hedge. The killer wore a dark hooded rain suit, glasses, a black Covid mask and thin vinyl gloves. Alex and the kids were only a dozen steps ahead as they went through the door.

The doorbell was right there, but . . . the door wasn't fully shut. The killer pushed it with a knuckle and as the door swung open, stepped inside. The gun was out and ready. With his off hand, he pushed the door closed behind him.

In the living room, Alex's back was to the

8

killer. Arthur saw the intruder, eyes widened in what might have been recognition, as the killer lifted the gun and fired two shots into Alex's back. Alex staggered and went down.

The boys tried to run, twisting, screaming, stumbling but the gun was right there, only six feet away. The killer shot Arthur first, in the hip, and the boy fell, crying out; Blaine was a step farther away, running toward the kitchen, and the killer shot him in the neck.

Alex had been hit low, and lay face-down on the Persian carpet, one hand blindly groping toward the ebony leg of the grand piano. The killer moved close, and shot him twice more in the back, through the heart. The boys were next, one shot each, the gun dangling from the killer's hand, only eight or ten inches from the boys' heads.

In the deafening silence after the murders, the killer heard the baby begin to cry in a side room used as a day nursery. He went that way. The baby looked up from her bassinet, little blue eyes hazy, lips stretched open and wide, the better to scream, as the killer hovered over her. . . .

A nightmare.

Like another one, on the very same day, full of the thunder of guns and the scent of blood on the ground.

Lucas Davenport crashed through a hedge and fired two off-balance shots at a fleeing killer who was too far away for his shotgun. The killer stopped, turned, and fired a long fully automatic burst back at him and Lucas was not too far away for an AR-15.

A bullet hit Lucas's right arm like a blow from a baseball bat and he windmilled the arm backwards as he went down. He screamed, "I'm down, I'm hit." He struggled to get back up, but his right arm hung uselessly. Pushing up with his left, he put the butt of the shotgun on the snow and used his good hand to jack a shell into the chamber.

Virgil Flowers ran up and shouted, "How bad?" and Lucas shouted back, "Go get him . . ." Again on his feet, his right arm flopping at his side, Lucas went after the killer, following Virgil, heard Virgil's shotgun booming in the night, and he kept going, shouted, "Virgil! Coming up behind!"

Virgil shouted something at him and Lucas saw Virgil was bleeding from a head wound, but they both went on, encountered an FBI agent hovering over a wounded agent, kept going.

Virgil was dragging one leg. Lucas realized that he'd been hit there, too, and they went on and then the killer turned again and unloaded another full magazine at them and Lucas got hit in the chest and leg and went down again, and this time, he didn't try to get back up.

He heard more shooting, Virgil's shotgun once, twice, and he thought, *Got him,* and then blacked out for a moment, came back, looking up at the bare branches of an overhanging maple tree, and the pain came.

The pain came like an ocean wave and dimmed his sight. He groaned, once, and sputtered, and it occurred to him that he might be dying. There was a scuffling nearby, and he turned his head, and saw Virgil crawling across the thin, hard-crusted snow.

He said, he thought, "Help me," as Virgil's face loomed, close, inches above his eyes, and he saw that Virgil was bleeding heavily from the head wound, the blood rolling down his face and into his eyes.

Virgil's face hovered and he asked again, "How bad?"

"I dunno . . ." And . . . blackout.

An *actual* nightmare.

When Lucas opened his eyes, he was almost pain-free, though there was an ache in his right shoulder. He was lying on his

11

own bed, in St. Paul. He was warm, safe.

Sweating. He could feel the sweat on his forehead and cheekbones without touching it. He groaned, "Jesus Christ."

He'd never quite pooh-poohed the idea of post-traumatic stress disorder and the flashbacks that came with it, but somewhere in the back of his hockey defenseman brain, he really thought PTSD mostly applied to guys who weren't quite tough enough.

He no longer thought that.

He lay in bed for a while, angry at himself for the flashback. He should, he believed, be able to get past them, if only he had the willpower. He also knew he was wrong about that, but couldn't help believing it anyway.

His wife, Weather Karkinnen, a plastic and reconstructive surgeon, had gone to work before dawn, as she usually did, leaving behind a stack of pillows that smelled lightly of her overnight lotion, a floral scent, maybe wild roses.

He sighed, rolled over, winced as his weight pressed on his injured shoulder, patted Weather's pillow for reassurance that everything was okay. With his feet on the floor, he sat checking for chest pain — almost gone, unless he put pressure on his rib cage — and leg pain. A series of X-rays the previous month confirmed that the leg bone had healed, with a slight deformity that the docs said wasn't important. Lucas wasn't sure he agreed: it still hurt when he jogged.

In the bathroom, he showered, shaved, and inspected himself in the mirror. He was a tall, square-shouldered man, two inches over six feet, with crystalline blue eyes and dark hair now threaded with gray. The gray was gaining but was not yet dominant.

He could see a fresh puckered scar from a bullet wound outside his right nipple, and another bullet scar in the muscle of his right arm, and a pink, six-inch-long surgical scar up the ball of his right shoulder. He had exit wounds on the back of his arm and on his right shoulder blade, another two bullet scars and a surgical scar on his lower right leg, but couldn't see those, only feel them.

He looked too thin. Lucas had two basic body styles: the square, two-hundred-pound light heavyweight boxer style, and the thinner, hundred-and-ninety-pound iron-man style. Usually, when he looked thin, he also looked tough, leathery, because he was training hard. Nothing like a fast, hard five miles before breakfast, his thinner self believed.

Now, at a hundred and eighty-five pounds, he looked too thin, and yet, puffy. Too much time on a couch, watching CNN or clicking through the streaming videos, eating Wheat Thins. He enjoyed working out, running hard, sweating hard, and had, all of his life. He hadn't been able to do either for almost nine months. In late July, with approval from the docs, he'd joined a local gym, started doing some lifting and treadmill work.

It helped, and it hurt.

This morning, after he'd cleaned up, he dressed in jeans, a University of Minnesota sweatshirt, and cross-training shoes. He ate a bowl of microwave oatmeal with a shot of whey protein, spent an hour reading five online newspapers and checking his stock portfolio on Morningstar. When he finished the last of the papers, he went for a walk to a Target store, as much for human contact as for the shopping. He carried an old-fashioned wooden-crook cane that he'd bought at a drugstore, just in case.

A deputy U.S. Marshal, Lucas had been shot the previous winter, during a chase through a fashionable suburb on Long Island. He couldn't believe his luck — both the good and the bad.

The shooter had been using solid core military ammunition, probably because his target would be standing behind triple-pane glass, and he'd worried that the instant expansion of hunting or defensive ammunition might deflect after the initial impact on the windows. Whether he was right or wrong about that, he'd efficiently killed the man standing behind the glass.

In the subsequent chase, he'd shot Lucas three times, using an AR-15 equipped with a bump stock, which effectively made it into a fully automatic weapon — a machine gun.

The first shot had hit Lucas's right arm and gone cleanly through, knocking him down in the process. The docs at the Long Island hospital had told him that when he was hit, he'd probably windmilled his arm backwards to break the fall and protect his head, and the impact with the frozen ground, not the bullet itself, had caused the bone to snap below his shoulder. That break was fixed in an operation that fitted a titanium collar around the bone, the collar held in place with eleven titanium screws.

So, three bullet wounds and a broken arm. Bad luck that he'd been shot at all; good luck that the slugs were solid, and the wounds hadn't been more serious. If he'd been hit with expanding hunting or defensive rounds, he most likely would have been killed or crippled.

Bad luck again that all three wounds were on the same side of his body. He hadn't been able to comfortably use crutches on that side, where he most needed the support, and he'd spent three weeks in a wheelchair.

The shooter himself was dead, having been shot by both Lucas and by Lucas's partner, Virgil Flowers. Virgil had been shot as well, hit in the thigh, but hadn't been hurt as badly as Lucas.

Good luck again, for them, anyway.

The shooter had killed a right-wing radio talk-show host, and two FBI agents. He'd wounded a third agent, a woman who'd been hit in the stomach, and who'd retired with a permanent disability. That's what a machine gun will do, when you don't know it's coming, and you get too close. Lucas and Virgil had gotten off easy, compared to the others.

Now, in early October, Lucas still hurt, especially at night. He'd had three months of physical therapy following the shooting, but didn't yet have full range of motion in his right arm, and he'd lost muscle from lack of exercise. The broken arm bone itself was largely healed, though he had continuous, nagging shoulder pain where the surgeons had cut through muscle to fix the bone. He'd played senior hockey for years, but now he couldn't skate, he had no slap shot.

He had additional significant pain in his upper right rib cage, especially when he lay down and his rib cage flexed. In the days after the gunfight, it had hurt simply to breathe; his breathing was now mostly pain-free, but sleeping wasn't, nor was anything but the most careful sex.

His lower leg was healed, but still complained when he tried to jog more than a few blocks. He was pushing that, both on the gym's treadmills and on the street.

Because he couldn't help himself.

Almost as troubling as the pain was the depression that came with the long recovery and confinement. At night, slipping in and out of a restless sleep, he would dream — or sometimes, he thought, simply remember — Virgil looking down at him as he lay on the ground, not knowing if he was dying.

Virgil's head wound, and blood-covered face, was the result of a slug that had hit a tree branch a half-inch above his head, blowing splinters into his scalp. The wound had bled like crazy but turned out to be not serious, although, Virgil told him, it had itched ferociously for two months. Lucas didn't know at the time that the wound wasn't serious, and he didn't know it in his flashbacks or dreams, either, and reexperienced the fear that Virgil had been shot in the head.

At the Target store, he browsed grooming supplies, lotions, and disposable razors. When he returned home, he popped a Vicodin and hobbled back to the TV room, where he dropped onto the couch, put his legs up on an ottoman — Weather refused to allow a La-Z-Boy in the house — and called up the streaming series called *Justified.* The main character was a deputy U.S. Marshal named Raylan Givens, who was apparently in the process of shooting everybody.

More interesting, for Lucas, was that he was close to an actual deputy U.S. Marshal named Rae Givens, though she'd never be mistaken for Raylan, as she was taller, black, and female. Lucas shared his interest in the streaming series with his adoptive daughter, Letty, who worked with the Department of Homeland Security as an investigator. They were texting daily, both appreciations and criticisms. He was still on the couch, watching a third consecutive episode, when Weather called.

"I've got a problem," she said.

Like this:

As Lucas was sinking into the couch, a six-year-old first-grader at St. Paul's Friedrich Nietzsche Elementary School had fibbed about his urgent need to visit the boys' room. Although his newly minted teacher had suspected that he was plotting to get out of the phonics lesson, she'd been so harried that she let him go with a stern warning to return as soon as he'd completed his mission.

He'd taken his time getting down the hall, taken his time using the low-hung urinal, carefully zipped up afterward — he'd already experienced the male affliction of an overly hasty zip-up — and on the way back to his classroom, poked his head into the open door of the teachers' prep room. There was a lot of interesting stuff in the prep room, including, unfortunately, a fascinating guillotine-style paper cutter.

That morning, Weather had done a rhinoplasty, which she would not allow Lucas to call a "nose job." From her office window at the University of Minnesota Hospitals,

19

she'd seen the hints of the incoming storm, not dangerous billowing orange clouds, like a summer thunderstorm, that might be hiding a tornado, but dark and murky, the arrival of autumn, several weeks late.

After lunch she'd harvested skin from a man's thigh and moved it to his forearm, to cover up the excision of cancer tissue that had been taken out earlier.

The skin graft was the last op on her schedule. That done, she'd changed out of her scrubs, into street dress, and returned to her office. Her assistant, Alice, was in her cubicle, on the phone to a prospective patient, while Weather met with a friend, an associate professor of history, about the pros and cons of breast-reduction surgery.

They'd gotten to the question of whether the professor's husband's desires were relevant, when a plastic surgery resident knocked twice, hard, on the office door then burst in without waiting to be invited.

"We got a good one," he crowed, excited, his voice like a truck horn, urgent, hoarse, too loud. "Elementary school kid chopped off three fingers of his dominant hand with a paper cutter. A teacher's aide picked up the fingers and iced them. Happened a half hour ago. They're on the way. Bulthorpe told me to get you. He's putting together a

20

team, whoever he can find. I'm on it."

Weather said, "Oh, shit," and to the associate professor, "We'll continue this later, Marie, but my bottom line is, you wouldn't regret it."

The prof said, "Go! Go!"

Weather went. Not to her first rodeo. On the way to the OR, she called Lucas, to tell him that she wouldn't be home for dinner, and probably not until after midnight.

As she talked, she could hear the television in the background: More *Justified.* She told him what she knew about the incoming emergency, as briefly as she could. She added: "How bad are you?"

"Not bad," Lucas said.

"On a one-to-ten scale?"

"Nagging. Maybe a two. I'm going to push it a little," he said.

"Not too much. Don't hurt yourself," Weather warned.

"Yeah, yeah, yeah. Go take care of the kid."

"You know where the Vicodin is." And she was gone, dropping down a stairwell to the women's locker room.

The kid arrived on a gurney, conscious and hurting, his father racing into the hospital a few minutes behind him, his mother five minutes behind her husband.

21

Nurses and orderlies moved the kid into the OR as the suits took care of the paperwork, and Weather, another plastic surgeon named Senat Morat, and two residents scrubbed up. Morat was very good, but Weather was the queen of the OR.

Over the next nine hours, the two surgeons, with assistance from the residents, an anesthesiologist and an anesthetist, two surgical techs, and three nurses, put the fingers back on. They first removed smashed tissue that couldn't be saved, trimmed the bones as little as possible, located and spliced tiny arteries and veins to get blood in and out, and rejoined nerves to make the fingers work.

The kid had been given a general anesthetic, knew nothing after he'd been wheeled into the OR, in pain, in shock, scared with pleading eyes. The gas passers were in and out during the entire procedure, watching the kid's heart and lung function.

Not exactly routine, but it wouldn't make the evening news, either.

For Lucas, the afternoon after Weather's call went like most days since the Long Island firefight: alone, bored, reading, watching television, suppressing the impulse to whine. He had friends, but they worked, and he wasn't feeling social.

He'd talked to Virgil every few days since the shootings, but Virgil had recovered, lived a hundred miles away, had a girlfriend, two toddlers, a dog, and horses, all of whom needed tending, and was chasing small-town criminals while writing a second novel and nervously awaiting the publication of his first.

Too busy to talk much.

Weather was usually home by three o'clock so they could eat dinner with the kids, or go out, but this day she wouldn't be back until late. He needed her to break up the feeling of loneliness, and to bend his mind away from the depression that had come sniffing around.

A run would be the thing, he thought, bored with the TV. He'd push it. Challenge the pain.

He put on a sweat suit, locked the house, and jogged north on the bike path across the street. He'd made most of a mile before he got back, happier, sweating, but his bad leg was on fire.

He popped another Vicodin, showered, and was back in the TV room when the kids got home from school, with Ellen, their live-in housekeeper, who'd gone to fetch them.

Gabrielle, the youngest, came to say hello. She had a cello lesson in two hours and hadn't practiced, so she was going to do that. Sam followed her in, chewing on a peanut butter sandwich, and said he was hooking up with his friend Jedediah to shoot baskets.

Lucas: "Shoot baskets down his basement on NBA 2K?"

"We're talking a lot about plays and strategy," Sam said, tap-dancing around the question. "Mrs. Clark asked if I wanted to stay for dinner and I said I'd ask you."

Right. He was talking about playing NBA 2K down the Clarks' basement. Lucas said Mrs. Clark was okay to feed him, and off he went. Gabrielle was sawing away on her cello in the family room, and Ellen would take her to practice and bring her back.

At five o'clock that afternoon, a bank of gunmetal clouds drifted in from the southwest, and his weather app said it would rain later in the day. Despite the pain in his leg, he decided to go for another walk, and did that, shambling along, stopping to chat with a neighbor and the neighbor's German shepherd. He could smell the rain coming, but it hadn't yet arrived.

He made himself a microwave dinner and went back to the couch, switching between

24

a John Connolly novel and West Coast baseball. Gabrielle got home from her cello lesson and talked on her cell phone to an endless list of girlfriends while she allegedly did homework.

Sam got home and hit the refrigerator, saying that Mrs. Clark had served her famous zucchini fettuccine — he stuck his index finger down his throat to illustrate his opinion of the food — and went to work on his math before he headed to bed.

As Sam went up to his room, the Sands were being murdered five miles away.

Lucas was watching CNN at ten o'clock when his phone rang: Edie Lamb, U.S. Marshal for the Minnesota District. Lucas looked at the phone screen and said, "Huh."

Lamb only called in off-hours when she wanted something. She wouldn't be calling to console him at ten o'clock at night, unless she was drunk. She did drink a bit, and sometimes, when sufficiently hammered, wanted to share her philosophical ideas about a life well spent.

He clicked on his phone and said, "Hey, Edie. What's up?"

Lamb: "How are you feeling?"

Lucas, wary about whatever was coming: "I hurt a little all of the time. I hurt a lot

25

some of the time."

"Gotta be tough," Lamb said, in the tone she used for insincerity. Lucas and Lamb liked each other; she'd replaced a marshal who didn't like Lucas at all. "Could you work?"

"Not if it involves fighting someone," Lucas said. So she wasn't calling about a life well spent. "Or long-distance running."

"How about brain work?"

"Nothing wrong with my brain, except that I'm still a cop," Lucas said. "I'd rather not travel. . . . What happened?"

"A federal judge and two of his three children were murdered a couple of hours ago in St. Paul. Close enough that you might have heard the sirens. They live up on Crocus Circle." Still using the present tense, for the newly dead. Everybody did it.

"Not that close," Lucas said. Crocus Circle was a wealthy twig off the slightly less wealthy Crocus Hill. He'd muted the television; now he picked up the remote and killed it. "Which judge?"

"Alex Sand . . ."

"Ho . . . man. Good guy, as far as I know," Lucas said. "Since you're calling, I'd guess the killer's on the loose?"

"Yes. There's a lot of verbiage being thrown around, but reading between the lies and bullshit, I'd say they haven't got a clue who did it."

"Who's *they*?"

"St. Paul cops, BCA, FBI. The usual. The locals will do the investigating as part of a task force, but the FBI will keep the hammer. We'll be observing. Not investigating. Yet. I'd like you to take a look. I'm all the way over in Minnetonka, with friends, finishing up a late dinner. I might have had a few. I'd appreciate it if you could get over there, show the flag. You still in a wheelchair?"

"No. Not for months. You sound a little pissed. I mean, pissed off, not drunk."

"I'm a little pissed both ways. Alex was a friend of mine," Lamb said. "He's got, had, nice kids. I talked to the FBI agent in charge, and he wouldn't tell me anything because, I suspect, he didn't know anything. I called the St. Paul chief and he confirmed my suspicion. I have some bare facts: the three of them were shot. Eight shots, four for Alex, two each for the boys."

"Since he was a friend of yours, I assume he was rich?"

"That's an insulting suggestion, Davenport, imputing to me a selection process for choosing friends that is not at all valid," Lamb said, slurring the longer words. "I

27

know poor people, and you're a friend of mine, so . . . oh, wait, *you're* rich. I'd forgotten."

"From the way you're avoiding the question, I assume that I guessed correctly: he's rich," Lucas said.

"Yes. Alex is quite well-off. Was. Why does that matter?"

"Because it suggests a motive. Somebody might have killed him because of his money. Because of his money one way or another. So, what do you think? What was he into? Cocaine, hookers, gambling . . . ?"

"None of those. He might have smoked a little weed back in law school, but who didn't? I don't think anything more than that, and not anymore," Lamb said. "From what I could tell, his marriage is solid. No fooling around."

"No hidden boyfriends?"

"I doubt it. He has always been . . . almost intolerably straight. Like me."

Right. Lucas knew — and she knew he knew — that she'd once been caught by her then-husband getting her bourbon-fueled brains banged loose by Elmer Henderson, a former governor and now the junior U.S. senator from Minnesota.

At the time, she'd been the number three bureaucrat in the Minnesota Department of

Public Safety. Henderson's influence had later gotten her the appointment as U.S. Marshal for the District of Minnesota.

Lucas assumed that she continued to be one of Henderson's intimate diversions. Lucas didn't care about that. And Lucas wouldn't admit it to Lamb, for reasons of bureaucratic self-protection, but he was immediately interested in the Sand murders. "I'm still in quite a bit of pain," he said, piously.

"Ah, for Christ's sakes, suck it up, Lucas. Getting shot is not optimal, and getting shot a whole bunch of times is worse, but you gotta get off your ass. It's time."

That was true, but Lucas let the silence stretch out. Lamb knew the game and said nothing. Lucas caved first: "I'll take a look," he said. "You might help clear the way. The FBI doesn't like me much."

"As I understand it, you haven't made yourself likeable. Besides, I've already cleared the way, since I knew you're a sucker for the big-media cases, which this will be," Lamb said. "Can you drive?"

"Not very well. Got hit in the fibula and if I have to hit the brakes hard, it's like getting shot again."

"A fibula is like an appendix?"

"It's a bone in my lower leg."

29

"I knew that. I even saw an X-ray of it and it's not the big bone, it's an appendix, in the broader definition of the word," Lamb said. She'd definitely had a few too many. "Your basic answer is yes, you can drive?"

"Yes. Again, with some pain."

"Since you're still getting a federal pay-check, show some guts and do a little work," Lamb said. "Let me give you Sand's address. You got a pen?"

He did.

After saying goodbye to Lamb, Lucas climbed the stairs to what Weather called a dressing room and Lucas called a closet, and changed into soft cotton blue jeans, a black flannel shirt, black running shoes, a blue rain jacket and a Dog Star Ranch ball-cap he'd gotten from a friend.

He went back down, climbed another set of stairs to the housekeeper's apartment, told her he was going out, collected an umbrella from a closet at the back entry, went into the garage, unplugged his Porsche Cayenne hybrid, and climbed inside.

A rap channel on SiriusXM was playing Everlast's "What It's Like." He was halfway to Crocus Circle when Weather called.

"I got a five-minute break," she said. "You okay?"

"Yeah. You remember a judge named Alex Sand?"

"I remember the name . . ."

Lucas filled her in on what he knew about the murders. "He's a friend, was a friend, of Edie's. She asked me to go over there and take a look."

"Good. That's really good, going back to work," Weather said. "Take it easy when you're walking around. I understand it's raining, you don't want to fall on your bad side."

"You mean my ass?"

"No, I don't mean your ass. I mean your shoulder and your ribcage."

She didn't say she was sorry about Sand because she didn't know him, and Lucas had been working murder cases since the day they'd met; too many unknown dead people over the years to be genuinely sorry about.

She did say they'd found and connected the arteries in the kid's fingers and were in the process of connecting veins. "I should be home in two or three hours."

"See you then," Lucas said. "I'm not officially on the case, and maybe I'll never be, so I shouldn't be out too late."

31

2

St. Paul is an old town, and weathered. Two or three affluent avenues were left over from the nineteenth century, where the rich had built their mansions — the railroad executives, the 3M people, the brewery owners.

There were smaller enclaves of newer affluent streets.

Most of the city, though, had been built of pine studs and Sheetrock, for workingmen, from the nineteenth century through the period immediately after World War II. In general, the houses were small and closely spaced, now dilapidated with worn and awkward additions that did not add to their beauty.

The city once had a geographically coherent black community, but that, of course, was where I-94 had been built, and the community had been atomized.

Lucas lived on one of the newer affluent streets, as far to the west as the city got.

Mississippi River Boulevard ran along the east side of the river. He couldn't see the river from his house because it was at the bottom of a steep-cut, heavily wooded valley; backing out of his garage, the mist-veiled houses of Minneapolis were visible across the gorge, glowing like miniature colored lanterns perched on a shelf.

Lamb had wondered if he could hear the sirens responding to the Sand murders, but his home was five miles from Crocus Circle, one of the old rich streets, so he hadn't. He took the river boulevard north and then turned east, windshield wipers squeaking away the rain, as the battery-powered car hissed silently along the dark streets.

He managed to hit almost every red traffic light between his house and Sand's home and got stuck behind a group of plastic-wrapped night-riding cyclists hogging a lane, and so took fifteen minutes to get to the murder scene.

There, he parked behind a collection of cop cars, both marked and unmarked. A forensic van sat directly in front of the house, on the wrong side of the street. A loose crowd of neighbors stood under umbrellas, watching the action.

As he fished his own umbrella out of the passenger-side footwell, he squinted through

33

the rain trickling down the windshield. The Sands definitely had been rich, he thought, or at least well-financed. In a city where housing prices were low, by American standards, the house where they lived would sell for at least a million, and probably more.

Two kids dead. Not a pleasant prospect. He'd seen a lot of ugly in his life, which might have contributed to his depressive episodes. He wouldn't quit what he was doing because what he was doing was interesting. He could be angered by the ugliness, but not undone. Lucas stepped out of the Cayenne, put the umbrella up, and walked across the street toward the house. A uniformed St. Paul cop moved to intercept him, stopped when he recognized Lucas, and said, "Hey, man."

"Hey, Steve. How bad is it?" Lucas asked.

"Bad enough," Steve said. A bulky man, he was wearing a knee-length raincoat and had a plastic wrapper on his uniform hat. His face was wet from the mist, and water droplets glittered from his eyebrows and glasses. "I haven't seen them."

Lucas: "Understand they were shot."

"Yup. All three of them. The wife found them," Steve said. "I'm told the judge got it four times, the kids twice each. The shooter made a real mess."

"Wife inside?" Lucas asked.

"Don't know. Haven't seen her and I haven't been inside. They put me out directing raindrops, soon as I got here. Forensics is already working it."

Lucas nodded: "Saw their van," and, "Take it easy, man."

"Yup. You, too. Hey: get well."

"I'm working on it," Lucas said.

He left Steve and shuffled up the redbrick sidewalk to the house, climbed three stone steps to the front porch, crossed it to the impressive two-panel front door. The door was covered with plastic sheeting, meaning the cops thought the killer might have touched it. A young cop inside the door said, in her best officious tone, "Stay inside the tape."

Lucas stepped into the house, found himself in an entrance foyer with twelve-foot ceilings, a wood-strip floor of some light-colored wood, and an intricate, circular red-and-blue Persian carpet under a modern cut-crystal chandelier.

Three small, framed watercolors of English country scenes hung on pale yellow plaster walls, above a darker-wood wainscoting. A three-foot-wide, blue-taped walkway led across the carpet deeper into the house.

He followed the walkway to the living

35

room, where a polished ebony grand piano sat in one corner — a basketball lay beneath the keyboard. A couch and six easy chairs, in two groups, were wrapped around coffee tables on another Persian carpet, this one at least twelve by eighteen feet, and threaded with gold.

Three bodies, one male adult and two male children, lay on the carpet, the adult seeming to grasp at a piano leg.

The room smelled of bloody flesh, not unlike the odor of a custom butcher shop, and beneath that, the incongruous scent of buttered popcorn and something else. A martini? A crime scene tech was using a video camera and an LED light panel to record the scene. A half-dozen people were standing inside the tape, looking at the bodies, or trying not to.

An FBI agent who Lucas didn't know, with an ID on a lanyard around his neck, glanced at him, nodded, then looked back at the bodies and the techs working around them. The St. Paul's deputy chief for major crimes raised an eyebrow to Lucas, and a BCA investigator named Gary Durey stepped behind the chief and said, "Didn't know you were working this."

"I'm not. I got yanked off the couch to look at it," Lucas said. Lucas had been a

BCA agent before he joined the Marshals Service and had known Durey for years. "You got anything other than the obvious?"

"Not much. I haven't talked to the wife yet; St. Paul has," Durey said. "She's not here. A friend took her in, with the baby."

"There's a baby?"

"Yeah. She was here — the baby was — during the shootings. The wife apparently found her screaming her head off when she came in the house."

"So the wife found the bodies?"

"Yes. Called 9-1-1. I heard the recording and I would swear on my sainted mother's grave, if she were dead, that there was nothing fake or calculated about it. She was freaked," Durey said.

The deputy chief said to Lucas, "Hey, guy. My wife saw you and Weather coming out of the bagel place on Grand. Said you still looked banged up."

"I've been told this will be good for me, a job," Lucas said.

"That sorta sounds like horseshit," the deputy chief said. "This ain't gonna be good for no one."

"We'll see. So what . . ." Lucas nodded at the bodies.

The deputy chief called, "Jimmy? C'mere a minute . . ."

37

A St. Paul detective had been talking with a forensics investigator. He broke away and stepped carefully out of the scene and onto the blue taped walkway, said, "Lucas. What's up?"

"I'm . . . observing, don't know exactly why," Lucas said.

The chief tipped his head at Lucas and said to the investigator, "Tell him."

Jimmy Russo, a short man with a bristly gray mustache and dark eyes, turned to look at the bodies, then back to Lucas. "The house has security cameras, and one of them looks at the front door. The cameras have microphones and speakers so if somebody's on the front step, you can speak to them from inside without opening the door. That means we've got sound, we got pictures, and we got the times, right down to the minute.

"At 7:41, Sand and his two sons, Arthur and Blaine, came around from the side of the house. Blaine was the older boy, twelve, Arthur was ten. Blaine was carrying a basketball," Russo said. He turned his head and nodded at the ball by the piano. "There was still enough light to shoot baskets and there's a net in the side yard behind a hedge. That's apparently what they were doing. It's just starting to sprinkle rain, in the video, you can see raindrops hitting on the porch steps. They go inside the house, half-ass shut the door — we can't hear the latch click on the video — and turn on some lights.

"One minute later, at 7:42, a man, close to six feet, maybe an inch more or less, looks like average build, not fat, walks up from somewhere, we don't know where, wearing a rain suit with a hood. I believe it's a maroon University of Minnesota hoodie like people wear to football games when it's wet. It's hard to see in the bad light on the porch, but it looks to me like it has a gold M on the sleeve. His hands were dead white, like he was wearing plastic gloves.

"Can't see anything of his face. He was wearing a black Covid mask and glasses," Russo continued. "He didn't ring the door-bell but it looks like he tried the door handle and the door opened. Sand apparently hadn't locked it when he and the boys went inside. The killer went in, closed the door, and in twelve seconds shot Sand four times, and the two kids, who tried to run away, toward the kitchen, twice each.

"Probably not a pro, because he wasn't a great shot, even up close. He shot Sand twice in the back, hitting him low both times. He shot the older kid in the neck and knocked him down, maybe killed him, we have to wait to see on that; the younger one he shot in the hip. He shot Sand twice more and then he stepped over to them and shot both kids in the head, once each, from six or eight inches — like he just let the muzzle hang down past his knee and shot them."

"How do you know the sequence?" Lucas asked.

"We don't, for sure, but we can hear the shots on the recording and that's what it sounds like," Russo said. "Bang-bang, that's Sand, two quick shots together, knocking him down. Then bang, bang, a little pause between shots, that's the kids; then bang-bang, that's Sand, higher up his back, through the heart, and bang, bang, the kids in their heads. The last four shots were more spaced, more . . . considered."

"Okay."

"He used a nine-millimeter automatic and left the +P shells on the floor where they landed. Commercial, not reloads. Not suppressed. Six minutes later, he walked back out the door, turning off all the house lights as he went. He was carrying one of those plastic shopping bags when he left, the kind you buy at Whole Foods or Trader Joe's, we think he got it from the kitchen. He turned left at the end of the sidewalk and strolled off into the rain.

"Sometime during the six minutes he was inside, he stepped in blood from the younger kid, and tracked it into the kitchen. We can see some tread, and the forensics guys say it looks like size eleven shoes, which is one of the most common men's sizes, I'm told. We should be able to identify the tread, but we're not there yet.

"We don't know where he went after he left, or if he walked or had a car. We're trying to figure that out now. We think he might have either been following the family or waiting for them from some spot outside the house, because they arrived so close together," Russo said.

He turned to look at the scene, thinking, made a rapid clicking sound with his tongue, turned back to Lucas.

"At 8:17, thirty-four minutes after the killings, Margaret Cooper, Sand's wife, drove past the front of the house and then past a security camera at the garage, around back. She parked inside the garage, walked into the house, saw the bodies, dropped a big bottle of olives on the kitchen floor, where it shattered."

"I thought I smelled a martini," Lucas said. "A jar of olives?"

"Yeah. Big one. She started screaming.

41

She called 9-1-1 still screaming, and we got here, on the security cameras, at 8:22 and found her standing on the lawn, in the rain, holding her baby. The baby was not injured, although, by the time we got here, might have been hypothermic. She's okay, though, the baby."

Lucas frowned: "Any idea of what the guy was doing inside the house for six minutes after the shooting? Anything missing or . . . ?"

"Let me ask you this — you've seen as many murders as anyone in the business. Does this look like a robbery to you?"

Lucas looked over at the bodies. "No."

Russo nodded, turned to the bodies. "Doesn't look like it to me, either. Too much well-planned violence for too little reward, as far as we know. The killer apparently took Sand's watch and his wallet. He went up to their bedroom and tore a closet apart, and two chests of drawers. Also the kitchen, dumped out a bunch of canisters. Dumped the refrigerator. Like . . ." Russo shrugged. "Like he was looking for dope or a stash of cash. I don't know — it's weird. The closet has two lines of built-in drawers, and Ms. Cooper had left a diamond ring, in a platinum setting, in a silver tray on top of one set of drawers. He yanked the drawers out, the ring must have been right in front of his nose, but he left it."

"Maybe too identifiable?"

"Pop the diamond out, sell it in LA. It's a big one," Russo said.

"Then why take the watch and wallet?" Lucas asked.

Russo spread his hands: "You tell me. . . . It's like he was faking a robbery to cover the motive for the killing."

"Okay. Now what?"

"After we get the bodies out of here, we'll bring Ms. Cooper back inside to check things out. Ms. Cooper told us that the baby was crying when she walked into the house and she wondered why nobody had gone to pick her up. I'm thinking that the kid started to cry when she heard the gunshots and the killer went in and looked at her, decided to leave her, but maybe had to think about it, soaking up a little time there."

Lucas: "What kind of shape is Cooper in? Can she talk?"

"She's *really* messed up. We put her and the baby in Regions, had the docs and a shrink spend some time with them. She didn't want a minister. She kept wanting to get back here, but we kept her away. She checked out of Regions about half an hour ago. I'm told a girlfriend picked her up and

43

took her to the girlfriend's home over in Edina. Katie McCarthy is over there with them, talking, but so far Cooper doesn't seem to know anything. This came out of the blue. She says."

Lucas: "Anything going on between her and her husband?"

"Not that we've been able to pick out," Russo said. "Tell you the truth, I spoke to Cooper for a total of five minutes. You know what? I agree with Gary about that. She didn't know anything about it. She has no idea who did this. Or why. I believe that."

Gary Durey, the BCA agent, had been listening, and said, "She really doesn't know what happened, Lucas. She just doesn't."

Lucas nodded at them: "Good. Thanks. Why do I smell popcorn? On top of the olives?"

"It looks like Sand and the kids made some microwave popcorn before they went outside to shoot baskets. There's still some left, and there's a microwave bag on the counter. They burned some of it."

Lucas spent another five minutes looking at the scene. The crumbled bodies of the dead children were disturbing, but nothing he hadn't seen before. Still, he felt anger rising, which was also typical.

Russo wasted a moment talking with the

chief and Durey, then stepped out of the blue pathway, going back to the bodies; Lucas said to his back, as he went, "I'll call you."

"Give me a little time," Russo said.

"Yeah."

There was nothing more to do inside, so Lucas nodded at Durey, said, "Catch you later," and headed for the door. He wasn't quite there when the chief called, "Lucas," and he turned and saw the chief coming after him, trailed by the FBI agent.

The chief nodded toward the porch and said, "Let's step outside."

On the covered porch, looking down at Steve, in the rain, the chief said, "There are going to be some complications with . . . all these people working the same case."

"The Marshals Service doesn't really do this kind of thing," Lucas began.

"Look. We've known each other for a long time. I'd appreciate your expertise on this, your experience, but I don't want my people to get run over. You know, in the press. On that social media bullshit."

"I don't need the credit," Lucas said. "If I get involved at all, I'll step back when the time comes."

The chief bumped him with an elbow. "Thank you. Maybe this killer screwed up

45

and we'll catch him tomorrow. If it goes on, especially if it goes on for more than a week, I mean, if you can find it in your heart to take a look, I'd facilitate that."

"I'll keep it in mind, Chief."

"Do. There's gonna be pressure, and here comes some of it now." Lucas looked up the street where an older Mercedes S-Class sedan had just pulled to the curb. Steve the cop looked in the passenger side window, then helped open the door.

Lucas recognized the mayor, Joe Hartcome, climbing out the passenger side; the driver he didn't recognize.

"Who's the guy in the hat?" he asked.

"That's one of our richie-riches, Noah Heath. He runs that Heart/Twin Cities charity."

"I think my wife gives money to them," Lucas said.

"As she should. Mayor's here because he knows the family and half his political donations come out of the Crocus Hill neighborhood," the chief said. "I don't know about Heath."

The two men scurried through the rain toward them, the mayor nodding to Lucas and the chief, calling them both by name, saying, "Noah and I were at dinner when we heard. I guess it's bad?"

"It's bad," the chief said. "I don't know if you'll want to go inside."

"Where's Maggie?" Heath asked.

"They took her to Regions, then a friend picked her up. She's with the friend."

The mayor carried the professionally sad look that mayors were expected to carry after an unexpected death. Heath looked genuinely distraught, wringing his hands, and he said, "A tragedy. A tragedy, my God, what is the world coming to, people cut down by madmen?"

The chief shook his head: "I don't know. This didn't happen back in the day . . ."

Lucas wanted to say, "Of course it did, all the time," but he didn't. Instead, he clapped the chief on the back, said, "Do good, man," nodded at the mayor and said, "Mayor, Mr. Heath, I gotta go," and limped down the stairs to the walk. The FBI agent followed, and called, "Davenport. Wait up."

Lucas turned and stuck out a hand and they shook, and the agent said, "John Howahkan. You're Lucas Davenport. I missed the investigation that got you shot up. I was out in the Dakotas, working a killing at Standing Rock."

"You missed an intense situation, then," Lucas said. "Though I'm told Standing Rock is an interesting place. Never been."

47

"You're a little too white to be poking around out there," Howahkan said. "Listen. I know about you, mostly good, from talk around the office. You're familiar with the local and state people working this. I'd just as soon you didn't tell them I was asking, but . . . Who in there is incompetent?"

Lucas turned to look at the men still on the porch. "Maybe the chief. He's an old-line copper, but he's mostly on a desk. He does outreach and political stuff, so no damage there," Lucas said. "Russo's very good. Gary Durey is better than competent. St. Paul forensics had some problems, but they've got that cleared up now, so they should be okay. On the whole, that's a good team. They won't miss much."

"Great. The SAC told me that we'd keep notional responsibility, but we're going to set it up as a task force and let the local people handle most of it. I guess I'm over here to make that point." He shrugged.

"I'm in the same position," Lucas said. "My boss said she wanted to show the flag."

Howahkan turned and looked back at the murder room and said, "Gonna be a lot of heat on this, lot of pressure. A federal judge, his kids."

"Yes," Lucas said. "But right now, we'd be in the way."

48

"Then we should go home," Howahkan said.

The crime scene belonged to St. Paul, and the mayor was the mayor, so they let him in to view the bodies. He would later relay the horror of the scene in a number of speeches, talks, and conferences, to let the voters know that he was on the job.

Left behind on the porch, Noah Heath stood, still wringing his hands, only half-listening as the chief, inside the door, detailed the killings to the mayor. Heath didn't care about the chief, the mayor, or the dead children, or the dead Alex Sand. He did care about Alex Sand's money. Sand had been about to cough up a hundred thousand or possibly a hundred and fifty thousand dollars to his latest Heart/Twin Cities project, called Home Streets, but hadn't yet signed the check.

Heath's mind was churning: Would Sand's wife, Margaret Cooper, honor that commitment? Would she go for the one-fifty? Might she go for more, as a way to honor her husband? God knows the family had enough money; she could drop a solid mil without noticing it. Unfortunately, Sand had mentioned that her interests tended to run toward the arts, rather than the poor.

But fuck Sand. Sand was dead. Fuck the children. The children were dead. They couldn't do anything for him at all. He had to find a way to get to Margaret Cooper.

He had his back against the wall of the house, and he slowly sank down it, until he was sitting on the porch floor, where he began to weep. Nothing faked about it, the tears were running freely down his face.

My money! My money! How can this happen to me?

The mayor came out of the house and saw Heath on the floor, was touched. He bent and patted Heath on the shoulder and said, "C'mon, Noah. C'mon. There's nothing more to do here."

Heath wailed, "Not Alex. Not Alex, oh, those poor, poor kids. . . ."

3

Two weeks passed.

Sand's wife, Margaret Cooper, had been taken back to the house the day after the shootings to see what, if anything, was missing. There were a few things missing that the cops didn't know about. Three laptops, one belonging to Alex Sand, the other two belonging to the kids, were gone. So were three iPhones.

She couldn't see anything else of significance and the sight of the blood puddles on the floor drove her nearly to collapse. She staggered, wailing, clinging to her girl-friend's shoulder. The cops got her out of the place.

A crime clean-up specialty company was brought in to clean the Persian carpet and the floor where the bloodstains had soaked in, and to patch eight bullet holes. That required the wood floors to be refinished, and the walls to be repainted. The technology was good enough that no sign of the crimes remained.

At the end of the two weeks, Cooper returned to the house, along with her friend, Ann Melton, at whose house she'd been staying with the baby. They did a quick walk-through, then went back out to the car and brought in some collapsed moving boxes, with packaging tape, and two suitcases.

Melton was charged with cleaning out the kitchen cupboards and the refrigerator. Most of the contents would go in the garbage, with the rest of it being moved to Melton's, where Cooper would stay for as long as she wished: she could not, at that point, stay overnight in her own house, Cooper thought.

Cooper dragged the two empty suitcases up the stairs, and down to the master bedroom, where she'd begin packing her own clothing. Alex Sand's clothing was all still hanging in their closet, and when she stepped inside, she could smell him.

She turned her head away, waited for a beat, then began pulling her own clothing out, laying it on the bed. She opened the closet safe, took out several pieces of jewelry, and closed it again. Got cosmetics, toothpaste, deodorant, facial creams and miscellaneous medications from the bathroom.

When the first suitcase was full, she began towing it down the hall to the staircase. The door was open on Arthur's bedroom and as she passed it, she glanced inside and saw Arthur sitting at his desk looking at a computer screen. Her son turned and looked at her. . . .

The vision hit her like a thunderclap and she staggered back from the door; Arthur vanished.

She'd been warned about the hallucinations. Many people had them: maybe most, after the death of a loved one, or even of a close but unloved one. They were called bereavement hallucinations and were the result of a well-known brain process. They were probably the origin of the belief in ghosts.

They were powerful and Cooper sank to the floor and began sobbing, her husband and children running through her memories. She was aware of Melton running up the stairs but couldn't stop crying, and when Melton asked, "What happened?" she said, "I saw Art. Oh, my God, I saw Art sitting there. He looked at me."

Another week passed. The days got shorter and colder, and there were snow flurries on a couple of cold nights, but the snow hadn't stuck. Not yet.

Lucas found stories about the Sand murders in the papers every day during the first week, three times during the second, and once during the third, because there was nothing new to report. Like all dead people, the Sands were receding into the past.

He talked to Russo twice a week, and got the same response every time: nothing new, except a growing feeling of desperation. Politicians did not like the idea that one of their class could be murdered, with no one caught, and the pressure was cranking up.

Then one morning Lucas woke late, yawned, rolled over and looked at the clock: 10:15. He lay in bed, half asleep, checking for any untoward body signals, found nothing alarming, got up, glanced out the window — cloudy, wet, but not actually raining.

He felt a touch of nonspecific foreboding, but then, he often did, and when recalled later, it turned out to be the precognition of a broken toaster or stubbed toe. Weather had gone to work at six a.m., her usual time, and the kids to school an hour and a half later. He could hear Ellen in the kitchen, cleaning up breakfast dishes.

Instead of taking two showers, one right

away, another after he got back from his run, he scratched his gut, yawned again, went into the dressing room, fished out an old gray sweat suit, pulled on his running shoes, got his cane, just in case, and headed out to the street. He'd tied a string to the cane so he could loop it over his back, out of the way, like a rifle.

His leg was improving. An inch at a time, but when you get enough inches . . .

He jogged north on the bike path along Mississippi River Boulevard, walked a bit, started jogging again, taking it easy. Weather had gotten him Hoka trail-runners with soles like marshmallows, to absorb impact. While he was still weeks away from his usual workout, at least he was out there. Maybe by Christmas . . .

He'd gotten to the northern end of his loop, a mile and a half out, when Virgil Flowers called. "Where are you?"

"Out for a run," Lucas said. "What's up?"

"You can run now?"

"Not well," Lucas said.

"Better than not at all . . . Listen, I got an early call. Henderson has been nagging the governor, the governor has been nagging Rose Marie, and Rose Marie has been nagging Cartwright." Henderson was a U.S. senator, Rose Marie was the state commissioner of public safety, Cartwright was director of the Bureau of Criminal Apprehension. As they say in the military, shit rolls downhill. "They want me to review the Sand murder. I just left the BCA, heading your way. I had them make two copies of the murder file. I thought you might enjoy some light fiction."

"I'm about ten minutes from that Starbucks at Marshall and Snelling and it's starting to drizzle. I need to get off the street and I'd like a look at the file; I haven't heard much."

"That's because there's not much to hear," Virgil said. "I'm on I-94, I'll probably get there about the same time as you."

"I'll limp fast. See you there."

Virgil's Tahoe was sitting in the Starbucks parking lot when Lucas arrived, and he could see Virgil at a window table looking at a bound file. The rain was coming down harder, with an occasional slice of sleet. He'd been using the cane the last couple of blocks, humping along, trying to take some impact off his leg. He hustled inside, pushed his wet hair back with one hand, nodded at Virgil and went to the counter.

The young woman behind the register gave him a kind smile and he said, "Gimme a Grande . . . Pike Place, and two vanilla scones."

He fished crumbled five-dollar bills out of a pocket and passed them across the counter. The young woman said, cheerily, "Oh, boy — I bet it's tough out there today, isn't it? Cold rain and all. Tell you what, I'll give you the two scones, but I'll only charge you for one."

That hadn't happened before. Lucas scratched one unshaven cheek, trying to figure out the con, decided there wasn't one, and said, "Okay. Thanks."

He got the coffee and scones, dropped the change into a tip jar and when he turned to Virgil, found Virgil trying to stuff the knuckles of his right hand into his mouth.

Lucas sat down. "What's funny?"

"A free scone?"

"Yeah." Lucas glanced back at the counter woman, who now was looking at them, and seemed puzzled. "What was that all about?"

"She thought you were a street guy. Spending money you collected at the corner. Wet sweatshirt and baggy-ass pants, the drugstore cane on a string, your hair is sticking up like the antennas on a '56 Buick, you're not shaved . . . She's wondering how you know the well-dressed blond dude. That would be me."

Virgil was as tall as Lucas, but lean, lanky, and blond, hair too long for a cop. He lived on a farm near the town of Mankato, a hundred miles south of St. Paul, as a regional agent for the Bureau of Criminal Apprehension. He had the best clearance rate in the agency and was sometimes pulled out of his territory to look at difficult cases.

"Ah, jeez," Lucas said. He glanced over at the woman, who was now ignoring them. "Maybe I oughta pay for the extra scone."

"Forget it. We've got to read this stuff, talk it over, get back to your place so you can change into something decent and get over to Minneapolis by two o'clock."

"What's in Minneapolis?"

"Margaret Cooper. Also known as Maggie," Virgil said, tapping the file. "She's still at her girlfriend's house with the baby. We need to talk to her."

"I'm not even sure I'm doing this," Lucas said.

"Oh, bullshit, you're doing it," Virgil said. "Stop wasting time and start reading the file. Is one of those scones for me?"

Virgil and Lucas spent an hour and a half at Starbucks, reading through the files, muttering at each other from time to time, looking out the window at passing cars and

58

walkers in the rain, like the cars or walkers might connect their thoughts. Because Lucas had grudgingly given Virgil one of his scones, Virgil bought two more, and told the counter woman to charge him for three.

He said, in a stage whisper, "I know he looks weird, but that guy is a really, really rich businessman. He's a little eccentric. He's got a sword inside that cane."

"Do not," Lucas called.

The woman puffed up her cheeks, exhaled in Gen-Z exasperation, and charged Virgil for three scones.

Lucas had begun reading about Cooper, Sand's wife. She'd been interviewed a half-dozen times by agents from three agencies, and somebody had put together a biography, with a selection of photographs, old and new.

Cooper was a tall, dark-haired woman approaching middle age, showing bones in her shoulders and elbows and knees, ungainly at first glance, but, according to her FBI biographer, a killer with a tennis racket in her hands.

A professor of theater arts at the University of Minnesota, she'd once, briefly, been an actress in Hollywood. From 2005 to 2009, she'd been a regular on a televised ensemble series modeled after *Friends* but not as good as *Friends.*

With deep brown eyes and a high-ridged nose, she might have played an ancient Roman or Greek, though her ancestry was resolutely Anglo-Saxon. On the show, she'd played an uptight accountant of uncertain sexuality. Lucas had seen a couple episodes on a streaming service, but had quit watching because they weren't very good. Even if they had been, they wouldn't have been to his taste.

She had been born and raised in Minnesota, the daughter of two doctors. She was a graduate of the Blake School and held three degrees in performance arts, two from NYU and a third, a PhD, from UCLA. She told interviewers that her talent for teaching was stronger than her drive to act, and when offered a job at the University of Minnesota, had happily returned home.

And there she'd met a youngish lawyer, also a graduate of the Blake School; Alex Sand had been two years ahead of her, and she hadn't known him well. After her return to the Twin Cities, they'd bumped into each other at a wine-and-cheese political event. The bump matured into courtship, marriage, and three children, two early in the marriage, followed by a trailer, a four-month-old daughter.

They were no longer quite so youngish. Cooper had become an associate professor, climbing the ranks, and Sand had been appointed as a federal judge by Barack Obama. Their marriage was solid, she said. They both loved each other and liked each other and loved their children. Though both were atheists, the family went to church on Christmas and Easter so the kids could have the experience of organized religion.

Cooper & Sand, as they thought of themselves, bought a family home, a much-remodeled house built in 1918, that didn't fit into a specific architectural style, but showed bits and pieces of several styles: stone and brick and creamy stucco with a slate roof and black shutters on the narrow windows. They were comfortable there, comfortable in the neighborhood. Any antagonisms between neighbors, and there were some, didn't include them.

Their house, Cooper told investigators, was too rich for a college professor and a judge, but Sand had chosen his great-great-grandfather wisely. His great-great-grandfather had owned Old River Mills, which eventually became a major component of General Mills — Cheerios, Wheat Chex, Betty Crocker, etc. A large chunk of money had taken up residence in the Sand family and had remained there for a hundred and fifty years. Alex Sand had been a millionaire as a toddler.

They had the usual disagreements of a husband and wife: the judge thought some of her closest friends were too arty-fartsy, she thought some of his had sticks way too far up their Anglo-Saxon rectums. They recognized these things about each other and about their friends, and even laughed about them.

They were as happy as successful people could be, right up until the bloodbath.

Into the file, Lucas said across the table, "They pushed on Cooper pretty hard."

"She inherits," Virgil said. "No prenup. She's five-ten and slender, which means she fits the physical profile of the shooter. What doesn't fit is her time profile. Or her foot size, for that matter. Her car's on cameras leaving the university, and arriving at and leaving Whole Foods, although you never see her face and you can't really nail down the driver's actual height. If she could have gotten somebody tallish to drive for her . . ."

"Then how would she have caught up with the car to drive it home?"

"Don't know," Virgil said. "There are obvious possibilities. Traded cars with the driver of her car, then traded back after the killings."

"Which means an accomplice."

"Yup. That seems . . . unlikely, to me," Virgil said. "If she did it, she did it herself without any help. Too smart to bring a second person into it."

"A lover?" Lucas suggested.

"No evidence of that."

"You'd have to be one goddamn crazy cookie to kill your husband and include your two little kids in the deal. Or to hire somebody to do it," Lucas said.

"Maybe that was why she was so distraught," Virgil said. "She didn't want the kids in on the deal, but the guy had to kill them because they were witnesses. They were twelve and ten, old enough to identify him."

"If he came through the door right behind them, he probably saw the kids before he was inside."

"True."

"Maybe she's distraught because she loved her husband and kids?" Lucas suggested.

"I think that's most likely," Virgil said.

"So you were playing devil's advocate, there."

"You know they had to poke her, Durey and Russo," Virgil said.

"Yeah."

A while later, Lucas said, "Whoa. Cooper says the killer did take something out of the house — laptops. And cell phones. Both the judge and the boys had their own laptops and cell phones and they're all missing."

"You didn't know that?" Virgil asked.

"No. When I talked to Russo at the house, he said they didn't know what was missing, if anything."

"Yeah. Sand had a work laptop, which he kept at his office. His home laptop was all personal stuff, including financial data and personal emails. All three laptops were Apple MacBook Pros. That's the expensive version," Virgil said. "If they were what the killer was after, he wouldn't have known which one belonged to who, so he apparently took all of them. Same with the phones. Cooper says the boys weren't allowed to be on their phones after seven o'clock. They had to put them in a basket on the breakfast bar and Alex Sand did the same thing. You know, to make a point with the kids."

"So the reason for the killing is probably in the computers or phones?"

"*Possibly* in the computers," Virgil said. "Most likely, one computer — Sand's. For which there was no backup. The boys' phones and computers were backed up to the iCloud. You know what the iCloud is?"

"Of course, I'm not a complete fuck-wit," Lucas said.

Virgil: "Fuck-wit. I think that's basically a British expression."

"Thank you, novel-boy."

"Anyway, the FBI got the backup data from the boys' phones and computers from Apple, and found nothing interesting," Virgil said. "From the phones, they got call logs, not the content, and the logs both showed identifiable phone calls to their friends and the older boy had calls to the Apple store and his friends, all routine stuff. He made appointments with the Apple expert bar, or whatever they call it."

"Why wasn't Sand backed up?" Lucas asked.

"Security. Cooper said Sand was security conscious, enough that he didn't want anything in the iCloud. Apple apparently allows us, 'us' meaning law enforcement, to look at backups, like the FBI did with the kids' stuff. Sometimes, apparently, the definition of law enforcement gets stretched. He kept private stuff in his computer, backed up to a thumb drive, and some of it printed on paper. Cooper says he kept the thumb drive plugged into his home computer most of the time — a slipup — and that's gone with the computer."

"Maybe the feds will come up with something."

Virgil: "Mmmm."

Lucas: "Yeah."

A moment later, Lucas said, "Wait — if the computer is password protected, the killer can't get at it, whatever it was. Cooper would probably —"

"You're so naive," Virgil interrupted. "One of your kids could bypass the password in about four minutes; and maybe the killer needed to destroy whatever it was, not get at it."

Lucas: "Why would you think that?"

"Because if he was desperate to destroy it, he already knew what it was," Virgil said. "He just didn't want anyone else to have the information."

"Good point. Got to be critical, whatever it is," Lucas said.

"Maybe. But maybe he took the laptops because he could get five hundred bucks each, on the street."

"Nope."

The discussion was occasionally cryptic, if overheard by an outsider:

Lucas: "Suppressor?"

"Probably not necessary. Raining, thick doors. It was cool, almost cold, so the neighbors would be shut up, too."

"He was familiar with the house?"

Virgil: "He was familiar with rich people's doors."

"Still loud . . ."

"Old couple who were out for a walk with their dog thought they might have heard the shots. They thought it was somebody remodeling with a nail gun."

Lucas: "Why does that sound like bullshit?"

"Actually, it sounds so much like bullshit, it probably isn't bullshit."

"Hmm. Athletic shoes," Lucas said. "Maybe an athlete?"

"Everybody wears them. Probably men's ten and a half or eleven, according to crime scene. So not a woman. Unless she was disguising herself with shoes. That goes back to Cooper again."

"This Carter guy," Virgil said. "You get there yet?"

"Just getting into it."

"Got out of FPC Duluth two months ago," Virgil said, flipping through pages. "Claims he was framed for the car thefts and the prosecutor knew it. Sand gave him five years."

"Released 216 days early for good behavior, so he did a little more than four . . . no history of violence," Lucas said.

"But if you look in the FBI investigation report on the car thefts . . . Carter's a shooter. An enthusiast. Had a big pile of guns at his home and had bought at least three suppressors. So . . ."

"I have a big pile of guns at my home," Lucas said. "If you have one gun, it's not totally unusual to have a pile of them."

"You also have a long history of extreme and unnecessary violence, and nobody does a fucking thing about it," Virgil said.

"It hurts me when you say things like that," Lucas said, with a yawn.

"Anyway, if you look at Carter's gun inventory, he liked concealed-carry guns, which means he wasn't a target shooter."

"Mmm."

"He was thinking that he might have to kill somebody. Maybe hoping," Virgil added.

"I'll buy that," Lucas said. He leaned back in his chair and gazed at the barista who'd given him the free scone. She was pretty, and ignored him. "Being a gun freak would explain why he didn't bother to pick up his brass. The lab report says there's no hint of a print or DNA on any of it. The killer cleaned it up before he loaded. He didn't want to have to crawl around picking up his brass."

"I saw that."

"Carter stole twelve brand-new Porsches and Audis over two years, before they caught up with him. Took them right out of the dealership," Lucas said, reading down the file. "They seemed to vanish. Took them on Saturday nights, the dealership was closed on Sundays, they'd be down in Mexico before the dealership knew they were gone . . . and if the pre-sentencing investigation is right, the cars were probably sold to cartel members. He either knew some seriously bad people or could get in touch with them. That might explain what could be a professional hit."

"Bzzzt." Virgil made a buzzer noise. "He's absolutely broke. Where would he get the money to hire a pro? Where would he even find one?"

"His alibi is, he was home practicing the piano when the killings took place. His wife was in Iowa visiting relatives, so there are no witnesses to the piano-playing," Lucas said. "He called his wife at 8:10 from his house and they talked for a half hour."

Virgil: "Hard alibi to crack, if he sticks

69

with it."

"He lives in Stillwater. He would have had time to get home and make the call after he did the shooting. If he did it. Would have been a *little* tight on time . . ."

They both went *"Mmmm"* at the same time.

And after a bit, Lucas said, "Russo doesn't think Carter was involved."

"I'm getting that," Virgil said.

"We'll have to talk to him anyway."

"He's threatening to sue for harassment," Virgil said.

"Good luck with that. We could ship his ass back to Duluth for stealing a cheese-burger."

"He still could sue . . ."

"If he wanted to take his case before a judge," Lucas said. "On an investigation in which another judge and his kids were murdered."

"True dat."

Russo, St. Paul's lead investigator, and the investigators from the BCA had determined that there were six more-or-less recently released convicts who'd been sentenced by Sand.

None were criminal geniuses. Only two had been convicted of gun crimes. One of those had an airtight alibi, having died of lung cancer shortly after his release. The second gunman had been attending a real estate license training course in Tempe, Arizona, on the night of the murders and had a dozen people to say so.

"Why didn't the shooter kill the baby?" Lucas asked.

"Because he didn't think it was necessary, and maybe he didn't want to make any more noise," Virgil answered. "He killed the two boys because they were old enough to be witnesses. The baby isn't."

"Did he know Cooper wouldn't be there? Maybe he was looking for her."

"Something to ask her," Virgil agreed.

"Here's a question," Lucas said. "When Sand and the two kids came back in the house, none of them were carrying a baby. So they left the baby at home, alone?"

"We talked about that this morning, when I picked up the files," Virgil said. "Cooper said Sand would never leave the baby alone, unless it was for one minute or something, to run out to the car or pick up a newspaper. Or maybe, to go out with the boys for two minutes and shoot some baskets, if the baby was sleeping."

Lucas thumbed through the pack of security photos. "None of them were wearing raincoats."

"Nope. They probably went out before the rain started."

"Did the camera see them going out?"

"No. They almost certainly went out through the garage. There's a back door in the garage," Virgil said. "The camera doesn't see it, because it's mounted above the door and is focused on cars and people coming up the driveway. If you go out that door and turn right, there's a flagstone walkway through a little secluded flower garden that opens out onto the side lawn. They walked out the door, turned right, shot some hoops, then ran around the house and went in the front door. Cooper said she saw the basketball in the garage before she went to work, so maybe that's why they did that."

"Sand didn't have a gun on him?" Lucas asked.

"Man, they were *shooting hoops* . . . No, he didn't have a gun with him."

"Does he even have a gun?"

"Yes. If you look further into the interview with Cooper, you'll see that she says they once had two guns. They'd even taken some lessons with one of them, someplace over in Wisconsin, the name is in there . . . But they never got carry permits or anything,"

Virgil said. "The main gun, that they took lessons with, was kept locked in a steel gun box hidden in their library. Ruger .357, hadn't been shot recently. The killer used a Nine, and . . . the second gun was a Nine, but she said Sand sold it in the parking lot of a gun show in Hudson, Wisconsin."

"That's convenient."

"Cooper said that it's embarrassing, that he would do that. She didn't know the brand. She says it originally belonged to Sand's father. Sand inherited it but didn't want it."

"Okay." Lucas scratched his head, reading about the guns.

"If you read down a bit, you'll see that Cooper said they didn't like shooting, and didn't much — a time or two after the lessons. The .357 wasn't fun to shoot, but, it'd do the job, they thought," Virgil said.

"That's true enough. If the .357 was locked up in the library, that would suggest that Sand didn't feel threatened," Lucas said.

Virgil: "Well, Cooper said even if they did feel threatened, they probably wouldn't have gone for the gun. She said they're not gun people. Even if they'd seen somebody snooping around in the yard, they probably wouldn't have thought of getting the gun.

They would have gone out to ask the guy what he was doing."

Lucas closed his copy of the file, rubbed his chin, squinted out at the street.

Virgil: "What?"

Lucas: "Revenge. Money. Sex."

Virgil: "Self-defense. Insanity."

"Does self-defense apply here?"

"It does if the killer thought Sand was about to do something to him," Virgil said. "Either as a judge or a rich guy with influence. Business and political influence. Social influence, maybe."

"Maybe we look at the cases he's been assigned but haven't come to trial yet," Lucas said. "The most extreme example of judge-shopping."

Virgil: "The FBI and us guys both looked at that. Came up dry."

"When you said 'social influence,' what are you talking about? You think he tried to keep somebody out of the Town and Country Club? Blackballed them?"

"He was at Somerset," Virgil said. "No known serious antagonisms over there. Russo checked with the members."

"All the members?"

"Yes. Russo actually got a list of all their male friends . . . and enemies, though there aren't many of those, and they're mostly people they simply didn't like, or who Cooper believed didn't like them. No real animus."

Lucas thumbed through to the list: "Twenty-two of them. He checked them all."

"They're doing everything," Virgil said. "The thing is, Sand was appointed by Obama. Some guys are thinking a right-wing nutcase . . ."

"A right-wing nutcase who killed Sand so a new judge could be appointed by Joe Biden?"

"Right-wing nutcases are not necessarily that good at critical analyses, as was demonstrated by the pizza shop basement fiasco." Virgil looked at his watch, and said, "We better get over to your place so you can change. Tell me one thing to think about."

Lucas considered, then said, "The killer sorta knew what he was doing. Two shots in the back to knock down Sand, one shot each to knock down the kids, then heart or head shots for all of them, to finish them for sure. He couldn't leave survivors. He figured that out before he went in. Rehearsed it."

"Yup."

"Now you tell *me* something," Lucas said.

Virgil thought for a moment, and said, "Like I said, self-defense. Or sex, somehow, but I can't see how, judging from what Russo got so far. Not money, because they had more than they needed and none of it is going out of the house because of the shooting. Not raving, delusional insanity — too carefully planned and he didn't kill the baby. I kinda don't think revenge, but it's a possibility. Psychopath or sociopath, for sure."

"Self-defense or sex. Interesting," Lucas said. "Let's go talk to the lovely Ms. Cooper."

"She's lovely?"

"She is — or was, anyway, to my eyes, judging from those photos," Lucas said. "After what happened, we'll see. If my kids were murdered, three weeks later I'd look like a fuckin' hobgoblin."

On the way out the door, the counter girl said, "I overheard some of that . . . I wasn't eavesdropping, I just . . . heard. You're cops, then?"

"We are," Virgil said.

"I thought about applying for the St. Paul cops," she said. She half turned away, with her eyes cutting back, as if she expected sarcasm.

"Well, they're hiring," Lucas said. "So is Minneapolis. So is everybody else."

"The problem is, I don't like cops very much," she said.

"Bad experience?" Lucas asked.

"I've had a lot of jobs like this, and they kinda . . . hit on me. A lot."

"Yeah, that's cops. Gonna be some built-in aggression. They're always pushing, especially new ones. Old ones mostly just want to get through the day," Virgil told her.

She laughed and said, "Well. Get through the day yourselves . . . have a nice one." Then she looked inside herself and added, "I say that all the time. The nice day thing. Cops don't have to do that, do they?"

Lucas: "We don't really deal with nice days. Not that often, anyway."

4

Virgil stood in Lucas's living room, yellow legal pad on top of the baby grand, rereading parts of the Sand file, making notes on interviews with Margaret Cooper.

Lucas was up and down in twenty minutes, shaven, wearing a lightweight gray wool suit, a French-blue shirt worn open at the neck, square-toed leather shoes, carrying a black half-length raincoat and a cane with a horn handle.

"I knew you must have a fashion cane somewhere," Virgil said, as he closed the legal pad. "Is there a sword in this one? Or a flask?"

"Fuck you."

"Yet another example of your flashing wit," Virgil said. He looked at his watch. "We've got twenty minutes. About right. Since you're no longer crippled, do you want to drive?"

Lucas did. As they walked out to the

garage, he said, "About that crippled thing . . . You've always been a flower child, concerned about oppressed people. I haven't been, so much."

"I've noticed that," Virgil said.

Lucas unplugged the car and as they settled into the Cayenne, he said. "I might have changed my views. I'm not passing out any flower blossoms, but, you know . . ."

"What are we talking about?"

As he backed the car out to the street, and dropped the garage door, Lucas said, "When I was back on my feet for a couple of weeks, I went downtown. I wanted to get up to the Skyways. I went in this bank building and the elevators were down because there was a power outage. I couldn't get up the stairs. I tried, but I couldn't do it. I made it to the first landing and I had to turn around and go back down. That wasn't the only time I had a problem, either. Weather and I'd go out for dinner, and I had to take the handicapped ramp at a couple of restaurants. I couldn't get up the steps without . . . ah, hell, never mind."

"No, I'm interested," Virgil said. "How'd you get up to your bedroom?"

"Funny you should ask."

"Not funny, huh?"

"No. I'd sit on the second step, pull my

good leg up to the first, and then push myself up two more steps," Lucas said. "Scooch my way to the top. I did that for . . . three weeks? Something like that. I refused to sleep in the study."

"You're saying you're a better man for the struggle?"

"I'm saying that I might hold a door for a crippled guy," Lucas said. "You know, if he looks like a decent guy who pays his taxes and he's crippled enough."

Virgil laughed. "Okay, some improvement. I wouldn't say a vast amount. I'm uncertain about the current social acceptability of the word 'crippled.' "

" 'Crippled' is okay. In my opinion. A long time ago I read this baseball autobiography by Bill Veeck," Lucas said. "You know who he is?"

"Ran the White Sox."

"Right. He lost a leg in World War II. He said he wasn't handicapped, he was just a cripple. Losing a leg didn't keep him from doing what he wanted to do, so he didn't consider himself handicapped."

"Strong worldview," Virgil said.

"Yeah. Crippled is better than handicapped. Being temporarily crippled taught me some things."

■ ■ ■ ■

They crossed the Mississippi at the Ford Bridge, threaded their way through south Minneapolis to Edina, a prosperous inner-ring suburb. The town was the subject of a limerick that began, "There was a young girl from Edina, who had a gold-plated vagina," universally known by Twin Cities poetasters.

Lucas recited the first two lines, said he could never remember the rest, and Virgil asked, "You know the avian one?"

"I do not."

"Same girl, rhymes 'vagina' with 'mynah.' As in mynah bird."

"Of course it does," Lucas said. "What's the rest of it?"

"I'd have to think about it," Virgil said. He pointed out the windshield. "Russo said it was a blue house; that must be it."

Cooper came to the door to meet them; another woman sat in the living room, on a pale green velvet couch, holding a baby wrapped in a blanket.

Cooper was tall and angular, but moved with a trained actor's grace; her dark brown hair was touched with auburn, either naturally or by a skilled hairdresser. Her hazel eyes were her most striking feature, not because of the color or set, but because of the sadness that lived there, along with a touch of wildness, fear, and loathing; the sadness extended to her mouth, which was wide and mobile.

She was wearing a gray silk blouse that chimed with her eyes, and black slacks; she was barefoot.

"Agent Flowers," she said to Virgil, extending a hand to shake.

Virgil took it and tipped his head at Lucas: "This is Lucas Davenport, a deputy U.S. Marshal that I work with sometimes."

She shook Lucas's hand and said to Virgil, "I know. When you called, I looked you up on the Internet and found pictures of you both, about that terrible shooting on Long Island. And I read you're a novelist now."

"I am," Virgil said.

"You were both shot," she said to Lucas. "You the worst."

Lucas lifted his cane: "It's getting better. I'm terribly sorry about what happened with your family, Ms. Cooper."

"Thank you. And . . . it's Maggie. To everybody."

"Are you all right?" Lucas asked.

"No. I'm a long fuckin' way from all right," Cooper said. Her face reflected that: she was without makeup, still pretty, but with a crinkling around the eyes that looked harsh and recent.

"It's the hardest," Lucas said.

"Yes." She had almost begun to vibrate, then suddenly seemed to relax, and showed a bit of a smile: "Well. Enough of that. Come in, tell me what you're doing. All the other officers seem quite capable, but from what I read on the Internet . . . you're the A-Team."

The house was warm and smelled vaguely of cooking, fading scents of lunch. The woman on the couch was Cooper's opposite, short, round and blond, pink cheeks. She was dressed in a brown cashmere sweater, fashion blue jeans, with cordovan dress boots. She said, "I'm Ann Melton, and this" — she lifted the baby in her arms — "is Chelsea Sand."

Virgil reached out and touched Chelsea's nose and said, "I've got a couple of these, a little older, boy and girl. Fraternal twins. The girl's just learned how to bite when she gets in fights with her brother."

"Good for her," Melton said.

Virgil leaned closer. Like all babies,

Chelsea looked basically like a loaf of bread, with hazy blue eyes. She looked incuriously at Virgil, and blew a bubble: Virgil said, "Mmm, Gerber's turkey with gravy."

Melton smiled and said, "You know your Gerber's."

Cooper sat on the couch next to Melton and pointed Lucas and Virgil at easy chairs. "I'll tell you anything I can and I won't lie about anything, no matter how painful. I told the same thing to the B-Team."

"We appreciate that," Lucas said, settling into a chair. "We'd like to talk with both of you, now, but we'd also like to talk to both of you individually, before we go."

Cooper looked at Melton, then back to Lucas: "I tell Ann everything. Even if we talk privately, I'll tell her about it."

"I'd do the same thing," Melton said.

"You can do what you want," Lucas said. "We'd still want to talk to you individually."

Melton said nothing. Cooper nodded. "Okay."

Whatever their relationship, she was in charge, Lucas thought.

Virgil: "We've read the investigation reports. These guys are good, meticulous — but they couldn't find anyone who would want to murder your husband out of revenge for his activities as a judge. You know, sending people to prison. . . ."

"That's what I understand. Alex would occasionally tell me about people who were angry because of the sentence he gave them, but . . . he said they were usually resigned and not surprised." Cooper leaned forward, hands on her knees; her fingernails were ragged, bitten down. "Here's something that I think somebody should do. They should look at the wives and girlfriends and children of the people he sentenced. That hasn't been done. You know, sometimes the Marshals Service . . ." She looked at Lucas. ". . . would seize what they called ill-gotten gains. Maybe that's not what they called it, but it was like that."

"Forfeiting the proceeds from illegal activity," Lucas said.

"Yes. Sometimes, even with low-level crimes like possession of drugs for sale, they would do things like seize a person's car or even a house, if they could show it was purchased with drug money. Alex would say that the man going to prison, he's fine. He's got housing, food, medical care, maybe even some friends inside. The people who were using the house and car might not be fine at all. They might be really screwed."

"But the killer wasn't a wife or child or

somebody's mother," Virgil said. "He was an adult male. From what we could see from the video, he wasn't a street person. We couldn't tell exactly how prosperous he was, but he was wearing what looked like a rain suit, a hoodie and rain pants. That's not what a low-level dealer would be wearing."

Melton spoke up: "The other team thinks that, too — but it seems to me that the man may have been consciously wearing a disguise, to hide something. His face, of course, but maybe his hands or . . . some physical thing. He didn't seem to limp in the videos . . ."

Lucas shrugged: "Hard to know, from what we've got."

"Something to consider," Cooper said. "The St. Paul officer who interviewed us said he thought the hoodie was from the University of Minnesota. I'm a professor there."

"We noticed that St. Paul was interviewing your friends and students at the U. Not kicking anything loose. Not yet," Virgil said. And, "Are you, have you gone back to work?"

"Yes. It takes my mind off these other things. I was told it would be good, if I could do it. I can."

Melton went back to the killer: "If he's not a street person, you think he was well-off?"

"Can't say that, but he didn't look poor," Virgil said. "We've identified the nine-millimeter pistol used in the murders as a Glock 17. Those are not cheap, and they're fairly big, for handguns, not easily hidden — they're not what you usually find on the street."

"Tool marks on the cartridge cases aren't necessarily definitive. How sure are you about the gun?" Cooper asked.

"Fairly sure," Virgil said. "It's true that there are sometimes problems — usually with the interpretation by the forensics people. Mistakes that are discovered later."

"But you don't think a mistake has been made," Melton said.

"We have no reason to think so," Virgil said.

"Which brings up the question of the missing pistol," Lucas said. "The nine-millimeter you once had."

Cooper threw up her hands: "I told the St. Paul and BCA investigators all about that, it should be in their notes. Alex got the gun when his father died, and he didn't want it around the house. There was a gun show across the river in Wisconsin, and he sold it there. That's all I know."

"Perfectly legal and easy to do," Melton said. "Legal at the time, anyway. It's the famous gun show loophole."

Lucas nodded. "Why did his father have it in the first place?"

"He was in the Army, and somehow, he got to keep it. Maybe he bought it. I don't know, maybe he stole it, though he wouldn't have thought of it that way. This was back in the late seventies, or early eighties. He was in the Army Reserve after that, a major, and got called up for Desert Storm in 1990. He talked about it endlessly."

Virgil looked at Lucas and said, "It wouldn't have been a Glock. It would have been a Beretta 92."

"If his father was in Desert Storm, and Alex inherited it, his father must have died young," Lucas said.

Cooper nodded. "Both his parents died young, they were both sixty-two. They were killed by a drunk driver outside a restaurant on Grand Avenue. Mowed down, crossing the street. Alex was already out of law school at the time."

"Actually, I remember that," Lucas said. "Must have been ten years ago. Fifteen?"

"Mmm . . . thirteen, now," Cooper said.

Nowhere to go with that.

Cooper was peering at Lucas: "When we were talking about wives and children, and ill-gotten gains, you thought of something. I saw it on your face."

"What I thought of is probably a coincidence. I won't talk about it until I check," Lucas said. "Almost certainly nothing."

"C'mon."

Lucas smiled and shook his head. "Maybe some other time."

"We understand that your husband had inherited wealth, which has to be tended to," Virgil said. "That brings up the question of whether he was involved in any business affairs, or investment affairs, where . . . you know, there might have been a problem. Like undiscovered fraud, embezzlement, some kind of scam?"

Cooper: "Not that I'm aware of. Alex was quite open about money, about our investments. I mean, between the two of us. If he'd spotted a problem, he would have told me. He insisted that I learn about the money in case something happened to him . . . which has. We gave a list of our financial advisors to the other team, and they've contacted them, but nothing came of it. Some of the interviews were perfunctory. I've been doing a review, looking for problems, but haven't finished with it yet."

"How soon will you finish?" Lucas asked.

"I have calls in this afternoon. One thing you should know is — this may be what has frustrated the other investigators trying to find a motive in the money — is that Alex didn't trust small companies," Cooper said. "Our money is placed with major companies and banks, where the investment supervision is done by teams. Crimes like embezzlement would be almost impossible to pull off, and if something did happen, the company would make good."

"That's what people thought about the Madoff firm before it went up in smoke," Virgil said.

"Madoff was small, compared to . . . I'm talking about J.P. Morgan, which has two and a half trillion dollars under management, not five or ten billion. And *we* own the stock and bonds — the companies don't," Cooper said. She unconsciously put a ring finger up to her mouth and nibbled on a fingernail, and Melton reached out and pushed the hand down. Cooper barely seemed to notice, and continued: "Even if the companies fail, the investments are ours. We have real estate investments where we have the deeds locked away. We don't manage it, but there's no question about who owns the properties. It can't simply be swindled away. Alex was extremely security conscious. He even took some seminars in how to protect your investments, especially from online thieves and scammers."

"So you wouldn't lose money, but an embezzler could go to jail if anyone found out what he'd done," Lucas said.

"Yes, exactly," she said. "I'll push it hard this afternoon and call you if I see anything suspicious. We consult extensively with one local company, Barnes and Blue, but they don't hold our investments. We pay them a fee for their advice, based on the value of the investments. They couldn't steal anything even if they wanted to."

Virgil patted the thick file he'd brought in with him. "Most of the financial information is in here, but Lucas and I haven't had a chance to review the details yet. What we really need from you isn't so much hard facts. The other guys piled up a lot of those. What we need is more like . . . stories. What you think, what you suspect, little things that may have popped into your head . . . In one of the stories that Lucas and I have talked about, we were wondering if *you* might have been the target. Because you got home late, the killer missed you."

"I got home late, but I didn't get home

later than I was expected," Cooper said. She stood up, turned around, restless, sat back down and reached over to Melton to touch the baby. "We have a play coming up and we rehearse late. Everybody knows that. Or, at least, anyone who was interested could find out."

"Is there anyone who might have profited, or might have thought he could profit, from his friendship with you, if Alex was gone?" Virgil asked.

"If you're asking if I had an affair, or if I'm having one, the answer is no. I haven't had an affair. As far as I know, nobody is enamored of me, although . . ."

She hesitated, rubbed her nose . . .

"Tell us," Virgil said. "Although what?"

". . . Although, you know, I teach theater students. Talented students. They can be quite emotional. Theater is an emotional calling," Cooper said. "From time to time, we will recommend certain student actors for auditions for commercial projects. Or, we have to decide who gets what role in a play — who gets to be a star, who carries a spear. We have to disappoint people. As I've said, they can be extremely emotional. Angry. Depressed. We've had people threaten suicide."

Lucas: "Okay, that's something. The BCA

has interviewed your students. These are the theater people, the actors?"

"Yes. The BCA did interview them, but in a general way. You know, checking alibis. They didn't have much to work with. The BCA isn't too invested in the idea that I was the target."

"Do you think you might have been?" Lucas asked.

"Thinking about it? Really? No, I don't. I don't think anyone dislikes me enough, hates me enough, and I don't know anyone capable of doing this killing," Cooper said. "I understand that people can suffer psychotic breaks, or perhaps are full-blown psychopaths and have kept that aspect hidden, but my whole life revolves around people who act . . . who create different characters for themselves. I would see a psychopath who was trying to hide his real character. I don't know any — I don't see any around me. I really see no profit for anyone in killing Alex and my boys. Certainly not to get at me, in any way."

"You probably *do* know a psychopath or two," Lucas said, mildly. "As many as two to four percent of successful business people are psychopaths . . . so . . ."

"That's a little shocking," Melton said. She turned her head to Cooper and said,

"I've had some questions about Calvin Crater. The way he looks at women."

"He's a little odd, but I've never heard anyone complain," Cooper said. "Except, you know, about that fucking accordion. And the fucking concertina."

Melton shrugged.

Virgil asked, "Who is Calvin Crater?"

Lucas answered him: "He's a psychiatrist. He plays an accordion in a New Orleans jazz band, and when the chamber orchestra needs an accordion, they get him, because he's good. He's not the guy we're looking for."

"You're sure about that?" Melton asked.

"He's about five-seven and portly. Maybe five-eight on his tiptoes," Lucas said. "He wouldn't be the shooter unless he was wearing stilts."

Cooper nodded: "That's true. How do you know him?"

"My wife is on the chamber orchestra board, and we know him that way," Lucas said. "We've been to the same orchestra parties."

Melton said, "Really. Your wife's name is Davenport?"

"Weather Karkinnen . . ."

Melton smiled and said, "Weather! This is really a small town. I met her years ago.

Haven't seen her in a while, but I still go to the chamber orchestra." To Cooper, she said, "Weather is one of the best plastic surgeons in the Twin Cities. Maybe the best."

"What do you do?" Lucas asked Melton.

"I'm an attorney. I'm a partner in Alex's old firm, before he became a judge," Melton said. "I've taken some personal time to . . . you know . . . hang out with Margaret."

"Nice. Good friends," Virgil said.

For the next hour, they plodded though the file, asking questions that came sideways out of the facts, pushing the two women to speculate. In the end, the women agreed to look more closely at Sand's financial affairs. Melton said she could help with that; Cooper thought it more likely that the killings were the result of something that happened in court.

Lucas asked Melton: "Is it possible that something happened back *before* Alex was a judge, something in his legal firm, came back to him? Something traumatic, a lost case?"

She looked up at the ceiling for a moment, then said, "He's been a judge for eight years, so that's unlikely. But, I'll have one of our paralegals pull all his cases going back, say, fifteen years. See if anything pops. The B-Team didn't ask that."

Lucas smiled and said, "Please don't call them a B-Team, at least where they can hear about it. They're good at what they do, and it'll piss them off. At Virgil and me. They'll think we started it."

Virgil looked at Cooper: "Could we get a couple of private minutes with you? Now?"

She nodded and Melton said, "I'll go put Chelsea down. Call me when you need me."

Lucas: "I've got to run out to the car and make a personal call. Back in a minute."

Out in the car, he called Weather, who was driving from her University Hospitals office to Regions Hospital in St. Paul, where she was also on staff. "You know an Ann Melton?"

"Sort of. To nod to, small talk before concerts. She's a regular. Her ex-husband is a radiologist, I knew him better. He goes to the concerts with his new wife."

"Ah. I didn't know she'd been married," Lucas said. "She's not now, I don't think. She doesn't have a ring and there's no sign of a husband around her house. I was going to ask you if she might be gay."

"Is that important?" Weather asked.

"It could be, if she had a sexual relationship with Margaret Cooper."

"Okay. Yes, I've gotten that feeling with her," Weather said. "That kind of testing thing — she's never hit on me or anything, but there's this . . . thing . . ."

"Vibration. I get it from gay guys, just checking," Lucas said.

"Right. She was married, her ex might have some ideas about her status."

"Won't be necessary. I'm gonna ask her," Lucas said. "Or Cooper."

"Tread lightly," Weather said. "I like her."

"But you like everybody."

"Not true . . ."

Lucas said goodbye and went back to Melton's house and let himself in. Cooper was still on the couch but Melton had gone. Virgil had asked if it were possible that Melton had had a relationship with Sand, when they worked at the same firm, and Cooper was in the process of replying that it was not possible.

"They were really quite friendly. And competitive, to some extent — Alex had the benefit of being wealthy and he was something of the firm's rainmaker because of his social contacts. She didn't have that. But she worked harder," Cooper said. "They were friendly enough, still were when Alex and the boys . . . you know. She was married, but never had children. She took an interest in ours. Like a godmother."

"Why did Alex accept an appointment as a judge?" Virgil asked. "His firm is well known in the Cities, he must have been doing very well there, financially . . ."

Cooper smiled: "The fact is — and it was resented, I'm sure — he didn't have to do well. He went in financially secure, so he didn't care how well he did financially. What he cared about was *time.* Being a judge can be difficult, but the job doesn't consume vast amounts of time. Being a law-firm partner does. We had our boys . . ." She stopped, teared up, wiped the tears away and continued. "We had two boys who were growing up, and he wanted to spend more time with them. His father hadn't spent much time with Alex. He was a go-getter, had the Army thing, got a law degree, big shot at 3M, had his cigars and his golf club buddies . . . a jerk, frankly. Alex didn't want to be that."

"Okay." Virgil turned to Lucas. "Any questions?"

Lucas edged closer to Cooper: "Is Ann gay?"

Virgil swiveled back to Cooper. A faint

blush appeared on her cheeks. "I . . . you know, that's a —"

Lucas: "Did you have a sexual relationship with Ann?"

Now she showed anger: "Why would that —"

"She might resent a husband, a husband with children," Lucas said.

"Does she look like she's six feet tall and thin?"

"So you're saying, yes, at some time you had a sexual relationship with Ann," Lucas said.

"I'm not saying . . ."

"Tell the truth," Lucas said. "You said you wouldn't lie about anything."

Cooper said, "Yes. We've had a relationship. Not serious, just fun."

"Was it just fun for Ann?" Virgil asked. "Or was it more serious . . ."

"I don't . . . know. Maybe it was," she said.

"How recently in the past?" Lucas asked. "This year?"

She looked at him for several seconds, then at Virgil and back to Lucas: "Yes. But like I said, it was just fun."

"Did Alex know about it?"

"No. I'm sure he didn't. Alex was very . . . conservative in his own way," Cooper said. "Too conservative. I really came of age in the theater business, where things are different."

Virgil and Lucas peered at her and she started streaming tears, looked down into her lap, then asked, "Do you have to push Ann about this?"

"Should we?" Lucas asked.

"No. I don't know. I don't see how . . . I don't see how she could be involved in anything, with murder . . ."

"Does she handle criminal cases?" Virgil asked.

"Not really. She mostly does estate work. The firm will do minor criminal stuff for wealthy clients — you know, people they want to come back. Like kids busted for shoplifting cigarettes, or whatever. Do you remember, a couple of years back, a boy murdered his girlfriend and another boy he thought was sleeping with her?"

They both did.

"That case came to Ann. She immediately sent it out to the firm of a man named Marvin Fingerhut . . ."

"We know him," Virgil said.

"Our firm, Alex's old firm, Ann's firm . . . they didn't want anything to do with it. That was going to be a big-money case. Lots of publicity. It needed specialist criminal defense attorneys. That's not what we did.

What Ann does."

When they'd pushed the questions about Melton as far as they could, Cooper asked, "Do you have to ask Ann about our relationship? Whatever you'd call it? It was just like a thing, you know, not . . ."

"Yes. We have to ask. We know two things now that the other guys apparently didn't," Lucas said. "You had a relationship with somebody who might be jealous of what you had with Alex and your boys; and she had at least some access to criminals. Perhaps had access to somebody who might be willing to do her a favor."

"Ah, God. This is awful."

When they called for Melton, she came and said, "Chelsea's asleep. Everything okay here?" She looked at Cooper's face, saw tears, and said, "Uh-oh."

"Talk to these two," Cooper told her. "I'll be in the back."

When she was gone, Melton settled on the couch and asked, "What happened?"

"We asked her about your sexual relationship," Virgil said. "We pointed out that you might have some animus directed at Alex Sand, if you were in love with Maggie — and because you occasionally deal with criminals, in your work, you might have access to somebody who'd do you a . . . favor."

Melton gaped at them. "A favor? A favor? You mean, murdering her family?"

Lucas nodded: "Yes. That's what we mean."

"Oh, fuck you," Melton shrieked. She pushed up to her feet, her face red with rage. She was shouting: "I would never do anything to hurt those people. They were my friends. Alex was my friend. I loved those kids, they were like my kids. You people go throwing accusations around —"

"We're not doing that," Lucas snapped. "We're not on TV — we're talking to you. Tell us why we're wrong to ask. Try not to get too deep into bullshit."

"Oh, this is going to get out," Melton shouted. "You're going to let it out, so you can bring some pressure. Mrs. Sand and her lesbo lover —"

Lucas, loud, talking over her: "We don't *care* what you and Mrs. Sand do in your love life. We're not interested in the sex, we're not interested how often you were in bed, we're not interested in whether it was having an effect on her marriage. All we're interested in is how much stress did Maggie's relationship with Alex place on you, and what you might have done about it."

"I didn't do anything about it." Saliva

trickled out of the side of her mouth, and she wiped it away with a finger. "We . . ."

Virgil: "Who else knows about the relationship?"

"Nobody!" Then she hesitated, and said, "Nobody now."

"What does that mean?" Virgil asked. "Now?"

Melton looked away from them, then took it down a notch, and said, "We were all in school together, Alex, Maggie and I. A couple of people, a couple of girls, might have known that Maggie and I were . . . affectionate. Experimenting. Not serious. We're *not* in love. Never have been. The sex is fun and recreational. Period."

Virgil: "You had no particular feeling about Alex?"

She shook her head: "No, I didn't." She turned away for a minute, then turned back. "Okay, that's not true. I liked him. We'd sit around after work and have a martini and tell stories. He was a good guy. I'm almost as screwed up about this as Maggie." She stopped, thought about that for a second, then amended, "Okay, that's not true, either. I'd have been a lot more screwed up if it'd been Maggie who got shot."

Lucas: "You never had any kind of physical relationship with Alex?"

"No. No. When I was married, the bottom line was, I really didn't much care about . . . accommodating him. My husband was a nice enough guy, a doctor, but I didn't care about the sex with him."

Lucas said, "You know —"

Melton interrupted: "I'd just like to say, for the record, that you're an asshole." She looked at Virgil: "You, not so much."

Lucas: "Thank you. I have to say, I tend to believe you. I want to believe you. But, we're going to have to dig into this enough that we're satisfied. We need to know where you were the night of the murders. We need to go to your law firm and ask for a list of clients you've worked for."

Virgil: "We'll tell them that it's all routine and even grasping at straws. But we *will* get the list."

"You want to see if I might know a killer," Melton said. "A contract killer . . . or somebody who owes me and who might become a killer."

"Yes."

"You're wasting your time, but go ahead," Melton said. "Since I know I didn't have anything to do with what happened to Alex, I'd appreciate it if you could do what you said — give me some cover with the firm."

"We will," Virgil said. "Now, give us a

timeline for where you were on the night of the murders. And did you hear about them from Maggie?"

They worked through the timeline. As she sat on the couch, eyes closed, casting back to the night of the killings, she came up with a half-dozen checkable people and locations, all in Minneapolis.

Lucas glanced at Virgil, who gave him a quick shake of the head: she wasn't involved.

When they were done, Virgil thanked her and said, "We may want to come back and talk to you some more."

"Yeah, that'll be a real pleasure," she snapped.

They called Cooper back into the living room; she came in carrying a cup of coffee, and asked, "All done?"

"For the time being," Lucas said.

"I gotta get away from them," Melton said, and she disappeared into the back of the house.

"Did you cut her up bad?" Cooper asked, as she watched Melton go.

"We asked the question," Lucas said.

"I sorta heard," she said. Cooper took a sip of the coffee. "I snuck up to the kitchen door and listened to parts of it. I couldn't hear all of it. Nobody . . . none of the other investigators . . . I mean, they seemed to know everything about the murders. Every fact you can imagine. They knew exactly, surgically, how my family died. What each individual bullet did. Who really needs to know that? What happened was obvious . . . they were shot and killed."

Virgil said, "The more you know, generally, the better off you are."

Cooper shook her head: "I don't believe that. They had an enormous amount of information that didn't add up to anything. That never had a possibility of adding up to anything. They told me Alex and the boys were killed with a nine-millimeter handgun. I went online and looked up nine-millimeter handguns and guess what? They're the most common murder weapon in America. So determining that meant absolutely nothing."

"It does mean something — it means we can't look for an unusual gun. It eliminated other guns," Lucas said. "Now we've learned it was a Glock, and even which model of Glock, so —"

"Oh, bullshit," Cooper said. "Are Glocks rare guns? Are they even uncommon?"

"No . . ."

"But, what I was getting at . . . You two came in here and picked up the relationship between Ann and myself," Cooper said. "That won't turn into anything, I promise you, but it could have. None of those fact investigators had a clue about that relationship."

She took another sip of the coffee: "You really are the A-Team," she said. "That gives me a little hope that you'll find the killer."

As Lucas and Virgil got up to leave, she asked, "Do you have cards? I have cards for everyone else. I'll try not to bother you. Annoy you."

"Sure," Virgil said, and he and Lucas handed her their business cards. "Don't worry about bothering us. We may wind up bothering you even more. If you think of anything, call. *Anything.*"

Driving away from Melton's house, Lucas said, "Nice that somebody thinks we're the A-Team. Nice that somebody thinks that there even *is* an A-Team."

Virgil: "Cooper said you thought of something, she could see it on your face. What did you think of?"

"That long list of people that Sand sent to prison. A guy named Larry Brickell was on it," Lucas said. "You remember him?"

"Mmm. Not offhand," Virgil said.

"Wasn't a real big deal. Two years ago, he was out on pre-sentencing bail after he was convicted of killing some wolves up north . . ."

"Got it. He didn't show up for sentencing. You guys went after him — not you, but some marshals — and there was a shootout," Virgil said. "Nobody hurt?"

"One of our guys got scuffed up, nobody got shot. Brickell went off to prison for the wolves and came back later for the shooting, pled guilty and got more time for ag assault. He's still inside, so nobody's paid attention to him. The thing is . . . I might be wrong . . ."

"Yes?"

"One guy thought it was Brickell's old lady who was shooting at them, if I'm remembering right," Lucas said. "Brickell pled to it, and said his wife was hiding behind a woodstove during the shooting. Our guy said he was fairly sure she was the one with the rifle. That went away when Brickell took the fall."

"You need to call your guy," Virgil said. "Uh, there's something else. Not sure how it applies."

Lucas: "What? About Brickell, or . . ."

Virgil said, "About Cooper and Melton. I've been mulling it over ever since . . . almost the beginning of the interview. Did you notice that they were aware of the small details of the investigation?"

"I did. I was even going to ask about it, but then it popped into my mind that they might have had an affair with each other. That sort of drove everything else out," Lucas said. "Like, I forgot to ask where they got the details."

"They knew that nobody went after the wives and girlfriends of people Sand sentenced," Virgil said. "They suggested that the killer might have disguised himself to hide some identifying infirmity, or some other characteristic. They referred to 'tool marks' on the cartridge cases — that's cop talk."

Lucas: "They said interviews with financial advisors were perfunctory. Even if they had a source inside the investigation, if somebody was keeping them informed, no cop would admit they'd done anything perfunctory. Not in a high-profile murder case."

Virgil said, "They've seen the case files. They're trying to be cops."

"Who'd show them?" Lucas asked.

"We could ask around . . ."

"Ask who? Nobody would admit it," Lucas said. "And we need to stay on friendly terms with the B-Team."

"Yeah. Interesting, though. That they're inside, somehow."

They rode in silence for a minute, then Lucas said, "You could be wrong about one thing — they might not be trying to be cops. They might want to know exactly what we're doing so they can dodge the cops."

"I don't think they're involved," Virgil said.

"You're ready to eliminate them?"

Virgil looked out the side window, thought about it: "No."

They drove on, and as they crossed the Mississippi, Virgil recited, "There was a young girl from Edina/Who stuffed avians in her vagina/One day she sneezed/And quick as you please/Out popped a sparrow, a wren and a mynah."

Lucas: "That's disgusting. I'll buy the sparrow and wren, but a mynah? C'mon."

5

Cooper stood at the door and watched, through a small diamond-shaped inset window, as Lucas and Virgil got in their car. Without turning, she said, "They're smart."

"Smarter than us?" Melton asked from the living room.

The Cayenne moved away from the curb and down the street, and Cooper turned to Melton, shrugged, and said, "Maybe as smart as us. And they have experience dealing with all kinds of criminals. Like us."

"We're not criminals yet," Melton said. "I guess if they found out about . . . I mean, John Larch gave me the BCA computer link more than a year ago, for the Karr kid, and it has nothing to do with the current situation. I doubt that John even remembers it. He thinks he was doing a good thing."

"Even if the Karr kid was a miserable little jerk, as he obviously was?" Cooper asked.

"Even miserable little jerks get to know

111

the exculpatory evidence, what the cops have," Melton said. "That BCA dickhead was holding out. It wasn't the first time, either."

"I don't want to argue," Cooper said. "Did you look at the file this morning before you went to work?"

"No. We can look now. I don't expect much. Kitchen table, make some smoothies."

Cooper went to the kitchen and got out the blender, along with an oversized tub of whey protein, a sack of frozen strawberries, and a quart of orange juice. Melton went to her bedroom and came back with her laptop and purse, set them on the kitchen table, and brought the computer up. Cooper dumped a handful of strawberries, a scoop of whey and several ounces of orange juice into the blender and hit Blend.

As the blender screeched and the computer went through its booting routine, Melton got her wallet from her purse and took out a limp dollar bill. She smoothed it on the table, and when the computer came up, she searched for a hidden file called CP5591, which was her father's initials followed by his birth year backwards, which wasn't hard to remember.

The file produced nothing but a blinking cursor. She spaced over two places, then entered E 26938920 I exactly as it appeared on the dollar bill she'd taken from her purse. The computer hesitated, decrypting the file, then burped up a link.

Melton carefully tucked the dollar bill back into her wallet and put the wallet back into her purse.

Cooper licked a spoon covered with strawberry smoothie. "Got it?"

"I do." Melton clicked on the link. Seconds later, as Cooper poured the smoothie into two glasses, she was looking at the BCA file on the Sand murder. The file contained photographs, which they never looked at anymore. It also contained a number at the bottom of the last page that indicated how many words were in the file.

"It's up four hundred words, more or less," Melton said. "Can't be much. Do you want to scan?"

"Might as well."

Scanning took fifteen minutes, because the file was fat. They found the additional four hundred words in an interview with a man named Ben Louis Pritchard, whose car had pulled off the road below the wooded bluff where the Sand house stood, a few days before the murders. A speed camera had picked up the license plate coming and going. Pritchard was not seen getting out of the car, and nobody was seen getting in. In the interview, Pritchard, a salesman for a barn-building contractor, claimed to have been talking to a worried horse owner about construction of a four-stall addition to her barn. He'd pulled over, he said, because he didn't have a hands-free telephone link in his car.

The horse owner backed him up. When the BCA agent asked why she'd called him so late in the day, between six and seven, she said, "I needed to get it done, the new stalls. Those people moved so slow it was like watching mold grow. I had three more horses coming from Europe."

Pritchard said, "She called me every fifteen minutes. I'm not saying she's nuts, but I'd say she was . . . worried. We got the job done on time. Almost."

He'd seen nobody on foot, as far as he could remember.

"Nothing," Cooper said, and Melton closed the file.

Cooper took a turn around the kitchen island, shook her head a couple of times, then said, "Davenport and Flowers aren't reporting. Flowers is in the system, but only on old cases."

Melton: "If they keep up with their paper-work, like they should, we'll be able to keep up with them. On the other hand, maybe they won't do that. They seem to work on their own."

"We could be blind to the competition," Cooper said.

"We have an advantage. Once they've identified a suspect, they won't go right at him, not unless they somehow find DNA and there isn't any question," Melton said. "Otherwise, they'll do a lot of running around, nailing down the suspect. If we can find out who that is . . . and we should be able to do that . . . we can move, as long as we're morally certain that they've got the right guy."

"But if it's Davenport and Flowers, and if they're really loners and keep it to them-selves . . ."

"At that point, when they believe they've identified the guy, they'll have to talk to their superiors at the BCA and it'll go in the file," Melton argued.

"I hope," Cooper said. "We've still got to get a gun."

"That's the scary part. I say we move now. Tomorrow," Melton said. "We've put it off long enough. We know where he is, and what kind of shape he's in. He'll go for it."

"I'll talk to him alone," Cooper said. "I don't want him to see your face."

"I'm good with that," Melton said. "When the cops kick down your door, I'll be your defense attorney."

"If we get caught at it, Davenport and Flowers will know what we're up to," Cooper said.

"We're either going to do it, or not," Melton said.

Cooper took a deep breath: "We're doing it."

"If Carter doesn't go for it, we might have to call the whole thing off."

"Nope. I won't do that," Cooper said. "We're gonna do it."

In bed that night, Cooper began to kick. She couldn't help it. The movement started with her legs, twitching, kicking, then her whole body would begin to shake. Not a random spasm, but a fight response. She was fighting, killing.

As long as she was talking, as long as she had a specific focus of some importance, she could function. Alone in bed, her mind began to churn, and her body followed suit.

She went from despair, to depression, and then to anger. The anger was always there, like a ball of fire in her belly. She'd been told she was suffering a variety of PTSD, created by her discovery of her murdered family.

But it was worse than that. Under any circumstances, stumbling on the murder scene would have been traumatizing enough. Her mind unreeled it, like a video, from stepping through the door from the garage, to the sound of the olive jar shattering as it hit the floor, and the sight of the bodies.

She and Alex had problems in their marriage, as all couples did, but Alex was a good man who loved her and loved their kids, and she loved them all back. At night, her mind would flow helplessly through the lost histories: one that recurred was the trip they'd taken when the kids were small, to western Nebraska, to see a total eclipse of the sun.

The trip was the first long car journey for the boys, but they'd been great, driving through the badlands of South Dakota, then through the crowds at Mount Rushmore, and hooking south to Nebraska to get into the path of totality.

The trip had been perfect, and hung in her mind like a postcard. There were other postcards and then came the horror movie.

117

There was one shattering image — the most awful thing of all, that her mind couldn't avoid as hard as she tried: when the bullet smashed through Arthur's head, it forced one eyeball out of its socket, and it came to rest on the floor, with a trail of bloody eye muscle or nerves or ligaments — she'd never asked which it was — and the single blue eye staring up at her.

Right at her, like an accusation: why weren't you're here to save me?

Irrational, crazy, but there it was, absolutely unavoidable, a flash of horror that came to her whenever she relaxed, whenever her mind lost immediate focus.

She tried to twist away from it before the Ambien pulled her under; tried to think of Davenport and Flowers, two men who'd made an effort to be thoughtful, but for whom the murders were simply a part of their jobs. They'd even seen worse.

They didn't live the horror as she did . . .

At eight o'clock the next morning, Cooper and Melton were moving, the baby dozing in a car seat in back. They drove straight east out I-94, to the St. Croix River, the border between Minnesota and Wisconsin. They turned north without crossing the bridge, to the old town of Stillwater, once a major stop for St. Croix and Mississippi steamboats.

In the light of day, Melton asked, "Are you sure?"

"I'm sure. If there's any doubt, I'll apologize and back away."

"I'm feeling kinda shaky."

"So am I, but I'm gonna do it anyway," Cooper said. They'd driven by the apartment on a scouting trip, and Cooper pointed through the windshield: "There it is. Take the car around the corner, where you're out of sight. I'll walk."

They found a parking space on a hillside, and the women looked at each other, and Cooper said, "Take care of Chelsea. If, you know . . ."

"I will. Go."

Cooper put on sunglasses and walked down the hill, nearly stumbled on broken concrete, turned the corner, trying to keep it casual and unnoticeable, and strolled down the block. Henry James Carter lived in a four-story condo on Stillwater's main drag, a red-brick building with dark glass windows looking out toward the river.

The entry opened to a lobby with a locked door to the interior. Cooper found Carter's name on a mailbox and pushed the call button above it. A man answered, "Hello? Who is it?"

"I'm a friend of the court, Mr. Carter. I need to see you on important business."

"What kind of business?"

"The kind you'd want to keep confidential. If you let me up, I can explain it all."

"You sound strange," Carter said.

"I assure you, this conversation will be greatly to your benefit, if you wish it to be."

Cooper could hear a woman's voice, apparently behind Carter, asking, "Who is it?"

"I dunno. I'm going to let her up."

The door lock buzzed, and Cooper walked over to the interior door and pulled it open.

Carter lived on the third floor. There was an elevator, but she took the stairs. At the top, she pushed open the door and saw Carter, in crazy-quilt patterned sweatpants, a black tee-shirt and suede slippers, standing in a doorway, looking down at her. He was balding and overweight. A pair of copper-rimmed glasses sat on his button nose.

Cooper walked that way and as she came up, Carter frowned and asked, "Who are you?"

"Elizabeth Cooper. Judge Alex Sand's wife."

"Alex Sand . . . put me in prison."

"I know. Now he's been murdered along

with my two young boys," Cooper said. "That's what I want to talk to you about. I have an envelope full of cash that I may give to you, for five minutes' conversation."

The woman, who was standing behind Carter, out of sight, asked, "What does she want?"

"Dunno," Carter said. He looked skeptically at Cooper, chewed his lower lip, then said, "All right. I'll listen, anyway. Come in."

Cooper followed him into the apartment, which was furnished in bland big-box-store furniture, tchotchkes, family photos, and framed Springsteen and Fleetwood Mac posters. The place smelled faintly of cigar smoke. Carter pointed Cooper at a couch, and she sat. The woman, who was wearing a quilted bathrobe, had reddish-purple hair showing some gray at the roots.

Carter said, "So . . ."

Cooper looked at the woman and asked, "Are you Mrs. Carter?"

The woman nodded: "Yes. Catherine."

Cooper settled in a bit, looked around the apartment, put her shoulder bag on the floor by her foot. The Carters were poor: the furnishings showed some effort, but no cash. Cooper rarely saw anything like it, except at the occasional grad-student party; and grad-student parties usually showed some creativity, which was absent here.

She turned back to the Carters. "Had you heard about my husband and sons?"

"Of course," Carter said. "It was all over TV news."

"Okay. Well, here's the situation." Cooper sat a moment, smoothing her slacks, then said, "When I learn who the killer is, I plan to murder him."

The Carters looked at each other, and then Catherine said, "What?"

"I plan to shoot him. My husband found Henry's case interesting," Cooper said. She looked directly at Carter. "He told me that guns were apparently your major interest in life and when you were convicted of a felony . . . that was the end of the guns."

Carter nodded and said, "I really call myself Jim, not Henry . . . I'm hoping to have my civil rights restored. I have a lawyer looking at what would have to happen, and he says it's possible. I was never convicted of violence of any kind."

"The lawyer's looking at the possibilities if we send him a check," Catherine Carter said. "Otherwise, we can go suck on it."

Cooper nodded. "I'm aware that Henry . . . Jim . . . has paid his debt to society, and I approve, certainly. Anyway, Alex told me that you had a federal firearms license, and in addition to being a car salesman, you dealt high-quality guns, far and wide."

"I did," Carter said. "All legal. And careful. I'd never sell to anyone under twenty-five, or anyone I thought might have violent tendencies. Like you."

"I hope you'll make an exception in my case, and I'll explain why, in a minute. Could you tell me, simply as a matter of information, if you needed to . . . access . . . a high-quality pistol equipped with a suppressor, how long would it take you to do that, and how much would it cost?"

Carter hesitated, then said, "If you're wearing a wire, you have to tell me. This sounds like entrapment."

"It's not. I'm not wearing a wire. Alex Sand's wife wouldn't be attempting to entrap somebody, and if you don't think I was really his wife, you could go online and look at pictures of me," Cooper said. "There are a lot of them."

Catherine Carter nodded: "I recognize you."

Cooper: "So, how long, and how much? I would pay you for a name and address if you could send me to the right person."

"That won't work. Anyone selling a cold gun with a suppressor . . . they'd want to know the face," Carter said. "Then, if you killed someone, they'd blackmail you."

Cooper thought that over for a moment, then asked, "How long would it take *you* to get one? Just, for instance?"

"Just for instance . . ."

Catherine Carter said, "Jack."

Carter repeated, "Jack. If he's home, and he almost always is . . . it'd take me thirty minutes to get there, thirty minutes back, depending on traffic, and we'd talk for a while to make the deal. Maybe an hour and a half, total."

"He wouldn't have a problem with your felony?" Cooper asked.

Carter laughed: "Where do you think the Minneapolis gangs get their guns? No, he wouldn't have a problem with the felony."

"He'd have an appropriate gun?"

"Yes, but it'd cost," Carter said. "It'd be cold, bought on the black market down in Alabama or Mississippi, cost maybe five thousand with the suppressor."

"Good quality?"

"Yes, most likely a Ruger or a Glock. Do you know guns?"

"I took some lessons years ago," Cooper said. "I still have a gun in the house, a revolver, but the police know about it and I can't use that one."

"That's wise," Carter said. He bit his lip. "What's in it for me?"

"I will give you the five thousand dollars, in cash, for the gun. I will give you, personally, twenty thousand to get it for me."

The couple exchanged quick glances: they wanted the money. "How soon?" Carter asked.

"Right now," Cooper said. "I won't pay until I have the gun and a box of the right ammunition."

"What if I went to the cops and said, 'I got a woman who wants to buy a gun to commit murder, and if you give me my civil rights, I'll tell you who it is'?"

Cooper smiled: "I'm deranged. Temporarily insane with grief. If you told the police that, as soon as they heard the name, they'd back off. They wouldn't want to have anything to do with it. A psychiatric worker might come to see me. And you wouldn't get twenty thousand dollars."

The Carters considered that for a moment, then Catherine asked, "What if you got caught, and they offered a deal. They'd give you time off if you gave up the dealer?"

Cooper shook her head. "First, I'm smart. I'd never do anything that might get me caught. If I did, I'd say that Alex bought the gun at a gun show years ago, because he thought owning a silencer would be neat. If you give me a gun that I could use to kill the man who killed my family, I'd be grateful forever. I'd never turn on you."

"How do you know that we wouldn't turn on you? If there was a reward or something?" Carter asked.

"Would you really admit to facilitating a first-degree murder?" Cooper shook her head again. "If this happens, we may never see each other again, but we'll be bound together. Neither of us would be able to testify to anything, without admitting murder or accessory to murder."

The Carters stared at her for a moment, then Carter said, "Twenty thousand for me?"

"Or a little more," Cooper said. "I brought plenty. And really, don't think about assaulting me and taking it away. I'm not here alone."

Carter looked at his wife, then said, "Let me and Cathy talk in the bedroom for a minute."

Cooper waited patiently as the two disappeared into the back of the condo; they were gone only three or four minutes. When they emerged, Catherine Carter said, "We'll do it, if we think we can be safe. You're smart, tell us how we can do that — be safe."

"First of all, don't use your phones for any of this. Don't call Jack to see if he's home, just show up," Cooper said. "I'll take any good-quality automatic pistol. With a suppressor, I guess they're called. A silencer."

"Yeah, but you've got to know they're not very silent," Carter said.

"I plan to get some practice before I use it," Cooper said. "After I use it, within the hour, it will be buried in a hole in a state park where it will never be found, so there's no way it will kick back on you. I'll give you your cash now, today, but you can't spend it on anything expensive, or noticeable, because the police or the IRS could get onto that and start asking questions. You could buy inexpensive stuff. You could go to estate and yard sales and flea markets, you could buy food and clothing and medicine, all of that. Anything where you can reasonably pay cash. Not a car."

"I see that," Carter said. "I pretty much lived that way when I was boosting those cars. I did hit some Indian casinos."

"You could still hit some native casinos, as long as it was small amounts of cash . . .

five or six hundred dollars and you spread it out between games. Maybe you'll even hit a jackpot."

Both the Carters nodded. They all looked at each other, and then Catherine said, "I heard lots of stuff about how your kids were killed. That's awful. We've got a son, he's at a community college, learning to build guitars. If anything happened to him, I'd be where you are. I'm so sorry about what happened."

Cooper: "Thank you. So?"

Carter said, "One way or the other, I'll be back in an hour and a half. You could go out and get a sandwich. There's a pretty good place right down the street. Lots of tourists, nice morning like this."

Cooper nodded. "I'll do that. How will I know you're back?"

"If it's going to happen, it'll happen in an hour and a half. Come back then. Bring money. I'll need some cash now . . ."

Cooper took a fat envelope from her shoulder bag, said, absently, "Most of the money is from my husband's emergency stash, so nobody knows I have it." She took a thick wad of currency from the envelope and counted out five thousand dollars in hundred-dollar bills. She arranged them in a neat stack, and passed them to him, and said, "Jim, don't mess with me, okay? You know you're talking to a potential first-degree murderer."

Carter seemed to take a step back. He said, "I'm fine. Just fine. I won't, I'd never . . ."

"Good." She gave him her movie-star smile and stood up. "See you soon."

She took the stairs again, emerged across the street from a modern office building with a strip of grass in front of it, spotted with fallen yellow leaves. Beyond it, the St. Croix was a cold gray ribbon. She walked around the corner, hurrying now, to the car.

When she was in, Melton asked, "How'd it go?"

"He's going for a gun now. We'll have it in an hour and a half, if it happens at all."

"What if he calls the cops?"

"That's not going to happen, believe me," Cooper said. "He's really hurting. His wife is all for it. They've got almost no exposure."

"Okay. Well, this is where the rubber meets the road," Melton said. "What do we do now?"

"He suggested we go get a sandwich. Which is one thing we won't do. Why don't we drive around the lake? We could stick our noses into a couple shops in Prescott, come back up through Afton."

"That should do it. Chelsea would like her bottle."

They were gone a few minutes more than the hour and a half, making the long loop through Wisconsin around Lake St. Croix, stopping on the way to change the baby's diaper. Back in Stillwater, Melton dropped Cooper around the corner from Carter's condo, and Cooper took a moment to compose herself, then walked into the condo.

Carter was there, with a grin. He had a gun, with a blued silencer sticking out the front, which he handled with an intimacy most people reserved for their sexual partners.

"Nine-millimeter Glock. Virtually new. Looks like it's maybe had a hundred rounds through it. It's safe, but no safety. Once you've cocked it — I'll show you how — you just start pulling the trigger," Carter said.

"I'm told my family was killed with a Glock 17."

"This is a 19, a little smaller, better for a woman's hands," Carter said. "It's safe, kinda quiet, and cold." He handed her two boxes of ammunition. "Don't forget to clean the shells before you load the magazine. Brass takes a perfect fingerprint. If you don't clean them, and the cops pick them up, they've got prints and DNA. You don't want that. Scrub them with alcohol and wear gloves while you're doing it, and loading the mag."

He gave a brief instruction on the specifics of the Glock, and then asked, "You got the money?"

"I do," she said. "I didn't know how much it would be, so I brought thirty thousand. I'll give you all the rest of it. Twenty-five."

She handed him the envelope, and he took it, bright-eyed, riffled the bills, and said, "Score. By God."

Catherine Carter said, sincerely, "No cars. Nothing expensive. We'll dribble the money out. No big purchases."

"Good. Thank you so much," Cooper said. She put the pistol and the cartridges in her shoulder bag. "Remember: we're welded together, now. No profit to anyone, even remembering this transaction."

"I've already forgotten it," Carter said.

Catherine reached out and put a cool hand on Cooper's forearm. "And Maggie: good hunting. Good hunting, dear."

6

After talking to Cooper and Melton, Lucas and Virgil split up, Virgil to spend the rest of the afternoon combing through the financial information in the BCA file, while Lucas tracked down the deputy marshal who'd been involved in the Brickell shooting incident.

The deputy was named Duane Kowalska. Lucas got his cell phone number from the Marshals Service office and was told that Kowalska had gone to Duluth to pick up a prison inmate. He was halfway back to the Cities when he picked up Lucas's call. "Hey, big guy? What's up?"

Lucas: "I've got an off-the-wall question for you. It's about the Brickell shoot-out."

"Remember it well," Kowalska said. "I got hit in the head with a car door."

"With a car door."

"Yep. Cut my forehead trying to crawl out of the car when the guns came out. Still got the scar. I was trying to get behind the engine block, because car bodies are now made out of toilet paper."

"That would be correct," Lucas said. "I even remember you walking around the office with a gauze thing on your head. A patch."

"Looking for a little disability downtime. Yankees were in town for a four-game stand," Kowalska said. "How are you, by the way? You working?"

"Maybe," Lucas said. "Listen, I'm not sure I got this right, but I heard around the office that you thought Mrs. Brickell —"

"That would be Ms. Cheryl Lundgren. She of the missing meds."

"Whatever. I heard that you thought she was the shooter, not Brickell."

"I still think that. I mean, I'm sure I saw her at the window," Kowalska said. "I was fifty yards away, but she's a blonde and Brickell has dark hair and anyway, he was wearing a red ballcap. I saw a blonde behind the gun. Shot a hole in the back window of the car."

"But that didn't go anywhere . . . You thinking it was Lundgard."

"Lundgren. No, it didn't. Because Brickell confessed," Kowalska said. "He was lying through his teeth to protect her. He was already going to prison, got a deal by pleading to ag assault on the shoot-out. I guess he figured what the hell, he could do the extra three. And then, maybe you gotta know Ms. Lundgren to fully understand it."

"She's not unattractive?"

"That's not it. She *is* unattractive. But she has a . . . pull. She latches onto you. She shot a hole in my car and before I finished talking to her, I felt sorry for her," Kowalska said. "Don't tell any of my fellow right-wingers at the office that I said that."

"She tall?"

"Oh, sort of, one of those tall skinny Scandinavians. Five-eight, five-ten, I'd say."

"How sure are you about the shooting? That she was the shooter?"

"Ninety-seven percent. No, check that. Ninety-eight-point-five percent," Kowalska said. "She tried to shoot me and Loren McCord. Loren never saw her at the window, he was eatin' dirt. What are you looking at?"

"Not sure. I may have to go up and see her," Lucas said.

"Careful. Stay away from her goats."

"Goats?"

"She's got a bunch of goats," Kowalska said. "She makes goat cheese for a living. She's got this one mean billy goat, went

134

after Loren. You know that thing about billy goats butting people? It's true. The god-damn things are dangerous."

"I'll be careful," Lucas said. "And I'll, uh, say hello from you."

"Do that. Tell her I hope she's doing okay."

Lucas went online to the Marshals Service and looked at the file on Brickell as well as the linked file on Lundgren. Brickell was a run-of-the-mill redneck asshole, more likely to use a baseball bat than a gun, apparently familiar with both the manufacturing and habitual ingestion of methamphetamine. Because of his attraction to underage girls, along with a history of dealing weed, he was no longer allowed closer than five hundred yards from the Paynesville Area Secondary School.

The county judge who issued the restrain-ing order referred to Brickell as a "spittle stain on the good name of Stearns County," which made Lucas think he might like the judge.

Lundgren also had a police record, all for involvements in bar fights, which she appar-ently started. Her mug shot made her look harsh, but then, it was a mug shot, and she had a split lip and a black eye.

Lucas sent a phone message to Virgil:

135

"Cecil's tomorrow at nine o'clock. Leave for Stearns County at ten. Bring a gun."

He got back a thumbs-up and no further message, not even a question of why they were going to Stearns County, which suggested to Lucas that Virgil was either deep into the financial matter, or working on his next novel.

Almost certainly the novel.

Virgil confirmed that the next morning, as they sat in Cecil's diner eating pancakes, and as Cooper and Melton were cruising around Lake St. Croix, waiting for the gun. "Everybody and his brother has been telling me that the second novel is where you fall on your ass. I'm trying to keep from doing that."

"Maybe Ms. Lundgren will give you another character."

"I've been working in southern Minnesota for ten years," Virgil said. "I've got more character models than I know what to do with. I could probably get five books out of Johnson Johnson alone."

Johnson Johnson — his father named him after an outboard motor, along with his brother Mercury Johnson and their sister, Evie (Evinrude) Johnson — had crashed every kind of vehicle known to mankind.

He was one of Virgil's two closest friends, along with Lucas. Lucas liked Johnson, though he was wary.

"You ought to help that crazy motherfucker write a memoir, though I doubt anyone would believe it," Lucas said. "We ought to take him up to Stearns County with us. He could probably seduce Lundgren right out of her goat farm."

"Johnson does get along with goats," Virgil admitted.

Lucas poked a fork at Virgil: "You figure anything out?"

"The pickings were thin, although there's one guy . . . I don't know exactly what the situation is there, but he's an investment advisor with that Barnes and Blue firm that Cooper mentioned. The advisory firm. He kept trying to talk Sand out of contributing money to a charity he called a scam. Sand wanted to kick a hundred thousand to this charity, and this investment guy was getting pretty hysterical about it."

"But . . . why?"

"I don't know. I got a bunch of emails and they both knew what they were talking about so they didn't go over it in the emails. The B-Team didn't look at it, not closely, because it was a negative thing — he was trying to talk Sand *out* of an investment, instead of into one."

"What's the company? That Sand wanted to invest in?"

"Home Streets," Virgil said. "The whole conversation got pretty tense, even though Barnes and Blue get some heavy fees from Sand. Sand sounded like he was getting pissed off about it. About the resistance he was getting from this guy."

"Was he gonna dump Barnes and Blue?"

"No, I don't think so. But it was tense," Virgil said. "The other thing is, the guy doesn't exactly have a rock-solid alibi for the night of the murders. He lives alone in a St. Paul condo. He says he was home, his phone was home — that checked out — the video camera got him walking out the front door at six o'clock, for dinner, he says, and back in the front door at seven-fifteen, and not out again. But, he could have gone down the fire stairs and out the back — no camera there."

"What about his car?"

"He walks to work, downtown. Eight or ten blocks from the condo. He has a car, but it was in an underground parking ramp the whole time. That *is* on video."

"You think he could walk to Crocus Circle?"

"Sure. Easy. It'd be the safest way to get

there, on a rainy night. It'd be dark, not a lot of people on the street. It's a little more than a mile from his condo to Crocus Hill. If he's in good shape, he could do the round-trip, plus the murders, in forty-five minutes."

"It's possible, maybe even likely, that the killer walked in," Lucas said.

"Yup."

Virgil started working on a pecan cinnamon roll, Lucas thinking about it, until he said, "A hundred grand would be chicken feed, if I understand Sand's total net worth. Barely worth arguing about."

"It is. I added up as much as I could, and I figure Sand and Cooper have something between a hundred and twenty-five and a hundred and fifty million, liquid," Virgil said. "That's not counting real estate, which I guess is extensive. Apartments. They own the land and buildings leased long-term to Walgreens drug stores. And, you know, other hard assets. Barnes and Blue is a big Midwestern advisory agency, offices in Chicago, Minneapolis, St. Louis, Omaha, and Kansas City, so a hundred thousand would probably be chicken feed to them, too. The overall Sand account wouldn't be chicken feed, though. They get three-tenths of a percent of the overall amount they

139

advise on — roughly a half million a year. And this guy might have been pissing off Sand. It's unusual enough to look at."

"We will, if we don't squeeze anything out of Ms. Lundgren."

Virgil wiped frosting off his mouth with a paper napkin, dropped it on his empty plate, and said, "Let's go squeeze."

Paynesville was two hours northwest of St. Paul, the first part of the trip through Minneapolis and its suburbs, then breaking out into open countryside. Once out of the urban area, Virgil synced his phone to Lucas's Cayenne and called Cooper, who was in her car and answered on the first ring.

"Agent Flowers . . ."

"Yes. I've been looking over the financial records in the BCA file," Virgil said. "Could you tell me if you've continued the relationship with your Barnes and Blue advisors?"

"Yes . . . Why wouldn't I?" Cooper said.

"I've been reviewing your husband's emails from the last month and it seems like the relationship with Barnes and Blue has gotten . . . mmm . . . somewhat tense, especially the discussion between your husband and a Barnes and Blue executive named Thomas Burston."

"Yes, Tom. Tom is aggressive. He'd annoy

140

Alex from time to time. Alex thought he was very good, though, very sharp, so we stayed with him. Tom didn't want Alex to invest in a housing charity. He said Alex would lose the investment, that the housing charity was mostly a sham built on PR."

"The amount, though, doesn't seem significant, for the size of your portfolio," Virgil said. "A hundred thousand dollars . . ."

"Rich people don't like to lose money," Cooper said. She made a rueful noise, almost a laugh, but not quite. "They *really* don't like it. We're richer than hell, and we both drive mid-level Mercedes for five years because Alex would go through agonies before spending money on what he called a sunk cost like an expensive car. He wasn't really cheap, though. He looked on this housing company, this charity, as doing something worthwhile, that St. Paul needed. That was the upside. Tom was only looking at the potential loss, the downside. That's what he's paid to do."

"Do you know Tom Burston personally?" Virgil asked.

"Yes, of course."

"Is he tall and thin?" Virgil asked.

Long pause. Then, "Yes. He is. Maybe not exactly slender, but he's in good shape. He's built like you. Big tennis player — he and I

141

team up in mixed doubles. We're quite good."

"Ah, but you, mmm, haven't . . ."

"He's gay," Cooper said.

"Okay. How do you feel about the level of antagonism or anything else he might have felt toward Alex?" Lucas asked.

"Hello, Lucas," Cooper said. "You know, like I said, Tom's tall, but I can't see any way . . . that he'd do something like murder. I can't see that at all. He's aggressive, he could get pushy with Alex over portfolio issues, but he didn't do it."

"Okay. What about this housing company or charity or whatever it is?"

"Home Streets. It's barely a real company. It was formed by the board of a St. Paul charitable organization called Heart/Twin Cities, as a subsidiary charity. I mean, it's not mafia, or organized crime, if that's what you were thinking. Alex was a board member. I've been asked if I will join the board to replace him, and I'm thinking about it. Alex and the other board members were planning to chip in starter cash to attract federal and foundation funding for housing for street people. Home Streets is trying to buy a tract over on the east side of St. Paul, some old railroad property."

"Then it really is a charity."

"Pretty much," she said. "What are you up to? Anything besides the financial stuff?"

"We took your suggestion and started looking at dependents of people Alex sent to prison. We're on the way to interview one," Virgil said. "I really can't give you a name or anything, it's confidential at this point."

"Okay. Good hunting, then," she said, unconsciously echoing Catherine Carter.

"Thanks. We'll be talking to you, Ms. Cooper. Maggie."

When she'd rung off, Virgil said to Lucas, "She didn't like the Burston idea."

"Not only that, she sounded like she knew what she was talking about. If a hundred thousand isn't worth worrying about in a portfolio, it's not worth killing for."

They drove on.

Minnesota was going tan and gray, losing its grip on the summer green. The soybean harvest was done, the fields bare and hard. Much of the corn was in, although some was being harvested as they drove past. Dozens and maybe hundreds of cows ignored them over barbed-wire fences; staring blank-faced as they chewed their cuds.

Virgil: "Cows have friends."

"Is that right?" Lucas's interest had a

depth of perhaps two inches.

Virgil: "They even have cliques."

"Amazing what you learn as a trained investigator," Lucas said.

Virgil: "They can communicate with each other both through vocalizations and their facial expressions."

Lucas: "Shut up."

Cheryl Lundgren didn't live in Paynesville, but a dozen miles southwest of town, in a four-square house probably over a hundred years old: a cube with a pyramid on top, two residential floors, a basement, and an expansive attic. A wide front porch with swing hangers, but no swing, faced the road. The main entry was on the side toward the back, next to the driveway.

The house must have been nice during its first fifty or seventy-five years, the headquarters for a prosperous farm. Now it was a lonely place with most outbuildings gone, barren soybean fields pushed close on the east and south sides, a blacktopped farm-to-market road in front, and a woodlot on the west side.

The woodlot had likely been there since the house was built, serving both as a windbreak and a source of firewood. The ground under the woodlot was a rough, well-creased mound left over from the glaciers. Covered by red oak and underbrush, except for a clearing of three or four acres, it was occupied by four small sheds and surrounded by a fence.

As they drove up to the house on a gravel-and-dirt two-track, they could see goats wandering around inside the fence, then gathering in the clearing to watch Lucas's car go past. Three more goats stood on the ragged dirt-scarred lawn, staring.

"Abraham Lincoln kept two goats at the White House, named Nanny and Nanko . . ." Virgil began.

"Shut up."

They were just getting out of the car when Lundgren came out the side door. She was dressed in a gray sweatshirt, blue jeans, and black Doc Marten lace-up boots. Her hair was an unkempt Einstein-like heap of dry blond strands, her eyes as pale blue as a bottle of Fiji Water, and piercing. Her face looked more than clean; it looked scoured raw.

And though she probably wasn't fifty, her cheeks were stitched with stress lines. She had a semi-automatic pistol in a black nylon holster on a gunbelt and Virgil, who was

145

closest, said, "Please don't touch that pistol."

"And if I do?" she asked.

"My partner will shoot you. He doesn't have a retention strap on his gun, so he can get it out a lot faster than you can."

"Want to bet?" she asked.

"No, I don't, because then we'd have to get the local deputies out here, and the coroner, and figure out who'd take care of the goats," Virgil said.

"And fill out all kinds of papers," Lucas said, as he came around the nose of the car, right hand inside his sport coat. "I'm a U.S. Marshal, my partner here is with the Bureau of Criminal Apprehension. We need to talk to you about the murder of Judge Alex Sand, three weeks ago down in the Cities."

She didn't quite do a silent-movies double take, but it was close. "Somebody killed Sand? How . . . ?"

"He was shot in his home, with his two young sons . . ."

"The kids were killed?" She seemed genuinely puzzled and appalled.

Virgil nodded. "We're talking to you because your friend Larry Brickell was sent to prison by Sand. You have a reputation for violence and the marshals who came here to arrest Larry believe it may have been you who opened fire on them."

The anger seemed to start somewhere in her chest, flow up through her neck to her head, and for a moment, Virgil thought she'd go for the gun. Instead, her hand came away from it as she poked a finger at him and screamed, "Did not! Did not! Larry confessed! You assholes know that! He confessed!"

"We have a witness —"

"I don't care what you got, dickhead," she swore through nicotine-colored teeth. "It was Larry that done the shooting! He's the criminal! He was always dropping me in the shit! He brought that little Carlson girl home and he was fuckin' her while I was down to Worthington. He's the dope-dealer child-fucker cop-shooter, not me!"

She took a step toward Virgil and Virgil took a step back, held up both hands: "Keep it together, Cheryl. We're here to talk. Where were you on Wednesday the —"

"Who said you could use my first name like you know me?"

"Easy . . ."

She'd shouted through Virgil's question, and her hand moved down toward the gun, then past it. She suddenly stopped screaming, saliva slicking down one corner of her mouth, and she wiped it away and said, "On

147

Wednesdays? I play canasta at the Bottle Cap. Starting at seven o'clock. Jerry has video cams good for thirty days. How's that for an alibi, federal assholes?"

"If you're on the video you're good," Lucas said.

"I'm on it. Ask Jerry."

"Where's the Bottle Cap?" Virgil asked. "And who's Jerry?"

"Paynesville, of course," she said. "What the hell else is out here? Jerry owns it."

"We'll check with Jerry," Lucas said. "How do you know he's got videos for thirty days?"

"Because they've used them in court when I got in fights," she said.

Virgil was amused: "Jerry hasn't banned you?"

"And lose fifty dollars a week in beer sales? I don't think so. He knows better than to fuck with me, anyway. I'll fight him. I'll punch him right in his fat fuckin' Swede nose."

Lucas said, "Cheryl, Ms. Lundgren, I don't want you angry with me, but I want to ask . . . you seem to have anger control issues. You've been arrested . . ."

She put her hands to the sides of her head and shouted, "Because nobody listens to

148

me. I know all kinds of shit, but nobody listens."

"The anger . . ."

"Yes, I have meds, but the meds fuck me up," she said, still shouting. "Everything feels dim, my brain goes dim, fades out. I go off them here, because all I got here is my goats. Goats listen to me. People don't listen to me. I take my meds when I go to court, and then they treat me like I'm an idiot because my brain is dim."

Lucas: "Okay. I think I understand that . . ."

"You don't understand shit . . ."

"I understand you make some pretty good goat cheese," Virgil said, a little obsequiously. "Love goat cheese, myself."

"Go get your own fuckin' cheese," Lundgren shouted.

"Well, we'll talk to Jerry," Lucas said, taking a step backwards toward the Cayenne. "If it doesn't pan out, we'll be back with a warrant and tear the ass off your house."

"Go check with him. If you get a warrant, you better bring more posse, because I won't put up with it," she said. "Now get the fuck off my yard. Don't run over any of my goats."

Virgil glanced at Lucas, who nodded, and they stepped toward the car and got in. As

149

Lucas backed down the driveway, Virgil, watching Lundgren, who stood with one hand on her gun, said, "Her life won't end well."

"No." Lucas told Virgil about Duane Kowalska's comment, that Lundren had pulled him in. "I felt that."

Virgil nodded: "She's ill, but she's working through it. Or trying to, anyway, trying to keep it together. Wonder how much cheese she makes. And who buys it?"

"Maybe neighbors . . ."

Virgil: "Goat cheese has anti-inflammatory and antibacterial qualities . . ."

"Shut up."

"I can't help it if I work out in the countryside," Virgil said. "This stuff rubs off on you."

Lucas: "That's fine, but you don't have to rub it off on me."

They drove back to Paynesville, found the Bottle Cap, and found Jerry, who did have a fat nose, Swede or not, who got on his computer and called up the canasta game from the night of the Sand murder. There were eight tables and Lundgren had a seat at the middle one, facing the video camera. She played right through the moment of the killing.

Virgil bought some peppered elk jerky on the way out the door, and said, as they headed back toward the Twin Cities, "The thing about elk is, some guy imported a bunch of them from the Rockies, where chronic wasting disease is endemic. They spread the disease to the Wisconsin deer herd, and now it's all through the Midwest. Could wipe out the whole whitetail population. I believe all the Cervidae are susceptible, and there are forty-seven species around the world . . ."

"Shut up."

"You're a little testy, and not in a particularly funny way," Virgil said.

"I know," Lucas said. "I can't help it, because Lundgren told me something important about who killed Sand, but I don't know what she told me."

"What? I didn't pick up a single thing from her," Virgil said. "We should go back and ask her."

"That's the problem," Lucas said. "I heard it, but I don't know what it is, and I don't think she'd know, either."

"Something about cheese? About goats?"

"No. Goats had nothing to do with it. I don't think."

7

On the way back to the Cities, they agreed that Lundgren probably couldn't or wouldn't help them, unless Lucas could figure out what he thought he'd heard, or deduced, from what she said.

"What about the Tom Burston guy, from Barnes and Blue? Worth a look?" Virgil asked.

"We should consult an expert," Lucas said. He called up the phone app on the car's video screen, and punched up the number for his adoptive daughter, Letty.

Virgil smiled: "Letty?"

"Master's in economics with a bunch of courses in finance," Lucas said.

"And she has a criminal mind. I always liked that about her," Virgil said.

"As long as you don't like it too much," Lucas said, as Letty's phone rang.

"Hey! I'm gonna get married . . . someday.

I have twins."

"Keep thinking about that," Lucas said.

Letty came up: "Hey, Dad."

"You busy right now?"

"Not this instant. What's up?"

"I'm in the car with Virgil," Lucas said. "We're looking into the murder of a federal judge."

"Alex Sand. I heard about that. You must be stuck, if you're calling me."

"Everybody's stuck. We've been invited in, but late in the game. Anyway, Virgil's going to tell you a story, and we want to hear your reaction."

"Go ahead, Virgie."

Virgil had taken his iPad out and called up a file on the B-Team's investigation. He told her about Sand's financial status, and about Burston: about the fact that Burston fit the physical profile of the killer, that he did not have an unimpeachable alibi for the night of the murders, and about the tension between Burston and Sand on the hundred-thousand-dollar investment.

He read through a dozen of the emails exchanged by the two men.

When he finished, there was a moment of silence, then Letty said, "That *is* odd. He certainly isn't as deferential as most finan-

153

cial advisors would be. Here's the thing: advisors advise — but the client makes the decision. Legally, anyway, unless the client gives the advisor a power of attorney, to make the investments on his own. That doesn't seem to be the case here."

"It's not," Virgil said. "Sand was involved all the way through."

"I agree that it's not much money for a portfolio as big as you say Sand had," Letty said. "A portfolio that size should kick off anywhere between seven and ten million dollars a year, if it's carefully balanced and managed. So . . . a hundred thousand would only be a fraction of what they'd earn annually. A small fraction. A percent and a half, if they're earning seven million. And half that if it's a legitimate charity and the contribution is tax-deductible."

"Burston plays tennis with Sand's wife, they're a doubles pair and apparently good at it," Lucas said.

Letty: "Uh-oh. If —"

"She says he's gay," Virgil said.

"Is he?"

"We'll ask around."

"Do that," Letty said. "Carefully. I don't think I have any ideas that you two probably haven't thought of, but I can give you my judgment, if you want it."

"We do," Lucas said.

"There's definitely something wrong. The question is, what? Does Burston have a powerful client who wants to stop the housing project? Does he have a personal problem with it, like, does he have property next to this low-income housing? Low-income housing, especially for street people, can devalue property for blocks around. You've heard of NIMBY . . ."

"Not In My Back Yard," Lucas said. "Now, *that's* an interesting idea."

"It is," Virgil said.

"If you don't have any more cases you want me to solve, I've got to go floss," Letty said.

Virgil called Cooper again. "Who runs this 'Home Streets' charity?"

"A man named Bob Dahl. Sort of. He's the director. Noah Heath is the chairman and is also the CEO and chairman of Heart/Twin Cities. Noah is the one pushing the housing initiative, the concept, but Bob would probably be better on the day-to-day details. Are you onto something?"

"Don't know, just poking around, Who'd know about the politics of it?"

"Either one. I'd talk to Bob. He lives with the daily issues. Noah is the one who rounds up the rich people and gets his hand in their pockets."

"Do you have phone numbers?" Lucas asked.

"Give me a minute, let me punch up my contacts list." They heard her fingernails tapping on the phone, and as she did that, she asked, "You have some kind of a break?"

"Not a break. More of an idea. Another one we can't talk about."

"I wouldn't tell anyone," she said.

Virgil laughed and said, "You're the one we don't want to know. The arm-twister. The squeaky wheel."

She found a listing for Heart/Twin Cities and read off three phone numbers, two for Dahl, a personal phone and one for his office, and one for Heath. Virgil thanked her, rang off, and punched in a number for Dahl. The call was answered by a secretary, and when Virgil identified himself as a BCA agent, she transferred him to Dahl.

Virgil identified himself again, explained that he was working on one aspect of the Sand murder. "Now that Alex Sand is gone, if Ms. Cooper decides not to contribute the hundred thousand that Alex was considering . . . what effect would that have on your project?"

"It'd be a kick in the pants," Dahl said.

"We have, we had, nineteen board members until Alex was murdered. We need at least a half million local dollars up front to pull in the grants we're looking at, and a million would be better. Twelve of our board members, uh, living members, are quite well off, but even for them, a hundred thousand is a stretch. It looks like we can count on maybe five hundred thousand from them. The other members might scrape twenty thousand between them. Frankly, I was hoping that Alex would increase his contribution a bit, to a hundred and fifty thousand. We were talking."

"He hadn't committed?"

"No, but he was leaning our way. We're hoping Ms. Cooper will honor that, but her charitable contributions have always been directed at arts organizations. So . . . it's all up in the air."

"Do you know what property you want to buy?"

"Yes. It's ten acres of old railway property on the east side of St. Paul. It has everything we need, and we've already got a commitment from the city council because it solves a lot of problems for them. Not much residential or small retail property around there that street people might disturb."

"Could you text us some addresses?"

"I can. At this number?"

"That would be fine," Virgil said.

When the addresses came in, Lucas said, "Do a search for the tax assessor's office, and call them."

Virgil did that, and as the phone rang, asked, "You have a name?"

"Yes, I do."

When a clerk picked up, Lucas identified himself and asked for Talullah Brooks, was put on hold, and he said to Virgil, "Old friend."

Brooks came up: "The same Lucas Davenport? The one struggling against declining sexual prowess and the curse of cataclysmic dandruff?"

"Must be a different one," Lucas said. "I'm the tall, dark-haired chick magnet, former hockey star, sidckick of the novelist Virgil Flowers."

"Ooo. Could I get an introduction?"

Lucas: "Say hello, Virgil."

Virgil: "Hello, Talullah."

"Really? Are you as big a bullshitter as Davenport?"

"We run pretty close," Virgil admitted.

"Unless you're looking for a double date . . . what do you want?" Brooks asked.

Lucas said, "We're working a murder case

and we're looking for a little information. There's a ten-acre lot that a charity called the Home Streets is trying to buy over on the east side, some railroad land, as we understand it."

"Yes. I know the property," Brooks said.

"I thought you would," Lucas said. "Who would like to sink the project?"

"That's an interesting question," Brooks said. "The parcel has poor access, which means the value is low and it's not exactly a great neighborhood to begin with. That's why Home Streets is interested. They could afford it. They're also wired into downtown influencers who'd like to see the street people sleep-overs moved out of downtown. But: if Home Streets can't buy it, and you had a big gob of front money, and very tight political connections to help you build access on the taxpayer's dime . . . you could pick it up cheap, throw up some condos and make a killing. There are rumors that a couple of different developers have been looking at it."

"Got names?" Lucas asked.

"I'd rather this didn't come back to me," she said.

"My lips are sealed. So are Virgil's."

"Tony Byrne, Arnold Drukker." She spelled the names. "Rival developers. Don't know how interested they really are, but they've collected maps and tax stuff, so I know they're looking at it."

"Are they crooks?" Virgil asked.

"They're developers," Brooks said. "Of course, they're crooks. Mostly in a white-collar way. I don't think they have leg-breakers — not actually on staff, anyway."

"Who could tell us how much potential profit would be in that?" Lucas asked.

"Donald Brooks could help out. He's a loan officer with U.S. Bank, and he can keep his mouth shut."

"Any relation?" Lucas asked.

"Yeah. My brother. I'll call him, ask him to give you a ring," Brooks said. "A murder case, you say?"

"Yes. And thanks. Please do that, and one more thing," Virgil said. "You've got that map database . . . could you look at the properties for a couple blocks around, see if any of it is owned by a Thomas Burston?"

"I can. I'll call you back. Shouldn't take long."

"Talullah, you're a princess among women," Lucas said.

"Then why am I working for the tax as-sessor?"

"Another of life's mysteries," Lucas said. "Call your brother."

160

■ ■ ■ ■

When they ended the call, Lucas asked, "Is Sandy still at the BCA?"

"Yeah, she pretty much runs the place now," Virgil said. "Nobody knows that but me."

Sandy had once been part of Lucas's BCA team. She was a computer hacker/savant and had once had a hasty affair with Virgil, in which Lucas's desktop had been involved. They'd immediately fallen out, and later yet had become friends without privileges.

"Call her up, give her Byrne, Drukker, and Burston. See if they hook up. She loves that shit, working out connections."

Virgil: "When you're right, you're right."

He called, but she didn't pick up; he left a message.

"Now for some lunch," Virgil said.

As he said that, they were passing a hog farm, with the associated stink, the most penetrating of barnyard odors. Lucas said, "Jesus. That'll take your appetite away."

"Think how bad it is for the pigs, they're right in it," Virgil said.

"I doubt that they have much reaction to it," Lucas said. "They're swine."

"Yes, but they're among the most sensitive of animals. They're smarter than dogs. They're even-toed ungulates, which means they bear their weight on two of their five toes. Two is an even number, that's why they're called even-toed, because 'two' is an even number. The whale family, including dolphins and porpoises, actually evolved from even-toed ungulates —"

"Shut up," Lucas said.

"I was thinking I might have a BLT, but now I'm thinking veggie burger," Virgil said.

They stopped at a grill off I-94 in Maple Grove, on the northwest corner of the Minneapolis metro area, and both stayed away from bacon, going with salmon (Lucas) and rotisserie chicken (Virgil). Halfway through lunch, Donald Brooks, the U.S. Bank loan officer, called back, and opened with, "Talullah said you'll keep me out of this."

"Absolutely," Lucas said. He and Virgil hovered over the phone, the volume turned down.

"Hypothetically, if somebody could get the permits, they could put maybe . . . I don't know exactly, but I'd say a hundred units in there. Medium-quality condos, most likely, retirement boxes, maybe throwing in a half-dozen low-income units to make the city council look good. It's not a high-end location, but it's got good access to downtown, if somebody would build the roads and a walkway and bicycle path."

"That's interesting. Any idea of the profit potential?"

"With the guys Talullah mentioned . . . they both have in-house designers and access to financing. The condo market is tricky, but at the hundred-unit point, all in, they might make two million after costs. Of course, they'd still take an income tax hit."

"A lot of money," Virgil said.

"A lot of risk," Brooks said. "Condo development is a good way to lose your shirt."

"But you know these guys. They're experienced, and they know what they're doing, right?"

"Yes, they do," Brooks said.

"And two million is two million," Lucas said.

"Yes, it is."

Brooks filled in a few more details of the condo-financing business, and again emphasized that he didn't want to be connected to the discussion. "We're already forgetting about it," Virgil told him.

Off the phone, Lucas said, "Two million. Can you say, *'motive'*?"

"Definitely pay for a professional, if you could find one," Virgil said.

"Don't think a pro would hit the kids, and might be a little reluctant to hit a federal judge," Lucas said. "Besides, the shooting was sloppy. Took eight shots. A pro would have taken three."

"Sure, if it was one of those mythical movie professionals," Virgil said. "If it was a dipshit with a gun who was willing to kill people . . . he might be a little sloppy."

"Good point," Lucas said.

Virgil looked around the restaurant, decided he could speak without being overheard, and said, "Okay: it's possible Burston was acting for Byrne or Drukker when he tried to discourage Sand from investing in the street-people housing. But it's also possible that he doesn't know those guys. Or that Burston has a direct interest, like a piece of nearby property. But you know what? Byrne and Drukker don't feel right to me. The killings have a personal feel. If the killer is one of those three, I'd bet on Burston. Acting on his own."

Lucas thought about it for a moment, said, "We've got some stuff going on. Without thinking about it too much, I'd say I agree with you. It feels personal to me, too."

"If it's personal, and not a pro, the killer

is stone cold," Virgil said. "Walking through like that, doing the kill shots on the kids?"

"He's a bad man," Lucas agreed.

On the way across the Twin Cities, the other Brooks called back, from the tax assessor's office. "I can't find Burston's name on any property within a half mile. The only property I find under his name is a downtown condo. But, there are quite a number of properties around the rail yard that are owned under corporate names, and I have no way to find out if he might be behind one of those."

When she rang off, Virgil asked, "What do you want to do?"

"I want you to keep digging through the finance files, and I'll get in touch with Sandy and push her on connections between Burston and the for-profit condo developers. I'll try to set up interviews tomorrow for Burston and that car thief guy out in Stillwater, whatever his name is."

"Henry Carter."

"Yeah, him."

Virgil: "Then, lay on your couch with a cool washcloth on your head, and try to remember what Lundgren said that makes you think she knows something."

Lucas glanced over at Virgil: "Goddamnit.

Encroaching old age. But I heard something. I did."

8

Virgil went back to his hotel, which was attached to the Mall of America, walked over to the mall and browsed through the thrillers at the Barnes & Noble store, bought a Mick Herron *Slow Horses* espionage novel that he hadn't yet read, got a Cinnabon, went back to the hotel and started digging through the financial records.

After an hour, he quit, read the Herron for an hour, then opened his computer and started revising chapters in the novel. He was confident in his dialogue, but the Herron novel highlighted what he felt was a deficit in his scene-setting and characterization. He needed to put some of that stuff in.

Virgil had written a lot of short outdoor nonfiction and several pieces of crime nonfiction for magazines. He'd learned, in two practice novels and one that was about to be published, that novel writing didn't work like nonfiction writing. His mother had a sewing machine that had a built-in zigzag stitch, which he thought of as a metaphor for fiction writing. It wasn't done in a straight line — you constantly went back and forth.

If something needed to be changed, enhanced, made-up, twisted . . . go back and do it. It's fiction.

Lucas called Thomas Burston, and after going through two secretaries, got him on the line, and made an appointment to meet him the next day. He spent another hour online, trying to find background on Burston, and read what BCA and St. Paul cops had gotten from earlier interviews. He did find some online information, but nothing of special interest. He went for a run, ate dinner with the family, and in bed that night, turned restlessly on his damaged shoulder, and tried to think what might have touched him during the Lundgren goat farm interview.

Whatever it was, he didn't find it.

The next morning, Lucas was waiting on the curb when Virgil picked him up. He climbed into the Tahoe, and asked, "Anything?"

"Nada."

"Me neither," Lucas said. "Burston has some online stuff, but it's mostly PR. Facebook, LinkedIn, like that. Nothing critical, that I could find, anyway. With St. Paul and your guys, he wasn't exactly stonewalling, but he didn't have a lot to say."

"I assume he was happy to hear from you?" Virgil asked.

"He was overjoyed," Lucas said. "You work on the novel?"

"Some. This case isn't helping."

"You gonna quit the BCA?"

"Maybe next contract," Virgil said. "I'll finish this book, and one more, then see what Esther can drag through the door in terms of money." Esther was Virgil's New York agent. "If it's big enough, I'll bail. I'll have enough time with the BCA for a state pension, no matter what happens."

"Ah, man."

"You quit, once," Virgil said.

"Yeah. Don't regret it, but I had to come back," Lucas said.

"You're addicted to the hunt. I'm not. I'll be ready to let go."

"Weather talked to Frankie," Lucas said. "Frankie said you've been looking at a cabin up north."

"I am. Made a bid on one, we should hear

169

in the next few days. Decent lake. Small, but deep. Muskies, walleyes. I don't have the big bucks, like you, but . . . it's a good place, the kind I always wanted."

In college and afterward, Lucas had written role-playing games with the help of friends, and several had been published, enough to buy a second-hand Porsche 911.

Pushed out of the Minneapolis Police Department — eluding a possible charge of brutality for beating up a man who'd church-keyed one of his informants — he'd written a series of computer simulations to be used in training 9-1-1 operators.

A college friend who'd majored in computer science had helped him transfer the simulations to PCs, and another friend helped him form a company to market the simulations. The company had done well but bored him nearly senseless; he'd sold out at the very peak of the Internet bubble.

With the earlier brutality charge effectively covered up, he'd gotten a political appointment that placed him back on the Minneapolis police force. Several years later, he'd moved to the BCA and started working with Virgil.

Lucas said, "You're different from me. If you let go, you won't be back."

"No, but I'll always be available to give you much-needed advice."

Barnes and Blue Investment Services had a floor on an older, but extensively renovated, red-stone building overlooking Mears Park in St. Paul's Lowertown.

They lucked into a parking place across the park from the building, fed the parking meter — Virgil put his BCA placard on the dash in case the interview ran long — and strolled over. The park was pleasant, green gone to tan, a good day: cold, clear, a mild leaf-shedding breeze carrying the faint odor of barbeque from a nearby restaurant.

They took the elevator to the third floor, spoke to a receptionist, who made a call, and a moment later, a young blond woman in a green dress came to lead them to Burston's office.

Burston worked out of a spacious cubicle with two wooden walls hung with certificates and art photographs, and two glass walls, one looking out at the park and the other inward toward the office.

He was a tall man, strikingly handsome, the right size to fit the killer; Lucas had the impression that he was heavier than the killer, but the killer had been wearing that rain suit, so it was impossible to tell for sure.

He had dark hair, well-trimmed and groomed, dark eyes, and a fashionable three-day beard on a square chin, as carefully trimmed as his hair. He was wearing a dark suit with a purple silk tie.

He'd been looking at a computer when they arrived at his door, and he stood, waved them in, and told the woman, "Close the door, would you, Barb?"

She did and they shook hands, and Virgil and Lucas took chairs in front of his desk, while he sat behind it. He looked, Virgil thought, exactly like a late-thirties' tennis player should: cool, smooth, tanned, and a bit slick.

He started: "Well. I know this is about Alex, but nothing else. I've already been interviewed by St. Paul police and an agent from the BCA. What can I do for you?"

Virgil said, "We're interviewing a lot of people around Alex Sand. You probably know from the other interviews that the killer was caught on camera outside their house. You fit that physical profile."

Burston look interested but unperturbed. He leaned forward, knitted his fingers on the desktop and asked, "How so?"

Virgil shrugged: "Same size and general shape, same shoe size. That's what first caught our eye. We also noticed that your emails with Sand were becoming contentious, for a financial advisor-client relationship. We were wondering why that was."

Burston nodded: "You might think it is, but that's not an exactly novel observation. Both the St. Paul detective and the BCA agent asked about that. And it's true: there was some contention. Alex didn't pay me to be kind, or slap his back, he paid me to tell him the truth. The truth is, he was about to dump a bunch of money into . . . might not exactly be a scam, but something that wasn't entirely real. Not what it said it was."

"The homeless housing," Lucas said.

"Yes."

"Margaret Cooper said that Alex accepted that he was really involved in a charity thing . . ."

Burston smiled, showing teeth, that changed his aspect from smooth and slightly slick to wolfish. "When you build housing, whether it's done privately or by a community group, large sums of money get paid out and effectively disappear. You understand what I'm saying?"

Lucas nodded and Virgil said, "Yes."

"Check the history of Heart/Twin Cities. That charity has made sizable amounts of money disappear. Alex was sure that as a federal judge he'd seen almost everything,

173

and as a lawyer who'd dealt with all kinds of business interests, he'd seen the rest of it. He didn't believe he could be conned. You know who makes the best mark for a con man? People who believe they can't be conned."

"You think he was being conned," Lucas said.

"I think the board would have put up a half million dollars, or a million dollars, including a hundred or a hundred fifty thousand from Alex, and they'd use that to campaign for more, maybe up to a million or so, from local people," Burston said. "That seed money would pull in something between five and ten million in grants, and in the end, you'd have three or four million dollars' worth of housing. And misters Heath and Dahl would be driving around South Florida, or someplace else that was warm and out of sight, in new Porsches."

"You're saying they're criminals?" Virgil asked.

"I'm saying that I went along with Alex for the original pitch for Home Streets . . . you know about Home Streets?" Burston asked.

"Yes."

"The people running Heart/Twin Cities aren't financial experts or real estate experts

174

or even nonprofit experts. They're hustlers. I can smell them. You expect some of that particular stink with people whose job is to raise money from rich people, but this was different. They're con men. They're the type of con men who take care of number one before they take care of anyone else. Alex couldn't feel that. Couldn't smell it."

"You've got no proof."

"No. I advise on stock investments for a living, and I'm good at it. In that milieu, you don't ask for proof, because there isn't any. You do your research and then you trust your sense of smell," Burston said. "During the little cocktail party after Heath and Dahl made their pitch, I heard Heath talking about the joys of driving a classic car. I made a point of watching him leave the meeting. He's driving a ten-year-old Mercedes S-Class. That's not a classic car — that's an old one. He's a bullshitter."

Virgil: "Okay. We will look into that . . ."

"You should," Burston said. "Even if they didn't kill Alex, there's something serious going on with their so-called charities."

They sat back and looked at each other for a moment, then Lucas said, "We understand from Ms. Cooper, Maggie, that you are tennis partners."

"Yes. We're good," Burston said. "Mixed

175

doubles. Not on the national level, quite, but we rule Minnesota amateurs."

"She told us you're gay," Virgil said.

"Yes."

Lucas: "Did you and Alex ever have a physical relationship?"

Burston leaned back in his chair, an amused smile flashing across his face. He said, "No. He was an attractive man, but he was . . . very, very straight. Something else: I made a little more than three hundred thousand dollars last year. If I were to have a sexual relationship with a client, and word got out, that would be the end of my job. I'd be out the door the next day. I like what I do; I wouldn't risk it."

Virgil: "You didn't murder Alex."

"No."

Lucas tilted his head: "Who did?"

Burston looked surprised by the question. He had three small terra-cotta flower pots on his desk, each with a selection of stone plants, lithops, that resembled pebbles. He reached out and touched one, and then another, his face down, studying the plants for a moment.

Then he looked up and said, "That's the question that plagues me. Frankly . . . This stays strictly between us?"

"It will," Lucas said.

"Frankly, I wondered if Margaret . . . but that's impossible. Why did it even occur to me? Because Maggie and Alex had quite different ideas about the money in the family — he wanted to preserve it and send it down to another three generations of Sands," Burston said. "She wanted to spend it. Some of it, anyway. She wanted a house in LA, or Malibu, or Santa Barbara, away from Minnesota winters. And maybe a pied-à-terre on Manhattan's West Side, walking distance from the Theater District. Maybe both. But like I said, she's not a killer. That's impossible. She loved Alex, and she loved her kids. She would have worn him down, eventually. She knew that. She'd have had her pied-à-terre. Also, she's a . . . kind person."

Lucas asked again: "If she didn't, then who did?"

Burston stuck a finger in one ear, wiggled it, turned and looked out the window, turned back and said, "Everything I have to say about that seems kind of stupid, in my own ears. It must be something Alex did, or maybe wouldn't do, as a judge. It didn't involve his money. Not directly, anyway. But the judge thing, I guess that's been seriously reviewed by the FBI, the BCA, everybody. I can't think of anything else. Unless . . . it was a walk-in-the-door madman. There's so much hostility in America . . . it could have been a crazy man."

Virgil: "Do you own any property or have any clients who own property around that rail yard that Home Streets wants to buy?"

Burston frowned, shook his head. "No. Not me. I don't own any real estate at all, except my condo. As far as clients go, I doubt it, but it's possible. I don't deal with my clients' real estate positions, unless it's in the stock markets, or REITs. But, I doubt it."

"Why?" Lucas asked.

"Because there's not much money to be made in that part of town. Not unless you're a building contractor who's overcharging and kicking the excess back to the developer."

"You think that happens?"

"I think that happens all the time," Burston said.

They talked for another twenty minutes, Burston getting out of his chair to roam around the office, stopping to peer at two large black-and-white flower photographs on the facing wood walls. He ran his hand through his hair, mussing it up.

He told Virgil, "The most shocking thing was to see Alex in the casket. The boys' caskets were closed, of course, but Alex . . . He was my age, a couple years older, but basically, my age, healthy as I am, hardworking, intelligent, and there . . . he's dead. You could see little rivulets of blood under the skin on his face. I guess the blood trickles down and hardens up in the veins after you die. You could see these purple death lines. The makeup didn't cover all of it. He just looked . . . fuckin' dead. I'm having a hard time dealing with it. I'm not sleeping. I keep seeing that casket face. I'm identifying with a dead man."

He looked at Virgil and Lucas, as though he wanted their help.

"It will get better," Lucas said. "If it doesn't, if you lie in bed at night, and your mind goes round and round trying to figure out what happened, and what you could have done about it —"

Burston jabbed a finger at Lucas: "That's exactly it! Exactly!"

"Then you may be suffering from the onset of a clinical depression. Talk to somebody."

Burston made a dismissive gesture: "If my bosses thought I was nuts . . ."

"See a decent professional and you'd be safe enough," Lucas said. "I've been through the depression thing twice, and believe me, pills are better than gutting it out. I could give you a name if you'd like."

"I'll think about it," Burston said. He hesitated, then, "Thanks. I'd like a name. I'm messed up."

Lucas reached across his desk, took one of his business cards, flipped it over, wrote a name and phone number on it, and pushed it across to him. "She's a nun, over at St. Kate's. And a serious shrink. If you need it, she'll help, and nobody else will hear a word about it."

"She's really good?"

"You'll notice I've memorized her phone number. Who does that anymore?"

As they were about to walk out the office door, Burston said, "This name you gave me, and the depression thing. Have you taken a close look at Maggie?"

Lucas turned and said, "We interviewed her once. With what happened to her, depression would be understandable . . ."

"This is something different," Burston said. "Something broke in her. She's changed . . . too much. In a bad way, an unstable way. I'm worried."

Back at the Tahoe, they agreed that Burston looked even less likely after the interview than he had before they talked.

"I gotta say, I believe most of what he said," Virgil said. "Though, he seemed pretty intent on siccing us on the Home Streets people."

"We need to take a look at them," Lucas said. "Cooper thinks that Sand was going to come across with the money. So did Burston. A hundred thousand, a hundred and fifty. Sand hadn't shown any sign that he was backing out. Even if the Home Streets guys are con men, would they kill the golden goose before he laid the egg?"

Virgil rubbed his nose, said, "No. It'd have to be something else, another reason. What if Sand did the research, the background, that Burston wanted him to do, and found out that they *might be* running a scam, and made the mistake of talking to them about it? They'd still want money from the others, but they might have to get rid of Sand to shut him up. They might collect from Cooper anyway, when Sand was gone. Wonder if Sand talked to them the morning of the killings, or the day before?"

"Good question," Lucas said. "I wondered the same thing, about twenty minutes ago."

"Bullshit. The question has my finger-prints all over it."

"Want to go jack them up?"

"Let's go over to the BCA and have Sandy

run them through the computer. See if anything pops."

At BCA headquarters, Sandy agreed to research Noah Heath and Bob Dahl, and suggested that she could probably pull a lot of information off the Internet about the charities under the Heart/Twin Cities umbrella and could get that done immediately.

Lucas and Virgil adjourned to the Parrot Café, for lunch, and when they got back, she had nearly a ream of printouts. Virgil still hadn't finished with the Sand financial information, so they got a conference room, divided the paper, and dived into it.

With two breaks for coffee, they read until four o'clock, when Virgil said, "I'm not getting anything new, and I'm going blind reading the small print. I'm gonna quit."

"Not a bad idea," Lucas said. He pushed a half-inch-high stack of paper across the conference room table. "Glance through this tonight, if you get time. This guy, Heath, has built a whole charitable structure. He keeps inventing new charities with cute names. The only thing he's missed, so far, is 'Puppy-dog and Kitty-cat Love/Twin Cities.' It's making me a little nauseous."

"Somebody needs to do it," Virgil said.

"Okay, flower child. You're as bad as Weather. I went online to our giving account at Fidelity, and she's given ten grand to the various Heart charities over the past couple of years."

"That's so nice of you," Virgil said. "I get tears in my eyes just thinking about it."

"Fuck you."

"No, really. I'm feeling a little emotional."

"Fuck you again. We're going home. Read that paper."

9

All the investigators on the Sand case had discussed the possibility that Margaret Cooper had either done, or had orchestrated, the murders. Some had decided that she had not; some were still on the fence.

She hadn't.

The killer had cruised the Sand home a half-dozen times since the night of the murders but had never seen a light in the house — it appeared that Margaret Cooper had moved out. Where she'd gone, he had no idea, and he was not the FBI, so he'd have to be creative.

He could stake out the house, he thought, but on that particular street, he'd be noticed and perhaps even questioned. He couldn't take that chance. Instead, he went online to the University of Minnesota, downloaded a class schedule, and found that Cooper taught a late afternoon acting class on Mondays, Wednesdays, and Fridays. Was she even working? He didn't know that, either.

The killer lived in a tiny St. Paul house that overlooked — if it overlooked anything — a narrow street in the front, and a set of abandoned railroad tracks in the back. He was a gig worker, employed at three different gymnasiums; none were willing to employ him long enough in any one week to be classified as full time, for which they'd have to pay more taxes and benefits.

His name was Hess. His house was a jumble of workout and electronics gear, a litter of dumbbells, laptops, stereo speakers, and an eighty-inch television that dangled beneath it three separate undisguised wires like kite strings. He had two leatherette easy chairs, pushed close together so he could put his feet on one while he sat on the other to watch television. The compact kitchen showed a stack of ramen noodle packages and also a large black tub of clarified whey protein.

He had no visitors.

Three weeks after the killings, he left his job at the noon gym and drove to the University of Minnesota, spotted what should have been Cooper's late afternoon classroom. There was enough movement around down the halls that he could hang out; he carried a spiral notebook and a

Nikon camera, was young enough to be a graduate student, and so fit in. Students moved past him without a second look.

At two o'clock that afternoon, he picked out Cooper as she walked down the hall toward the classroom, a brown file folder in her hands, a young woman walking next to her, talking rapidly, Cooper's head tipped to listen. Hess turned away, because if she saw his face, it might spark a memory.

An hour later, he returned, watching from a distance as she left the classroom; he followed her to an office, where she disappeared inside. She showed no special wariness, which was a good thing. According to the schedule, her teaching day was over, so she should be moving.

There was a bench down the hall, outside another office, and Hess sat down, opened his notebook and began drawing a cartoon race car. He'd done that since high school, a way to kill boredom. A young woman came along, carrying a backpack over one shoulder, and asked, "Are you waiting for Dr. Seigel?"

He shook his head, smiled, said, "No," and moved to the end of the bench so the woman could sit down. "Waiting for my friend."

Ten minutes later, the door they were sit-

186

ting next to opened, a bearded man poked his head out, looked at the woman and the killer, said, "Christine?" The woman stood up, gathered her purse and a notebook, and followed the man into his office.

Cooper appeared a minute later, her face turned away from him, walking down the hall, carrying her purse and a leather satchel. He followed her, at a distance, to a parking garage, which, it turned out, would be a terrible place to commit a murder. There were always people around, some of whom you couldn't immediately see, lots of cameras, and the few escape hatches were all well-lit. Metal doors banged open, people called to each other, the echoes reverberating through the garage. A gunshot would sound like a cannon.

That would be a no-go.

He watched her as she got in her car and left the garage. He couldn't follow, because he was on foot.

Hess didn't particularly *desire* to murder Margaret Cooper. Not like a psycho, with his mouth watering in anticipation. He wouldn't *mind* killing her, it wouldn't bother him, but it was a risk, and the risk bothered him. Plagued him. So far, he'd committed an *almost* perfect crime.

Lying awake at night, reviewing everything

he'd done, he could find only a single flaw: Cooper hadn't been there. He'd carried out the shooting perfectly; had arrived and departed invisibly. He'd gotten rid of the gloves, the shoes, the rain suit, Sand's wallet and watch, three cell phones, all at the bottom of the Mississippi, in separate packages. He'd thought he might keep the watch, until he'd looked at it and found Sand had been wearing an old Seiko quartz watch. An Internet sales site would sell him a better one for $306.

He'd taken the things from Sand because he'd hoped the cops would look on the killings as a robbery. Had they done that? He didn't know. He'd seen the video the cops had released, of his arrival at the house, and his departure, and guess what: the cops had nothing.

Though he suspected it was a mistake, he'd kept the Mac laptops, because he couldn't afford new ones of his own. He'd crack the passwords when he got around to it and wipe the hard drives, then find a way to trade or sell them online. He needed the cash, and besides, he thought, if the cops ever searched his house, he was already done for.

The gun — he still had the gun, but it was wrapped in plastic bags and buried under the abandoned railroad tracks behind his house, where it could never be found, not even with a metal detector, and where he could quickly retrieve it to use again, if he decided that was necessary. The gun should also be in the river, he knew, and it would be there, sooner or later. He'd stolen it, from a near stranger, who'd have no reason to connect him to the theft. He'd kept it because . . .

Because the murders were almost perfect. Almost.

Except that Cooper was alive. If Cooper were given his name, a light might come on. Life could get difficult. He didn't know if there could ever be enough evidence against him to bring charges, but the criminal justice system was quirky, and prosecutors were known to play dirty.

Of course, he was a white man, and blond, so he had that going for him. Made him smile when the thought passed through his head.

So. There was a risk in killing her, and a risk in not killing her. He weighed those things, without making a final decision.

Two days later, before work, Cooper had gotten up early and had driven to an informal gun range in Wisconsin, a borrow pit, where she and Alex had taken lessons with their revolver.

This time, she was shooting the Glock she'd gotten from Carter. She'd watched video instruction with the gun, had un-screwed the suppressor and was shooting without it.

At the borrow pit, she pinned a target to the dirt wall, walked ten feet away, took a breath, and began shooting. She shot care-fully, remembering the instruction she'd taken with the revolver, and the recom-mendation on YouTube. She did well, she thought, grouping her shots, after the first wilder ones, in a hand-sized pattern.

The gun was much easier to shoot than the .357, with a lighter trigger pull and far less recoil. She worked through twenty-two rounds. Nobody else had shown up to shoot, so she walked back to her car, screwed the suppressor on the gun barrel, and fired three more shots. The suppressor made the gun a little more awkward to handle but did cut the noise.

Still, it was loud. Carter had warned her of that, and he was right.

Done with the shooting, she packed up the gun, and drove to work.

That same day, Hess parked his Subaru two

blocks from Cooper's classroom building and walked over, lingering until Cooper left class, followed her to her office, watched until he was sure she was heading for the parking garage, ran to his car and waited.

When she drove past him, he let three cars get between them, and then followed south across Minneapolis. She drove to a house in Edina, parked in front of a two-car garage, and used a key to get in the house. Now he knew where she was. He would have to think about that.

He went home.

Cooper used her key to open the front door and was met by Melton, carrying the baby.

"You look annoyed," Cooper said, looking at Melton's tightened face. "Very annoyed."

"Mary didn't show up," Melton said. She was patting the baby on the back. "I called her and she said she thought she might have the virus again. This would be like the third time. I've been here all day."

"Ah, jeez, I'm sorry," Cooper said. "You should have called, I could have run home between eleven and two. Are you okay at work?"

"I got most of it done by Zoom. The hard part is the paper," Melton said. "I have the paper couriered over. This idiot I'm dealing with right now doesn't like the Internet . . . If I'm going to keep doing this we need to get an office printer in here."

"We'll hit Office Depot tomorrow morning and I'll call Mary tonight. This is unacceptable."

"Yes, it is. We need to find somebody else. So: how did the shooting go?"

As they exchanged reports of their days, Cooper took the baby and carried her around the kitchen; she remembered that Virgil Flowers had identified the exact Gerber's baby food that Chelsea had eaten that day. She couldn't do that yet, but the baby smelled like something dark and root-vegetable-like. She asked, "Anything on the BCA? Or Flowers and Davenport?"

"Yeah. I tapped into the system an hour ago. They interviewed a woman up north . . . I can't remember the exact town, two hours away. Anyway, she was the girlfriend of a man Alex sentenced to prison. She's violent, but they cleared her. Turns out she plays canasta in a bar that keeps a video record. She was playing cards when Alex and the boys were killed."

They now used the phrase "Alex and the boys were killed" without flinching.

"We hadn't heard anything about that

woman from the B-team, I wonder how they found her," Cooper said. She jiggled the baby and added, "I need some coffee. That goddamned Mary. We pay her a lot."

"She gets sick too much," Melton said. "I wondered if it was drugs or alcohol, but I don't think so. I think she just gets sick. Or maybe, she doesn't like the work."

"Thank God it's not drugs or alcohol and we're leaving Chelsea with her," Cooper said. "Anyway, Davenport and Flowers found somebody we hadn't heard about, this woman, and took it seriously enough to go interview her. I feel like . . . they're out there operating. *We're* operating."

"Yes. Flowers wrote the report for the BCA and added that they'd be talking to Tom Burston. That would have been today. They haven't filed a report on that yet, so I don't know what happened."

Cooper looked at her Rolex. "Tom might still be working . . . I wonder . . . Take the baby, will you? I'll give him a call."

She handed the baby to Melton, took out her phone, punched up her contacts list, found Burston's office number and tapped it. Two minutes later, she was talking to him: a hundred and fifty million dollars, liquid, will do that for you.

"I wanted to touch base with you," she

said. "I'm still . . . pretty messed up . . ."

"You gotta be," Burston said. "I'm having trouble with it myself."

"I know I've got to deal with things," Cooper said. "I need to schedule a meeting with you and the staff, see where we are. My attorney is looking at the estate documents, Alex's will. There are some bequests that will come out of the account. Not too many, and not too much."

"I understand. I didn't want to press you on that until you were ready," Burston said.

They made arrangements to meet the next week, and he asked her to bring copies of the estate documents. "You know Alex was thinking of giving some money to Home Streets? And that I opposed it?"

"Yes. That's another thing we need to talk about. I don't know those men very well. Heath and Dahl."

"You know," he said, "I was interviewed by two more law enforcement officers today, a U.S. marshal and a BCA agent . . ."

"Flowers and Davenport . . . we've met them."

"They were interested in what I had to say about Noah Heath and Bob Dahl. I think they're going to look at them. Maybe we'll get an actual, you know, law enforcement perspective," Burston said.

"That could be helpful," Cooper said. "Davenport and Flowers. What was their reaction to you . . . and yours to them?"

"They wondered if the stress between me and Alex, over Home Streets, might have made Alex think about pulling your account out of Barnes and Blue. I assured them there wasn't that kind of stress."

"I told them the same thing," Cooper said.

"I appreciate that, Maggie. They knew I was gay, did you . . . ?"

"Yes. I told them that we were doubles partners," Cooper said. "They wondered if you and I had an affair — and if one of us might have killed Alex so we could run off together with his money."

"Ah, jeez. Lucky I'm gay, huh?"

"We've had that discussion, we don't need to have it again," Cooper said. "What was your impression? You think they've got something going on?"

"They were smoother than the other cops. Especially Davenport," Burston said. "Flowers has this shitkicker thing going on, he was wearing some kind of lizard-skin cowboy boots. But he's no shitkicker and he won't miss much."

"Good. I've got some hope, then."

"Listen, one more thing," Burston said. "This might sound really awful to you.

Crass, or something."

"Go ahead, I'm sure I've heard worse."

"Uh . . . What kind of shape are you in to hit some balls?" Burston asked. "I don't, you know, expect to make this season, but January . . . Maybe it'd help take your mind off everything. God knows we both could use that."

Cooper laughed, and Melton looked up at her. She hadn't really laughed for weeks. "Actually . . ." She looked over at Melton. "We've got some babysitting arrangements to make, but I'd like that, Tom, a lot."

"We'll talk about it next week."

She clicked off and asked Melton, "Where'd we put Davenport's card?"

"Over by the spoons pot."

Cooper found the card under the ceramic pot, called Lucas. Lucas came up: "Ms. Cooper."

"Maggie," Cooper said. "Have a minute to talk?"

"Of course. Something come up?"

"I called Tom Burston to talk about the estate documents he'll need, and the account, and bequests in Alex's will," Cooper said. "He said you'd interviewed him today. What do you think?"

"About what?"

"Did he do it?" she asked.

"Don't quote me," Lucas said.

"I promise."

"I believe you were right about him. He seemed seriously affected by the killings and it looked genuine; he's feeling some grief," Lucas said. "I don't believe he killed your family."

She exhaled, then said, "All right. After a while, you begin to doubt your own judgment, but . . . All right. That makes me a bit happier."

Nightfall came around seven o'clock. Hess didn't know a lot about guns, but since every idiot in the country seemed to know how to use one, he was confident in his ability to make it go *bang!* He'd taken lessons in his specific gun, a Glock, on YouTube, so he was good to go.

He left his house as the sun disappeared below the western horizon, driving across the Cities to Edina. The night was cold, and he'd gone warm and dark and in the required uniform: a black hoodie over black jeans and black boots, the gun in the pocket of the hoodie.

He made a preliminary pass at the Edina house. There were lights on, most intensely in the back, maybe a kitchen. The area around the front door was more dimly lit. The tension was climbing up his back to his neck; he'd have an overnight headache for sure. *Why was he even doing this?*

Around the corner from the house, he could look past a row of bridal wreath bushes and across a neighbor's yard to the back windows of the Cooper house. As he hovered there, waiting on the street, he saw Cooper walk past a back window with a cup in her hand, wearing a red blouse. She appeared to be alone. Washing dishes, maybe.

The line of houses that included Cooper's all faced the same street; each house had a moderately-sized backyard, most skimpily landscaped with shrubs and trees, some with children's playsets or basketball hoops. The backyards ran slightly uphill to a line of fences, where they met another set of backyards, attached to houses facing the opposite direction, to another street.

Most of the houses showed lights, but the backyards were dark; a waxing first-quarter moon was well off to the west, throwing enough light between the scudding clouds to give the neighborhood the gritty feel of the northern Halloween.

He choked, nearly chickened out. He drove

198

around the block again, and started around again when he noticed, a hundred yards or so from the house where Cooper was staying, a house that was dark, but with three newspapers on the driveway. *Why was he doing this? If the cops caught him . . .*

Nobody home. He drove around the block again, beginning to quite literally sweat, smelling the odor welling up from under the hoodie.

Thought: *Just do it.*

He pulled into the driveway, waited to see if a light came on — none did. He touched the gun in his pocket, cool and hard like a tool, like a hammer head. He got out of the car, took a deep breath, and began jogging down the block like a night runner.

Cooper said, "I've wondered whether the shootings had any effect on Chelsea. Sometimes, she seems to fix her eyes on something and then just not move them. Staring into space. Not asleep, but . . . she sometimes seems stunned."

"She's an infant," Melton said. "Every once in a while, she goes back to the womb."

"Change of topic," Cooper said, taking a sip of tea. Talking about children tended to inflame the ball of rage that sat below her heart, spinning her off-balance. "Did I tell you what Delonia did today? She comes out on stage in an orange kind of chiffon blouse, *really* thin, probably rayon. Maybe silk, but thin, whatever it is. Unbuttoned to her god-damned navel. No bra, it's cool in there, her nipples were sticking out like pencil erasers. The kid I was telling you about, Colin? He's gotta be a virgin. I don't even know if he's seen a nipple outside a porno. He takes one look and before he gets half-way across the stage, you can see he's already working on a . . ."

Melton's phone rang, and she looked at the screen, frowned. "Neighbor. Old lady in the back. She hardly ever calls, I'm her emergency responder . . ." She pushed Answer and the speaker button at the same time and said, "Shirle?"

Shirley said, in a rusty old voice, "Annie! Annie, there's a man in your backyard. He looks like he's . . . he looks like he's looking in your window. I'll call 9-1-1 if you . . . He's hiding in a bush and he's looking in your back window, he's dressed all in black."

Cooper waved Melton off and said, "Shirle? This is Annie's friend, the one stay-ing with her? That might be a friend of mine. Before you call, let me check out there . . ."

"I'll be watching, dear," Shirley said.

"Thanks, Shirle." Melton touched the phone to ring off, and half stood. "You think?"

"Gotta be. Gotta be," Cooper said. The ball of rage now had her by the throat. "Let me, let me . . ."

She could hardly speak. She stood and walked quickly into the back of the house, to her room, where she dug out the pistol that she and Alex had kept in their library. A .357 revolver, the simplest, they'd been told, to operate. She stopped one moment to think: *There's nothing to think about: point and shoot.*

She walked into the kitchen and snapped, "Get the baby into your bedroom. Get down on the floor . . ."

Melton said, "Nope, nope, nope, I'm in on this. Don't do anything for a minute, let me . . . stay away from the fuckin' window . . ."

"No! Get back in the fuckin' bedroom . . ." Cooper gestured with the gun, at one point, the barrel wobbling across the line of Melton's forehead.

Melton said, "Hey! Hey!" She put up a hand as though to deflect a bullet, and Cooper jerked the gun barrel away. Melton hurried toward the back of the house with the baby, put her down in a bassinette,

201

crawled across the kitchen floor to a storage drawer, took out a foot-long black Maglite and said, "I'll light the fucker up. You watch from the window in the hallway next to the back door. If you see him start to move away or point a gun . . ."

"Then *I'll* light the fucker up," Cooper said, using a phrase they'd heard on a cop show. She'd been standing well away from the window, and now, as Melton had done, she got on her hands and knees and crawled across the kitchen to the back door, and the window beside it.

Melton was braced by the kitchen window. She asked, "You ready?"

Cooper said, "Wait! Let me unlock the door." She did it. "Okay. Light him up."

Melton peeked around the side of the kitchen window, put the flashlight against the glass, and turned it on. The Maglite lit up the backyard like a movie set and Cooper hit the back door, gun first.

Hess hadn't gone straight into Cooper's backyard. He'd chickened out again, and had circled the entire block, jogging, feeling the weight in his pocket bouncing up and down. He'd almost run back into the driveway that held his car, when he passed it, but he slogged on another hundred yards, and then, holding his breath, swerved to his left, crossed a white board fence into the yard next to Cooper's house, where he froze.

No reaction from anyone. No shouts, no questions. He slinked across the yard, keeping as many trees and bushes between himself and the house as he could. The house next door showed only a couple of lights, plus the pulsing colors of a big television played against a curtain.

When he'd gotten a grip again, he continued across the yard and slipped over the board fence into Cooper's yard, stopped again to listen, then crept forward to a stone circle that contained a flower garden with a tall, slender cypress tree at its center. There was little light, except what came from the line of windows up and down the block.

He knelt there, eyes fixed on the kitchen window. He could see Cooper's head and shoulders; she was apparently sitting at a kitchen table and now seemed to be talking to someone. The chatter continued, then Cooper got up and moved away from the window.

He was worried about shooting through the glass of the window. He decided several fast shots followed by a quick flight up the block, that should work. For a moment, he considered slipping back out of the yard, going home, and seeing what YouTube said about shooting through window glass. Had to be something. And he thought about crawling from the flower circle across the lawn, to pop up right next to the window, no more than five or six feet from Cooper, when she came back . . .

Not a good idea. Too exposed. He waited for her. A curtain moved at the kitchen window. What? And then, without warning, he was pinned like a bug in a brilliant light and he lurched to his feet and turned to run . . .

Cooper hit the door and saw the man in black crouched next to the cypress; she could only see the bottom half of his face beneath a monkish black hood, but he turned and she screamed something, not a word, but a sound, high and shrill, like a baby screaming in an airplane seat. The gun was already up and she began squeezing the trigger, but nothing happened, until she squeezed extra hard, and the gun went off, jumping in her hand.

She regripped with both hands and fired again, flinching and closing her eyes as she did, then again and again and again, trailing the running figure across the backyard.

He went over the neighbor's fence and

then turned, still moving, sideways, from her point of view, missed by all those shots, and his arm came up and he fired a gun and she caught the muzzle flash and pointed her own gun at the flash and pulled the trigger and it went *click*.

She'd used all the ammo and didn't even know where she'd put the rest. The man's gun flashed again and she was aware of whacking noises, and realized that she was hearing bullets hit the house.

Too close, too close, too close.

She lurched back inside and fell backwards on her butt, letting go of the gun as she did, and it clattered across the kitchen floor.

Melton, still with the flashlight in her hand, screeched, "Get the gun, get the gun . . ."

Realizing that Melton didn't know the gun was empty, Cooper let it go and crawled to the door and slammed it and shouted, "Gun's empty, we can't let him get in, no bullets, push the table, I'll get the front door."

Melton shouted, "Okay," and she began pushing the small kitchen table toward the door and Cooper scrambled to the living room and began tugging and then pushing a sofa into the entryway.

With the door blocked, Cooper ran back

to the kitchen and Melton grabbed her and pulled her down.

"What, what?" Cooper was gasping, trying to get up, but Melton pinned her and screamed, "He's shooting at us, you idiot."

Not anymore. The shooting had stopped and the man was gone and Cooper pushed Melton off and crawled low across the kitchen floor and Melton shouted, "Check the baby?" and Cooper shouted back, "Go in the bedroom, we can barricade the door with the bed."

Melton followed her into the bedroom where they rolled the guest bed across the doorway. The baby was crying and Melton shouted at Cooper, "Check the baby, check the baby, I've got my phone, I'm calling 9-1-1."

Cooper checked the baby — crying, but not hurt.

Melton had 9-1-1 on the line and the operator asked, "Is this an emergency?"

"Yes! Yes! A crazy man is trying to shoot us."

"Is this the home of Ann Melton? Is this Ann Melton?"

"Yes, I —"

"Your neighbor called. Patrol cars are on the way," the operator said. "Remain in your house, stay below the windows. We're coming. Less than two minutes now."

"Tell the officers to be really careful, this man shot a lot," Melton said, breathing hard. "He's got a high-capacity gun and I think he must have shot at us twenty times . . ."

"I will pass that along," the operator said. Her voice was cool, the most routine thing in the world. "No injuries in your house?"

"No, we're all okay."

Melton heard the operator say to someone, "No injuries." Then, "Stay on the line while I pass your information to the patrolmen . . ."

Cooper, staying low, crawled out of the bedroom to the back window, peeked. Lights were coming on down the block and the elderly woman in the house across the backyard came out on her back porch and shouted, "I called 9-1-1."

Cooper shouted, "Thank you, thank you." And she turned and shouted to Melton, "The cops are coming."

And the cops *were* coming. Lots of them. Hess never saw them. He made it back to the car. He kept jabbing the key at the ignition, kept missing, because he was shaking so hard. Couldn't believe that Cooper had apparently emptied a gun at him. She must have been waiting, must have had a gun in her hand. Couldn't believe that he'd actually stopped to shoot back: "Stupid stupid stupid," he said to himself.

He pulled the car out of the driveway and headed into the night, following narrow streets to a traffic light, then into the stream of cars. He was wearing a blue shirt, and at the next stoplight, he pulled the hoodie off and threw it into the back, in case the cops were stopping Subarus, looking for a man in a hoodie.

But if the cops were coming, he never saw them.

As they sat on the floor, waiting for the police to arrive, Cooper said, "I had the most ridiculous thought, halfway through the shooting, after I ran out of ammunition."

"And that was?"

"I saw this dumb bumper sticker on a pickup truck that said 'Point and Click Means You're Out of Ammo.' That just happened to me! I pulled the trigger and it went click and I was out of ammo."

"Sounds like a life lesson," Melton said. "Believe bumper stickers."

They began giggling and didn't stop for a

minute, then Cooper said, her voice gone dark, "I'm hysterical as shit."

Cooper called Lucas.

Lucas answered on the third ring, and he must have put her name in his contacts list, Cooper thought, because he answered with, "Maggie: what's up?"

"Lucas! The killer was here and he tried to kill us!" She was loud, but not shouting.

"What!"

"Oh my God, oh my God, I just shot at him and maybe I shot him —"

"What!"

"Pay attention, pay attention," Cooper now shouted. "The killer was here, he tried to shoot me . . ."

"Anybody hurt? Are you okay? Are you still armed and loaded?"

"Yes. No. He ran away. He ran, the cops are coming, a neighbor called the cops, I don't know where the killer went, he ran away but I shot at him with my revolver. I ran out of bullets, I don't have any more, I mean I do, around here somewhere, but I don't know where —"

"I'm coming," Lucas said. "When the cops get there, meet them in the street. Leave your gun in the house, meet them empty-handed. Tell them right away that this is part of the Sand investigation. That they need to find out where the killer went and if he had a car, what kind of car it was, what direction it went. Do you understand?"

"Yes. Tell the cops about the Sand investigation."

"Leave the gun in the house. Empty hands, can you say that to me? Ann, too. Say it!"

"Empty hands, empty hands."

"Good. The baby's okay?" Lucas asked.

"The baby's okay. Lucas, you can't believe this, I kept shooting at him and shooting at him and he never fell down or anything, I thought you were supposed to fall down . . ."

"Hang tight. Talk to the cops. I'm on the way."

Lucas called Virgil as he drove across the Mississippi, told him about the attack and, "I'll see you there."

"I'll be right behind you," Virgil said.

At Melton's street, the cops tried to wave Lucas off, but he hung his marshal's badge out the window until he got somebody to look at it, and got the name of Edina's lead investigator. There wasn't one, yet, he was told, but she was on her way. In the meantime, the patrol cops were freezing the scene. Virgil showed up as Lucas was talking to the cops, and Virgil pulled in behind Lucas's Cayenne.

Lucas went to meet him and Virgil asked, "Talked to her yet?"

"No. I've got the okay to go inside. They've got some cops sitting with them."

They went in the house, found Cooper, Melton, and the baby huddled in the living room, watched over by two patrolmen. Lucas and Virgil identified themselves for the cops and Lucas said to Cooper, "Well, this is another fine mess."

Cooper looked at them with a wan smile and said, "Laurel and Hardy. But there were actually about a dozen variations on the line."

Melton asked, "What are we going to do? The killer knows where we are."

"We'll start by either finding you another place to stay or getting extra security around this place."

"Since he knows where we're at . . . we should move to my house," Cooper said. "More protected, stone and bricks, fewer cars, security system. I could hire a security service to watch over us."

Lucas nodded: "That would work. I could get you a service."

Virgil: "Tell us the story."

■ ■ ■ ■

Cooper began the story, starting with the call from the neighbor woman. She'd gotten to the point where Melton lit up the backyard, when the Edina lead detective arrived, a bulky woman named Marsha Moss, who was not happy to find Lucas and Virgil already interviewing Cooper.

After some semi-heated rank pulling, she conceded that they knew more about the case, and would be working it harder than she would be, and she settled in to listen.

Cooper: "I pushed open the back door and he was right there and I could see he had something in his hand which I thought was a gun, and it was a gun, he shot it at me a bunch of times . . ."

She hadn't actually seen a gun, but she and Melton had agreed, before the cops arrived, that it might be a good thing to say that she'd seen one. And anyway, it had been one.

"Bullet holes all around the door . . ." Melton interjected.

Moss to Cooper: "Do you have any idea of how many times you fired your weapon?"

"Yes, of course," Cooper said. "Five shots. I'm such an airhead, I have a box of bullets around here somewhere, I brought them when we came here, the next day after Alex and the boys . . . Five shots, I fired them all."

"You don't think you hit him?"

"He didn't fall down or stagger or anything, that I could see, but I was . . . freaking out, is what I was doing," Cooper said. And, "I don't know. What do I know? I've never done this. I fired five times and he fired a bunch of times and that's all I know."

Moss looked around, poked a finger at a patrolman and said, "Junior, get some guys and talk to all the neighbors. We need to know that there's nobody lying dead in their houses. Or shot up."

Junior nodded: "On it."

"We need crime scene here right away," Lucas said to Moss. "Look for blood. If we got blood, we got DNA. Maybe she hit him . . ."

Lucas and Virgil stayed at Melton's house until the two women began to settle down, and arrangements were made to place Edina officers outside the house and another inside, until the next morning.

When they left, Melton was making grilled cheese sandwiches for the cops. In the yard, crime scene crews were still crawling around the yard under tripod-mounted work lights, looking mostly for blood spatter, without finding any, but picking up eight ejected shell casings.

On first examination, the shells appeared to be identical to those found at the Sand-Cooper residence. Slugs taken from the door frame where Cooper had been standing were also recovered and would be compared to those taken from the Sand-Cooper residence.

As they walked out the door, Cooper caught Lucas's jacket sleeve and said, "It was me he was after. Alex and the boys got caught by mistake."

Lucas shook his head and said, "Don't jump to conclusions. That's one reading. The other reading is, you know something that Alex also knew, and he doesn't want it to get out. You're now in charge of the family money. That has to count for something, too."

Virgil: "Lucas told me that you talked to Tom Burston this afternoon . . ."

Cooper: "Yes, I did."

". . . and you mentioned something about bequests in Alex's will. Would the bequests be large enough that somebody might want to hurry them up? Or would the recipient believe that Alex was unlikely to die naturally before the recipient did?"

Cooper looked down, dragged her fingers across her mouth, looked up and said, "Yes . . . though I'd hate to think that anyone on his list would commit murder. There are three individuals and two organizations that would get a million dollars each."

"We need that list," Virgil said.

"I'll get it to you in the morning," Cooper said.

Lucas looked at Virgil: "But why would they come after Maggie, if Alex is already dead? They wouldn't get more money . . ."

Virgil looked at Cooper: "Would they?"

Cooper thought again, and said, "Well . . . one would. I'll get that to you tomorrow, as well."

Before they broke up for the night, Lucas and Virgil stopped by their cars to talk. Lucas said, "We've still got to talk to the car-theft guy in Stillwater. Carter? Though he's sort of . . . receding in my thoughts. Killing Sand is one thing, but why would he come after the wife?"

"Ah, yeah. I've sort of written him off, but I guess we ought to talk," Virgil said. "Maybe get breakfast tomorrow, and then run out to Stillwater. Back before noon."

"If Maggie's moving to the Sand place tomorrow morning, we could stop there after Stillwater and get the list of bequests from her. Maybe go over to Home Streets and check out Dahl and Heath tomorrow afternoon," Lucas said. "Sandy should have some returns on those guys, though I haven't heard from her yet. We can call her in the morning, give her a push."

"I'm more interested in the people who would inherit from Sand. I should have thought of that sooner," Virgil said. "I might bump them up ahead of the Home Streets guys. Then, there's Maggie's students at the U. We haven't even started on that . . ."

"We can sort it out tomorrow," Lucas said. He looked up at the sky: no moon anymore. "It's late. We can hit Cecil's about nine o'clock. Drop your truck at my place, I'll drive."

"Deal," Virgil said. And, "You think this guy, this shooter . . . think he'll quit? That he might have had enough tonight?"

"I don't know," Lucas said. "What I'm afraid of, is, he'll pull back, lay low, and then a month from now, or two months, make another run at her, if we haven't caught him. He's got some reason for doing what he's doing. Why would we think that reason will go away?"

"There's a happy thought to end the day," Virgil said. "See you tomorrow."

They got in their cars, but before Lucas could pull away, Virgil flashed him twice with the Tahoe's headlights, got out of the truck and walked down to the Cayenne. Lucas rolled the window down and Virgil said, "I try really hard not to be a cynical asshole."

"I don't do therapy after sundown," Lucas said.

"Not asking for therapy, I want you to tell me that even if I have asshole-like, cynical thoughts, I'm not really a cynical asshole."

"All right. Tell me."

"We had two shooters, and we know where they were. Maggie was at the kitchen door, the shooter started out by that flower circle and then over by the neighbor's fence, right?"

"That would be correct," Lucas said.

"Maggie fired five times. The shooter fired at least eight shots at her, apparently emptied his gun at her, first from twenty feet, and then from what, forty or fifty? And neither of them hit anything. Nothing. Nada."

Lucas closed his eyes: "I'm afraid I see where this is going."

"There were at least thirteen shots fired

from close range and none of them even broke a fuckin' window, Lucas."

"What happened was, the shooter just proved that there's a killer out there, and it's not her. That's very, very good — for her," Lucas said.

"Tell me I'm not a cynical asshole."

"Well, you are, but you're also right," Lucas said. "The shooter hit to the right of the door, and to the left of the door, but he never hit the door where Maggie was."

Virgil looked back at the house, still lit up like a Christmas party, with cops still crawling around the place. "We may have to stop calling her Maggie and start calling her Ms. Cooper again. You know, like a suspect."

"Ah, man," Lucas said. "I'm too tired for this shit. I gotta go to bed."

"Yeah." Virgil slapped the door panel and said, "One more time — see you tomorrow."

10

Tomorrow turned out to be cold and dark, with a chill wind jabbing at exposed necks. They got breakfast and then headed east out of St. Paul to the old town of Stillwater. Henry James Carter, former car salesman and later car thief, now an unemployed ex-con, lived in a condo on Stillwater's main drag.

"How's your leg?" Virgil asked, as they went.

"Another indication that something is seriously wrong with me — ever since I started working again, I don't hurt so much," Lucas said.

They rang Carter's apartment from the lobby, and a woman answered. They identified themselves, and after some talk between the woman and a man in the background, she buzzed them up.

Carter met them at the apartment door.

He was a burly man, running to fat, balding, three inches under six feet, clean shaven, wearing a tee-shirt, shorts, and Nikes. A pair of copper-rimmed glasses perched on his nose. His file said that he was fifty-six, and he looked ten years older, with a pale, flaccid face.

At the door he asked, "What'd I do?"

Virgil shrugged and said, "I don't know. Did you do something?"

"Nothing except look for a job." He backed into the condo, where the woman, who matched Carter in size and weight, stood, mouth half open, waiting for the worst. Virgil and Lucas followed him in. "If you guys don't mess me up, I got an offer from Fleet Farm. I start next Sunday."

"Good for you," Lucas said. "We understand you were interviewed by the BCA and St. Paul police about the murder of Alex Sand . . ."

"Is that what this is about?" He glanced back at the woman, ran a hand through the remnants of his hair, and said, "They know I didn't do it. The police. I mean, I was here. They know I was talking on my phone . . . besides, I had nothing against the judge. It could have been any judge. The sentence could have been longer. The judge wasn't like a judge, he was like a clerk. All he did was give me the sentence that got worked out between the prosecutor and my attorney."

"He had nothing to do with it," the woman said. She began to cry, and walked backwards into the living room, and sank down on a sofa. Carter looked at her, saw the tears gathering in her eyes, and Lucas said, "Look. Give us ten minutes."

They asked about the phone alibi, about the piano practice. He showed them what might have been an expensive Roland keyboard, if the keys on the top and bottom octaves had worked.

"I'm trying to fix it in my spare time, which I got a lot of," he said. "At least for now. I'm hoping for some decent overtime up at Fleet Farm, I'm a good salesman. If I can get the piano going, I might have a gig at a golf club, you know, Saturday nights."

The woman said, "He is a good salesman. He'll never do anything like that again. Like the cars. He got hooked on the Indian casinos, that's what made him do it."

"How about gun deals?" Virgil asked. "Made any recently?"

Carter was indignant. "You guys ever spent any time in a federal cage? Locked up? Gives me the creeps just thinking about it. I go out on the street here, breathe the free air. I gotta tell you, I'm never doing anything that might get me sent back. Never. No fuckin' way. I'm trying to get my civil rights back, so maybe I can get back with the guns. Until then, I won't touch one. I swear."

"Please, just leave us alone. We're trying to get on," the woman wailed.

"There's fifteen minutes I won't get back," Virgil said, when they were on the street. Virgil looked back at the condo. "By the time we left, I wanted to give him money."

"A sad sack," Lucas said. "You notice his feet?"

"Size fourteen?"

"At least. And about a hundred pounds too heavy for the killer. So: he's out?"

"He's out," Virgil said. "We should go talk to Cooper — see if she's moved back into her house."

In the condo above them, the Carters watched them walking away. Catherine put her arms around Henry's waist and gave him a big squeeze. "They bought it. I promise you," she said.

"Let's grill a couple of steaks and then go roll them bones," Carter said, and he laughed aloud, something he'd started to do since meeting with Cooper.

■ ■ ■ ■

Lucas and Virgil drove back to town, talking about Cooper and Melton on the way, and how long the threat against Cooper might last, if there actually was a threat. "I appreciate your cynicism, but I decided before I went to sleep last night that Ms. Cooper didn't set us up," Lucas said. "I mean, how would she ever have convinced the shooter to come back? If the guy'd been caught last night, he'd have had a hell of a time convincing anybody that he wasn't the Sand killer."

When they arrived at Cooper's home, they were met at the door by a very large man, ten years older than Lucas. He had gray hair, a two-day stubble, a Navy tattoo spreading out from under a tee-shirt, a peanut butter sandwich in one hand and a 9mm in the other.

Lucas: "Jesus Christ. What are you doing here, Pelz?"

Virgil: "Hey, Binky."

Pelz had spent thirty years as a St. Paul street cop, and though in theory a devout Catholic, he hadn't been known for his acts of Christian charity.

He pulled the door all the way open, swallowed some sandwich and said, "I'm guarding some bodies. They told me to shoot first and ask questions later, but I had a peanut butter sandwich in my hand when I saw you two mooks coming up the walk and I couldn't rack the slide."

"At least the sandwich is well protected," Virgil said. "Is Ms. Cooper here?"

"Yeah, she and Ann are upstairs in the office looking at documents. They said you might show up. How you guys doin'? Virgil, you need to eat more. Davenport, word is around that you got your ass shot off."

They talked about the New York shooting as he led the way through the house to the stairway going up to the second floor. Lucas noticed as they walked through that there was no sign of the recent violence. The Persian carpet where the bodies had fallen had disappeared, to be replaced by something less Persian and more Craftsman.

Virgil hadn't been in the house and as they climbed the stairs, muttered to Lucas, "Dark house. Good place for a murder. If you're Agatha Christie. Or any kind of novelist."

"Shh."

The office contained a business-sized walnut desk and, to one side, a long walnut table with two comfortable-looking business

224

chairs. The women were sitting on opposite sides of the table, with stacks of paper between them.

Melton looked up when they walked in and she said to Cooper, "The cops," and Cooper turned to look.

Cooper said, "We're going over the estate stuff."

"We were hoping you'd have the list of beneficiaries," Virgil said.

"We do," Cooper said. "They were all carefully identified in the estate documents, so we have names, addresses, and phone numbers, as of the last update, which was two years ago."

Melton had started digging through the paper when she saw them, produced a page with a printed list and handed it to Lucas.

"That's great," Lucas said. "How are you guys doing? Since last night?"

"We're okay," Cooper said. She glanced at Pelz and said, "I hired Ben to provide extra security. He'll be here until we lock up, and after that, we won't open the door to anyone. Even if we know them."

Virgil: "Good. Though I never heard Binky called Ben."

"Binky?"

"You had to tell them, didn't you?" Pelz said.

"We're old pals from the St. Paul cops," Virgil said. "He taught me about golf, I taught him about police work, how to read without moving his lips, and women."

"You might have missed some essential information about women," Melton said.

Pelz: "I desperately want to shoot somebody, but I don't know where to start."

Cooper, with gravel in her voice: "I desperately wish to shoot someone, too, if we could only find him." And she looked like it, eyes staring and fixed for a moment, before she broke free from the thought.

That put a temporary cloud over the conversation, but they talked for a while longer, and Virgil asked Cooper if she knew anything personal, that might be useful, about Bob Dahl or Noah Heath, of Home Streets.

"Bob is kind of a weenie, a suck-up, but that might go with the job. Noah's a trust-funder. I don't think he's ever really had a job. He's got this rich-man shell, but underneath it, he's . . . what?"

She looked at Melton, who said, "Obsequious."

"Neither one is particularly likeable, but I have to say, Noah has done a lot of good in the community, over the years," Cooper said. "He's made a hobby of doing good, which is better than spending his money on crap, I guess."

"Are you going to give him a hundred and fifty?" Lucas asked.

"No. He stays at a hundred thousand. He will get that as soon as I'm satisfied that Home Streets is a real thing. Alex thought it was, Tom disagreed, but I want to know. On my own."

"So there'd be no advantage, to him, in . . . attacking Alex. Or you, last night."

She shook her head: "I don't believe so."

Back outside, with the list of beneficiaries from Sand's will, Virgil said, "We need to talk to Sandy, see what she's got on the Home Streets guys."

"You know, if it was Homey Streets, it'd be like a rap boy-band," Lucas said.

"There's something wrong with your mind," Virgil said.

Sandy Hayward started out as a hippie and never grew out of it. She was a soft, thin woman with an easy-smiling face, blond hair usually frizzed-up, dangly jade earrings that she made herself, body-hugging dresses in shades of beige with unnecessary frills; hot librarian glasses.

A vegetarian hippie with multiple cats and

a hipster boyfriend who led the Twin Cities in man-bun hair styling, she'd originally been hired by the BCA, at the urging of Lucas, to do computer-based research. She enjoyed nothing more than tracking down people she called rat-fuckers.

Her wide and growing knowledge of federal and state data systems, and her willingness to sidestep what she saw as unnecessary bureaucratic restrictions on data access, made her a valuable resource.

The BCA had paid her not much, as a part-timer, until she threatened to quit, and now she was a full-timer with a small glass-enclosed office, an excellent salary, three computer screens, and two printers, one for text, one for photos. She was in her office, her feet on a waste basket, eating an apple, when Lucas and Virgil walked in.

She looked up and said, "Well, there goes the morning."

"It's almost afternoon," Lucas said. "What do you have on the Home Streets boys? Besides the Internet shit you gave us yesterday?"

"I got quite a bit, actually."

She kicked her feet off the waste basket, turned and poked a key on her computer. The screen lit up, and her fingers rattled across the keyboard and a file came up. "I will give you an oral summary. If you want a printed version, I would have to do some redaction so it couldn't be used as evidence."

Virgil: "Uh-oh."

"Don't ask. I will tell you that Noah Heath has been involved in eight other charities that I could find, some now defunct, some still active," she said. "His family apparently had quite a bit of money at one time. Some of it sent Noah to Dartmouth, and from what I can tell, he's been living on Dartmouth creds and a modest inheritance for most of his life. For the last thirty years, as chairman of boards of charities that he started himself under the umbrella of Heart/Twin Cities."

Virgil: "Uh-oh. Again."

"All of the charities actually accomplished things, but it looks to me that the accomplishments were considerably short of the original goals," Sandy said, peering at her computer screen. "They made up for that with PR. I might be the only one outside of Heart/Twin Cities who knows that."

"Give me an example," Lucas said.

"He created one of the early prosthetic-aid organizations for disabled soldiers returning from the oil wars," Sandy said.

"From what I can tell — and this may not be the whole story — all the prosthetics were sourced through a single company, and that company was founded shortly before the charity. His name is not involved in the company, but it seems that the company was a pass-through thing."

"What's that?" Lucas asked.

"They bought the prosthetics from established companies, and then sold them to Heath's charity at a markup," Sandy said.

"Classic hustle," Virgil said.

"Maybe. Can't prove it yet," Sandy said. "Also, the charity folded after four years and the statute of limitations has run out, even if we could prove it."

Virgil: "So you're not ready to declare him a rat-fucker."

"Well. His next charity, where he was also chairman of the board, was to supply very high-priced drugs to sick people who couldn't afford them," Sandy said. "It was called Minnesota Meds. The idea was to import prescription drugs from the Bahamas, where the prices are controlled and considerably lower, and supply them at much lower prices, or free, here. He ran a fund-raising campaign to buy the drugs. That went on for five years before the office burned down. After the fire, Minnesota

Meds evaporated."

"And the fire took the charity's records and accounts with it," Virgil said.

Sandy nodded and said, "A tragedy. There was still forty thousand dollars in the bank account, which was distributed to local hospitals to great acclaim. He was given the key to St. Paul."

"The next one?" Lucas asked.

"Big Grin. That's the name," Sandy said. "Raises money to send surgeons to third world countries to fix cleft palates. That'd be a harelip to you, Virgil, since you're not married to a plastic surgeon and live out in the weeds."

"I know what —"

She continued, interrupting: "That one's still operating. Apparently out of the same office as Home Streets because they have the same director, this Bob Dahl guy. I can find six real surgeons who have actually done some of the work. However, there are five more that I can't find — not to say that they don't exist. They come from countries where I don't have access to the data. I just have their names from annual reports. If they all got paid at the same rates, the five volunteer surgeons would have gotten around a half million dollars for expenses, supplies, and paid assistants, nurses, who aren't named."

Virgil: "So you're saying . . ."

"Yeah. He's a rat-fucker," Sandy said.

"How about Dahl?" Lucas asked.

"He's definitely a crook," Sandy said. "I just don't know what kind. 'Bob Dahl' isn't his real name, but I don't know what his real name is. There was a Robert Dahl, called Bob, long juvie record, who ran away from home in East Bumfuck twenty years ago, and supposedly went to California. That Bob Dahl and this Bob Dahl share a Social Security number and a birth date, but they don't look much alike. I've seen both their driver's license photos."

"People change in twenty years," Virgil said.

"Eye color and height? Our boy is three inches shorter than the original."

"Okay . . ."

"I suspect the runaway is dead, and that the Home Streets Bob Dahl knew the original, or found out about him, somehow, and used him for the name change. When that would have happened, I don't know. I do have a driver's license renewal for the current Bob Dahl, and that includes a home address in White Bear."

Lucas looked at Virgil and said, "Dumpster dive."

Virgil, "Ah, shit. Which one of us is gonna dive?"

Lucas pulled his jacket open to show off the labels: "I'm wearing a fifteen-hundred-dollar sport coat from Zegna. You're wearing a shirt-jac from Filson."

Sandy said, "If you can get me some prints, IAFIS can get back to us in two hours or less, if I tell them it's a murder check. If he's in there."

They called Dahl at the Home Streets office from an anonymous burner phone, one of several that Sandy kept in her desk. The secretary asked for Lucas's name, and he said, "Mike Bennett." She said, "Just a minute, I'll ring you through."

Lucas hung up and said, "Okay. He's at the office."

Virgil read through Cooper's list of beneficiaries on their way out of town, and said, "There's one guy, Martin Wye, who'll get a million from Alex Sand and another million from Maggie, if she doesn't change it before she dies. It appears that he runs some kind of wildlife rescue center up in Ely. Wolves and so on."

"And nobody's interviewed him?"

"Nope. Not yet."

"Sandy needs to look him up."

Ten minutes farther on, Sandy called. "Do you guys know a reporter for KSTP named Daisy Jones?"

Virgil: "Ah . . . yeah. What does she want?"

"Have you ever slept with her, Virgil?" Sandy purred.

"No. Jesus, Sandy. I never slept with her," Virgil said.

"Okay, then. That's one that we know of."

Lucas laughed until Sandy asked, "How about you, Lucas?"

"No. Never." He laughed again. "I like that line about Virgil, though. 'That's one we know of.' "

"Sandy . . . what do you want?" Virgil asked.

"Jones called and asked me if it's true that you and Lucas are working the Sand murder together. I told her I didn't know and suggested that she get in touch with you guys. She said she tried Virgil's number, the last one she had, and it's now assigned to somebody who never heard of Virgil. She said if you don't call her back, she'd have to go with the rumor that you're on the case and have identified the killer and expect to reveal the name in the next couple of days."

"Goddamnit, she's blackmailing us," Virgil said. "Gimme her number."

Virgil called Jones, identified himself, and asked, "What do you want?"

"Is Lucas there with you?" Jones asked.

Virgil looked at Lucas, who shrugged and said, "Yeah, I'm here, Daisy."

"Good. Who's the killer?" she asked.

"We don't know. We really don't have a clue," Virgil said. "That's the truth, Daisy. You know I've never told you a direct lie."

"You've sort of danced around a lot of them, though," Jones said.

"So have you. But: honestly, we have no idea who did it. We're flopping around like fish out of water."

"But you are both working the case," Jones said.

"Yes, we are," Lucas said.

"Good. I can deal with you guys," Jones said. "Those stiffs from St. Paul and the BCA won't even talk to me about Sand. So I'm going with the new fact that you're working it, and I won't add anything really delicious. For not doing that, I'll expect a call."

"We don't know if we'll ever find anything," Lucas said.

"I have faith," Jones said. "Oops, gotta go. Somebody's crying in the corridor."

235

■ ■ ■ ■

When they were sure she was gone, Lucas said, "You know, when Sandy said, 'That's one we know of,' that would imply that you and Sandy . . ."

"Shut up."

"I wondered what the hell happened to my desk that one night. I came in the next morning and there were pencils all over the floor, and what looked like a smear . . ."

"I'm not listening . . ."

"I had to wipe the desk down with a paper towel. I mean, jeez."

Dahl lived in a modest split-level house in White Bear Lake, north of St. Paul. They cruised the place twice, Lucas driving, Virgil checking out the house with binoculars. "Looks dead."

"That's great, but what about the garbage can?" Lucas asked.

"Behind the fence, I think. That'd be the logical place."

A woven board fence extended out from the garage to the next property, and then turned down the lot line along the backyard.

"I'll knock," Lucas said. "If you sorta want to hang back . . ."

"Wait a minute, I'm getting the gloves on," Virgil said. He began rolling some tan vinyl gloves up his fingers. When he was ready, he said so, and "I hate this. I always wind up smelling like tomato sauce and rotten bananas."

"Face it; that's your lot in life," Lucas said. "I, on the other hand, smell like Tom Ford's *Oud Wood.*"

"So that's what it is," Virgil said. "I thought you might have had a hooker in the car."

They were on Dahl's block, and as they came up to the house, Lucas pulled in at the far right side of the driveway, as close as he could get to a gate through the woven fence. Lucas got out, walked to the front door to ring the doorbell. Virgil unfolded a plastic garbage bag and waited.

Lucas rang the bell, stood looking at the door, rang again, listened, opened the screen door, and knocked on the interior door. Nobody came to answer the knock, and Lucas turned to look at Virgil, and nodded. Virgil climbed out of the car, walked to the gate in the fence, worked the handle, stepped behind it, where he found two blue trash cans.

He lifted the lids on both, saw some Pepsi

cans. He gathered them up, handling them by the rims, and dropped them in the garbage bag. He added an empty orange juice bottle and a waxy microwave pizza box. That looked like the best of it, so he dropped the trash can lids, closed the gate behind himself, and walked back to the car.

Lucas: "We good?"

"If we have the right address."

Virgil called Sandy on the way back to the BCA, told her to crank up the latent fingerprint unit for a crash examination. She said she would do that, and the fingerprint tech was waiting when they arrived. He took the bag and disappeared.

Lucas said, "Late lunch."

"Parrot?"

The Parrot Café was a half mile from the BCA office and an agent hangout. They settled in for sandwiches and used their cell phones to look up the recipients of money from Sand's will.

Martin Wye was an adjunct professor of environmental studies at the University of Minnesota Duluth and an authority on North Woods predators. He'd founded and still operated the Center for Predator Studies in the town of Ely.

Virgil: "Says he wrote the definitive papers on fishers. Sounds kinda legit."

"I don't want to drive all the hell the way to Ely to talk to him . . . and if you went, you'd probably be towing a boat and get lost for a week."

"True," Virgil said. "I suggest we put him on our list, but down a way."

"With the other beneficiaries," Lucas said. "I don't . . . I don't see that panning out. I think Heath and Dahl are looking like a better shot."

They were finishing the last of their French fries when Gary Durey, the BCA agent leading the investigation, came through the door, trailed by another agent. Virgil lifted a hand to them and Lucas turned to look and Durey ambled over and asked, "You figured it out yet?"

"Probably take another twenty-four hours, give or take a month or two," Virgil said.

The other agent, George Pope, said, "Lucky you guys are working it. I mean, Durey couldn't find his own ass with both hands and a flashlight."

Lucas said, "Look, Gary, we really don't want to step on your toes."

Durey waved them off: "Happy to have you. Okay, not outrageously happy, but honest to God, we're not finding much at all.

239

You guys seeing anything?"

Lucas: "We're looking at the beneficiaries of Sand's and Cooper's estate plans. You know there's a guy who'll get a million because Sand went down, and another million if Cooper does?"

"Jesus, that's not bad, especially not after last night," Durey said. "You chasing them down?"

"Ah, maybe next week," Lucas said. "Virgil's heading back to Mankato tonight, spend some time with Frankie and the kids. And probably work on another fuckin' novel."

Durey shrugged: "If you're not gonna get right on top of them . . . We could take a look at them."

"Good with me," Virgil said. Lucas nodded. Neither of them mentioned Dahl or Heath. Lucas took the folded paper out of his jacket pocket and passed it to Durey. "Hot off the presses."

As they were leaving the café, Sandy called: she'd gotten Bob Dahl's real name from IAFIS — the FBI's Integrated Automated Fingerprint Identification System. "Real name is Darrell Hinton. Has a juvie record in Minnesota, lived in West Bumfuck, so he probably knew Bob Dahl. Went to California, got in trouble, five arrests over fifteen years, all for various nonviolent hustles. Did eighteen months in Susanville, Level 2, for running a home-rental scam . . ."

"We're on our way in," Virgil told her. "We'll want to see all the paper."

11

Sandy had the paper ready for them when they got back to the BCA. They skimmed through it, then Virgil called a friend, Random Cosby, at the California Bureau of Investigation.

Cosby did a fast search for Darrell Hinton, as they waited on the phone, and came back with, "Yup. We got him, if it's the right Darrell Clark Hinton, 02-22-1987."

"That's the one," Sandy said.

"We've got a warrant for him, issued, mmm, six years back now, running a credit-card points scam through Amazon," Cosby said.

"How'd that work?" Virgil asked.

"Let me read this . . ." Cosby went away for a minute, then came back. "Okay, he was working at a computer repair service. He'd check to see if the computer had an automatic link to Amazon. If it did, he'd check to see if the owner had accumulated points through a credit card. American Express was big. If there were a bunch of points, he'd use them to order stuff, have it delivered to a Whole Foods drop box, and then resell it. Looks like a lot of people didn't even know they had points. If the merchandise was bought with points, payments wouldn't show up on credit card bills."

"How much did he get?"

"The LA cops managed to track down forty-two victims, their hacked accounts, but there would have been more. Total take was around fifty thousand dollars over the course of the year that he was working at the computer place. The computer owner was cooperating, but Hinton disappeared. Not a sniff of him since then."

Virgil: "Does his sheet show any violence?"

"Mmm . . . nope."

"You guys still want him?" Lucas asked.

"You'd have to talk to LA, but the case is pretty old, trying to track down witnesses and all. Be expensive for not much return . . ."

Lucas said, "Got it."

"Make an excellent threat to hold over his head, though," Cosby said. "I can send you a copy of the warrant, if you want to print it out. Get it to you in five minutes."

"Do that," Virgil said.

"Okay!" Sandy said. "We've thrown one rat-fucker on the barbie, as the Aussies wouldn't say."

Virgil looked at Lucas: "How do you want to do this?"

Lucas shrugged: "The usual."

The "usual" involved backing Bob Dahl/ Darrell Clark Hinton against the wall to see if he'd turn on Noah Heath, the chairman of the board. Previous investigators had noted that Heath was as tall as the killer, although he was also described as "chubby." The killer hadn't looked chubby in the security video, but the rain suit could have disguised the weight.

"I'm not doing anything now," Virgil said. "As long as we can get him alone."

The headquarters of Home Streets was in an appropriately down-market building off an I-94 frontage road, one slot in a rehabbed warehouse, stuck between a laundromat and a dog groomer.

Lucas parked in a space in front of the dog groomer, and when they got out of the car, wet-dog odor got all over them. The door to the Heart/Twin offices had a sign

244

with a list of charities, including Home Streets and Big Grin — "Putting a Smile on the Children of the World."

Inside the office, which carried a hint of wet dog, a big-haired receptionist with purple-rimmed glasses waited at a desk, behind "In" and "Out" boxes, a wired phone set, and a plastic plaque that said "Doreen Pollard." Her chipboard desk guarded four visitors' chairs that faced each other over a coffee table covered with *National Geographic, Reason,* and *Atlantic* magazines.

Pollard: "Can I help you gentlemen?"

"We're with the Bureau of Criminal Apprehension and the U.S. Marshals Service," Virgil said. "We need to talk with Bob Dahl."

The rear of the space held two fabric-walled cubicles, and farther back, a windowed office with a door. The back office was unlit and appeared to be empty.

The receptionist said, "Let me ring Mr. Dahl . . ." but as she said it, Bob Dahl popped out of one of the cubicles and said, "I've got it, Doreen." He walked toward them through the office and said, with a friendly grin, "We'd actually be more comfortable out here. My cubicle is a little tight. Is this about the tragedy?"

"Yes, the tragedy," Lucas said. "We'd prefer a place a little more private, to talk."

Dahl, a middle-sized man with a square build showing what might have been gym muscle under his short-sleeved shirt, looked from Lucas to Virgil and then back to Lucas, then to Doreen and back to Lucas, and finally said, "I guess we could use Noah's office. He's not in at the moment."

"That would be good," Lucas said.

As they passed between Dahl's cubicle and the cubicle across the aisle, they looked into the two spaces; Dahl's had a disorganized stack of paper on the desk, and an older desktop computer and printer. The other cubicle appeared to be unused, no paper, no computer.

Heath's office was larger than either of the cubicles, and much better furnished. An expansive wooden desk, maybe cherry, a conversation area of four chairs around a matching wooden coffee table, a late model Windows computer, and a printer. A high-back leather chair sat behind the desk. Two pictures hung from the wall, one of a man shaking hands with another man, who was accepting a framed certificate of some kind. Lucas recognized the pictured Heath as a younger version of the man he'd met at the

Sand murder scene. The other was a photo of a blond woman holding a miniature white poodle.

As they sat down in the conversation area, Lucas pointed at the first photo and asked, "That's Noah Heath, right?"

"Noah's on the left," Dahl said, turning in his chair to look. "He's getting a certificate of appreciation from, mmm, I think the Rotary. Or the Chamber, one or the other."

Virgil got comfortable in his chair and asked, "How much have you and Heath stolen from your charities?"

Dahl was shocked. "What!"

Lucas: "You heard him, Darrell. We're gonna need some cooperation here, or we'll ship your ass back to LA on the fraud warrant. You know about that, right? The computer hustle?"

"I don't know what . . ." Dahl began. "I should have a lawyer . . ."

"Darrell, we've got the fingerprints, the Social Security number you're illegally using, the photos on your driver's licenses going back to California," Virgil said. "You can ask for a lawyer, if you want one, when we ship you back to LA. You want to go back to LA?"

"No," he mumbled.

"We even know who Bob Dahl is, though

we think he's dead. Did you have anything to do with that? Dahl's death?"

"I never . . ." He stopped talking for a moment, looking down at his thighs. Lucas and Virgil waited. Then, quietly, "What do you want?"

"One thing we don't want," Virgil said, "is to spend Minnesota money to put your ass in jail and send you back to LA. But we'll do it. We will. You gotta believe that."

Hinton nodded. "Okay." And, "Goddamnit. Goddamnit."

"Was the real Bob Dahl murdered?" Virgil asked. "What can you tell us about that?"

Hinton — Dahl — shook his head: "Bob wasn't murdered. He died of an overdose in Glendale. The Glendale cops didn't know who he was and didn't care because he was a street addict. His only busts had been small-town juvie, and his prints weren't in the system, so they couldn't find out. They cremated him and put him in a mass grave out there. You could check that. I could give you the time, date, and place."

"And you know all that because . . . ?" Virgil asked.

"Because I knew him from back home . . . here in Minnesota. We went to the same high school."

"California? What happened there?" Virgil asked.

"I was staying in a motel, a flophouse was what it was, but with separate rooms. Out in Glendale. On days when it was raining or cold, I'd let Bob inside when it was late, and he'd sleep in the stairwell," Hinton said. "I wouldn't let him in my room — I mean, I did once, and he stole some of my shit, so I didn't let him in after that. But I let him into the stairwell when it was cold or raining. Sometimes I let him use my shower, as long as I could watch and make sure he didn't steal any more of my shit."

"You're a saint, Darrell," Virgil said.

Lucas prompted him: "The motel, and then . . ."

"And then, he croaked. Heroin with fentanyl or meth mixed in, and it killed him," Hinton said. "The guy who ran the motel came knocking on my door and said Bob was tits-up in the stairwell. I ran to see and told the manager to get the cops. While he was gone . . . I was in some trouble out there . . . and I got this idea and I took his wallet."

"And came back here as Bob Dahl."

"He didn't need the name anymore, and I sure as heck did," Hinton said. "I wasn't too long out of prison, had a hard time getting a job, and when the computer business went down, I knew I'd be back for a longer stay if they got me."

"So you got lucky with Bob," Virgil said.

Hinton looked down at his shoes again and mumbled, "I guess."

"How did you hook up with Heath?" Lucas asked.

"Just . . . accident," Hinton said. "Or maybe I saw that he was a hustler. He was running this medical thing, bringing in medicine from the Bahamas. I was working part time for UPS and I'd deliver to his office and we'd get to talking . . . I said something about the fact that the way the medical thing was set up, a guy could take some cream off the milk. He kinda looked at me, and a couple weeks later, I was working for him."

"He was taking some cream off the milk?" Lucas asked.

"The cream and half the milk," Hinton said. "It took me a while to figure out the numbers, but I'd done some hustling. I know a good one when I see one."

"We know about those," Virgil said. "Let me tell you up front, the prisons here are not like the rest home at Susanville. What I'm saying is, you best stay on our right side."

"I'm trying, I'm trying," Hinton protested. "Susanville wasn't a rest home, either. They were teaching me to fight forest fires, for Christ's sakes. Do I look like a forest-fire fighter?"

Lucas agreed that he didn't, and asked, "You know why we're talking to you?"

"When you said who you were, I thought it would be about the Sand contribution to Home Streets."

"It's a little more about the fact that Heath is the right size to be the killer, and that Sand's financial advisor was trying to talk him out of investing with Home Streets," Lucas said. "Sand might not have contributed, but his wife still might. You told me on the phone that you hoped she would."

Hinton sat back in his chair. "Oh . . . boy. I never thought of it that way."

"How were you going to steal the Home Streets money?" Virgil asked.

Hinton cocked his head and frowned at Virgil for a moment, and then said, "You're a little bit of an asshole, aren't you?"

"A little bit," Virgil said, "but that doesn't answer the question."

"I wasn't going to steal anything. I get a paycheck," Hinton said. "I'd get a taste of the action if it worked out. A small taste. I keep the job because Noah knows that I know what he's doing, and he doesn't think I'd turn on him. It's a nice racket."

"You never thought about blackmailing him?" Virgil asked.

"Thought about it, never did anything. The problem is, you blackmail somebody like Noah, who has influence, and you might have a couple of crooked cops coming around to talk to you," Hinton said. "If they got my fingerprints, I was toast. I couldn't risk getting sideways with the cops."

"Pretend we believe that," Lucas said. "How much was Heath going to steal? I mean, from Home Streets?"

Hinton closed one eye and tipped his head to the side, thinking. "That's . . . flexible. When it's all said and done, he might get ten percent. He'd overpay the architect and general contractor and they'd kick the money back."

"And how much would the project cost?" Lucas asked.

"However much we could raise," Hinton said, as though that were obvious. "The deal is, you can get money for street-people housing from the governments — state, federal, some from the city — but most of it comes from do-gooder foundations. The foundations want a local charitable buy-in, maybe ten percent. Noah thinks if we get the ball rolling downhill, with big shots like Sand buying in and recruiting new money, we can raise a million. That might be a ten-million-dollar project. If he raises eight hundred thousand, it'll be an eight-million-dollar project. And so on."

Virgil whistled. "He'd take out a million? How would he get it clean?"

"He plays poker in Vegas. He wins. I mean, not really. He doesn't actually play. He buys the chips with cash, takes back checks when he cashes out, so he has the checks from the casinos to prove his so-called winnings. Declares it on his income tax. Not all of it, but a pretty big chunk. He spreads that over two or three years."

"What about the rest? The undeclared cash?" Lucas asked.

Hinton spread his hands: "Look at his checkbook and credit cards. He doesn't spend anything on food and clothing or gas or travel or any of that, because he uses cash whenever he can. He's probably the last guy to use a travel agent, because he gives his travel agent cash, and they buy all his tickets for him, pre-pay for hotels. He has a place somewhere down in the Caribbean, on . . . Arugula? Something like that. He bought an Arugula passport back a while ago, he goes down there in the winter. Might have a boat of some kind. I don't know, I'm not invited. Probably pays cash on a mortgage down there, if he didn't buy it outright. I understand cash is welcome in the Islands. That's where he'd probably take a big payout from Home Streets."

"Nice," Lucas said.

"How many of the harelip . . ." Virgil began.

Lucas interrupted: "Cleft palate . . ."

". . . cleft palate surgeons are real?"

"Not sure, because I issue checks, I don't recruit the surgeons. Noah does that. But, I believe at least three are phony, and maybe five, all from Cuba. Cubans who supposedly work in Central America. Hard to track down. We pay five Cuban surgeons and five surgical nurses, plus travel and supplies, and it comes to between three hundred and fifty and four hundred thousand a year."

"Jesus, if the guy wasn't rich, he's getting that way," Virgil said.

Hinton nodded: "It's a good gig. Not something I could have pulled off. You had to have some status in the community to do it. You need a Noah Heath, and they're not that easy to find. He has the big house, used to have the hot wife until she died . . . Oh. Hey."

Lucas looked at Virgil, then back to Hinton and asked, "How'd she die?"

"Fell down the stairs and broke her neck. Noah was supposedly at some kind of dinner when it happened," Hinton said. He pointed at the photo of the blond woman and the dog. "That's her. He had that alibi, but . . . I mean . . . I'm not sure anybody figured out exactly how long she'd been dead when he got home and found her . . ."

Lucas said, "Yeah."

Virgil: "Do you think he might have murdered her?"

Again, Hinton closed an eye and tipped his head, then his mouth turned down at the corners and he said, "I hate to disappoint you, but I don't think so. He's kind of a pussy. What if he'd pushed her down the stairs and she *hadn't* broken her neck? Then he'd either have had to club her to death, or . . . make up some kind of excuse for pushing her. Like he stumbled, and who's going to believe that? Not her. She was one mean woman. She would have put his ass in jail and sold the house and moved to Miami."

Virgil: "So . . ."

"He's too smart and too much of a pussy

255

to have murdered her. I think he got lucky because the marriage was in bad shape," Hinton said. "She'd figured out he wasn't as rich as she thought, when they hooked up."

"You had to think about it — whether he'd murdered her," Lucas observed.

"Yeah, I did. Noah . . . Noah's been running big rip-offs for years and years. Years! I mean, I gotta admire the guy. The best I ever did was like being a porch pirate, stealing computers and TV sets and reselling them. Amazon shit. Heart/Twin Cities sponsors a Monte Carlo Night at a hotel over in Minneapolis. Tickets are two hundred and fifty bucks each, you get two hundred and fifty chips. Noah gets one of the Indian casinos to bring in craps tables and roulette wheels and blackjack. You know — all that real casino stuff, and for free. Then he gets local businesses to donate prizes. Can't be money, but anything else — TVs, vacation trips, whatever. If people pay and lose, they can buy more chips right on the floor. Anyway, the last one of these he did, there were three hundred people there. Three hundred times two-fifty per ticket, what is that?"

Virgil rolled his eyes up. "Seventy-five thousand."

"Right. He probably had ten thousand in overhead. So he clears sixty-five. Guess how much of that got to the harelips."

"Cleft palates," Lucas said.

They talked for a while longer, got Heath's wife's name, and an approximate date of death.

When they got up to leave, Virgil held up his phone and said, "We've got a record of all this. A recording. There's a good chance that if Heath falls, either for ripping off these charities or for killing Sand or his wife, the prosecutor will want to talk to you. You'll be able to make a deal and walk away. Or mostly away. Do not run. Do. Not. Run. If you run, we'll track you down, and there won't be a deal."

Hinton: "You really are an asshole. Why don't you take a lesson from this guy . . ." He nodded at Lucas. ". . . and relax a little? Don't go through life as an asshole."

"Good advice," Lucas said. "I've told him he should try to model himself on me."

"And you should," Hinton told Virgil, with apparent sincerity.

Outside, Lucas took a minute to laugh as they got in the car, said, "Virgil, somebody finally figured you out. You asshole."

"Yeah, yeah. I'll tell you what, I'm gonna

257

want to look at an autopsy report on Helen Heath."

Lucas nodded: "If he did his wife, he could have done Sand and the kids. But I don't know. Hinton is a con man. Con men know psychology. He thinks Heath is a pussy and would be too smart to murder her. Especially like that, falling down a stairs. That's got some weight to it."

"It does, unless Heath is a psycho. We know the Sand killer must be one," Virgil said. "Psychos can hide it. Maybe even from con men."

They'd worked late into the afternoon. They sat in the parking lot for a while, talking about what to do next: Virgil wanted to go home to Mankato, which would take an hour and a half, but promised to be back in the morning, when they could go after Heath.

"I'd rather transcribe the talk with Hinton and get that on the record, before we hit Heath," Virgil said.

"Fine with me," Lucas said. "My only problem might be if Hinton warns him that we're coming."

"Yeah. But he could be on the phone, right now. Maybe we should have busted him on the warrant . . ."

"Then he'd lawyer up and we wouldn't get another word out of him for a month," Lucas said. "Nah. We got him scared. He won't go anywhere. Probably."

Virgil smiled: "Probably." He took his phone out. "Gotta call Frankie and tell her to brace herself."

"You do that, big guy," Lucas said.

They were on their way back to Lucas's house, when they took a call from the BCA duty officer. "We got a call from a woman who wouldn't give her name, with a message for you guys. She heard on the *Jonesing for News* show that you two were working the Sand murder. She has what she said was an important tip."

"Did you get her number?" Lucas asked.

"Yes. It's a pay phone at the university," the duty officer said.

"I didn't think they had those anymore," Virgil said.

"They do, but they're rare, and mostly used by drug dealers," the duty officer said. "You want the message?"

"Sure, why not," Lucas said. He had little faith in anonymous tips.

"What she said was, 'Watch season four, episode six of *The Old Pals* streaming series on Netflix.' That's it."

Virgil: "That's it?"

"That's it."

"I got Netflix," Lucas said.

At Lucas's house, they trooped into the family room and turned on the television, went to Netflix, found *The Old Pals* streaming series, and went to season four, episode six.

One minute in, Maggie Cooper walked into the apartment set, where two of her old pals were obsessing over the possibility that another old pal was cheating on the old pal he was supposed to be dating. The story line was absurd, way dumber than *Friends,* but their interest perked up when Cooper's character decided to stupidly disguise herself to spy on the possibly philandering old pal.

She did it by putting on a dark hoodie and black sweatpants. Hanging around a stoop outside the apartment of the man she was spying on, she was a dead ringer for the Sand killer.

Virgil: "Ah, man."

"But she was in her car . . ." Lucas began.

"Or Melton was. Never could see who it was, on the garage and Whole Foods videos. Cooper leaves the U early, driven by Melton, who drops her off away from the house. Cooper walks to the house in the dark and waits. Melton goes back to the U, gets Cooper's car, drives to the Whole Foods, buys some olives, to establish the alibi, then to the house and parks in the garage.

"Cooper has already done the shooting," Virgil continued. "She walks off the porch, then around the house past the basketball net to the garage. Remember how you never see Sand and the boys leave the house through the garage access door? Because the camera in the garage looks the other way, down the driveway? In the garage, Cooper takes the jar of olives and finds the bodies. At the same time, Melton goes out that door, through the yard and disappears."

"I don't believe it," Lucas said.

"But it's possible. And it would explain a lot of stuff, like we can't find any sign of the killer after he leaves the porch. There were people walking around the neighborhood when the rain started, but nobody saw him, nobody knows where he went. He's like smoke, he vanishes."

"But that leaves Melton here in St. Paul. Miles from her car at the U. What, she walked there?"

"She could have," Virgil said. "Five or six miles, maybe? Maybe she caught a bus part of the way. I don't think an Uber, that'd leave a trail . . . Or maybe she pre-positioned her own car over here. I mean, she really doesn't have a perfect alibi."

"Not perfect, but pretty good," Lucas said. "Besides, I still don't believe it,"

On screen, Cooper was back in the *Old Pals* apartment set, now showing a ridiculous bushy mustache and hexagonal steel-rimmed glasses. The camera switched to another old pal, then back to Cooper, by the door.

Virgil: "Look at her shoes."

Lucas. "Yeah. They look big."

"Maybe even size eleven," Virgil said.

12

After Darrell Hinton showed Lucas and Virgil to the office door, and when they'd safely driven away, Hinton turned to the big-haired receptionist and said, "Those guys were cops, Doreen. They know all about Noah and the charities. I'm getting my ass out of here. If I were you, I'd do the same."

Doreen didn't argue. She leaned sideways and picked up her purse. "Is Noah gonna call Ron?"

"I doubt it. Two fires would be one too many. But, who knows?"

"Well, if he's gonna call Ron, I'd come by and grab my chair and computer, you know?" Doreen said.

Hinton shook his head. "I wouldn't do that. If the cops figured out they were missing, they'd know you knew what was coming. If you grab anything, make sure it's something that would burn, so they don't know it's missing."

Doreen was already moving and as she passed Hinton, she said, "Okay, smart guy. I see what you mean. Are you gonna see Noah? Warn him?"

"Yeah, probably."

"Tell him that I don't know nothin' about nothin'."

"I will," Hinton said. He saw her out the door and locked it behind her. When she was in her car, he hurried back to Heath's office. Heath didn't know it, but Hinton had once put a GoPro on a bookshelf and had gotten video of Heath opening the office safe. Just in case.

Now he knelt in front of the safe, punched in the combination, turned the crank and opened it. Heath kept what he called his "persuader" in a brown envelope, and Hinton took it out, relocked the safe and carried the envelope to his cubicle.

Sixteen hundred dollars, in twenties and fifties. Less than he'd hoped, more than he'd feared. He put it in his back pocket. He pulled the bottom drawer out of his desk, which had metal catches to keep it from popping all the way out. He reached under it and stripped out the two passports that were taped to the bottom of the drawer, one in the Dahl name, one in the Hinton name.

The cops had warned him not to run, but he'd learned through hard experience not to trust any cop, ever: they lied like a fish breathes water. He'd squeeze more money out of Heath, steal some license plates at a Walmart, and hit the road. He'd be in Florida in two days, unload the van, get a new one, start working on a new name. He knew how to do all that, because he'd already done it.

First, he'd stop at home, load up the good stuff. The house and furniture were rented. If he kept moving, with God's help and a matchbox full of black beauties to keep his eyes open, he'd be in Kentucky before the cops woke up in the morning.

Noah Heath was a tall, brooding man, with heavy brow ridges, high cheekbones, and a rounded chin with a narrow cleft. He wore glasses with photochromic lenses that never became perfectly clear in dim light, giving his pale eyes a yellowish cast.

He'd taken a sauna, and then a shower, and was wearing boxer shorts and a tee-shirt when he decided that he could use a piece of toast; maybe two pieces. He had naturally dry skin and was rubbing lotion into his face as he walked down the stairs to the oversized kitchen.

Heath lived in St. Paul's premier neighborhood, along Summit Avenue. The house was a bit of a pile, redbrick and clapboard and tile, with a long curving rosewood stairway that led down toward the front door. When Helen was alive, and they'd host a party, she'd always wait until most of the guests had arrived, and then make her entrance down the stairway, shimmering in the latest of her party dresses.

Until the day the staircase bit her in the ass. Ah, well. Shit happens.

His slippery, lotioned hand on the stairway handrail reminded him of Helen's last trip down the stairs . . . He'd come home from a chicken dinner and found Helen at the bottom of the stairs with her neck bent at an infelicitous angle, her eyes open, blank and staring at the ceiling.

Heath had spent time in the sauna thinking about Margaret Cooper. The hundred thousand, he thought, was pretty secure. He'd been hanging back, not wanting to hit her for the extra fifty thousand until the mourning was over. Was three weeks long enough to wait? A month might be better. This was all very delicate.

Could he somehow leverage his discovery of Helen, dead on the stairs, with Cooper's discovery of Alex and her children, the shared agony, into a bigger bite?

He'd push her a bit: maybe . . . some kind of memorial to Alex and the children at the Home Streets project? Not a statue, or anything that elaborate or expensive, but maybe . . . a plaque? Or a plaque on a memorial fountain?

He was thinking about it, had popped up the toast and was scraping on butter when the doorbell rang. He glanced at the kitchen clock: ten after four. He wasn't expecting anyone.

Carrying his toast to the front door, he peeked out a window panel and saw the man he knew as Bob Dahl standing there, bouncing nervously on his toes. Something about his face suggested bad news.

Heath unlocked the door, pulled it open and poked his head out. "Bob? Is there a problem?"

"Yeah, you might say that. We got hit by the cops this afternoon and I think they'll be coming to see you," Hinton said. "About your charity scams. They seem to know all about them."

Heath had had nightmares about this moment; they'd begun shortly after he'd set up his first charity. In his nightmares it hadn't been Dahl breaking the news, but two thuggish cops in bad suits. In some of them, they simply arrested him and dragged him away to be thrown in jail with foreign-looking drug dealers; in others, they were looking for a handout, or even a partnership, asking half of what he was making. Half! Ridiculous!

Heath stepped back from the door, staring in horror at Dahl, and Dahl asked, "You okay?"

"Are you sure?" Stupid question. He took another step back and Dahl followed him into the house and shut the door.

"Of course, I'm sure. I even heard of one of them, this Davenport guy, U.S. Marshal, killed a bunch of people. You can look him up on the Internet."

"Davenport? What'd they say?"

"They were pushing me to talk about you, but I told them I didn't know anything," Hinton lied. "I was just a clerk, I said. I don't think they bought it, they'll be back. I told you about California. They had a warrant."

"A warrant? Then why aren't you in jail?"

"Because they didn't want me, they wanted you," Hinton said. "They wanted to turn me. They wanted me to say you had something to do with murdering Alex Sand."

"Alex? That's crazy talk," Heath said.

"I told them that. I told them that we were relying on Sand to help with the Home Streets project, that him dying was a disaster for us. That we could only hope that Ms. Cooper would honor his intentions, but that was no sure thing. The problem is, they were asking a lot of questions about Home Streets and Big Grin and the other charities. About the finances."

Heath wandered in a circle inside the reception area, running a hand through his hair. "Do you think . . . they knew anything?"

"Oh, yeah. They were asking me about the names of the Cuban surgeons with Big Grin. They asked how much you were going to skim from Home Streets. They asked about the other charities, too, about the fire, about your wife falling down the stairs . . ."

"My God! That was an accident!"

"Yeah, well, they're cops," Hinton said.

Heath was out of it, Hinton decided. He said, "Listen, Noah, you might not be as far up shit creek as you think."

"Shit creek?" Heath said wonderingly. "My parents, my father, he was one of the prime movers in this town. I followed him . . ."

"Yeah. Noah, try to focus," Hinton said. "Here's the thing. They have the warrant. They got my ass in a crack. They said if I cooperated . . ."

"Cooperated?"

"Yeah. You know, talked about the charities. Talked about you. They said that would be taken into account by the prosecutors. I'd get off if you went to prison. Well, bullshit. They were lying, of course, and I'm out of here. Tonight."

"Where are you going?"

"Never mind about that," Hinton said. "I need some money from you."

"Money?"

"Yeah, you know. Dollar bills. Twenty-dollar bills. Fifty-dollar bills. I gotta tell you, Noah, if they grab me, I'm gonna tell them everything I know. I been to prison and I'm not going back if there's any way I can get out of it. I believe I can get away from them, change my name, get a job somewhere, but I need cash and I know you got some."

Heath whined, "My money? My money?"

"Yeah. You can always get some more. Sell this house and move to Arugula or whatever that island is called."

"Antigua? I'm a citizen there, I don't —"

"Don't bullshit me, man, I once saw you take five grand out of the safe in your of-

270

fice," Hinton said. "I know you got it. I know you can get more. If I disappear, they got nothing on you. Doreen don't know shit."

"Doreen?" One thing Heath suspected: Doreen *did* know shit. Maybe more than Dahl.

"Noah! Get your shit together," Hinton said. "Get some money! I gotta get out of here. I'll be three states away before they come looking for me."

"My money," Heath said, then he took a breath and said, "I suppose we should go upstairs."

"There you go," Hinton said.

Heath took another breath, snapped the elastic on his boxer shorts, and said, "Come along."

They climbed the stairs and took a turn into the East Wing — a small brass sign on a walnut panel said "East Wing" — and walked down a long hallway to his office. The office held an expansive rosewood desk and a line of matching file cabinets against one wall. One of the file cabinets was actually a hardened, fireproof safe with a keypad.

Heath looked at Hinton in exasperation and a little fear, then bent and used his body to cover the keypad as he punched in the code. When the top drawer unlocked, he took out another brown envelope and thumbed through it. "I can't give you all of it, I gotta keep some handy."

"Nope, nope, I gotta have it all," Hinton said, extending a hand. "If I run, you're good. If I don't, you're screwed. I need to get far away and I need cash to do that."

Heath reluctantly handed over the envelope. Hinton opened it and thumbed through the wad of cash, asking, "How much?"

"Five thousand dollars, or a little more," Heath said.

"Goddamnit, Noah. You got more than that in there. Gimme it, or I swear to God I'll make a deal with the cops. I can't run on five grand."

"*I have to live, too.* My bank account's low . . ."

"You don't seem to understand what's about to happen, Noah. You're going to Stillwater prison," Hinton said. "It's Minnesota's butthole, is what I've heard. A rich guy like you ain't gonna do well. They don't serve no butter croissants."

Heath began to tremble, put a hand to his mouth, bit on the knuckles, staring at the impatient Hinton. Then he turned, opened the bottom desk drawer, and took out a much fatter envelope. "That's it," he said.

"That's all of it from the last Vegas trip, twenty-two thousand. I'll have to go to the bank just to eat . . ."

"Better than getting those free meals, the ones at Stillwater," Hinton said, satisfied now. He turned and walked through the office door, into the hallway, with Heath trailing. "I've got to make one more stop, and then I'm outta here. You won't be hearing from me again."

"Listen, leave me five thousand, Bob. Bob? Is that your real name?"

"Not exactly. I started out as Darrell Hinton and the cops know that. You can explain that you did a background check on Bob Dahl and never found anything, that you didn't know me as Darrell Hinton. Blame the hustles on me."

"Okay, but . . . five thousand to keep me going? I've got money going out for the surgeons, I can speed it up a little . . ."

"Hey, fuck that," Hinton said. "You're a cheap asshole, Noah. Take the money out of the bank. Sell the house. I don't care."

"If I sell the house, people will know that I'm broke," Heath whined.

"Well, tough shit. That's your problem."

Hinton had reached the top of the stairs and turned to go down, and Heath, coming up from behind him, consumed with fear and anger, lifted one of his long legs and thrust it into Hinton's back.

Hinton's body arced down the stairway, like a Labrador retriever going into a lake, and Hinton dropped the cash envelopes and put out his hands to break his fall, but neither his hands nor his arms were nearly enough to defeat the law of gravity: his head hit one of the stair treads with the sound of a baseball bat hitting a cantaloupe.

He bounced twice and rolled and finally crumbled into a heap near the bottom. At the top, Heath, breathing hard, said, "Oh, good Lord." He stood motionless for a moment, then hurried down, stepping carefully past Hinton's unmoving body. "Bob, Bob, I'm so sorry, I tripped . . ."

But it was a body, now, a corpse, Heath thought; given the size of the dent in Hinton's balding skull, and the blood pooling on the steps, it seemed unlikely that he could still be alive.

But he was.

He didn't move, but he groaned, and Heath, transfixed, didn't think it was some postmortem exhalation, it was a genuine groan; and then Hinton did it again, and one arm twitched.

Heath: "Oh, my God."

He felt for the pocket where he always had

his cell phone, and found, to his surprise, that he was wearing boxer shorts. Of course he was, he'd only gone downstairs to get a piece of toast. He turned and ran back up the stairs, stepping over Hinton's body. His cell phone was on the bathroom counter, where he'd left it after the shower.

As he picked up the cell phone — intending, he thought later, to call 9-1-1 — he noticed the transparent plastic sack inside the bathroom waste basket. The sack was empty, having been emptied by the housekeeper that afternoon. He stood staring at the bag, said, "Huh," then put the phone back in his pocket and pulled the bag out of the wastebasket and carried it back down the stairs.

He got below Hinton, who was now obviously breathing. Heath didn't want to actually touch him, so he carefully pulled the bag over Hinton's head and then tightened it around his throat.

And waited.

Three or four minutes passed, seeming like an eternity. Hinton's breathing stopped and his body began to shake, trembling, dying. Heath gathered up the cash envelopes, ran back up the stairs, put them in the office safe, locked it, and pulled on chinos and a sweatshirt, socks, shoes. Got his wallet, keys, the gold pinky ring inherited from his father, which he always wore for good luck.

Back downstairs.

Thinking hard, all the time. How would he do this? Had to get rid of the body . . .

Hinton was now thoroughly dead. Heath went to the garage, climbed up a ladder to a loft, got a little-used sleeping bag, brought it back down, carried it to the stairway. After taking Hinton's wallet and car keys, he spent a frantic, heart-thumping five minutes stuffing Hinton's body into the bag.

That done, he dragged the body to the garage, and left it near the access door. Outside, he got in Hinton's van, which Hinton had parked in the driveway, and drove it to the garage access door. The back of the van was stacked full of clothing and other junk.

He spent three minutes taking it out, throwing it on the floor. He dragged the sleeping-bag-wrapped body to the van and hoisted it inside. He added a spade from the garage wall, in case that should be the disposal solution.

Bury it in the woods or a lonely piece of nonagricultural prairie. No, wait: he knew a place, where that idiot Morton had recruited him to launch his silly fuckin' stripper canoe down below Hastings . . . Of course, he'd taken twenty-five thousand out of Morton for the Big Grin, for what that was worth.

Bury the body, maybe leave the van at the airport, catch a cab home. Throw all the crap from the van in a dumpster somewhere . . . or just throw it on a sidewalk in a less desirable part of town, from whence it would instantly disappear.

A lot to do and not much time to do it.

He had to be calm. None of this was his fault, this was on Dahl. Hinton. Entirely on Dahl. Hinton. And Hinton had been right about one thing: if Hinton disappeared the cops would have nothing on him.

Well: there *was* Doreen.

He edged the van into the street and turned left.

13

Heath got to his office early the next morning. Doreen wasn't in, not due for another hour. Heath began pulling up computer files, selectively deleting many of them, moving others to flash drives, which he would put in his car for later reference and possible editing.

Although he'd never actually had a job, Heath prided himself on membership in the executive class, and the night before, he'd executed. After recovering from the *accident* on the staircase, he'd realized that it would be more convenient for almost everybody if Hinton simply disappeared. Disappearing the body hadn't been hard, one of the advantages of living in a largely rural state.

After loading Hinton's body into the van, along with a gardening spade, he'd driven south along the Mississippi to a remote boat launch, dragged the body well away from the launch, and buried it in the muck. It was hard work, and he wasn't accustomed to physical labor, but he got it done. He was careful not to make the hole too grave-like: he carved out a square, dug down four feet deep, and folded Hinton's body into it.

Adrenaline had helped. When Hinton's hips were two feet below the surface, he threw the piled dirt back in the hole and tramped it down.

Good enough.

On the way back north, thinking about it, he wound up stopping at the Mall of America, heading for an athletic wear store, specifically one that featured the University of Minnesota's Golden Gophers.

Wearing a hat and Covid mask, he scored.

That done, and with growing confidence, he drove the van to Minneapolis-St. Paul International, left it in the Gold Ramp. He took a cab back to St. Paul, got dropped at a small shopping center, and did the long walk home.

He'd scrubbed the steps clean. He shredded the paper towels he'd used and fed them through the garbage disposal, followed by fifteen minutes of hot water and heavy doses of all-purpose cleaner and a shot of Drano. All the crap Hinton had in the van he dropped at a homeless encampment along an I-94 frontage road.

Then he spent the night actively forgetting about Hinton. Had rehearsed and re-rehearsed the deposition of Hinton's body, over and over and over again, until it all became boring. Became distant. Became something he'd only imagined. By morning, though he was tired, he was confident that if anyone asked about Hinton (or Bob Dahl), he'd be puzzled: Why no, I don't know where he is. He should be here by now . . .

At nine-thirty, Doreen still hadn't shown up. She didn't have any critical files on her computer, other than calendars. He sat at her desk and began pulling them up, and again made some selective deletions. No reason that the police, if they were to take the computers, needed to see entries like, "Noah to Antigua" or "Call Mickey about Noah's Antigua tickets."

He stopped to wonder if Hinton had told them about Antigua; and thought, well, if he had, the cops could ask. He didn't have to volunteer the information.

At ten o'clock he went back to his own office and started calling up YouTube music videos, and then some golf instruction videos, and then looked at some TikTok jiggling-girl videos, and a little later, the door opened and looking through his windows, he saw two men walk in and look around, and spot him at his desk.

Police, he thought, and he was right.

Relax. Relax.

Lucas followed Virgil through the office door and said, quietly, "No Hinton."

Virgil: "Must be Heath back there. Doreen's gone, too."

They could see Heath through the office window, looking out at them. "Goddamn Hinton better not be running," Lucas said, keeping his voice low.

Virgil: "We need to poke this guy."

As they walked toward the back of the office, Heath stood up, stepped into the hall and called, "Can I help you fellas?"

Virgil: "Are you Noah Heath?"

"I am."

Virgil held up his BCA ID, identified himself and Lucas, and said, "We talked to one of your employees last night, Darrell Hinton."

Heath looked nonplussed. "Hinton? I've only got two employees . . ."

"Bob Dahl," Virgil said. "His real name is Darrell Hinton."

"Hinton?"

Lucas: "You didn't know that?"

Heath was offended: "I did not. Where is

he? He should have been here an hour ago. Where's Doreen?"

As Virgil and Lucas got closer, they didn't slow down, and Heath retreated into his office. Lucas and Virgil followed him in, without asking, and took the two guest chairs across Heath's desk. Heath sat down and asked, "What has he done?"

Virgil: "Hinton told us about your Big Grin scam, the fake surgeons, which we're gonna have to talk to you about, sooner or later. Right now, we want to know whether you murdered Alex Sand and his sons."

Virgil had seen the phenomenon, once or twice, as the blood in Heath's face seemed to drain away, leaving him as white as printer paper. He sputtered, "What? What? I never . . ."

Virgil leaned forward and touched Heath's desk and said, "Of the two of us, I'm the polite one. I gotta tell you politely, a guy like you, stealing from charity money, that's about as low as it gets. You're a dirtbag and we're gonna hang you out to dry. But right now, we need to know where Hinton is. You didn't kill him, too, did you?"

Heath's eyelids fluttered and his hand clutched his chest, then he pushed back from his desk and stood up and shouted at them, "I don't know where he is. I didn't kill . . . I want you out of here. I'm calling my attorney — my civil attorney, the one that's going to drag the two of you into court and get every dime you ever earned. Throwing accusations, you're crazy . . . I'm a serious man in this town . . ."

Lucas: "Ah, shut the fuck up. Is Hinton running? Are you hiding him?"

"Hinton? Hinton? I don't know any Hinton," Heath shouted. "Get out of here. Out. Out. Out."

Lucas yawned, turned to Virgil: "He never denied killing Sand and the boys."

Virgil: "I noticed that. He's the right size and shape for the killer. Look at those shoes. They must be close to size elevens."

"My shoes, my shoes . . ." Heath picked up a piece of paper from his desk, balled it up and threw it at Virgil's head. Virgil leaned sideways to let the wad fly past, and said to Lucas, "Ag assault on a police officer. If a corner of that paper had hit my eye, it could have put it out."

"I'm a witness," Lucas said. "Wanna put the cuffs on him?"

"Maybe we could call 'CCO before we do that," Virgil said.

" 'CCO? I've got friends at WCCO. I know all the anchors," Heath shouted. He was on his feet, pointing at the door. "Now you — out! Out! Out! I'm calling my attorney."

Lucas tipped his head toward the door and Virgil followed him out. On the sidewalk, Virgil looked back into the office, and said, "Jeez. Did you see his face when I asked him if he killed Hinton? He really did look like he was having a seizure."

"We need to find Hinton," Lucas said. "I'm kinda worried here."

As the cops left, Heath collapsed in his office chair, breathing hard, his heart pounding. He'd felt the blood drain from his face at the first accusation, and now it came flooding back, so he could feel the actual capillaries in his cheeks swelling almost to the bursting point. A flop sweat began a moment later, the perspiration rolling down from his hairline, and he wiped it away with the heel of his hand.

But he'd told them. He'd told the fuckers, and he'd gotten away with it. Without Dahl, Hinton, whatever his name was, they had nothing.

Well. They still had Doreen.

He licked his lips and picked up his car keys. He was back at the house in five minutes, and walked around the place, looking, and wound up in the garage, at the

284

workbench, which he couldn't remember having ever opened. The bench was more for the staff, when there was a staff: he'd been reduced to a single Hmong woman twice a week. He looked in one drawer, and then another, finally opening a drawer that held two hammers, including a ball-peen. He liked the heft of that one.

White Bear Lake was twenty minutes up Highway 61, the one Bob Dylan had revisited; Hinton's house was dark, still, curtains pulled across the fifties-era picture window. They knocked on the front door, pushed the doorbell button but didn't hear it ring. Hinton never appeared. They walked around the house, looking in the windows that weren't covered.

The house next door had a patio table with four chairs, and Virgil went over and knocked on the front door. A woman came to the door and asked, "Yes?" and he held up his ID.

"We're worried about Bob Dahl next door. A federal marshal and I are trying to see inside. We're . . . worried. Could we borrow one of your patio chairs?"

He could.

Virgil dragged the chair across the lawn and put it next to a rear window, climbed up, looked in, and Lucas asked, "What?"

Virgil jumped down and said, "He's running. That's a bedroom and I can see an open closet door with nothing in it."

"Goddamnit. We need to get inside," Lucas said.

"There's a warrant for him, from California. He's a fugitive," Virgil said.

"Interstate flight to avoid prosecution, even if California really doesn't want him," Lucas said. "That's federal. I'm gonna kick the door."

Virgil looked past Lucas's shoulder. "Uh . . . hang on a second. We got a cop."

A White Bear Lake patrol car, which was black-and-white, like a patrol car should be, had stopped in the street and a cop was watching them standing by the chair.

"Hope he doesn't shoot us," Virgil said.

Lucas took his marshal's ID out of his jacket pocket, opened it, held it up so the cop could see it, then walked over to the car. The cop rolled down his window and asked, "What's going on?"

"I'm a U.S. Marshal, we got a runner, a guy who called himself Bob Dahl here, but he's actually a fugitive from California named Darrell Hinton."

"Huh. You going in?"

"Yeah, I just don't want to get shot by one

of you guys. My partner here is with the BCA."

"Mind if I watch?"

"Feel free. We're gonna kick the back door . . . Did the neighbor lady call you about the chair?"

"She thought the blond guy was suspicious. Hair's too long," the cop said, looking at Virgil.

"That's true," Lucas said. "Be sure to tell him that."

The neighbor woman had come out on her lawn to watch. The cop pulled his patrol car to the side of the street, and Lucas walked over to Virgil, who said, "Hinton . . . I don't think he owns this place. Maybe the neighbor would know who does."

"Good," Lucas said.

He led the way to the woman, who crossed her arms as they came up, and Lucas explained what they were doing. She did know that Hinton was renting, and she knew the landlady, a real estate dealer with an office downtown.

"If you can get her, she could be here in five minutes," the woman said.

"Better than kicking an innocent door," Virgil said.

They called the real estate office, spoke to the dealer, who said she'd be there as soon as she could. Ten minutes later she showed up, and found Lucas, Virgil, the cop, and the neighbor sitting on the neighbor's patio drinking Dr Pepper.

The landlady let them into Hinton's house, and it was clear that he was running: there was still furniture in the house, but nothing personal.

"There goes the security deposit," the real estate woman said, looking around. "Wonder what I should do about his furniture? It's crappy, but it's his."

"Leave it," Virgil said. "This is a crime scene now, we'll probably want to process it, to get DNA. Won't take too long. And you got the deposit. Besides, it looks kinda rented."

"It does, doesn't it?" she said. "I don't think regular retail stores sell dill-pickle-colored couches."

They locked up the house and on the way to the car, Lucas said, "We need to call the DMV for his license tag, get it out there. See if we can chase him down."

"What else?"

"We need to think of a way to push on Heath," Lucas said. "Without Hinton, it's gonna be tricky. Get Sandy to find out who's on the Heart/Twin Cities board of directors, nail down the scam."

"You don't think he killed Hinton?"

Lucas had to think about it, then said, "I don't know. I have a hard time visualizing that. It's like Hinton said, he struck me as a pussy. If he killed him, what'd he do? Gun him down? Why? When? But then . . . we know we're talking about a psycho. If he's a psycho, all bets are off."

"Psychos don't have hissy fits like he was having," Virgil said. "Unless maybe they're faking it. Or have an alternative personality."

"Which he could have. He's got the motive," Lucas said. "If he thought Sand was about to dump him, but that Cooper might still come through with a hundred or a hundred and fifty thousand . . ."

"Goddamn Hinton. Maybe we should have busted him."

"We'll find him. He won't be running to California. I'm thinking Miami."

"If he's alive," Virgil said. "The more I think about it . . . Heath was panicking. We need to find Doreen. Now."

14

Virgil called Margaret Cooper and got the name of Heart/Twin Cities board vice-chairman, George Whitman, and his work phone number. Virgil called, pulled Whitman out of a meeting at the agriculture commodities company where he was the chief financial officer, and got Doreen's full name, which was Doreen Pollard.

"Is there a problem with Home Streets?" Whitman asked.

"I'd hold off a while before making any further financial commitments," Virgil said.

"Oh . . . no."

The next call was to Sandy at the BCA office. She went online with the Minnesota DMV, which produced a driver's license. Sandy sent the image to Virgil's iPad, and the license photo was good enough to confirm that they had the right Doreen Pollard and her address.

■ ■ ■ ■

Two hours after they'd left Heath in the Home Streets office, they arrived at Pollard's apartment complex in West St. Paul, a town that lay directly south of St. Paul. Following Virgil's iPhone navigation app, they missed, by twenty minutes, the departure of a blood-and-bone spattered Noah Heath.

Heath was talking to himself as he hunched over the steering wheel of his aging Mercedes-Benz. He'd parked it a block from Pollard's apartment, and had walked over, empty-handed, except for the ball-peen hammer he'd stuck down the back of his pants, the head of it hanging over his belt.

He was saying to himself, as he drove away from the apartments, "Had to do it, Dad, had to do it. Had to make the call, make the decision, make the move. Sometimes, people need to be fired for the sake of the entire company. You hate to do it, but it's got to be done."

The running commentary was done in a sing-songy voice, and before he got home, he thought, in a moment of clarity, that he sounded like a complete fruitcake. He had

291

to stop talking, but he couldn't. He kept going: "It's hard, but somebody has to do it. You know it'll be tough on the employee's family, but not removing the person is hard on the entire business . . ."

He'd never know how close he came to meeting Lucas and Virgil in the parking lot. When he got home, he parked the Benz in the garage, stood back, and considered what the aging car represented: the end of the Heath lifestyle, going back to 1945, when his grandfather came back from World War II and built his first motel, or, as he called it, a motor hotel.

One way or another, Heath thought, the charity business was done. He'd sell out and vanish. His chin trembled with the thought. On the other hand, Antigua was a fine place to spend the end of your days. He'd have influence there.

Pollard's apartment complex was weathered, with fake-brick-looking fiberglass siding covering the bottom half of the buildings and green-painted clapboard above. Each building appeared to have about twenty apartments; the structures were arranged in a rectangle with an empty swimming pool in the middle. A battered child's bicycle, possibly thirty years old, leaned against the nearest building, with weeds growing up through the spokes of one bent wheel; several television satellite dishes were perched on the roofs.

"She was not paid well," Virgil said, as they got out of Lucas's Cayenne. "Either that, or she spent her money on something else."

"Boiled cabbage," Lucas said, using a key fob to lock the car, then locking it a second time.

"Boiled cabbage?"

"That's what it will smell like inside. Boiled cabbage and baby formula."

Virgil nodded. "And dryer exhaust, from the in-house coin laundry."

They were right about all of it.

Pollard's apartment was in Building 2, which had double glass doors opening into a small lobby with brass mailboxes; the doors had prominent locks but didn't lock.

Lucas and Virgil pushed through into the lobby, were hit with the odor of boiled cabbage, with an overtone of boiled carrots, climbed a narrow, carpeted stairs to the second floor. Pollard's apartment, 251, was at the end of the hall. As they walked toward it, they heard music from one apartment, and two women arguing in another.

They knocked on Pollard's door, got no answer, and knocked again, and harder. Nothing.

"Feels empty," Virgil said.

A door opened at the next apartment back down the hall, and an elderly woman peeked out. "Who're you?"

Lucas: "U.S. Marshal, looking for Doreen Pollard."

"You got a badge?"

"I do," Lucas said. He took his badge case from his pocket and showed it to her. "Have you seen Doreen?"

"I know she's home. I got a plumbing problem and the manager opened up my wall and there's nothing between me'n Doreen but wet Sheetrock," the woman said. "I heard her talking on her phone, not more'n half an hour ago. And she hasn't left, or I woulda heard her, the way she bangs that door. What'd she do, anyway?"

"Where's the manager? Here in the building?"

"In Building 1, if the lazy shit isn't having a rent nooner with May Ann Wells, that slut, which he probably is," she said.

"It's not noon," Virgil said.

"Nooners are good anytime between nine and five," the woman said, with a rattling cackle. "Especially when it saves you eight hundred bucks a month."

"Could you call him, and ask him to come up here with a key?" Virgil asked.

The woman said she could and closed her door after saying she didn't want any strange men in her apartment. "I'll come back, one way or the other, after I call."

"We'd appreciate it," Virgil said.

They waited three or four minutes before she came back, still speaking through the cracked-open door. "I got him. Told him the marshals were here, and they wanted to talk with him. He'll be over as soon as he gets his pants on."

"He say that?" Virgil asked.

"No, he didn't say that, you dummy," the woman said. "He thinks nobody knows about his little hobby. What do you want Doreen for?"

"Some questions about her job. She's not answering her door, so we're a little worried."

"Didn't hear no gunshots," the woman said.

"That's a good thing," Virgil said.

The manager, a rotund man with sparse brown hair and a pointed, ratlike nose, with a ratlike mustache beneath it, came hustling down the hall five minutes later. Lucas and

Virgil identified themselves and asked him to open Pollard's apartment.

"Can you do that without a warrant?" He was wearing a plastic name badge that said "Warren."

"We can if we think there may be a crime in process, or that one has been committed," Lucas said. "We've been told she's home. We've knocked, and she hasn't answered."

"I haven't heard her either," the elderly woman said, "though I did a while ago. She's still in there."

"Okay, sounds reasonable," Warren said. He kept his keys on his hip, with a pull-out retractable cable. He pulled out the key ring and sorted through the keys.

Virgil: "Is Warren your first name, or your last?"

"Warren Dodd," the manager said. He found the pass key, slipped it in the lock, and unlocked the door.

Virgil said, "You know . . ." He carefully reached behind the doorknob and used the knob's shaft to open the door. When it unlatched, he used an elbow to push the door open.

Doreen Pollard lay on a rag rug inside the door, face-up. Most of her skull above her nose had been crushed, and her eye sockets were islands of liquid blood.

Virgil blurted, "Jesus," and Lucas turned away and said, "I hate it when this happens."

"Not funny," Virgil snapped, walking backwards into the hall.

"I wasn't trying to be funny," Lucas snapped back. "That's the worst."

Dodd peeked around Lucas's shoulder, his ratlike nose twitched, and he said, "Holy fuck knuckles."

The old lady, still behind her door, asked, "What do you see, Warren?"

"Somebody killed her. She's . . . this is awful. Beat her head in. This is gonna kill our rep."

Lucas stepped over to the body, careful not to get blood on his shoes. Blood and pieces of bloody skull bone were on both the rag rug and the tile floor around it. He looked at Pollard's chest, to see if there was any sign that she was breathing; there wasn't.

"She's dead. Let's close it up," Lucas said, backing toward the door. "We need the West St. Paul cops, Gary Durey, and the BCA crime scene guys."

They made the calls from the hallway. When everybody was on the way, they sent Dodd down to the parking lot to direct the cops and the BCA.

"What do you think?" Lucas asked Virgil, as they waited.

"That fuckin' Heath," Virgil said.

"Really? I was looking for something a little more complicated," Lucas said, leaning back against a wall. "We've got a missing guy, we've got Heath, who fits the physical description of the Sand killer, and we've got a dead Pollard, but as far as I can see, the pieces don't fit."

"Who's Heath?" the old lady asked.

Lucas didn't answer the question, but asked her, "You didn't hear anyone come down the hall since you heard Ms. Pollard on the cell phone?"

"Nope. I was probably on the pot. I've got an overactive bladder. The doctor can't fix it. Not that she gives a shit."

Virgil said, "I have to talk to the marshal. Why don't you go back inside and shut the door?"

"Because I want to hear what you say. I've never been around no murder. First murder in this building."

"Go inside," Lucas said.

When she was inside, with the door closed, Virgil said, "Cheap door. Probably has her ear pressed against it."

"Do not," the old lady called.

Virgil pointed down the hall. "Why don't we . . ."

They walked down the hall and Virgil said, "The pieces *do* fit. Heath kills Sand because Sand was going to drop his donation to the Home Streets scam, but he hoped he might still get money from Maggie Cooper. But: Hinton knew something that tied Heath to the murders, and after we started busting his balls, he went to Heath and either asked for help, or threatened him, and Heath kills him and dumps his body. Then, because Pollard also knew too much, he gets rid of Pollard. With, I have to say, what must have been a hammer, or something like a hammer."

"That's an intriguing theory," Lucas said, "If you've conveniently forgotten that Heath was having dinner with a half-dozen people at the Town and Country Club when Sand was being murdered, and one of his witnesses is the mayor."

"How do you know that?"

"Because Heath showed up at the Sand murder scene while I was there. He showed up with the mayor — they'd been having dinner with a bunch of other people when the Sands were murdered," Lucas said. "He was interviewed, but he was never a suspect and he had a solid alibi with several eyewitnesses."

Virgil said, "Huh. You never mentioned that."

"Yeah, huh. You got anything else for me, that's not useless?"

"One thing," Virgil said. "Dodd said, 'Holy fuck knuckles' when he saw the body. I'm always looking for expressions like that. I'll use it in the novel."

"I meant about the Pollard murder," Lucas said.

"Nah. You shot me down. I got nothin'," Virgil said.

The West St. Paul cops arrived first, four patrolmen and an investigator. Lucas warned them about going inside the apartment or touching the doorknobs on either side of the door but allowed the investigator to push open the door, to look at the body.

"That's about as dead as you can get," the cop said. "Anything alive inside? I mean a cat could . . . you know. Take a bite."

"Maybe we should leave the door open," Virgil said.

They made small talk with the investigator and a couple of uniform cops until Durey arrived. He looked at the body, and said, "Crime scene is on the way. They were getting in the van when I left the office. Do you guys have any idea of what's going on?"

"Lots of ideas," Lucas said. "After crime scene gets this, Virgil and I oughta go back to the office and make statements. It's complicated."

Virgil: "It's possible we caused this by poking around."

"Give it to me in two words," Durey said. "Did the Sand killer do this?"

Virgil and Lucas looked at each other, and then simultaneously shrugged. "We don't think so, but it's not impossible," Virgil said.

"Thanks for that," Durey said. "Let me write that down in my notebook."

The BCA crime scene crew arrived, and Lucas and Virgil backed away, leaving Durey to run things. "I want your statement, quick as you can," Durey said. "Everything you've done since you started working it."

"We'll coordinate and give you one statement from both of us," Lucas said.

"That'll work."

Virgil took a last look at Pollard's body, shook his head, and followed Lucas down the hall.

They almost made it to BCA headquarters. A half mile out, they took a call — from

BCA headquarters. The duty officer said, "You guys put in a request that we track a van owned by a Bob Dahl? It's at the airport. The airport cops are trying to find it, but they picked it up on the automatic plate reader coming in, and it hasn't gone out."

Virgil: "We're on the way."

The duty officer called back as they took I-35 south: "Gold Ramp, level 2. They got it."

When they got to Gold Ramp, level 2, they found an airport cop named Rex Drummin waiting for them. There were no empty spots, so they pulled to the side, parked, and got out.

Drummin walked over and said, "Haven't touched it. The BOLO said the guy might be a runner."

"What are the chances that you might have video of him?"

"About a hundred percent," Drummin said. "We got cameras everywhere, and we've got the exact time of entry from the plate reader. You want to look at the car first?"

"Yeah."

Virgil went back to Lucas's Porsche and got a pair of gloves from the equipment bag, walked back to the van and tried the passenger side door, which popped open.

"That's not something you see every day," Drummin said. "They're usually locked up tight as a . . ."

Lucas and Virgil looked at each other and Virgil said, "A drummin?"

"I didn't want to say that," Drummin said.

Virgil opened the door, and Drummin shined a flashlight over his shoulder. The van's keys were sitting on the passenger seat, which explained the unlocked door. The van was empty, except for the usual paper litter.

"Not much," Virgil said. "Let's look in the back."

They popped the cargo doors. The back of the van was empty, except for what looked exactly like a hand-sized blood stain on the carpeted floor.

"Oh, boy," Virgil said.

"We need to get the BCA crime scene crew here," Lucas told Drummin. "We need the car locked up tight, and we need somebody to sit on this area to make sure nobody messes with it. Can you do that?"

"Absolutely. Let me get on my radio."

Drummin made the call, and they all waited until an airport cop car arrived with two cops inside. They explained the situation, and when they were sure it was understood, followed Drummin to police parking, and then to the on-site operations headquarters on the baggage level.

Since the van's arrival was recent, and the time precise, it didn't take long to find the relevant video.

Lucas looked and muttered, "Sonofabitch."

"That's not right," Virgil said. "That can't be right."

Drummin: "It's right. You recognize the guy?"

The man who got out of the van was tall, wearing what appeared to be a dark University of Minnesota waterproof hoodie, a black Covid mask, and glasses. His hands were unnaturally pale, as if he were wearing plastic gloves.

Lucas: "Not exactly. Can we see where he goes?"

They tracked him to the cab stand and lost him. "We need the cab driver," Lucas told Drummin.

"We can give you his tags . . ."

"We'll take them," Lucas said. And to Virgil: "Call Durey and fill him in. California collects DNA from all felons, so we need to get DNA on the blood. As quick as we can."

"If we can jump the line, it'll still be a day

or two," Virgil said. "But I've had stuff take months, because of the line."

"The line can be jumped," Lucas said. "A rich federal judge murdered with his two sons and the TV stations are hovering like flying weasels, talking about a law enforcement clusterfuck; we can jump the line."

"You had me at weasels," Virgil said. "I'll call Durey. You call about the taxi driver."

Lucas called the cab company and was told the driver was in his car working what was probably an illegal daily 12-to-12 shift. His dispatcher got him on the radio, and he agreed to drive to the airport to meet with Lucas and Virgil at the operations center.

A thin, tall, gray-haired Ethiopian man named Oromo Belay, the cabbie spoke a soft Minnesota English with a school-teacherish precision. He remembered the passenger because of the black Covid mask.

"I don't know what he looked like, he was wearing his Covid mask. Black mask," Belay said. "He was taller than me. I'm one meter eighty-two . . . almost six feet."

"Did you talk to him?" Virgil asked.

"Not much. I didn't want him breathing on me. I thought maybe he wore the mask because he had Covid. I asked him if he did, and he said no. He said he wore the mask so he didn't get it. He asked me if I was vaccinated, and I said, 'Of course.' I still didn't trust him."

"When you did talk, did he sound like he was from here?" Virgil asked.

"Oh, yeah. He sounded like a Minnesota man."

Belay had dropped the masked man at a small shopping center on Ford Parkway, which he thought odd, because it was late, and the shopping center was closed.

"He told me he was meeting a friend who worked late at Target," Belay said.

When they'd wrung him out, and had gotten his personal information, including his cell phone number, they told Belay that another investigator might want to talk. With Belay back in his cab, Virgil got his iPad and called up a map program.

"It's about three-point-three miles from Target to Heath's place. An hour's walk."

"Long walk," Lucas said.

"Suppose you weren't trying to prove you were innocent — you were smart enough to try to build a case intended to defeat prosecution," Virgil said. "Suppose you'd seen the tape of the Sand killer on TV like everybody else, and knew where you could get a U hoodie . . ."

Lucas nodded. "You think Heath is that smart?"

"He didn't strike me as a wizard, but he's probably smart enough. He's a Dartmouth grad, for whatever that's worth. He set up those phony charities and ran them for years, we know he's a con man, and most con men have at least some brains. He killed Pollard silently, so not even a snoopy neighbor heard it."

"So Hinton's in the river, or a hole somewhere, Pollard's got no skull, and Heath is a psychotic killer who didn't kill Sand," Luca said. "We've got two murderous psychos and no proof of anything."

Virgil nodded: "That's the way I see it."

15

Jimmy Russo, the St. Paul cop who'd briefed Lucas the night of the Sand murders, steamed into the operations center. Lucas saw him first and said, "Uh-oh. Here we go."

Russo spotted them and stalked over and asked, "What are you two doing? I'm leading this thing and you're not even talking to me." He jabbed a finger at Lucas and said, "I didn't even know you'd gotten involved until Durey called me and told me about this Pollard. I run my ass over there and he's already leaving because you called him about this Hinton's van."

"We're not trying to go around you," Lucas said. "Virgil works for the BCA and I'm sorta tagging along. Not even my boss knows I'm out here."

"Bullshit, Davenport, I've known you since you were on the Minneapolis cops, you don't tag with no one." He looked at

Virgil: "And what's this guy doing, fuckin' Flowers, anyway? He's usually down investigating some pigsty full of hayseeds, yokels, and retards."

Virgil: "Am not."

That made Lucas laugh, which made Russo angrier, and then Durey showed up and Lucas said, "We told you not to rat us out to that fuckin' Russo."

Durey glanced at Russo and said, "Keep me out of it."

"How's the Pollard situation?" Virgil asked.

"Still dead. You guys were supposed to be writing a report," Durey said.

"We got a call about the van," Virgil said. "We took a look."

Lucas said to Drummin, who was listening in amusement, "Show these guys the tape." To Durey and Russo: "There's blood in the back of the van. We think it's probably Hinton's. But you got to look at the tape."

They looked at the tape and Russo said, "No, nope, no way."

"You know what's weird?" Virgil said. "It wasn't cold or raining last night, and this guy is bundled up like an Arctic breakout is coming through."

"He's trolling us," Lucas said.

"Who is?" Russo asked.

"Noah Heath. He probably killed Pollard, he probably killed Hinton."

"Noah Heath? The rich guy? The mayor's pal? Probably?"

"That's the guy," Virgil said. "Of course, we've got no proof of that and he's wearing the costume like the Sand killer to jack us around. But, he did it. Probably."

Durey scratched his head right at the hairline, eyes closed, face down, then sighed and said, "You two . . . please go write a report and get us up to date. We've got Pollard covered, we'll cover this van, whatever it is. Get crime scene to sample the blood and get the DNA going. But we need your report."

"You'll have it before we go home. You can pick it up online," Virgil said.

"Just go," Durey said.

Russo: "Yeah, go."

Lucas and Virgil spent three hours writing the report, Virgil typing while Lucas paced back and forth, sat in an office chair with his good leg on a desk, or lay on a couch.

"We look like a couple of guys in a movie, writing a screenplay," Lucas said.

"I've thought about writing a screenplay,"

Virgil said, looking up from the computer screen.

"Tell me about it when the movie gets made," Lucas said. "As for this report, I think we should be more . . . circumspect . . . about Heath. If we put all this shit in there, and the report gets out, there'd be a substantial stink, and guess who'd be in the middle of the odor?"

"Nothing to be done about that," Virgil said. "We want some serious focus on the guy."

"Sure. But we leave his name out of the report. Call him Subject A," Lucas said. "We know that Maggie Cooper has a leaker — but nobody knows who Subject A is, except Russo and Durey. If that leaks to Maggie Cooper . . ."

"Then it has to come from Russo or Durey. We're setting a trap for our friends," Virgil said.

"If it snaps on somebody . . . we don't have to say anything about it. We'll just know."

"Hope it's Russo," Virgil said.

"Because he hurt your feelings with that hayseeds, yokels, and retards bullshit?"

"No, because Durey's a friend. Even if he's a little pissed off at me now."

They finished a half hour later. Virgil

checked the time and said, "I'm going home. I'll be back tomorrow at ten o'clock."

"You could always bag out at my place . . ."

"Finding a place to bag out isn't a problem," Virgil said. "Dealing with Frankie is a problem. I'll spend the night there, get refreshed, be back at ten."

Ann Melton was nearly asleep when Maggie Cooper came into the bedroom, grabbed one foot and shook it. "Lucas and Virgil filed a report. It's online. It's freaking me out."

"I'm coming," Melton said, struggling to get out of a tangle of sheets.

Out at the kitchen counter, Melton started reading the report, and after a couple of minutes, muttered, "My God, my God." And, "These guys are out of control." And, "Beat her to death with a hammer? Who is Subject A?"

"When you read the whole report . . . I mean, you wouldn't believe me if I told you."

Melton looked up: "You know?"

"I suspect. I've been talking to George Whitman and he thinks Lucas and Virgil are investigating Heart/Twin Cities and Home Streets. Two Heart employees are either dead or missing. Subject A has got to be Noah Heath."

"Noah? I know Noah, he's a big chicken," Melton said. "I can't see him beating somebody's brains out. The report says it looks like it was done with a hammer or something similar. That is *not* Noah Heath."

"Think about it overnight," Cooper said. "You'll see."

Melton said, "I'm thinking about it now." She thought about it, pressing an index finger to a lower lip. "Okay, wait. Noah's always creeped me out a little. There's something about him." She peered at Cooper. "Do you think he's insane?"

"If what Lucas and Virgil are saying is accurate, he's set up five or six charities specifically to rip them off, to embezzle money," Cooper said. "He's stealing money from kids with harelips, for Christ's sakes."

"Cleft palates," Melton said. "That's bad. That's bad enough to kill Alex, but why would he?"

"Well, he didn't," Cooper said. "He was having dinner with the mayor and some other people when Alex and the boys were murdered. That's in there, too."

"I'm going to need some time to read the whole report."

"Wait until you get to the end. There's a

313

punch line."

"Let me read."

Cooper let her read, stuck her head in the refrigerator, closed it, opened the freezer drawer, took out a raspberry popsicle, peeled the paper off, propped herself against the kitchen sink, and waited.

Melton got to the end and said, "What! The killer gets out of the missing guy's van?"

"Told'ja," Cooper said.

Melton paged through the report again, skimming backwards, and finally asked, "What do *you* think?"

"We've got to talk to Lucas and Virgil again. They're the real deal. They got more in a week than the other guys got in a month."

"If this report is correct, they might also have gotten two people killed."

Weather left for work at six in the morning, as usual, but Lucas wasn't an early riser. On this day, his phone rang at seven-thirty, and he groaned, woke up, thrashed around, and after five rings, the phone went to voice mail, and he subsided, relieved.

For thirty seconds. Then the phone started ringing again. This time, he was awake enough to get it. He looked at the phone's screen: Virgil.

314

"What the hell?"

"Maggie Cooper called me. She won't admit it, but she's got our report," Virgil said. "The one we put up about, oh, twelve hours ago. She called me because you mentioned you like to sleep late, but I lived on a farm, so she figured I got up with the chickens. She called at seven and I gave you the extra half hour."

"Do you? Get up with the chickens?"

"No. I worked until one o'clock last night. Then . . . never mind."

"You got laid until three o'clock? You only gave her two hours?"

"Let me talk. Maggie's seen our statement," Virgil said. "The whole thing. She even knows that Subject A is Heath."

Lucas didn't exactly know how to respond, so he didn't for a moment, then he said, "We need to jack her up."

"Jack *her* up? She's demanding that we come to her house. Like, now. She's jacking *us* up. I told her I couldn't get there before eight-thirty or so. If I'm going to be miserable, I thought you should be, too."

"Goddamnit . . ."

"You want me to meet you at her house, or pick you up at yours?"

"Pick me up. We'll hit the Caribou Coffee before we go."

Virgil arrived, and they took his Tahoe to Caribou Coffee. On the way, Lucas called Sandy, who was still at home. "How hard is it to identify an IP address?"

"Well, if it's a naked IP, not too hard. If it's run through a VPN, it's hard. It can be hard in the sense of impossible."

"Could you look at Internet accesses to BCA data files, specifically, the report that Virgil and I filed last night? We left there at seven o'clock and access was probably last night or very early this morning, if it happened. And it would be coming in from outside."

"Yeah, I can do that," Sandy said.

"How long will it take?" Lucas asked.

"Mmm, five, six minutes."

"Sandy, I will give you four dollars if you can get it to me in five minutes," Lucas said.

"Call you back," she said.

She called back as they were waiting for their coffee: "Yup. Somebody came in. Strong protection with a VPN, so I can't tell you who it was. Came in at eleven o'clock with a sign-in password I don't recognize. We had two other hits, one internal from Durey, and another external, from the St. Paul cops."

"Russo," Lucas said. "Thanks, Sandy."

"You said something about money. Four dollars, I believe."

"I'm a little short this week, so, remind me someday," Lucas said.

Virgil: "They've got their own access and password. I'd like to know how that happened."

"Every reporter in the Twin Cities can get into DMV files, so . . . the state's security is crap. We even know it's crap, but nobody does anything."

A barista called their coffee, and they took it out to the Tahoe. Lucas took a sip, burned his lip, and asked, "How do we play it?"

"We don't tell them we know," Virgil said. "We might find a use for the information. You know, later."

"Good. That's good. The fact that she did something to get inside . . . she must have bribed someone. I still can't see her for the murders."

They'd finished the coffee by the time they got to Crocus Circle, and Virgil pulled to the curb. Cooper opened the door as they got out of the car and she walked barefoot down the frosty walkway and rasped, "Did he kill my boys? Did he hire it done?"

"Who?" Lucas asked.

"Noah Heath. His secretary was murdered and the director can't be found and Gary Durey told me you're investigating them for fraud, stealing from the charities. Tom was right! They're crooks!"

"We have no evidence that would hang him, not with the director missing," Lucas said.

"I don't remember the director, this Dahl, I only saw him once. Does he fit the killer's profile? Is he tall?" she demanded.

"He's kinda short," Lucas said. "After we talked to him, he cleaned out all the personal stuff in his house, so we figured he was running. Then we found his van at the airport with blood in the back. We think it might be his."

"Noah killed him to get rid of witnesses! It's obvious!" Cooper said.

"Go inside before your feet get frostbitten," Virgil said.

Cooper looked down at her feet, as though she hadn't realized she was barefoot, did a little dance, and turned and hurried back toward the house, with Lucas and Virgil trailing.

Inside, in the living room, she said, "It's obvious!"

318

"Where's Ann?" Virgil asked.

"At work," she said. "What I want to know . . ."

"He didn't kill Alex and the boys. His alibi is good. Could he have hired it done? Maybe. He apparently has the money, but the killings weren't professional, they were sloppy," Lucas said. "If he hired it done, he hired somebody who didn't know much about guns."

"Which would be weird," Virgil said.

Cooper ran her hands up through her hair, then shook her head, as though she were trying to clear it. "I don't know," she said. "Maybe we'll never find out. I was up half the night, trying to break through the wall: What could Alex have done? What could he have done, or been planning to do, that would cause somebody to take such a huge risk? It doesn't seem like the money thing could have been enough. . . . Of course, if Noah Heath killed two people, I guess the 'not enough' theory goes out the window."

"Money is always enough," Virgil said. "Especially in large amounts."

"But killing a federal judge and two children in cold blood? That's life without parole, in Minnesota," Cooper said. "If he's charged by a federal prosecutor, he could be executed. What did Alex do? We talked all the time, if he had hidden concerns, I should have at least picked up that he was hiding something . . ."

She looked at Lucas and asked, "What?"

Lucas turned his eyes away from her and said, "I don't know."

"Yes, you do," Cooper said. She could read his mind; he was almost afraid to look back at her. "You just thought of something this very minute. Do you know who did it?"

"No, but . . . you might." He turned to Virgil. "I just thought of what I picked up at Lundgren's place, but she ran past it so fast, it didn't stick."

To Cooper, Virgil explained that Lundgren was a violent family member of a man Alex Cooper had sent to prison. "You suggested to us that maybe a family member would be upset . . ."

"I remember that. The ill-gotten-gains thing," Cooper said.

Virgil looked at Lucas: "So tell us."

Lucas had closed his eyes as he leaned back in his chair. After a moment, he said, "Fuck me."

Cooper: "What?"

Virgil: "Maybe we should step out on the lawn."

"No, I want to hear it," Cooper said.

"She has to hear it," Lucas told Virgil. "It explains why the killer came after her. Because she knows him. She could figure out who he is. She probably would, sooner or later."

"What!" Cooper demanded.

Lucas: "When we were talking to Lundgren, and suggested that she might have been the one who shot at the marshals, she said something like, 'Larry is the criminal. He's the dope-dealer, child-fucker, cop-shooter."

Virgil: "Yeah? So what? I do remember that . . ."

"What if it wasn't Noah Heath, or anything to do with Noah Heath? What if it didn't have anything to do with Alex Sand? What if it was all about the kids? About a child-fucker?"

Cooper frowned. "The boys?"

Virgil: "Oh, shit." He lurched out of his chair, took a turn around the living room. "Man, that could be it."

Cooper looked from Lucas to Virgil and back to Lucas. "Please," she said.

"If you're looking for a motive, something that could get someone sent to prison for a very long time . . . maybe forever . . . sexually messing with a child, or dealing with child porn, that would do it," Lucas said.

321

Cooper turned pale, touched her fingertips to her mouth: "Oh, no."

"We've got to look at it," Virgil said. "It would explain a lot. It would explain why the whole family was murdered, because somebody in the family might be able to identify the predator. Why he killed Alex and both boys, and then came back after you."

"Oh, no," she said again.

Lucas leaned forward, reached across the space between them, and touched her on the knee. "Think of somebody who would have access to the boys. A tall male, size-eleven feet, which is about all we know. But if it's a sexual crime, he would have to have been in a place where he's seen the boys . . . unclothed."

"Unclothed? Oh, my God."

Virgil was staring at her, moved up, and said, "I saw it in your face, like you saw it in Lucas's. You have an idea."

She stumbled: "No, I, I don't. I really don't. Maybe a gym teacher at school? But they don't take their clothes off. They took swimming lessons . . ."

They pushed, but she gave them nothing but the swimming lessons. They were still pushing when Durey called.

"We don't have DNA yet, we're working

on it," Durey said, "but the blood type is Hinton's."

"He's dead and Noah Heath did it," Lucas said.

"Probably," Durey said.

"You gonna pick him up?"

"I'm meeting Russo at Heath's house in twenty minutes. You want to be there?"

"We're on the way," Lucas said. He clicked off and said to Cooper: "You have to tell us."

"I don't know anything," she wailed. "I don't, oh my God, what, what . . ."

Lucas watched her perform and finally said, "I don't believe you. I don't know why you're covering for the guy, but Virgil and I will be back to talk about it."

"I don't know . . ."

Lucas to Virgil: "C'mon. We gotta go."

As they stood and walked toward the door, Cooper cried, "Wait! Wait! They took basketball lessons, too. At the Greenway Rec Center."

"Greenway," Lucas said. "Got it. And the swimming lessons."

Virgil and Lucas hurried out to the truck; Heath's house was five minutes away.

When Cooper saw them pull away from the curb, she called Melton at work: "I know who did it," she said. "And I know why."

16

"She has an idea about who did it," Lucas said, as they pulled away from Cooper's house. "Specifically, who did it. She has a name."

"I know. Why won't she tell us?"

"I'm afraid she might try to do something herself," Lucas asked.

"She's not that dumb," Virgil said.

"She's not dumb at all," Lucas said. "That's the problem. The murder clearance in St. Paul, is what? Fifty percent? Half? It's a lot less than that in Minneapolis. Most of those are done by people dumber than a bag of hammers and we're lucky to catch half of them. If she works at it, she'll get away with it."

"How would she do it? We're talking about a large male suspect who used a gun, who has a gun and is willing to kill."

"She'd . . ." Lucas looked at Virgil. "What are you getting at here?"

"She's smart. You just said so, and I agree. If she's going after someone, she'd do it with a gun. She has a gun, and possibly two, a Nine, which Alex Sand, we're told, sold at a gun show. Maybe he didn't. Maybe she's got that hidden. But. She told Durey and Russo on the day after the killings that Alex had sold the gun. She'd still be in shock. I doubt she would have jumped to the idea of murdering somebody so quickly."

"That would be quick," Lucas agreed. "Keep talking."

"If she's planning something, revenge, who would she know about, from the investigation, who might have a good idea of where to get a cold gun?"

"Carter," Lucas said.

"Yes. But I keep thinking, if a likely suspect gets killed . . . then she'd automatically be a leading suspect in that murder," Virgil said.

"If she does it right, she hires the best defense attorneys in the state — she's got the money to do that — and says not a single fuckin' word to us. She's gotten rid of the gun somewhere we'll never find it. She'll be guilty as hell, but she'll be prosecution-proof."

They thought about all that as they drove, and then Lucas said, "You know what? You could describe Heath the same way. Unless we get some of Hinton's DNA from the house, or maybe Heath's from the van, we're sucking wind."

Durey was waiting under a barren maple tree on the verge outside Heath's house. When Virgil and Lucas got out of the Tahoe, he walked over and said, "He's in there. I saw him in a window. Russo will be here in a minute or two."

"We, uh, just had an interesting session with Margaret Cooper," Lucas said.

"Yeah?"

"Yeah. We think she knows who killed her family," Virgil said.

"What? What? What the hell is going on, Lucas?" Durey asked.

Russo arrived and Virgil said, "Let's wait, get Jimmy in on this."

When Russo had parked and walked over, Durey jabbed a thumb at Lucas and said, "You need to hear this."

"Ah, God, no. I don't like the way you said that."

Lucas told them about the interview with Cooper; he didn't mention Sandy's discovery of a computer intrusion that might go back to Cooper, or the question of where Cooper might get a gun. When he finished,

Russo said, "I believe you guys. It could be the kids, and if you saw her react . . . I don't think you'd make this kind of a mistake."

Durey was staring up into the branches of the maple tree. "Let me see . . . Basketball lessons and swimming. Maybe . . . the Y? Would they send their kids to a Y?"

"Not by themselves, I don't think," Virgil said. "Besides, they're rich. If they sent them to a gym, it'd be a private one."

"We can cover all of those in a couple of hours," Durey said. "Still, we won't know who she's thinking of, if she's got one guy in mind."

"We gotta find a way to put pressure on her," Russo said. "Maybe I'll park a car outside her house for a couple of days. You know, to protect her."

"She could call the mayor, sic him on you," Lucas said.

"Nah. He needs the Federation more than he needs her," Russo said. "All she's got is money, we got the votes. Most he'd do is call and ask a question."

"Then we're good," Virgil said.

Russo looked up at Heath's house, with a deep-set door inside a stone front. "Let's do Heath. If you don't mind, I'll lead."

Lucas: "Fine with us."

They trooped up to the front door and

Russo leaned on the doorbell. No answer. Leaned on it again and they felt a vibration from inside. Heath's face appeared at the door window, then he cracked the door and asked, "What do you want?"

Russo identified the four of them, and said, "We need to interview you about your employees. One was murdered and the other disappeared. We're aware that you're a respected citizen, but we could use your help in working through this."

Heath pointed at Lucas and Virgil, and said, "I don't want these Nazis inside. They virtually attacked me at my office."

Russo said, "Ah, well, you know, you don't have to talk to any of us, if you don't wish to. If you do decide to discuss this problem, Lucas and Virgil have information about your employees that you may not be aware of, and you may find interesting. And, sir . . . it may help you, help us, to determine what happened to them."

"I don't know . . . could I have an attorney monitor the conversation?" Heath asked.

The dreaded attorney question. "Of course," Russo said. "Wouldn't have it any other way, sir, if you think it's necessary." He started lying: "We got some funky video from Ms. Pollard's apartment, camera was a piece of junk, but we've sent it off to the

FBI lab and their techs think they can clear it up. That should help. But. Sure. A lawyer, *if you think it's necessary.*"

As in, *if you think it's necessary* because you're guilty.

Heath worked his lips in and out, then said, "I'll let you in, but you ask me any questions with untoward implications, I swear to God I'll throw the whole bunch of you out and I'll sue all your butts into oblivion."

He pulled the door open a couple of feet, turned away, and stepped back into the house. The four cops glanced at each other and simultaneously suppressed smiles: no lawyer.

Virgil muttered, "Well done," as Russo led the way inside.

Heath's living room was a carefully color-coordinated grouping of 1900s furniture of the mission kind; grainy oak tables with earth-colored sofas and cushioned chairs. Undistinguished hand-colored prints of British country scenes, usually with a red-colored dog, hung on the walls.

The walls were a dark oak-leaf green, the carpet a muted geometrical craftsman reproduction. The cops checked the room, looked at each other with tipped heads, and found chairs. Heath took a high-backed chair that, with a squint and a sense of humor, might have been mistaken for a throne.

"I have no idea what my employees do in their off-hours, or where they might have gotten to," Heath said. "I believe it's possible that Bob and Doreen may have . . . once had some kind of personal relationship. When you find Bob, you might ask him about that. I don't approve of office relationships, but they were adults, and not even young ones, at that."

"Was their relationship angry?" Russo asked.

"I believe it was over," Heath answered. "That Bob had broken it off."

"By Bob, you mean the man you knew as Bob Dahl, whose real name was Darrell Hinton," Durey said.

"Yes, yes." Heath waved the correction away, like a fly. "These two persons" — Heath gestured at Lucas and Virgil — "came to my office and accused me of abusing our charitable funding. I bitterly resent that. Bitterly . . ."

Heath departed into a goofy-sounding monologue, suggested that he was more a figurehead than a manager, that his job, as specified by the board of directors, was to use his social status to identify donors and encourage them to support the charities.

"That is a full-time job. More than full time. Bob's job . . . this Hinton, you say — his job was to keep the books, make sure everybody got paid, and to inform the board about business concerns. He shared some of those duties with Doreen, who had a business school background. I personally paid little attention to that aspect of the work . . ."

They listened for a while, and when asked why Heart/Twin Cities had hired Hinton in the first place, he sputtered, "You want to know why? Because he seemed to have some qualifications and because he was *cheap*. You seem to be under the illusion that we're a big-money operation. I can assure you, we're not. We do wonderful work, but we do it on a shoestring."

Russo: "We found Hinton's van at the airport. We found Hinton's blood in the back. We don't think we're going to find him unless we get very lucky. We suspect he's in the Mississippi or in a hole out in the woods. We have more video of a man getting out of the van at the airport. He's tall. About your size."

"Is that an implication . . ."

"No, no, an observation," Russo said.

"You're observing that I could be a murderer," Heath said. "Why couldn't this guy be the murderer?" He pointed at Virgil. "Same shape and size as I am."

"But I don't have a motive," Virgil said.

"Neither do I!" Heath slapped the arms of his chair with both hands. "The furniture in this room is worth more than any amount of money I might have stolen."

Lucas: "Really? It looks like repro . . ."

"Repro? Get out, get —"

Virgil: "Wouldn't you like to know why we are here?" He took his cell phone from his pocket. "I made a recording . . ."

"Which, I suppose I should tell you, Agent Flowers transcribed and included in a report to the Bureau of Criminal Apprehension," Durey said.

Virgil put the phone on the coffee table in front of Heath, who looked at it like he might have looked at a rat. With the heavy drapes, cushioned seating and carpet, the room was very quiet, and when Virgil clicked on the recording, Hinton's voice was clear to them all.

Heath listened to the recording until Hinton said:

". . . I don't recruit the surgeons, Noah does that. But, I believe at least three are phony, and maybe five, all from Cuba. Cubans who supposedly work in Central

America. Hard to track down. We pay five Cuban surgeons and five surgical nurses, plus travel and supplies, and it comes to between three hundred and fifty and four hundred thousand a year."

Virgil's voice: "Jesus, if the guy wasn't rich, he's getting that way."

Hinton: "It's a good gig. Not something I could have pulled off, because you know, you had to have some status in the community to do it. He has the big house, used to have the hot wife until she died . . . Oh. Hey."

Heath stood up. "All right. All four of you, out. Get out. I'm calling my attorney. I won't speak to you again. The charges are ridiculous. Hinton was covering for himself."

Lucas: "Did he hit himself on the head with a hammer and bleed into the back of his van?"

"Out! Out!" Heath pointed at the door.

They stood, and Durey took a paper from his inside jacket pocket and thrust it at Heath.

"Search warrant. We're entering your office right now. We're seeking another for your house, but the judge hasn't quite decided yet. Don't try to remove anything.

When you drive out onto a public street, you'll be stopped and your car will be checked. I don't want to see any smoke coming out of your chimney."

"Outrageous!"

"Tell that to KSTP. They should be showing up anytime now," Russo said. "The station made a Freedom of Information request, and under state law we had to comply. I think they're at your office right now."

"Out," Heath bellowed.

Out on the sidewalk, Virgil said, "I hope he doesn't kill himself."

Russo was looking toward the front window, where Heath stood watching them. "Why? The guy is a waste of air."

Lucas: "You agree with us? You think he killed Pollard and Hinton?"

"I do now," Russo said. "I've probably interviewed a thousand guilty guys. I know the smell and I could smell it on him."

Durey: "He's not only guilty, he's crazier than a crack-house cockroach."

Lucas: "But can we convict him?"

"Not yet," Durey said. "I'd really like to get into his house with a crime scene team."

"The judge won't go for it," Russo said. "I picked my favorite guy to ask, and he said we're not that close. We need one solid thing. We don't have it. We can do the office because both the victims worked there . . ."

Durey held up a hand to Virgil and Lucas: "Don't be strangers."

As they were walking toward their cars, Lucas stopped, turned and called, "Hey, guys! Wait."

They all walked back together, and Lucas said to Russo, "You were talking to a Minnesota state judge about that search warrant?"

"Yeah?"

"Try the federal magistrate. You'd have to get an FBI agent to front for you, but . . . that could be done."

"Why couldn't you front for me? You're a federal law enforcement officer."

"I've got too much knowledge of the case," Lucas said. "I'd know going in that the application was bullshit."

"But why . . ."

"Give the FBI guy the murders of Hinton and Pollard and tell him why we suspect Heath. And then . . ." Lucas smiled.

"What?"

"Show him the video of Sand's killer, and then the video of the guy getting out of Hinton's van at the airport."

336

Russo touched his lips. "Oh . . . ."

Durey: "We know Heath can't be the Sand killer."

"I wouldn't necessarily mention that to the FBI," Lucas said. "As far as I can tell, they're barely monitoring this thing."

Durey: "Jesus, Lucas, when that came out, the magistrate would put *us* in jail."

"A federal magistrate dealing with the murder of a federal judge," Lucas said. "If the search turns up something, he's not going to throw it out, because his old buddy Sand is the victim. If it doesn't turn up anything, well, the warrant goes in the wastebasket. There'd just be no return. The magistrate would probably never know that he'd been bullshitted."

Russo: "Oh, man. I mean, that's . . . tempting."

"How long you got to retirement?" Durey asked.

"Never mind my retirement," Russo said. To Lucas: "You're a fed. Who's the dumbest FBI agent you know?"

"I'm not sure you want a dumb one," Lucas said. "You want an ambitious one. You'll have to ask around."

"I'm not involved with this," Durey said. "But if you do it, I won't mention it to anyone."

They talked about it for a while longer, and Russo said he'd sleep on the idea before making any moves.

17

When they left Russo and Durey, Virgil said, "Still early. I say we drive out to Stillwater, get lunch, and hit Carter. See if he's talked with Cooper."

"That's a plan. I gotta tell you, this damn thing is getting away from me," Lucas said. "The two-psychos idea. We may even have a third and fourth, if Cooper and Melton are planning to kill somebody."

"I don't know if I'd class them as psychos," Virgil said. "I mean, if somebody killed your family, Weather and the kids, I'm not sure how far I'd trust you to go with the letter of the law."

"You're suggesting there's such a thing as a situational psycho."

"Yes."

"You might be right. But. When I look at Maggie Cooper, I see sadness, but I don't see depression. If somebody killed my family, I'd go right over the edge. Depression,

339

anger, I'd be out of control. What I see in her, on top of the sadness, is calculation. She and Melton are up to something."

They talked about Cooper's mental state on the drive to Stillwater; they had lunch at a place on the river called The Dock and talked more about Cooper, the possibility of a federal search warrant, and Virgil's new novel.

"Cooper is a goddamned Hollywood liberal. How could she justify killing another human being? I don't see it," Virgil said. "What I could see is some kind of Miss Marple deal, where she sleuths around and someday expects to pop up and hand us the evidence, and then we go arrest the guy. In other words, a fantasy."

"Nah."

"Good point," Virgil said. "Cogent."

Lucas ticked a salad dressing-covered fork at Virgil's nose: "She's an actress. She's been in four movies and a bunch of TV shows and one long TV series. I believe you're right about Hollywood. How many Hollywood movies have you seen where somebody's family is kidnapped or murdered and the surviving spouse goes after revenge? That's what she's got in her Hollywood head. She wants to kill somebody. She actually said that out loud, when we were sitting there, talking with Binky."

Virgil wondered if Russo would really try to suck the FBI into backing a federal search warrant of Heath's house.

"Russo's not a lawyer," Lucas said. "He doesn't have to worry about being disbarred. He's not the one who'll go to court. If he can show the evidence to the feds without answering any questions about whether Heath could really have done it, it's a possibility."

"There's the possibility of a galactic-sized pissing match, is what there is," Virgil said. "One of my many tenets of life is, 'Don't fuck with federal judges. Or magistrates.' They pretty much consider themselves right there next to God."

"True."

"Where are you at in the new novel?" Lucas asked.

"Halfway, or a little more. Fifty-two thousand words," Virgil said. "I went to a book signing once, and this famous author said books have three parts: the set-up and the climax, and then in the middle, the swamp. He said he wanders around in the swamp like a lost soul. I now know where he's coming from."

"If you were writing the Sand case, where are we? In the swamp?"

"Yeah, we're in the swamp, but we're edging into the big build-up to the climax."

A moment later, he added, "Thanks for reminding me." He took out his cell phone and laboriously typed in a note with his thumbs.

"Reminding you of what?"

"The novel. Durey said something about Heath being crazier than a crack-house cockroach. I can use that."

The restaurant didn't like people in their parking lot unless they were eating, so after lunch they drove around the compact downtown area until they got lucky with a parking place three blocks from the Carter condo.

They walked over, a sunny brisk day with a bare edge of ice on the wind. Virgil was enjoying the autumn until Lucas said, "Say, is that Janey Small up there?"

Virgil flinched and looked. Judging from the woman's hair, size, and ass, it had to be. Virgil stepped into a doorway. "Get in here," he said. "She'll see you."

"I don't care. Why should I care?"

"Do it because you're my friend," Virgil said. Janey Klein, previously Janey Small, and some husbands before that, Janey Flowers, was not somebody to trifle with, although Virgil had, in fact, trifled with her even after they parted ways. She was the second of his three divorces.

"Ah, Jesus." Lucas stepped into the doorway. "Why did you ever marry her in the first place?"

"Did you even *look* at her ass?" Virgil peeked around the corner of the doorway. Small had ambled another hundred feet farther down the sidewalk.

"That doesn't seem like a reliable predictor of marital success, though it is an architectural marvel," Lucas grumbled.

"What would you know? You've only been married once."

Virgil peeked again and Klein was getting in her car. A moment later, she pulled away from the curb and was gone in the traffic.

"Close call," Virgil said.

"Instead of screwing around with novels, you ought to write a memoir about your failures with women," Lucas said. "You'd go to number one on the bestseller lists."

"You know the big problem with women?" Virgil asked.

"Yeah. They're all good," Lucas said.

Virgil led the way across the street to the condo. Inside, they buzzed the Carters, identified themselves to Catherine, who answered, and she buzzed them up.

Carter was waiting by the door when they got out of the elevator. "Now what?"

"Couple more questions," Virgil said.

Catherine poked her head past her husband: "We can't keep doing this. If you keep coming at us, we'll have to move."

"Not outside the state of Minnesota, not until Henry's parole is up," Lucas said.

"Yeah, we'll move to International Falls and you can drive up there when you want to talk," she said. But she looked frightened.

"C'mon inside," her husband said.

They went inside; the apartment hadn't changed. Lucas and Virgil sat in the same chairs they'd taken the first time, and Lucas said, "Have you been talking to Margaret Cooper?"

Carter was mystified. "Who?"

"Judge Alex Sand's wife," Lucas said.

"Alex Sand's wife. Why would I . . ."

"She bought a gun from you, right?" Lucas said.

"What! I don't *have* any guns. I don't *want* any guns. Why in the hell would I sell a gun to anybody? Why would I sell a gun to the wife of a guy who put me in prison? If I did that, I'd go back to prison myself." His voice was climbing, and finally he shouted, "What the fuck is going on here?"

"If you *were* gonna sell a gun to Margaret

344

Cooper, where would you get it?"

Carter looked away from them, shook his head, and finally said, "I'd go on Express Heat, and order one, I guess. That was before I lost my federal firearms license. But if you're . . . I guess I could go to a gun show, but I don't think there've been any lately, not close around here. What's going on? Did Mrs. Sand, Mrs. Cooper, shoot somebody?"

"No, she hasn't," Virgil said.

"Then what are you hassling me for?" Carter asked. "I gotta talk to my parole officer about this. I'll have him call you. I've been walking the line."

"If you had to get a cold gun . . ." Lucas began.

"Look. Check my trial record," Carter said. "There's nothing there about firearms. Not a thing. I was a straight-up, legit gun dealer. Kept the records, did everything right. Would you ask some clerk in a pharmacy where to buy heroin? Same thing with me. I never bought a hot gun in my life. Or a cold one. I have no idea where to get one."

As they did the first time, they sat on the couch and asked the same questions in twenty different forms until they were all tired of it. When Virgil and Lucas were walking out the door, Catherine Carter

345

squawked, "Hey! Don't come back!"

Out on the street, Lucas asked, "What do you think?"

"I sort of believe them . . . but I sorta don't. They didn't seem shocked enough by the question. They had all the right answers, but it was like they were braced."

"So, you think it's possible that they sold Cooper a gun?"

Virgil looked up at the windows of the Carter apartment. "Twenty-five percent. Or fifteen percent. I guess I don't really believe it."

Above them, in the apartment, Catherine Carter asked, "Did they buy it?"

Carter looked at her and said, "Shh."

Back in the car, Lucas said, "Too early to quit. What do you want to do?"

"Go back to the BCA and look at some-body else's paper, see what they got. Russo and Durey were going to start running checks on gyms where the boys might have gone. Maybe there's something in that. I'm wondering if Russo is talking to the FBI."

"Hope so," Lucas said. "Because I'm run-ning out of ideas. We could hit up Maggie Cooper again."

"In the morning," Virgil said. "Maybe if there's nothing else."

"Where's the climax you think is coming?"

"It's coming, one way or another," Virgil said.

In a borrowed office at the BCA, they looked over the latest reports from Durey and his agents on interviews with Cooper's students. There was a note that Durey himself would interview Cooper again about what the two boys might have known.

They were still looking through the interviews when Durey showed, leaned in the office door and said, "Can't find Cooper. Her phone goes to voice mail and she's not at home. The babysitter says she's at the university, but she doesn't have a class today. So . . ."

"We'll try her tomorrow, early," Lucas said.

"Okay, but I got a call from Russo. He said the feds are looking at a search warrant for Heath's house. He got his ass out of there before they could ask too many questions."

Virgil: "Holy shit. They're going for it?"

"Could happen," Durey said. "They're supposed to be providing support on the case, but they haven't done much. This looks like a spot they could jump into."

"Jumping into the hole in an outhouse," Virgil said.

Durey straightened up. "My grandpa's farm had a three-holer. One for each of us: St. Paul, BCA, FBI."

"Gotta say, I like the metaphor," Lucas said to Virgil. "Maybe you could use it in the novel."

18

Cooper had a new child-care helper, a young Mexican woman named Fatima Diaz. As Virgil and Lucas were driving to Stillwater to confront the Carters, she left the baby with Fatima and the ex-cop, Binky Pelz, and met Melton at a Starbucks on the University of Minnesota campus. They wedged themselves in a corner with their lattes.

Melton asked, "Where's Binky?"

"Still at the house. I told him I wanted him to keep watch, in case the killer showed up again. That I'd be okay in the car and in crowds, and I wanted him with Fatima and Chelsea. I'll call him when I'm close to the house, so he can cover the garage area."

"Okay. This man . . . Don Hess? You're sure?"

"Almost positive. Not quite a hundred percent. Everything fits, though. He's the right size and shape, he was around the kids . . ."

Hess, she told Melton, worked at the Silver Star, a boxing gym that had a special class for younger kids. Hess did the kids' classes, with special equipment including the softest gloves, helmets, rhythm bags.

"I went there and talked to him. I didn't want my kids getting concussions or beat up or any of that. I didn't even want them to take the classes, but Alex pushed it really hard. He wanted the kids to be able to stand up for themselves, not be afraid about physical confrontation. Hess showed me what they did. Actually, let me box. Then I was okay with it, because it felt confrontational, but wasn't really rough. Nobody was going to get hurt."

"Still sounds crazy to me," Melton said. "Men hitting each other. Boys."

"It's hormones," Cooper said. "The boys actually liked it. But. There was something about Hess. This kind of . . . seminary student thing. That sounds bigoted, but you know what I mean?"

"He was a seminary student?"

"No, no. But he had that well-groomed, kind of unctuous, I don't know . . . *thing,*" Cooper said. "He had the kids doing all kinds of exercises, you know. Push-ups, sit-ups, they had some little dumbbells. Squats. Then they'd put on their gloves and helmets

and either hit these big mitts that were supposed to be like somebody's head . . ."

"I've seen those in movies . . ."

"Or they'd box with each other," Cooper
said. "There'd be these taped squares on
the floor mats, instead of a ring . . ."

"Were there other adults around?" Melton
asked.

"There was a whole adult area. The kids
had their own space, and a little locker room
with showers. They'd pick up a towel when
they came in, just like the big guys, the
adults," Cooper said. "Art and Blaine were
in the nine-to-twelve group, then there was
a thirteen-to-fifteen, and a sixteen-to-
seventeen. Older than that, they worked out
with the adults. The different kids' groups
worked out on different days, once a week.
There was a girls' group, but I'm not sure
who ran that."

"So the kids would be alone with this Hess
guy."

"Well, there was another guy there, an
older guy. The kids called him The Wiz, and
he had a 'The Wiz' name tag. But he wasn't
the killer. He was built like a concrete block,
and short. Maybe a little dumb, or punch-
drunk. He seemed okay to me. Hess,
though . . . It stuck in the back of my mind
that I kind of didn't want him alone with

351

the boys."

"But you're not sure."

They stared at each other, the coffee ignored, and then Cooper said, "No. Not one hundred percent."

"I'm not willing to kill somebody that we're not absolutely sure about," Melton said.

After a moment, Cooper said, "Neither am I."

The best way to deal with Hess, they decided, was to track him, see when he was home, when he wasn't. What they'd do with the information, they would discuss later.

"Is he full-time at the gym?" Melton asked.

"I'm not sure. I know he's there every evening, because he's got all these kids' groups, he and The Wiz."

"How long are the classes?"

"An hour or so. The kids start arriving around six-thirty, get changed. They'd box until eight, then they shower if they want to, and change clothes again, that's another half hour. So, he's probably there from six to eight-thirty or so."

"We'll go to the gym tonight. My car. You can point him out. Can Fatima stay late?"

"She'll take as many hours as we give her.

I'll check. She's a lot better than Mary was about that. She's a sweetheart."

"So . . . I've never tracked anyone . . ."

Cooper leaned across the table. "When I was waiting to come here, I looked up surveillance techniques on YouTube. There are lots of videos. Most of them are sort of . . . bullshitty. Some of them have good ideas, though. When you get back to your office, you should look at them. Do you have binoculars?"

"Sure. They're not great."

"Alex had a really good pair, I'll dig them out. One of the videos I saw suggest that you stay pretty far back from the target. You also have to be careful not to make passersby suspicious of what you're doing. . . . Go watch some videos."

Melton smiled. "I'll feel like an idiot."

"Well, yes. Oh, and we need some of those cell phones you pay for. Burners, you pay for so many minutes. I think you can get them at Walmart. I've never been to one."

"I have. I'll get a couple," Melton said.

"Pay cash. And don't sync them to your car."

The Silver Star gym — named after a military medal supposedly won by the founder — was located on St. Paul's West

Seventh Street, a mixed commercial area not far from Cooper's house. There were a number of restaurants nearby, and parking was sometimes hard to find in the evening.

Melton met Cooper at the house at five o'clock. Cooper had made arrangements with Fatima to take care of the baby until ten o'clock, explaining that she and Melton would be in and out during the evening. At forty dollars an hour, overtime, Fatima was happy to stay.

Outside, Melton took a burner from her purse and handed it to Cooper. "Not a problem. Pay and walk. But: there are cameras all over the Walmart, so they'll have picked me up. We can't let them, the cops, get the phones. They have to be broken up and dumped somewhere nobody can find them. I've already programmed the numbers in."

The women went to the Silver Star in separate cars, found parking spaces, after a while, on both ends of the block with the gym, on opposite sides of the street and several storefronts away. The combination of streetlights and store lights brightly lit the sidewalk in front of the gym; Hess arrived at six o'clock, for the six-thirty boxing class.

He was a tall man with short, neatly cut blond hair, pale eyes and skin. He walked with a long stride, hurrying, not paying much attention to his surroundings; his eyes seemed fixed on the Silver Star sign.

Cooper spotted him, pressed the Favorites selection on her phone. Melton answered: "Is that him? Tall guy, tan jacket?"

"Yes. Can you see his face?"

"Yes. Not bad-looking. But sort of petulant. Did you see him get out of his car?"

"No, he was walking when I saw him," Cooper said.

"Maybe he lives around here."

"I don't know."

Hess pulled open the door to the gym, took a step back to let a man come out, carrying a gym bag, then disappeared inside.

"That should be it, for three hours or so," Cooper said. "Let's go back to the house and get a bite to eat. Back at eight."

"I feel like one of the PIs on YouTube," Melton said.

"We're not there yet, girlfriend," Cooper said.

At the house, they had Trader Joe's salads and French fries, and handled the baby after watching YouTube recommendations that suggested handling would socialize the child. At eight o'clock, they turned Chelsea over to Fatima again, and rolled back down the hill to West Seventh Street in their separate cars.

When they found parking places, boys were already coming out of the Silver Star, carrying gym bags, to be picked up by their parents. When the last of them had gone, they waited, burner phones locked together, until Hess appeared with his own gym bag. He was walking toward Cooper's car, so Cooper slid low in her car seat, while Melton got out of her car and tagged along behind him, trying to keep at least one night walker between them.

He walked around a corner and got into a silver Subaru that was facing Melton. She put her head down and the phone to her ear as Hess drove past her and took a left at West Seventh.

"He'll be going away from you," Melton told Cooper. "Little silver car. Turning now."

"I see him. Hurry and catch up," Cooper said. "I'll be behind him."

Melton jogged back up the street to her car, had to wait for traffic, and followed. "I can see you," she said, "but I'm way back."

"He's two cars ahead of me. Can you pass?" Cooper said.

"I'm coming, I'm coming. I'm driving like

a maniac."

A slow maniac, but she eventually pulled up behind Cooper's car. Cooper said, "I'll take the next left if he doesn't."

"Okay . . ."

Cooper took the next left when Hess didn't, and immediately did a U-turn, went back around the corner, and fell in three cars back from Melton's. The car behind Hess's slowed and took a right, leaving Melton directly behind him. "I'll take the next left if he doesn't," Melton said.

"Okay . . ."

They played tag to Davern Street, where Hess took a right and then a left on Field Avenue, eventually parking in front of a small postwar house. Melton followed, went on by, Hess ignoring her. When he was inside, lights on, she went back and made sure she could pick out the house in daylight.

"I got him, he's inside his house," she called to Cooper, who waited at the end of the block. "We should go back to your place and look at the computer."

Cooper: "Lights, camera?"

"Nothing that I saw. He had to go inside to turn them on. And it looked like he went straight in, he didn't stop, like he was turning off an alarm. He went right to the back, lights coming on. No cameras that I could see."

"Okay. Meet you back at the house."

At the house, they said good night to Fatima. The baby was already asleep, and they went up to the home office, opened the computer and called up Google Maps, went to Street View on Field Avenue, and walked the images down the street, looking at houses until Melton spotted Hess's.

They took down the address from the front of the house, went back up in Google's sky, selected the satellite view, and studied the neighborhood around the house. They couldn't see everything because of trees, but they could see most of it.

"I see two possibilities," Cooper said after a while. "Either one, we wait until we see him go inside the Silver Star for a class. The first possibility is, you drop me off outside his house. I walk around to the side and break through the back door."

"People could see . . ."

"Or we sneak," Cooper said. She tapped the computer screen, where a set of old abandoned railroad tracks ran behind the houses on Field Avenue, with a heavy screen of trees between the tracks and the houses. "That's the second possibility. We both go in along the tracks, in the trees. We cut across Hess's back lawn and crack the back door."

"How do we do that?" Melton asked.

Cooper frowned. "I don't know . . . tools, I guess. A claw hammer or a screwdriver. I've got those. I might even have a crowbar. We'll look at YouTube."

"What about masks?"

"Same thing the killer used here," Cooper said. "Covid masks, stocking caps to cover our hair, maybe reading glasses from the drugstore. Dark clothes."

"We need to go past there a few times, both in daylight and at night," Melton said. "What if there are street people back there?"

"That's a risk we'll have to take," Cooper said. She brushed hair out of her eyes. "If there are two of us, and we have a hammer and a screwdriver . . ."

"Maybe the gun? With the silencer?" Melton suggested.

"Probably not. We wouldn't want to shoot a neighbor who spotted us, somebody innocent. And it's loud. I shot it both with the silencer and without it, and the silencer is quieter, but it's very loud. Still sounds like a gunshot."

Melton had been leaning over toward the computer. Now she stood up, shook out her back. "We're getting close to doing this. It's getting scary."

"Don't back out, please," Cooper said.

"I won't — but I'll be scared. Breaking into somebody's house? That's sort of worse than shooting him. I can see us doing that. Knock on the door, he answers, we get inside, saying we want to talk, and bang! He's dead. Walk back out, drive away. Three minutes. If we break in to search the place, we have to stay a while. If we get caught . . . that's the end of the whole thing. And it's the end of our jobs. We'll be ruined."

Cooper leaned back in her chair. "I've been meaning to say something about this, but I was afraid you'd be offended. So if I could say something . . ."

"Go ahead."

"All my assets . . . I've got something like two hundred million dollars, total. A hundred and fifty million liquid. If we got caught breaking in, we could tell everybody we only did it because we know he killed my family. We might lose our jobs, but we wouldn't go to prison. If that happened . . . I can give away something more than ten million with no immediate tax consequences for either of us. I will do that. I would give you ten million dollars. You wouldn't need your job."

"I'm not doing this for your money," Melton said.

"I know that. Of course, you aren't," Cooper answered. "But you shouldn't be financially ruined because you're doing this, and you won't be."

"If we kill him . . ."

"That's entirely different," Cooper said. "If we get caught doing that, *really caught,* the money won't keep us out of prison."

Melton shrugged. "We're doing it, so we should try not to get caught. And hey, Maggie: about the money. Thank you."

Cooper: "When do we do it?"

Melton scratched her neck, thinking, then said, "Quick. Right away. Davenport and Flowers are too smart. They know that you have somebody in mind. I'll scout the train tracks early tomorrow before I go to work. And you should do that before you go to the university. And maybe after you get back. Look to see if there are street people back there. If there's anyone around. We need to know who could see us. Where we can park the car. We need Fatima to take the baby. But let's do it. Get it underway before we chicken out."

"This calls for YouTube again," Cooper said. "How to break into a house. Bet there are a dozen tutorials."

19

Virgil's eyelids seemed to be stuck shut with some kind of sleep glue, nasty to think about, but he pried them open and looked around the hotel room. There was one bright line of sunlight slicing between the blackout curtains, and directly across where his eyes had been. He rolled over, picked up his phone: seven-fifteen. He punched the Favorites tab and called Frankie.

"Everybody's just fine, except they desperately miss you — the kids, the dog, the horses," Frankie said. "I personally don't care; I've been chatting with Olaf."

Olaf was the rural, but louche, postal carrier; he was good-looking, and knew it, and may have delivered more than mail along his rural route, but Virgil wasn't worried. Frankie had dealt with louche, and louche had come in second.

"I'm yawning," he said. "Listen, I'm hoping to get out of here this afternoon, depending on what happens. Lucas can do all the running around. If the FBI bites on this whole search-warrant thing, I might have to stick around for a while, but I'll try to be home before dark."

"You should take everybody out to eat," Frankie said.

"Red Lobster?"

"You know how to woo a girl, you rascal."

Virgil got out of bed, cleaned up. In the shower, soaping up, he ran his hand over the lump of scar caused by the bullet wound he'd suffered when he and Lucas had been shot. It no longer caused him any pain, but hurt a little then, as he touched it, as though he'd wakened it. But not much, and he forgot about it.

Out of the shower and dressed, he opened his laptop and started working. He'd written two unsuccessful novels before the third one sold, and one thing had become piercingly clear: he had to do the work. Every day, including Sundays and holidays.

Naturally restless, he could keep his ass in his chair for three hours, but after that, his brain was cooked. When he was working his day job, he wrote at night, when everyone was in bed. If he wrote until one o'clock, he could still be up and around by eight, which was good enough for government work.

When he was traveling, he had to grab the time when he could. To make sure he actually wrote, he kept a small red Moleskine notebook with his laptop, in which he recorded the number of words written each day. He hated days when there were less than a thousand.

He was into the flow, an hour and fifteen minutes, 1,047 words downstream, according to Microsoft Word, when Durey called. "You probably won't believe this, but the feds are going to get the search warrant for Heath's place."

"Uh-oh. Somebody's gonna get in trouble," Virgil said.

"But not us, which is the important thing," Durey said. "Russo did the sales job, and he doesn't care — he considers the feds a bunch of time-wasting bureaucrats anyway. As we understand it, they'll hit the house about eleven o'clock. We're invited. And Lucas, if you want him."

"I'll give him a call," Virgil said.

Partly because he had a kind heart and knew Lucas slept late, but mostly because he wanted to get another four hundred and fifty-three words written, Virgil didn't call Lucas until nine forty-five, when he'd gotten past the morning's writing goal.

Lucas claimed to be already up, which Virgil didn't believe, but let it go. "Okay, if you're up, I'll pick you up in fifteen," Virgil said. "It looks like the FBI bought your idea about the guy getting out of the van. They're gonna hit Heath at eleven."

"We got time, then," Lucas said. "Give me forty-five minutes. I'd like to get a couple miles in, loosen up."

"You lie like a Persian carpet," Virgil said. "See you in forty-five."

Lucas got out of bed, dressed — jeans and a pullover, with cross-trainers, because he might be digging around some unusual areas of Heath's old house, if the FBI would allow him to do that — and made pancakes for himself. He made no effort to get in two miles.

"You get your two?" Virgil asked, when he knocked at the door at ten forty-five.

"A little better than that," Lucas lied. "Balance still isn't as good as it should be. Especially with the shoes Weather bought me. Big fat soles. They save your knees but can kill your ankles, if you land wrong."

Virgil had Apple CarPlay going, and they listened to Otis Taylor's *Banjo* album as they made the short trip across town.

"Music for writing?" Lucas asked.

"Works for me."

"You ever looked at the video for Elton John's 'Tiny Dancer'?" Lucas asked.

"I don't think so."

"The music combined with the video might be the best thing ever done about LA," Lucas said.

"I'll look it up," Virgil said. "I've been watching a little Post-modern Jukebox . . ."

They were still chatting about music as they rolled down Summit Avenue; they arrived at Heath's house at eleven o'clock with no federal cars in sight, and nobody moving outside the house.

Virgil called Durey and asked: "Where's everybody?"

"It's the FBI," Durey said. "They're running late. Give them another fifteen. They're on the way."

"Where are you?"

"About a block east of the house. You just went by me."

"All right . . ."

They turned back and parked behind Durey, waited, listened to more tunes, talked about Cooper, and soon enough a parade of large, dark SUVs rolled along the avenue, which might have been a famous rap star with entourage, but turned out to be the FBI.

366

Virgil fell in behind them and parked behind the last of the federal vehicles. Agents were already getting out, one of them leading the way to Heath's front door, while the others waited at the SUVs or were strung out behind the leader. The leaders were wearing suits, but the actual searchers wore vaguely tactical pants and shirts.

Durey pulled up behind them as they got out of the Tahoe, and two agents in suits walked toward them, one of them making shooing gestures with his fingers.

Lucas held up his marshal's ID, and when the agents got close, said, "Marshals Service, BCA, and probably St. Paul cops."

"We'll ask you to wait here until we've made contact with Mr. Heath."

"That's fine," Lucas said.

A minute or so after the first agent rang the doorbell, Heath came to the door and the agent handed him the warrant and signaled those still on the sidewalk to come up.

When the agents broke away from the SUVs, Lucas recognized one of them as John Howahkan, the agent he'd met at the Sand murder scene. Howahkan spotted him, and stepped over, and they shook hands. "I guess we're in it. I thought it'd be all you guys."

"Your teams search better than anyone, and since the FBI is technically in charge of the operation, I guess St. Paul decided to go with that," Lucas said. "Of course, the fact that you guys still have the death penalty might be useful in prying information out of people."

"Okay. I thought you guys might be up to something slippery."

They both smiled at once, and Howahkan nodded: as he'd suspected, something slippery was going on, but he didn't yet know what it was.

"The St. Paul cops doing something slippery? Seems unlikely," Lucas said.

"I'll find out eventually," Howahkan said. And, "You all the way back yet?"

"Close, but not quite. Still hurt some. Not enough to slow me down. It's nagging."

"Like three days after somebody punches you in the mouth."

"Like that, but nine months later."

Virgil had already disappeared inside, and when Lucas and Howahkan caught up with him, Virgil asked, "Wonder how you get in the garage?"

"You think he put Dahl in there?" Lucas asked.

"No. I . . . There's who I'm looking for."

Deeper in the house, they could see Heath on his phone, probably calling a lawyer, and behind him, a diminutive Hmong woman, holding a vacuum cleaner and looking frightened.

Virgil went that way, Lucas trailing, while Howahkan stayed with the FBI agents. Heath was talking rapidly in his phone, frowned at Virgil and Lucas and turned away from them. Virgil brushed by him and went to the Hmong woman. He smiled at her and asked, "Could you come over here . . ." He gestured at a small side room with a bay window overlooking the backyard.

The woman hurried over, carrying the vacuum. When they were away from Heath and the surrounding FBI agents, he asked, "Could you show me Mr. Heath's tools? Where he keeps his tools?"

"He doesn't have too many," she said, shyly, still with some fear in her eyes.

"That's fine. Where are they?" Virgil asked.

"In the garage," she said.

"Can you show me?"

"Mr. Heath fire me . . ."

"You go by yourself," Lucas said. "We'll wait until he can't see you, and then we'll follow you."

She looked from Lucas to Virgil, nodded,

and walked out of the room, carrying the vacuum, stopped to retract the power cord, then disappeared into the opposite side of the house.

Lucas said, "His tools. We're looking for a hammer."

"And maybe a shovel," Virgil said.

They walked past Heath, still on his phone, and the circle of agents, into the other side of the house, after the housekeeper; Howahkan broke off to follow them. The woman was stuffing the vacuum into a closet in the kitchen, and she gave them a come-along hand signal and they followed her down a hallway and through a door into the garage.

Howahkan: "What are we looking for?"

"Nothing," Virgil said. "At least, I think it will be nothing." He turned to the woman and said, "We need to find Mr. Heath's hammers."

She said, "There are two . . ." and led them to an old-fashioned wooden work bench at the back of the garage. There, she pulled open a drawer that showed a neat arrangement of hand tools — screwdrivers, pliers, a socket wrench set, three crescent wrenches, a set of Allen wrenches, and one hammer, a short-handled sledge of the kind that might be used to drive stakes into the ground.

The woman made a puzzled face and said, "Should be two. The other one, right here."

She touched a space inside the drawer that might once have held a hammer.

Howahkan: "Ah. Nothing it is."

Virgil looked at the woman. "Could it be somewhere else?"

She shook her head. "Mr. Heath, he doesn't use tools. I saw it here last week when I came to get a screwdriver."

Lucas: "You're sure?"

"I'm sure."

Howahkan said, "I'll get somebody to put her on the record."

"Do that," Lucas said. He bent over the small woman with another smile: "Where does Mr. Heath keep his shovels?"

"Over here." She pointed to the side of the garage. They walked around the nose of Heath's Mercedes, to where three shovels and a spading fork, all old, were racked between two-by-four studs in the wall. "All here," she said.

Virgil and Howahkan knelt by the shovels. Two had bowl-shaped blades, one long-handled, the other short-handled with a grip. The blades on both were dry and lightly crusted with garage dust and dirt.

The third, a spade with a short handle and square blade, was clean.

"No dust," Howahkan said. "It's been washed, and not long ago."

The three men looked at the woman, who said, "Not me. I didn't shovel since last spring, in the flower garden. Also raked."

Howahkan took out his iPhone, turned on the flashlight. The blade of the spade was welded to a triangular steel socket that held the end of the handle. Tipping the light from one side to the other, he said, "Okay. He got the blade clean, but there's dirt along the seam of the weld. It doesn't look entirely dry. I gotta get one of the technicians in here to bundle this up."

To Virgil, he said, "That's a nice catch. With a little more education and good hard training, you could be an FBI intern, if only you were better-looking."

"He'd need different clothes," Lucas said.

"That's true."

The woman looked at them and asked, "What?"

Back inside the house, Virgil told Heath, "You left some dirt on the spade. That could hang you. Federal offense, you could get the needle."

As the words came out of his mouth,

Heath's attorney, Jon Radcliffe, showed up, pointed a finger at Virgil and said, "Stop talking to my client."

Virgil stopped, and to Heath, Radcliffe said, "Not a single word, except to me. We need a private space to talk."

Heath said, "They're tearing the place apart. We could go in the pantry?"

The agent who was leading the search approved the pantry, which had already been worked through, as a private space, and the two men went inside and shut the door.

Russo showed up and asked about the search, and everybody shrugged; Howahkan told him about the spade. Virgil and Lucas drifted through the house, watching the searchers. There were seven rooms on the first floor, seven on the second, and an expansive attic.

As they were walking down from the attic, Lucas said, "He's broke. He's got two good rooms of furniture, and the office is nice, but everything else is crap, and there's nothing in the attic except junk. He's sold almost everything that was worth anything."

"Unless his parents did."

"I don't think so. From what I understand from Russo, his father was genuinely successful, and well-off. I think Heath's never done anything in his life, except run hustles and spend his inheritance."

The spade from the garage had been bagged and taken away, as was Heath's computer and iPhone. The search was interesting to watch but turned up nothing else that seemed relevant to the murders of Pollard and Hinton. Lucas and Virgil hung around until four o'clock, when a young woman associate of Radcliffe's hustled through the front door carrying what appeared to be a copy of the search warrant, grabbed Radcliffe by the shirt sleeve and said, urgently, "We have to talk."

She, Radcliffe, and Heath went into the pantry and shut the door. Russo watched them go, then stepped over to Lucas and said, "I feel a problem coming on."

"Might be time to turn things over to the feds," Lucas said. "And get the fuck out of here."

They got Durey and headed for the door. Outside, Russo asked, "Any of you guys talk to Cooper today?"

Nobody had.

Lucas held up a finger, dug out his phone, punched in her number. No answer, but ten seconds later, his phone rang: Cooper. She sounded out of breath. "My phone was across the stage, in my pocket."

"We need to talk again," Lucas said. "Me'n Virgil and Durey and Russo."

"Ah. You're ganging up on me," Cooper said.

"When can we get together?"

"I'm at the U in a rehearsal. I've got an hour more to go, maybe a little more."

Lucas looked around. Russo shook his head, no, and Virgil turned his hands palms-up, another no.

"How about tomorrow morning? Later in the morning? Me'n Virgil."

"At my office at the U? I need to be over here for a nine o'clock meeting with teaching assistants, that'll probably go until eleven, but then I'm free until one o'clock."

"We'll see you then," Lucas said. "Unless you want to tell me what you know, or suspect, right now."

"Lucas . . . damnit, if I knew anything, I'd tell you. Cross my heart."

"Talk to you tomorrow," Lucas said.

Virgil and Lucas headed back to Lucas's house; Lucas decided it would be a good day for a run, and Virgil wanted to get home. Durey drove to the BCA, Russo went downtown to police headquarters.

As they pulled away from the curb, Howahkan stepped out on the walkway in front of Heath's house, looked at Lucas as he drove by, in the passenger seat, and shook his head.

To Virgil, Lucas said, "I believe the shit has hit the fan."

20

Six-thirty.

Melton slipped into the garage where Cooper was waiting. "If they're watching us, they're better than I am. I don't see anything or anybody, except those old people and their dog."

"How about Hess?"

"I saw him go in. He was carrying his gym bag."

Cooper stood on the steps for a moment, then said, "It's now or never."

Fatima had the baby; they could hear her crooning softly in Spanish, a soothing, quiet song. Pelz had been well paid, with a bonus, and told he was no longer needed. They had a gun, they had locks, they doubted the man would come back again after nearly being killed. He disagreed, but they thanked him and sent him on his way.

Now Cooper shut the door, cutting off

the sound of Fatima's singing. She had a leather tote bag over her shoulder, containing the largest screwdriver from Alex Sand's tool chest, four smaller screwdrivers, two flat-blade and two Phillips, a claw hammer, a flat pry bar, two black Covid masks, and vinyl kitchen gloves. If they were stopped by cops . . . she didn't want to think about it.

They'd made a half-dozen trips past the Davern Street intersection with the railroad tracks and had spotted a likely place to leave the car, a block away. They were both dressed in navy tracksuits and running shoes, a possible alibi if stopped. That would work only if they'd ditched the tools, but it might save them, too, so they went with it.

They'd talked about the burglary a half-dozen times during the day, back and forth, back and forth: now, on the way to Hess's house, they barely spoke. The drive took only ten minutes, and the carpark space was empty. Melton pulled in, asked "Your phone's off?"

"Yes"

"Give me a kiss."

They shared a quick kiss, got out of the car, locked it, and jogged, slowly, looking around, to the tracks. The only sound was that of cars passing on West Seventh Street, a couple of blocks away. At the tracks, they took a last look around. The tracks were edged by a thick line of trees, and after miming two women taking a break from a long run — bent over, hands on knees, watching, listening — they stepped back into the brush.

And waited some more. Three minutes, four minutes, and Cooper said, "Go!"

They walked along the tree line, having agreed beforehand that they'd move slow, watching for movement in the trees or on the other side of the tracks. When they were behind Hess's house, they stopped, squatted, and listened again.

"I'm scared," Melton whispered.

"So am I."

"I don't hear anything . . ."

Slow, slow, slow, moving from tree to tree, walking toe-down, trying to get through the underbrush and fallen leaves as silently as possible. The night was crisp, not quite cold, but not a night when windows and doors would be open. Hess's house had a tiny backyard, more dirt than grass, with a concrete patio extending out from the house. They moved on, the only light coming from windows in adjacent houses, the windows covered with shades and blinds.

The house had a side entrance, and also sliding glass doors that led out to the patio.

Cooper whispered, "Try the glass doors. Put the gloves on."

They took the gloves from Cooper's bag, pulled them on. "Ready?"

"Yes."

They crossed the lawn, still moving slowly. At the sliding doors, Cooper put her hands against the glass of one of the doors and pushed. It moved, but only an inch, then hit an obstruction with a quiet *thud.* They'd agreed not to take a light with them, because they might be tempted to use it, so they couldn't see the obstruction.

Cooper muttered, "Shit," gave the glass another push, but it didn't move at all. She stepped over to the next door and pushed. It slid two inches and stopped with another *thud.*

Melton took hold of Cooper's shoulder and pulled her close, put her mouth next to Cooper's ear and whispered, "I think there's a piece of wood in the door track. You know how that works . . ."

"Yes. Let me see if I can get my hand inside."

The space between the edge of the door and the wall was no more than two inches wide, but Cooper's hand slipped through. With her other hand, she passed the long screwdriver through, and using her fingers to hold it, pushed the blade along the interior track until she hit the obstruction.

"It's wood, all right," she whispered. She tried to slip the wood out of the track, but it fell back inside. She tried again, the same result. And again, and this time, it stayed out. "Push the glass."

Melton pushed, and the door slid open a foot. She gave it a harder push, and it opened another four or five inches, and they were in. They stopped, pushed the sliding door closed.

The house was dark and absolutely silent. Groping across what must have once been the living room, Melton nearly tripped over something she couldn't see, a dumbbell. She caught herself and they went on toward the front of the house. Cooper unlocked the front door to give themselves an alternative way out, then stepped over to a window, slipped a finger between two curtains and looked out at the street. A car rolled by; just one. Then quiet.

One of the YouTube burglary videos warned against using a flashlight once inside a dark house: nothing catches the eye like a flashlight on a curtain, the black-turtlenecked "security advisor" warned. He'd also warned that he wasn't teaching burglary, he was teaching defenses against burglars, to which Melton had said, looking at the video screen, "You big fat liar."

"Gonna do the lights," Cooper said.

"Okay."

Cooper turned on the lights and they looked around. They were inside a small living room with a couch, an easy chair, a television, a weight bench with a dozen dumbbells, and a small desk with an iMac desktop computer.

They could see the kitchen down a short hall to the right of the front door. A door to the back left led to a small bedroom; another door opened to a set of steps that went up to a tiny bedroom/attic.

"I'll take the bedroom and bathroom," Cooper said. "You take the living room and kitchen."

Melton tried the laptop first, pushing the power button: it asked for a password, and she shut it down again. She had no idea how she could bypass it. She looked behind the TV, and then felt along the back edge, and found nothing. The room had an old wall-to-wall carpet, and she crawled along the edges looking for a place where it might pull up. . . . She rattled all the power outlets to make sure they were solid and identical. She moved to the kitchen, opened a storage cabinet and found a plastic box full of keys.

"I got a bunch of keys," she called. "Should we keep one in case we want to come back?"

"Try the side door."

Melton took the most likely keys, opened the side door, and tried them. One group of three identical keys on a key ring worked, and she took one and put it in her pocket and returned the rest of the keys to the cabinet.

"Got one," she called.

Cooper opened the bedroom closet and searched all the pockets in the shirts, coats, and pants. She looked behind the clothes for any kind of box or container. She shook out shoes. She looked under the bed, under the mattress. They'd been searching for twenty minutes when Cooper worked through a small chest of drawers, feeling through the socks and underwear and sweatshirts.

A silk orchid, in full bloom, sat in a plastic pot on top of the bureau, and it occurred to her that she'd seen nothing else that looked like plant life in the house. She picked up the pot. It was too light for its size, and looking at the fake orchid, she picked it up at the base of its stem and lifted. The plant came cleanly out of the pot, and beneath it she found three tiny silver SanDisk USB flash drives, none more than an inch long and a half-inch wide.

"Got something," she called to Melton.

Melton hurried in to look, frowned and said, "Shit. We didn't bring a laptop. We should have brought a laptop."

"Can't get in his?"

"No, it's got a password, I don't know how to get past it. What should we do?"

"I don't know — he hid them, they must be important," Cooper said. "Maybe I should put them back, for now. If the place gets searched, we can make sure they're found."

"God, I hate to. They're something," Melton said.

Cooper put them back in the pot and said, "We've got some time to think about it."

They worked through the kitchen, then Melton climbed the stairs to the attic/guest bedroom. She'd been in the room only a minute when she called.

"Maggie! Maggie!"

Cooper, in the kitchen, hurried up the stairs. The room was nearly empty, with a flat, ancient mattress in the middle of the floor, on iron legs. There were four suitcases against one wall, one flopped open and empty, and a broken IKEA desk.

When Cooper stepped inside, bending

under the low, slanting ceiling, Melton said, "Look."

She lifted one side of the mattress, where three MacBook Pros sat on the woven bedsprings.

"Oh, Jesus," Cooper wailed, a hand slapping over her heart. "Oh my God."

She knelt on the floor and lifted one of the computers off the springs, opened the lid. Inside, there was a Banksy sticker showing a black-and-white chimp wearing a sign that said "Keep It Real."

"Art's," she breathed. She pushed the power button, and when the computer asked for a password, she typed one in. "We made the kids give us passwords in case . . . we wanted to know what they were looking at," she told Melton.

The computer accepted it.

"Now we have a working computer," Melton said.

Cooper looked at her and nodded: "Yes, we do."

They carried it down the stairs, took the USB drives from under the silk orchid, and plugged in one of the drives. The drive was full of MP4 video files. They clicked on the first one and as it began running, Cooper said, "Oh, no."

They clicked on more, faster and faster,

just a few frames of each one, then Cooper ejected the drive and said, "Okay, we suspected that, he's a kiddie porn freak. There's nothing from the gym . . ."

But the second one . . .

The second one was in the boys' locker room in the gym, and was full of naked kids, with Hess, fully clothed, moving among them.

"I can't watch this," Cooper said.

"I can," Melton said, grimly. "You go away."

Cooper stepped away. Melton clicked through the files, then said, "You should come look at this one. Let me rerun . . ."

She reran. The video, from a fixed point, showed a boy getting out of the shower, followed by a naked Hess, who showed a wobbly erection. "He's in there with them, naked."

"But he's in there alone with that boy . . . I don't know who that is."

"I need to look at the third one," Melton said. "I haven't seen Art or Blaine."

The third one contained more commercial kiddie porn, and Melton closed it down.

"Nothing with your boys," Melton said. "I wonder . . . I wonder if maybe one of the boys just *knew* about it. Knew about it and said something, and Hess decided he had to get rid of them."

Cooper said, "We'll talk about it later. We should get out of here. I want to run upstairs for a minute."

Melton closed down the MacBook. Cooper was running back down the stairs and came through the stairway door holding the other two Mac laptops. She picked up her tote bag, crawled across the carpet to a cold air return register, knelt beside it, and took a screwdriver out of the tote.

"What are you doing?" Melton whispered.

"I'll explain later. This is a return air register. I learned about them when we were doing our remodel."

She took out the two screws that held the register in place, pulled it loose, pushed the stack of laptops inside. "Give me the flash drives," she said. Melton handed them to her, and she put them with the computers, and screwed the register back in place. "Get me a couple of damp paper towels."

While Melton did that, Cooper used the screwdriver to scrape the paint out of the grooves in the screws that held the register in place, and to scratch the area around the screws.

"Making it so a search crew couldn't miss it, but Hess will," she said.

Cooper cleaned up the chips with the

damp paper towel and put the towel in her tote bag. "All done. Time to go home."

The front door had a keyed lock, but the side door would lock automatically when it was pulled closed from the outside. Cooper closed the sliding glass door they'd come through, but left the wooden safety block on the carpet outside the tracks. Then she stepped into the bedroom and tipped over the silk orchid, leaving the plant and pot lying on their sides.

Melton: "What are you doing?"

"I'm telling Hess that we've been here," Cooper said.

"What?"

"C'mon."

They turned off the lights, went out through the side door, and crossed the backyard into the trees and through them to the abandoned railroad tracks. Sticking close to the trees, but moving faster than they had coming in, they got back to the car and inside.

Melton said, "Jesus Christ, I'm shaking like a leaf."

"So am I, but now we know for sure," Cooper said.

Melton started the car and pulled wordlessly into the street, and drove out to West Seventh, took a left.

"Tell me what you just did," Melton said, when they were back in traffic.

"I'm making sure that Hess will come after me again," Cooper said.

"Are we going to kill him?"

"That's still the plan," Cooper said.

"I know it *was.* We could tell Lucas and Virgil who he is, that you suspected it all along, and they'd find a way to go in there and find the computers."

"And then what?" Cooper asked. "A trial where he might pull some crazy shit and get off?"

"As one of your lawyers, I can tell you he won't get off. Not as long as those computers are still there when the cops go in," Melton said.

"What if he ditched them? Like tonight?"

"Well . . . We'd know, but . . ."

"If that happened, and if he got off, we'd find him and kill him. But I don't want to go to prison and when I saw those computers, it all came to me. Like I was struck by lightning. What we'd do next."

"Tell me," Melton said.

Hess got home at nine o'clock, flipped the lights on, took a step inside and suddenly felt that he was not alone. He neither saw nor heard anything, but he smelled something: what was it? Sweat? Or . . . deodorant? Perfume?

He called, "Hey! Hey! Hello? Who's there?"

Nobody was there. The loose wooden safety bar stopped him: he was sure that it had been in the door tracks. The door itself was closed . . .

But when he went in the bedroom, he saw the orchid the instant he was inside. And the empty pot.

"No, no, no . . . oh, no."

He turned around in the bedroom, picked up the silk flower, hurled it at the wall, walked out to the living room and smelled it again . . .

Perfume.

21

The next morning, Virgil was halfway back to the Cities when Durey called.

"Heath's attorneys apparently went steaming into the U.S. Attorney's Office this morning. They want the search warrant and everything it produced to be quashed. The FBI's Special Agent in Charge called in the guy who is supposed to be supervising the overall investigation, and he called Russo . . ."

"Cut the introduction and get to the movie," Virgil said.

"Russo claimed that Heath's alibi wasn't watertight," Durey said. "That the mayor and the other people eating with him the night of the murders agree that Heath went to the bathroom a couple of times and did some table-hopping, so he wasn't right under their eyes the whole time. It only takes three or four minutes from the restaurant to Crocus Circle, so maybe . . ."

"It would take a bizarre piece of luck to leave a restaurant, drive to Sand's house at exactly the right moment, kill three people, and get back without anyone noticing," Virgil said. "The killer was inside for what, five or six minutes? He would have been gone for a minimum of fifteen minutes."

"Yeah, we all know it's bullshit, but it got us inside Heath's place. Anyway, what I'm calling to tell you is that the U.S. Attorney is trying to protect his ass. He called the magistrate judge who signed off on the warrant, Coffman, and apparently a shit-fit was thrown. Coffman wants everybody in his chambers at eleven o'clock. Can you make it?"

"Yes, I'm halfway there now. So the federal courthouse?"

"Yeah. Call Davenport and tell him about this, and tell him to get over there, too. Russo's carrying the water on this, but it was Davenport's idea."

Virgil and Lucas met at a Minneapolis Starbucks to decide what they'd say, if the magistrate had questions for them. Lucas argued for innocence: that the man in the video getting out of the car at the airport looked exactly like the Sand killer, even to small details of dress — the University of

392

Minnesota rain hoodie, the Covid mask, the size of his shoes.

That they had good reason to believe that Heath had been involved in long-running charity frauds and that his two associates or accomplices were either murdered or missing.

"Coffman's not stupid," Virgil said. "If he knows Heath's alibi is solid, he could throw out anything we found."

Lucas said. "Luckily, we didn't find anything, except the dirt on the shovel."

"That's already in the lab . . ."

"Your lab, or the FBI lab?" Lucas asked.

"Ours," Virgil said. "We're good on Minnesota dirt."

"Call them. Tell them to work it now. We need whatever they've got, *right now.*" Lucas checked the time. "We better walk on over to the courthouse. We don't want to miss any of the action."

Whatever the action was, they were going to miss it. Coffman didn't want anyone in his chambers except the attorneys. The rest of the gathered cops and FBI agents were left to stand around in the hallway, trying not to look at each other. Heath was in the hallway with the rest of them, standing by himself, bouncing on the balls of his feet, looking at the ceiling or the floor, anything but the cops.

Inside Coffman's chambers, the magistrate had his clerk bring in a folding chair. Coffman was in shirt sleeves, a lanky man in his fifties with tight gray hair, black glasses on a narrow face, an angular nose over thin lips. He had a metal coffee cup warming his fingers as he put Heath's two attorneys facing the U.S. Attorney and the assistant U.S. Attorney who'd approved the warrant.

When everyone was settled, he took a last sip of coffee, put the cup aside, and asked U.S. Attorney Jackson Morely, "Is this going to make me angry, Jack?"

"That is possible, sir, which is why we are here. Early this morning, Ms. Cynthia Clayton and Richard Roverson" — he nodded at Heath's attorneys — "called me at my office and said that a search warrant for the residence of Mr. Noah Heath had been improperly and, actually, fraudulently sworn to by a St. Paul police officer. It came to you because the FBI has overall jurisdiction in the case, although the actual investigation is being done by local authorities, with monitoring by the FBI . . ."

"Why isn't the FBI doing the actual investigation?" Coffman asked.

"Frankly, because the local authorities are very good with crime scene analysis and have the manpower for what seemed like it would be a wide dragnet of dozens of possible suspects."

"Go on."

"That happened — the warrant application — the day before yesterday and we applied for the warrant on an emergency basis," Morely said. "You granted it yesterday morning, if you'll recall."

"I do recall," Coffman said, nodding.

Morely said that Heath's attorneys' claim of fraud or misrepresentation was serious enough that he thought Coffman should consider the problem, although, he added, "There are good reasons to maintain the warrant as is, though the evidence in support of the warrant is perhaps less sound than it was represented to you yesterday. We thought this problem should be discussed before we went any further with this investigation."

Coffman was calm enough: "And why is the evidence now weaker than yesterday?"

"There is the possibility that we had a certain amount of . . . gaming by the police, specifically by St. Paul police sergeant Jimmy Russo."

"Is Sergeant Russo here?"

"Yes sir, he's out in the hall, if we need him."

Morely went on to summarize the evidence for the warrant, the same evidence that the judge had heard the day before.

"All of that evidence, with one exception, is still relevant," Morely told Coffman. "However, one piece of it, which you may or may not have considered to be critical, involved a man seen leaving a van at MSP. The man in the video was dressed identically to the Sand killer. There was other evidence, which was not presented to us at the time, and that the FBI had . . . mmm . . . apparently forgotten, or hadn't seen, that suggests that Mr. Heath could not be that man. In fairness, I'll ask the attorneys for Mr. Heath, Ms. Clayton and Mr. Roberson, to tell you about that."

Clayton made the presentation. A mid-sized, gray-haired motherly woman with small steel-rimmed glasses, she presented Coffman with a list of witnesses who said that Heath was with them at the time of the Sand murders.

"The FBI has had jurisdiction in the case, but most of the actual investigation was left to a task force of local law enforcement officers led by Detective Russo and Gary Durey of the Minnesota Bureau of Criminal

Apprehension," Clayton said. "They knew that Mr. Heath could not be the Sand killer, and if the man seen getting out of the van was the Sand killer, it couldn't be Mr. Heath — but they presented that as evidence to get the warrant."

She argued that the warrant should be vacated, that any evidence seized from the Heath house be suppressed, and everything taken from the house be returned.

When she finished, Coffman said, "I'd like to hear directly from Detective Russo. Could we get him in here?"

The Assistant U.S. Attorney hurried to the door, stuck his head out, and called, "Sergeant Russo?"

When Russo was inside, Coffman gave him a quick review of the claims of Heath's attorneys, and then, "Detective, what do you have to say for yourself?"

Russo said, "Your Honor . . ."

"Speak clearly, so we can all hear," Coffman said.

Russo said Heath's alibi was not as solid as had been represented by Clayton. "Heath was at that dinner, which involved several people, and I've now talked to them all. It was political, with people moving around, laughing, back-slapping, drinking, and table-hopping. Heath went to the men's room at least twice and maybe more often. The dinner lasted four hours and all he needed was three minutes to drive to the Sand house . . ."

That began a three-way argument among Morely, Clayton, and Russo about timing, and at the end of it, Coffman nodded. "All right, I've heard the arguments —"

Russo interrupted and said, "Sir, one more thing you should hear . . ."

"What is that, Detective?"

"I'm St. Paul's lead representative to the FBI's task force on the Sand murder. I know this isn't an evidentiary meeting, but there is one more piece that hasn't been referred to, in support of the warrant, and that you haven't heard. I hope you can take the time to do that. But it's absolutely critical."

Coffman turned to the U.S. Attorney: "Mr. Morely?"

"I don't know what Sergeant Russo wants to present. We didn't manage to talk before this hearing."

"We didn't have time," Russo said.

Coffman thought for a minute, and one of Heath's attorneys said, "This is very irregular . . ."

"With all the confusion here . . . I guess it can't hurt to see this evidence."

"Uh, hear it, Your Honor," Russo said. "It's a recording. I gotta go outside and get Gary Durey, he's the BCA representative to the task force."

After more objections, Coffman decided they would listen. Durey was brought in, carrying a briefcase. He took out a portable CD player and two small speakers, already wired into the CD player, set them up, and pushed Play.

The recording was from Virgil's iPhone interview with Hinton. The full recording took fifteen minutes, and when it finished, Durey told Coffman, "This was a voluntary interview, and this is the man who is missing and is now believed to have been murdered. We are now checking the DNA from the blood from his van against DNA taken from his home. We do know that the blood in his van, type A, is the same as Hinton's blood type."

Coffman glanced at Heath's attorneys. Clayton said "Your Honor, this is ridiculous. We don't know the history, the provenance, of this supposed confession . . ."

Coffman interrupted: "We do know, however, if Agent Durey is trying to pull a fast one with a faked-up interview, I'll put him in jail." He looked at Durey: "Is that clear?"

"Very," Durey said.

Coffman stood up: "I'll think all this over and have a ruling by the end of the day. In the meantime, Mr. Morely, there will be no further action on this warrant. You will not do any further search at Mr. Heath's home. Is that understood?"

"Yes, sir."

"And you will so instruct the investigators?"

"Yes, sir."

"So let's all go to work," Coffman said. "I will have my clerk contact the U.S. Attorney and Mr. Heath's attorneys before the end of the day, with my decision."

There was a chorus of thank-yous, and Coffman picked up his suitcoat and went out a side door.

The attorneys, with Durey and Russo, adjourned to the hallway where Lucas, Virgil, and a half-dozen other cops and FBI agents were waiting. Heath's attorneys walked over to him, and as the U.S. Attorney stood poking a finger at Russo's chest, Heath, who'd been listening to Clayton, erupted:

"I've never had anything like this experience," he said, so loud that everybody else shut up to listen. "I am the victim of some of the worst, most vile, police work you could possibly imagine. They arranged for their accusations to be leaked to the television stations. Even though I'm innocent of all these ridiculous charges, I believe I am already ruined, in the eyes of the public. There's no way back from that."

Clayton: "We'll talk about some possible civil remedies . . ."

"Civil remedies? Will they go to social media and repair my reputation? No."

His face was glistening with sweat, and he dragged a jacket sleeve across his forehead. "I've done nothing but good with my charities; I've never taken a nickel from them. I don't need to take a nickel. I'm quite . . . well off. And now, I find myself crucified. Crucified!"

Lucas plucked Virgil's shirt sleeve and said, "We gotta move."

"What?"

"We need to talk to the guy who does your dirt for you," Lucas said.

Virgil: "Are we in a big hurry?"

"Yes, we are. We need to have this done before two-thirty."

The dirt guy, whose name was Yin, was at lunch when they left downtown Minneapolis. Virgil asked the duty officer to find him and get him back to the BCA. He was waiting when Virgil and Lucas walked through the door, and he was not happy.

"I have not finished the analysis. I should have that done in the next few days, but . . ."

"Do you know anything? Anything at all?" Lucas demanded. "Forest, farm, ditch . . ."

"I've seen algae in it," Yin conceded. "Under a microscope."

"Algae?"

"Yes. It's very dark, floodplain muck," Yin said. "Not from a lake, from a river. That's one thing. And the algae."

To Virgil, Lucas said, "You've got to have your guys scrape the dirt out of the tread of Hinton's van. See if it's floodplain. See if it matches the shovel."

"Because Hinton's buried in a floodplain," Virgil said. "And if the warrant's quashed, we won't be able to use the shovel dirt to develop more evidence, but if it hasn't been quashed yet . . .".

"Exactly. We can still use it. Maybe." Lucas checked the time again. "Okay. I'm gonna make the call."

"You worry me sometimes," Virgil said.

Virgil and Lucas were back in Virgil's Tahoe. Lucas made the call to Daisy Jones, the talking head of *Jonesing for News.* He got a receptionist, then a producer, and finally Daisy herself.

Virgil said, "So Daisy, what kind of boring bullshit are you putting up this afternoon?"

"Flowers. You're selling something, aren't you?"

"I'm sitting here with Lucas — we're on the truck speakers — and he said, 'Why don't we go on that *Jonesing* show and give Daisy an exclusive?' I said, 'Why, do you have something going on with Daisy? 'CCO has a lot bigger audience.' Maybe we should go to them . . .'"

"I can put you on right at the top of the hour if you can get here by ten-to-three. Tell me what you might say . . ."

Jones was a sexy chunk of woman whose brain could slice open a guest like a watermelon if he or she didn't take care. Lucas and Virgil had known her for years, from the time she was a young cop reporter working the streets in her off-hours, looking for the sensational or, failing that, the touching.

She'd once done a story that involved a fluffy white street puppy with one blue eye and one silver that had gone national, making her almost famous; Virgil had once alleged that she'd stolen the puppy for the story, the only time he'd ever seen her lose her cool. With her long nails, he'd feared for his eyes.

They arrived at the studio at two-forty, plenty of time for Jones to push them into the makeup chair. "I'm going to start with a brief couple of lines about the other guests, then I'm going straight to you. Who wants to go first?"

"Virgil's a better bullshitter than I am," Lucas said.

"Virgil it is," Jones said.

With the makeup on, they walked down to the broadcast studio where they were hooked into lavalier mikes. The floor manager sat them too close together on a couch, while Jones took the red chair facing them and looked at a heavily scrawled legal pad and muttered her opening lines a couple of times. That done, she looked up and said, "You've both been on before. Remember to talk to me. Don't talk to the cameras."

The floor manager counted off the time and fifteen seconds out, Jones shouted, "Ray, I'm going straight-faced serious . . ." and to Virgil and Lucas she said, "Don't smile, I won't. Be cops."

The floor manager thrust a finger at her and she looked at a camera and said, "Good afternoon. I'm Daisy Jones and we have a very serious request from two of the best-known law enforcement officers in Minnesota, two men who were both terribly wounded in a famous shoot-out in New York's Hamptons last winter . . . We will get to them in one second. Later on the show . . ."

When she came back, she looked at Virgil and said, "Virgil Flowers, a Minnesota Bureau of Criminal Apprehension agent known for his fantastic clearance rate . . . Virgil, what's going on here?"

Virgil told her about the discovery of the van at the airport, and the blood on the floor. He didn't mention Heath, but did say that the van owner was believed to be dead, murdered, and, because of some timing considerations, that his body was believed to be buried within a two-hour drive of the Twin Cities.

She introduced Lucas as a U.S. Marshal. "And Lucas, you believe that dirt taken from the van could be a clue," Jones said. "You want this program, and our audience, to help find the dead man?"

"That's right, Daisy," Lucas said. "A BCA expert on Minnesota soils tells us that the white Chevrolet van recently had been driven across marshy soils typical of floodplains. He found algae within the soil, the type of algae found in river floodplains. We

405

believe it's quite possible that the murdered man is buried very close to a river — one that occasionally floods over the burial area."

"How can we help, Virgil?"

"You can ask your audience, the audience that lives near a river within an hour or so of the airport, if they saw lights, car lights or van lights, where there shouldn't have been any, the night before last, between about four and six. The van had no trailer hitch or roof rack, it couldn't have been pulling a boat or hauling a canoe. It would be a vehicle very close to a river, on the floodplain, without a trailer of any kind. And it would have been there for a while. And it might have been in an obscure place, where not many people go."

"Is this related to the murder of Alex Sand and his children?" Jones asked.

"It may be, Daisy," Virgil said. "There are a couple of murder investigations going on simultaneously. They may be linked."

"You say there may have been more linked murders than just the three at the Sand house?" She looked amazed.

"We can't expand on it, but that is the case," Lucas said.

She had more questions, and when it was

over, they went to a commercial break and Daisy said, "Thanks, guys. That was good. I'd give you each a Snickers bar if I had two more. I need a sugar hit."

She took a Snickers bar out of a bag hidden behind her chair, took a bite, put the bag back behind her. Virgil and Lucas got untangled from the lavalier mikes and were shepherded toward the exit by a producer. As they left, they heard Daisy shout, "Ray: have I got caramel on my teeth?"

Outside, Virgil asked, "Do you really think this will produce?"

"I think it'll be picked up by all the other stations, and probably the papers. It can't hurt. If Coffman hasn't ruled against the warrant yet, then we're not using the fruits of an illegal warrant to ask for help. If he decides it is illegal. And goddamnit, your dirt guy better pull some algae off those van tires, as backup, in case we have to swear where the dirt came from."

"I'll make sure that's being done," Virgil said, and he got on his phone.

22

After discovering that the flash drives were gone, Hess had run up the stairs and lifted the mattress on the bed. The computers were also missing. After an hour or so attempting to quiet his initial panic, he lay on his bed, lights on, forearm across his eyes, and thought about it.

Key fact: he wasn't in handcuffs. If any cop had found that stuff, he'd be in a dungeon somewhere. Fact: he'd smelled that odor when he first walked in. Ethereal, but there. Perfume. Women.

After resisting for a long time, he'd come to a conclusion: Cooper had been there. She'd thought of him, in relation to the boys. Now that she had the proof, what was she going to do?

If she was going to turn him in, where were the handcuffs? Was it possible that she was going to come after him herself? To go for revenge, rather than call the law?

Just barely possible. If so, then he had to strike first, recover the flash drives, recover the computers, get rid of all of it.

Get rid of Cooper, and the woman she was with.

Cooper and Melton had to go to three different Cabela's stores to get the two items that they needed. Melton went in, bought them, paid a lot of cash, apologetically.

Two Armasight generation-3 night-vision monoculars. She bought them the morning after the burglary, and they tried them out that evening. Melton had been skeptical, Cooper insistent, and both were surprised that they worked so well.

Cooper had the house gun ready. They wouldn't use the Carter gun for this ambush, only if it became necessary to kill Hess at his home. The plan was simple: they'd see Hess coming — they were fairly sure he would be — and Cooper would ambush him. When they were sure he was dead, they'd call 9-1-1 and begin screaming for help.

The baby would be in bed a little after dark, would awaken later for a feeding, and then sleep until dawn. Hess would come before then, and Cooper would kill him.

"From the office window I can cover the

whole front of the house. From the Zen room, you can cover the whole back of the house. He can't come from either side without showing himself to one of us," Cooper said.

"Could be a long wait," Melton said.

"I don't think it'll be long. He'll figure out that I took the flash drives. He'll have to come, and soon."

Melton sat in the Zen room, named, Cooper said, by the family who owned the house before them. With windows that bulged out from the back of the house, to catch both the rising and setting sun in the winter, she could see the backyards of all the adjacent houses. That, she thought, might well be where he'd come from.

The other option was up the hill from the street below the bluff, and Cooper should catch that. He'd come, they both thought, before they'd be expected to go to bed. The house was a fortress, and he'd either ring the bell, or knock, or slip a crowbar into a door and force it.

He knew the house. If they were upstairs, in bed, and he forced a door, anyone on the second floor would have time to lock one of the heavy bedroom doors, and get a gun, if one was available. He'd come when the lights were lit on the lower floor, when he could burst in and be right on top of them.

Much like he'd done with Alex and the boys.

Cooper sat in the darkened office, watching. Nothing happening on the street below. The occasional car, two old people walking their dog, as they did every night.

After a while, her mind shifted to a new gear, the mental video of the bodies on the Persian carpet, and finally her son's single blue eye looking up at her. It was the nightmare, but she was awake, seeing the video out over the street . . .

Then Hess came and the nightmare blipped out, like a burning piece of film.

Hess came up the heavily wooded hill, from the street below, at eight o'clock. He was dressed in black pants and a dark blue sweatshirt, and was nearly invisible in the dark. The hill was steep, but not long, and at the top he stopped to watch. The Sand house was to his left, with lights on the lower floor.

She was back.

The house on the corner, across from his spot, was dark except for a single light on the top floor, in back. A bedroom or bathroom. The house on the other side of the

411

Sand house was lit both up and down. He'd have to be careful, there.

He watched for a while but could see no movement in the Sand house. The curtains had been pulled and wouldn't show anything, anyway. He felt the lump in his pocket: he was carrying the gun he'd used on the Sands, retrieved from beneath the railroad tracks. If he were caught hiding here, lurking, he'd be in trouble.

He couldn't decide if he should cross the street. That afternoon, and on the way over, he'd come up with several different plans; the only one that would give him everything he wanted, everything he had to have, would be if he were able to get inside the house without being seen or heard. He had to take Cooper, preferably alive, and then find the flash drives and the laptops.

With an actress and a kitchen knife held to her face, and the promise not to mutilate her if she gave up the drives and the laptops, he should be able to recover them. And, then, of course, he'd kill her.

If he could get inside. On this night, in the dark of the moon, he'd slip across the street, and circle the house, looking for a weakness. If a door were open, unlocked, he'd do it. If not, he'd think of something else, but he wasn't sure what it would be.

■ ■ ■ ■

Cooper called, "Ann! Ann! He's here."

Melton came quickly. Cooper was looking out a narrow space between a window blind and the frame. Melton could hear her breathing, excited, stressed: "He's right at the corner. Look maybe fifteen feet to the left of the street lamp, by that round bush . . ."

After a moment, Melton said, "I got him. Yup. I got him. Oh: here he comes."

"Which door?"

"He's going to the hedge . . . I can't see him anymore . . . he's by the hedge . . ."

"Let me see, let me see . . ."

Melton stepped away, Cooper looked out. She could see no motion at first, but then, a sudden step and Hess was in the side yard, where the basketball net was.

"I don't know, I can't see him anymore, he's too close to the house. He could be coming in the garage door, but he could come around to the front . . ."

Cooper considered, then said, "I'm going downstairs with the gun. You stay here. I should hear him if he comes in, and if he doesn't, you should see him run away. His car must be around here somewhere, and he'll go back down the hill to get to it."

"That's scary," Melton said. "Are you sure . . ."

"I'm going. You watch."

Cooper was sure she'd hear him coming. The front door was stout and thoroughly locked this night. The back door, between the house and the garage, was also solid. The door into the garage from outside was much weaker and had windows that could be broken to reach the doorknob lock. She decided to set up in the kitchen, leaving the door to the garage open just a crack. She could slam it in an instant, or let him come in, so she could kill him.

She could feel the burning ball in her chest. She cocked the gun, absorbing the cold steel beneath her fingers and palm. Sitting on the floor, she called Melton on her burner phone. When Melton picked up, she said, "Keep the connection. We can talk . . . if you see him."

A few minutes after she'd found her spot, Cooper heard what sounded like somebody testing the garage door.

She said to the phone, quietly, "He's trying the garage."

The noise stopped. She stood, and backed up a bit; a streak of light should be cutting

414

across the garage floor, an invitation to come in. She stood behind the kitchen counter, her elbow on the counter to support her gun arm, the revolver cocked and pointed at the door . . .

She said, in a whisper, "C'mon, c'mon, c'mon."

Hess, peering in through one of the windows in the garage door, saw the stripe of light on the floor. Why? Why was that door open, unlocked? Could be carelessness. Or it could be a trap.

He looked at it for ten seconds, turned away, turned back for another ten, then walked around the house into the side yard, feeling the sweat at his temples. He stopped behind the hedge, checked the street, saw nobody, and jogged across the street to the edge of the bluff, and dropped into the trees.

Melton, now in the office, shouted, "He's running. He's running across the street and into the trees."

Cooper ran up the stairs, too late to see Hess's retreat. "You're sure?"

"Of course, I'm sure." She waved the monocular at Cooper. "Saw him plain as day. He took off."

"Shit. Shit. Shit. I left the kitchen door open just an inch. I wanted him to see an open door if he looked in the garage, but . . ."

"You spooked him."

"I think so. Goddamnit."

"He can't be sure it was a trap," Melton said. "He'll be back."

"We should lock up," Cooper said. "So close. So close. He wasn't twenty-five feet away. If I'd been in the garage, I could have shot him through a window. Maybe next time."

Hess slipped down the hillside, moving from tree to tree, then walked across the street below, which was actually a long off-ramp from I-35, and continued just inside the tree line to an intersecting street, turned the corner, and hurried to his car.

He should have gone in, he thought. Could have. But: tomorrow was another night.

Melton said to Cooper: "He'll be back. You might have spooked him, but he'll think about it, and he won't be sure. He did get away tonight, so that might make him feel safer. We know he's looking around back. Tomorrow night, we'll be in the garage."

"I need to kill him, Ann. I need to know he's dead."

"I know. I'm with you."

23

The highway patrol never got an exact count on the number of tips it got about where the body might be buried, but the number was in the high double digits — eighty, ninety, something like that. The patrolmen checked them out and found a lot of wet weeds plus two inebriated catfishermen trying to get a jon boat out of the Mississippi.

However.

John Jacob Orregon, owner of Orregon's Port-A-Potties, called to say that the night before last, he'd been headed down County 18 Boulevard between the Vermilion and Mississippi Rivers. He was on his way to the Tipsy Turtle Bar and Grill when he saw the white van pulling away from a dirt boat launch on North Lake.

North Lake was a backwater off the Mississippi, and as Orregon told the trooper he spoke to, Russell (Rusty) Craft, "I could touch the bottom of that lake with my dick and not get my balls wet. Don't know why anybody would be down there, and the van weren't pulling no trailer. No canoe on it, neither."

The trooper, who'd earlier sat in a café with two other patrolmen cursing Flowers and Davenport for being large pains in the ass, had already checked out two remote, wet, nasty, stinking water meadows.

"You're sure it was at the boat ramp?"

"No place else to go down there," Orregon said. "That 190th is a dead end. Nothin' but a couple of farm fields and the boat ramp. If he wasn't pulling out, or puttin' in, I don't know what the hell he must've been doing."

"All right, I'll take a look," Craft said.

The location was just north of the Treasure Island Resort and Casino, and Craft thought it was most likely that a drunken gambler had taken a wrong turn down the gravel road.

He called in, told his dispatcher where he was going. Driving through a swirling snow flurry, he headed south toward the Prairie Island Indian Reservation, took 200th Street, which turned into County Road 18 Boulevard, then off on 190th. He was kicking up a storm of gravel under his fenders:

Craft was a fast driver and the car was owned by the state, so he didn't care about gravel dings.

He parked at the boat launch, zipped up his coat, put on his gloves, and walked down to the water. Nothing. He shook his head, turned his face into a stinging north wind, and started back up the dirt ramp. Halfway up, he noticed what appeared to be freshly crushed weeds leading off toward some trees. He followed the trail, stepping carefully, because he halfway thought he knew what he'd find at the end of it: the spot where a fisherman had taken a dump.

That's not what he found. What he found was a square of disturbed black earth, probably three by four feet, now speckled with snowflakes. He exhaled in exasperation, but at the same time, felt the hair rising on the back of his neck. He could deal with a bloody road accident, had seen way more than his share of dead people, but digging up the dead? Not in his psychological wheelhouse.

Besides, it might just be a bunch of deer guts or something.

Craft carried a short spade in the back of his patrol car. He went over to the car, popped the trunk, got the spade and started digging, but not for long.

About eighteen inches down, he struck a lump, soft, but resistant. The ground was wet and he didn't want to use his hands, so he scraped away a layer of muck and found himself looking at the pocket of a pair of blue jeans, and after a minute of further exploration, determined that there was a buttock under the pocket.

By the time Lucas and Virgil got to the scene, there was a crowd, including Gary Durey from the BCA, three Goodhue County sheriff's deputies, two highway patrolmen — Craft was one of them, telling people how he'd done it — a field investigator for the Southern Minnesota Regional Medical Examiner's Office, a BCA crime scene crew, three officials from the Prairie Island Community, and a guy with a canoe who hadn't been allowed to launch into the lake, but stayed around out of curiosity, and was expertly and surreptitiously making a video with his iPhone. The video would wind up, later, on the *Jonesing for News* show.

They'd learned the night before that Coffman had vacated the search warrant. In the morning, when Durey called about the discovery of the body, he was told the U.S. Attorney might ask that the warrant be reinstated if the body was Hinton's.

"Coffman said it was a close call, but . . . he was not amused by Russo pulling the wool over the FBI's eyes," Durey told Virgil. "This might change his mind."

The crime scene team was busily excavating the body which was butt up, head down, folded like a greeting card. The second jean pocket they uncovered contained a wallet with a Bob Dahl driver's license.

"I can never figure out whether you're a genius or the luckiest guy in the world," Durey said to Lucas, as they watched the diggers.

"With what happened last winter, it's probably not luck," Lucas said. "I'd go with 'genius.' "

"If this hadn't turned up, with that *Jonesing* stunt, we would have looked like a couple of dopes," Virgil said.

"That's never held you back," Durey said. "Either one of you."

The crime scene crew took two full hours to get the body out of the ground. Hinton's body was covered and penetrated with muck, but they could all see the plastic bag tied around his head. Virgil prodded the medical examiner's investigator, who he knew because they covered the same southern Minnesota territory, to give them an opinion on the exact cause of death.

"The bag, right?"

"Can't tell you," the investigator said. "His hands aren't tied, no ligature marks, no tape, so they don't look like they were tied or cuffed, but he didn't try to get the bag off. He's got a skull fracture, I think, there's a pretty good groove across frontal bone. Might have been hit by something with an edge . . . then the bag was pulled on because he was still breathing."

Lucas: "Wonder why there was a blood spot in the truck if he's got a bag around his head?"

"Bag leaked," the investigator said, pointing. "You can see where blood was running down his neck under the bag."

"Need to know how he was killed, as fast as you can do it," Durey said. "We're going back to the federal magistrate for a search warrant, and he's already pissed off at us."

"I'll call the doc on the way in," the investigator said. "Tell him the problem."

"We don't need the chemistry right away, but we do need to know what kind of object he might have been hit with," Virgil said. "What we can look for, if we get the warrant."

"I will tell him."

"And DNA," Virgil said. "Anything that might have foreign DNA from the killer."

The investigator shook his head: "That body's got so much foreign DNA it'd take a million years to sort it out."

The cops had blocked off the dead-end 190th at the intersection with County 18 Boulevard, and three television vans were waiting there as the unnecessary cops, including Lucas and Virgil, began leaving the crime scene.

Daisy Jones was there with a crew and she tried to wave them down, but Virgil rolled his Tahoe on through the line. Daisy gave them the finger when they didn't slow down, and when she called them one minute later, they didn't answer. "Done enough for Daisy," Lucas said, with a smile. "Besides, I like teasing her."

"But now what?" Virgil asked.

"Why don't we go see Maggie again? I know damn well she's got some idea of who the killer might be. I'd like to figure out exactly what she's up to."

Virgil was good with that, and Lucas called her. She was at the university, in the middle of a class, she said, but she picked up because she thought he might have some news. He told her about the discovery of the body and askcd, "Can we come over and talk? When are you between classes?"

If they came soon, she said, they could take her to lunch; she had a meeting at one o'clock.

They wound up in a semicircular corner booth at a place called the Beacon; the waitress asked Lucas and Virgil, "Say, didn't I see you on *Jonesing*? Looking for a body?"

Virgil: "Must have been two other really, really good-looking guys."

"Did you find the body?" she asked.

"Watch *Jonesing* this afternoon," Lucas said. "Seriously."

The waitress went away with their orders and Lucas and Virgil turned to Cooper. Virgil said, "We know you've got an idea of who might have killed your family. We want to know why you won't tell us who it is. And we want a name."

"Before we get to that . . . you did find a body?"

Virgil nodded: "Yes. There'll be a lot of TV. People are still out there, but it's Darrell Hinton, who you probably knew as Bob Dahl."

Cooper sighed, slumped, then said, "Okay. I'll tell you what I'm doing, if you don't go all law-enforcement on me. Be a couple of parents."

"I don't like the sound of that," Lucas said. "But go ahead. We won't put it in a report."

"I think I might know who it is. Ann and I went to his house the night before last when . . . we thought he might be going home," Cooper lied. As an actress, she could lie as well as any cop. "He *was* going home, and we let him see us. We cruised his house three times, and we know for sure he saw us the first time, and we think the third time, too."

"Goddamnit, Maggie," Lucas said. "I see what you're doing. You're trying to pull him in to your house."

"Yes. So far, he hasn't shown up. We're waiting. If he tries to break in, I'll kill him. I've got my revolver. He can't break in through the front door because it's solid and two inches thick. He probably has to come in the back. When he does, he'll be three feet away. It won't be like what happened at Ann's place, where I was shooting a long way. I'll be shooting this close . . ."

She made a pistol finger and pointed it at Lucas's chest. "Bang."

The waitress was there with Diet Cokes and coffee. She looked from Cooper to Lucas: "Bang?"

When the waitress had gone again, Lucas said, "You can't do that, Maggie."

"Of course I can — you just crook a finger." She made the pistol finger again and crooked her finger, as though it were on a trigger. "It's what you'd do, Lucas. And probably what you'd do, Virgil. If your families were murdered, would the killer survive?"

"That's a hypothetical," Lucas said. "What you're doing isn't hypothetical, it's the real deal."

"You're being evasive," Cooper said. "Answer the question: would the killer survive?"

Virgil looked at Lucas, then shook his head: "Maybe not."

Lucas said, "Maggie, if you kill someone, it will alter your whole life, and maybe ruin it. Do more damage than has already been done. You have a daughter, you need to take care of her, and you need to be with her to do that."

Virgil: "You're talking about a gunfight and I believe you're thinking about it in TV terms — you'll win because you're the good guy. Last year, Lucas and I were in a gunfight that left two FBI agents dead, another one so badly injured that she had to retire, maybe permanently crippled, and Lucas and I all shot up. By one guy. One guy with an AR-15 with a bump stock. All of us, every one of us, were good with guns. Experienced with guns. *Nothing* says the good guy is going to win. You could lose, and then what happens to Chelsea?"

She wouldn't give them a name, wouldn't give them a hint, and when they pressed her, she said, "As far as I'm concerned, all your arguments are bullshit. I'm going to kill him."

When they left the restaurant to walk to their cars, it was snowing again, more than flurries this time. Virgil, who lived in the countryside and so tracked storms, looked up at the iron-gray sky and said, "They're saying we might get an inch, but it'll be gone in a couple of days. Gonna be cold, though."

Cooper said, "We live in Minnesota."

Lucas: "Maggie, I . . ."

She held up a finger: "I've heard it all. You can stop talking about it."

"Goddamnit . . ." They walked along for a half block, and then Virgil asked, "Are you going back to the U?"

She looked at her iPhone, checking the time. "No, actually. George Whitman called me, he's the vice-chairman of the Heart/

Twin Cities board. There's a board meeting this afternoon. The first order of business will be to elect me to the board, as a replacement for Alex. As the second item on the agenda, Noah Heath will present an emergency report on the murder of one employee and the disappearance of another. He plans to say that the disappeared employee did the murder. He apparently doesn't know what you guys dug up."

"Heath murdered them," Virgil said. "We're trying to get the search warrant reinstated. I doubt we'll find much, but it cranks up the pressure on him."

"I believe all of that," Cooper said, hunching her shoulders against the snow and wind. Her cheeks and nose already looked raw with the cold. "The third order of business will be to dismiss Noah from the board. Alang Thao, a board member, will make the motion, there'll be discussion, so Noah has a chance to defend himself. Then Noah will be asked to leave the room, and there'll be a unanimous vote to dismiss him. He'll be called back in, told that he's gone. The last item of business is authorizing a complete audit, and the executive committee — I'll be on that — will be authorized to release the audit to the attorney general."

Lucas: "You're headed for a dogfight, then."

"Noah doesn't know it, but the dogfight is over," Cooper said. "All that's left is to clean up the dog poop."

24

Back in the Tahoe, Lucas said, "I smell smoke. You must be thinking."

"Yeah. Maggie seemed too certain that the killer is going to show up. One way or another, I think she's baited her trap. I don't know with what."

"I agree," Lucas said. "What do we do about that?"

"A little ratiocination," Virgil said.

"Fuckin' novelists and their word-a-day calendars," Lucas grumbled.

As they crossed town, they agreed that the killer, if he went after Cooper, would come at night, but before bedtime, before the lights went out in Cooper's house. They also agreed that they could be wrong — that while Cooper might know who the killer was, she wouldn't wait, but planned to go after him.

"Damnit. We're talking a stakeout," Lucas

said. "If a killer goes after Cooper, we need to see him coming. If she goes to him, we need to track her."

"We need to re-scout her house. See where we can sit where she won't see us, and neither will the killer."

Lucas: "If we have to sit outside, we're gonna get colder than a well-digger's ass. Temp's going down to twenty tonight and there'll be some wind."

"We could go talk to Russo or Durey and let them run the stakeout," Virgil said. "They could be convinced that we're onto something."

"Who could they get who'd be better than us?" Lucas asked.

Virgil said, "Nobody."

"You talk to Frankie, I'll talk to Weather, tell them we'll be out late," Lucas said. "Cooper's not stupid, if she set a trap, he'll be coming, and soon."

Cooper would be occupied by the board meeting, so they went to her house, and rolled through the neighborhood. Crocus Circle was not exactly a circle, but was more of a square with well-rounded corners. They talked about a couple of potential stakeout spots, but because the neighborhood was well-lit and patrolled, and cars weren't left on the street at night, neither place was exactly subtle.

Virgil pointed to a well-preserved clapboard Victorian at the far end of the block, which was surrounded by a raised lawn dotted with oak trees. "That's our best shot. We'd be out of the car."

"We'd need parkas and hunting boots," Lucas said. "Nothing to get behind except trees. Couldn't even move."

"Maybe we could talk to the owner, show him our IDs, explain at least part of the problem to him, and see if he'd let us sit in the window over the porch."

Lucas looked at the blue-and-cream mansion, shrugged, and said, "It's worth a try. If the owner is a friend of Cooper's, though . . . he might squeal on us. But it'd be a hell of a lot warmer in there than out on that lawn."

When they were talking about the Victorian's owner, they kept saying "he," but when they knocked on the door, the owner turned out to be a she, who, after a first look, appeared to be as old as the house.

Martha Muller, widow, looked at their IDs, as they stood on her porch, and said, "Wait here for a moment."

She came back with a pen and a notepad, wrote down their names, and said, "I'll be

432

right back." She shut the door in their faces. They stood around, shuffling their feet, for five or six minutes, talking about nothing, then Virgil's phone rang and the BCA duty officer asked, "Are you talking to a lady named Martha Muller?"

"Yeah, we are," Virgil said.

"I've got her on the other line. She's confirming your identities."

"Well, why don't you do that?" Virgil asked.

He did that, and Muller came to the door and invited them in. "What's up? I know about you two, by the way. You got shot last winter. Does this have something to do with Picky-Arc?"

Lucas and Virgil looked at each other, then Lucas said, "I'm sorry. I don't know what Picky-Arc is."

"Hmm. Okay, it's the St. Paul Police Civilian Internal Affairs Review Board. No, not board, Commission. Picky-Arc. I'm on the commission."

"No. It's not about that." Virgil looked around the living room, into which they'd moved from the doorway. Thoroughgoing Victorian: high white plaster ceilings, walls painted a pale lemon yellow with white baseboards. Landscape paintings and over-stuffed furniture around a coffee table completed the furnishings. The faint odor of burnt toast hovered around them. "It's complicated. Can we sit down?"

They sat and Muller asked, "If it's not about Picky-Arc, it must be about the Sands. You don't think Maggie bumped off her husband and kids, do you?"

Lucas said, "Uh, no. But it's about that case."

"Good. Because she didn't. They were fine parents with nice boys. What a tragedy this is," Muller said. "I will tell you one thing, though. I've heard so much bullshit from cops, I'd really appreciate it if you wouldn't bullshit me."

Virgil asked, "If we tell you a secret thing, could you keep your mouth shut?"

She smiled: "Of course. That's one reason I'm on the Picky-Arc. I do love a good secret."

Lucas turned to Virgil: "We gonna tell her?"

Virgil scratched the side of his nose, judging Muller. "Yes," he said.

They told her what Cooper planned to do, and why she shouldn't. That she might get killed trying, and that even if she didn't, if she didn't do everything perfectly right, she could be charged with murder.

"I don't see how it would be murder . . ."

"If the guy showed up hoping to talk, to explain something, to claim he had nothing to do with the murders, and he is empty-handed and she panics and shoots him . . . that's murder," Virgil said. "I can tell you, she's so angry, and so fixed on revenge, that could happen. She's blinded by it."

Muller leaned back in her chair and said, "I can put you up above the porch. There's a microwave in the kitchen, I've got cocoa and coffee and some burritos in the freezer. Vegetarian, beans and cheese. Or you could bring your own."

"Ms. Muller, that would be great," Virgil said. "Your driveway goes around behind your house. We'd like to park there so if we needed the car in a hurry . . ."

"Feel free," she said. "Would you mind if I spent some time up there watching with you? Be better than another streaming video. Get to watch some actual police work."

"Of the unbelievably boring kind," Lucas said. His phone rang, and he looked at the screen. Durey.

"We got the search warrant reinstated," Durey said. "The feds are heading over to Heath's house right now, if you want to come along."

"He won't be there," Lucas said. "He's at a meeting of the Heart/Twin Cities board, where he'll be fired. He doesn't know that yet. Cooper told us. I don't know where the meeting's at . . ."

"We don't need him. We're going in. Russo's there already, I'm about to leave here. If you want to come . . ."

When she left Virgil and Lucas, Cooper drove to St. Paul, to the University Club, where the Heart/Twin Cities board met in the library. Heath, who didn't yet know what was about to happen, met her with a smile, but the smile faded when she avoided his hug, turned her back, and plunked her shoulder bag on the long table and nodded at George Whitman, the vice-chairman. Four other members were already there, and eight others showed up in the next few minutes.

The board, Cooper thought, was a group so mixed that it had to be done with a fine sense of the twenty-first century appropriate: nine women, ten men, four blacks, two Hmong, an Ethiopian, and eleven standard-issue St. Paul white people. They even had a homeless board member, but he hadn't shown up, and his phone number no longer rang.

When everybody was seated, and the secretary had turned on his tape recorder, Heath called the meeting to order and after the usual routine of approving the minutes of the last meeting, turned to Cooper and said, "I've spoken to several members about electing you to replace Alex, and I think we've agreed, but I'll have to ask you to step outside while we take a formal vote."

Cooper nodded, unsmiling — she'd been on other boards — and stepped outside. As she was closing the door, she heard Heath say, "Do we have a motion . . ."

Two minutes later, Whitman came out and said, "You're on the board. Unanimously. Noah has no idea of what's about to happen, but he really wanted you on the board. Wants that hundred thousand."

"Still planning to ask him to step out while we discuss whether to get rid of him?"

"Alang is so unhappy about what he's heard . . . I think he's just going to pull the trigger. Get ready for it."

Back inside the room, Heath congratulated her on her election to the board, paused, then said, "We have a good deal of tumult in Heart/Twin Cities, as I'm sure you all know. First came the murder of our beloved Alex Sand, with his two young sons. Now we're dealing with the apparent murder of Doreen Pollard. And the disappearance of Bob Dahl, our director. I think the two events are connected. I believe Bob somehow . . . went off the rails. He had a previous relationship with Doreen . . ."

He went on for a while, concluding with, "We carry on. That's what we've always done. I personally have been the victim of a scandalous charge by two police officials implying that I may have some involvement with this disaster. They even obtained a search warrant for my house, which turned up nothing, of course. The warrant was later found to have been illegally, fraudulently obtained, and has been quashed."

He looked around, said, "That is my report. Now, what to do?"

After a moment of silence, Alang Thao, who had been sitting with his hands linked on the tabletop, listening to Heath's summary, raised a hand, and when Heath gestured to him, said, "I move that we dismiss Noah Heath from the board of directors, effective immediately."

Heath half stood and shouted, "What!" and Cooper said, "I second the motion."

Heath turned to her and opened his mouth again, sputtering, but before he could say anything, Cooper looked at the rest of the board and said, "Noah apparently hasn't been watching television, or what's about to be on television. Bob Dahl's body was found buried near a rural boat ramp down by Prairie Island. He appears to have been struck in the head with an edged object of some kind, and, to make sure he died, a plastic sack was then tied around his head. The police have been quite explicit in suggesting the murders were committed by Noah."

She looked up at him now and he screamed, "No! No! I did not do this, I had nothing to do with this, you can't push me out — this is my charity! My charity! I own this charity!"

Whitman said, calmly, "No, you don't, Noah."

Cooper said, "I've been talking rather extensively to law enforcement officers investigating the murders of my husband and two sons. One of them made a recording of Bob Dahl confessing to a series of embezzlements of Heart/Twin Cities funds, by Noah Heath. He said that it has been going on for years . . ."

Whitman said, "I don't think Noah can actually function as chair given the circumstances, so I will call the question on Al-ang's motion that we dismiss Noah as a member of this board . . .”

“That’s illegal,” Heath shouted, saliva flying down the table. “You don’t have the gavel, I’ve got the gavel . . .”

Whitman said, “All those in favor of dismissing Noah, raise your hands?”

All the hands went up.

Noah shouted, “No! This is illegal! I’ll have my lawyers on you, you can’t do this!”

Cooper was closest to him, and the accumulating anger in her gut pushed her to her feet and she shouted, “You’re a goddamned murderer, Noah. The police know it, and I know it. Bob Dahl was cooperating with Davenport and Flowers and he was going to send you to prison . . .”

Heath snapped.

He launched himself across the table at Cooper, reaching for her throat with his hands. The edge of the table caught him at the thighs, and he went sprawling across it as she lurched away, but then he slid sideways around the corner of the table and knocked water glasses off the table as the male board members tried to get to him.

Cooper backed into one of the men as she tried to get away from Heath, and bounced off him back toward Heath and he again reached for her neck and she went down backwards with Heath on top of her, a tumbling water glass between them, and the back of her head hit the floor, hard, the glass shattered on her face as Heath's body landed on top of her, and then the men had Heath and pulled him away and one of the women board members screamed, "I'm calling 9-1-1 . . ."

The men wrestled the still swinging Heath out of the library room as one of the women knelt next to Cooper and said, "Your face is cut, you're bleeding . . ." and in the other room a man had his arm around Heath's neck and was chanting, "Calm down, calm down, Noah, stop this . . ."

The woman looking at Cooper's face said, "Stay down, you're hurt, we need to call an ambulance . . ."

"Is my face . . ." She touched her face with a hand, and pulled it away to look at it; her hand was covered with blood.

"It'll be okay," the woman said, in a way that made Cooper understand that it wouldn't be okay.

Outside the library, Heath had gone slack, and when released, looked around, clutched his chest and staggered to a couch and fell on it. He cried out, "Not this, not this . . . Oh, my Lord . . ."

Inside the library, a groggy Cooper was half sitting, hand on her bleeding cheek, and she said, "Purse, give me my bag . . ."

"You need to lic back down . . ."

"Give me my bag . . ."

One of the women handed her the shoulder bag, and she dug out her purse, took out a compact, opened it and looked at her cheek and said, "Oh, Jesus . . ." She had two bloody slashes below her eye on her right cheek. One of the cuts was a full three inches long, and deep, the blood flowing freely. The other was shorter, at an angle to the first, and also bleeding heavily.

She said, "Phone, where's my phone . . ."

The woman found Cooper's phone in the shoulder bag and she thumbed through her contact list and found Lucas's number and called it. Lucas picked up and she said, her voice now as calm as she could manage: "I was attacked by Noah Heath. My face was cut bad, and Ann said your wife is the best plastic surgeon in the Twin Cities . . . I need her . . ."

Lucas: "Where are you? Can you drive?"

"University Club in St. Paul. I have people here . . . they've called an ambulance."

"I'll call Weather. I'll call you back in one minute."

The women around her said, "Maggie, lie down . . . lie down."

She did, clutching her phone. A headache

was clawing at her temples from the impact with the floor. A minute later, Lucas called back: "Go to Regions. Weather will meet you at the emergency room."

"I'll go . . ." she said.

Police arrived.

They took a look at Cooper, listened to the men, and to Heath, who was apologizing, the words tumbling out in an unending cascade, good as a confession. They arrested him, and when the ambulance arrived, led the paramedics into the library past a gathering audience. The paramedics put a brace on Cooper's neck when she told them about the head pain, loaded her on a gurney, and took her out to the ambulance.

Ten minutes later, she said, "Hello," to Weather, who looked at her and said, "Yeah. We can fix that. We're going to take some pictures of your neck and head, first, to make sure we don't have anything else to deal with."

"That sounds . . . okay," Cooper said.

Virgil and Lucas were standing in Heath's front hallway when Cooper called. Virgil had listened to Lucas talking to Cooper and Weather, and when Lucas had finished, he asked, "What the hell happened?"

"Heath attacked her during the board

meeting. She couldn't give me details, except that she got cut bad. We're five minutes from the University Club . . ."

The cops were still talking to witnesses when Lucas and Virgil got to the club, but Cooper was gone. There were three patrol cars in the driveway, and as they parked in the street, they saw Heath being escorted to one of the cars by a cop, his hands cuffed behind him. He was talking rapidly to the cop, who seemed to be paying no attention.

Lucas and Virgil showed their IDs to the sergeant who was managing the scene and warned him that the attack was part of a much larger and complicated situation.

"I already got that from these board members," the sergeant said. "They think this Heath guy killed a couple people."

"So do we," Virgil said. "You know about that body dug up this morning . . . that's the victim."

"Hoo, boy." The sergeant looked back at the crowd of board members. "I guess we nail down everything."

Virgil and Lucas talked to the board members about the fight, got Technicolor descriptions, then Virgil called Durey and Lucas called Russo, to fill them in. Russo said he'd come to the club. Virgil called Ann

Melton. Melton was in Minneapolis, said that she'd immediately go to Regions Hospital, and that Chelsea was with Fatima, the child-care helper.

Lucas and Virgil went to Regions. They were both familiar with the hospital, and a nurse told them that Cooper had been through imaging and was being taken to surgery.

"Weather Karkinnen is my wife," Lucas told the nurse. "If she's not scrubbed up yet . . ."

"I think she's scrubbing now," the nurse said. "I can take you down there."

Weather was standing over the scrub sink with another doc, working on her fingernails, turned and saw him coming.

"You had a look yet?" he asked.

"Yes. Two cuts. They're deep, but clean. I'm told they were made by the edge of a broken water glass. I didn't see any debris. We really haven't done any exploration yet."

"She's an actress, or was . . ."

"So you said. If she's patient with the healing, she won't have any scars that can't be hidden by a dab of makeup. The docs here took some pictures, she says she's got a headache but they didn't see any neck or skull problems, no whiplash, no displacement in her spine. You can probably see her in the morning."

"Be careful with her . . ." Weather rolled her eyes, and Lucas said, "Okay, okay. I'll go away now."

"Do that."

Back in the car, Virgil said, "This has officially gotten weird. Still want to do the stakeout?"

"Sure. I don't think this will make TV until the ten o'clock or tomorrow . . . so how's the killer going to know?"

Durey called: "Don't bother to come back. We're down to picking up hair on the staircase."

"What?"

"The doc down at the Mayo says the impact wound on Hinton was caused by a scuffing blow to his forehead that could have been caused by a fall. Since Heath's wife fell down the stairs . . ."

"All right. Good luck with the hair," Lucas said. He rang off and said to Virgil, "Why don't we pick up something to eat and head over to Martha Muller's?"

With sundown coming shortly after six o'clock in the evening, they rolled down Muller's driveway at six, went through the back door, put a couple of chicken wraps from Whole Foods in the refrigerator, along

446

with Diet Cokes for Lucas and cans of coffee for Virgil.

Virgil poured one of the cans into an oversized cup and Muller ran it through the microwave. That done, they all went upstairs to a darkened room with a window overlooking the street.

"Best stakeout ever," Virgil said. They moved chairs to a spot where they could all see the front of Cooper's house, and down the street that curved around from hers. They couldn't see anyone coming in from the other side, but from that side, a stalker would have to go through five backyards, and from their side, he'd only have to go through one before he got to Cooper's. And if he came up the bluff, they'd have a front-row seat.

They told Muller what had happened with Cooper, and she was astonished. She got on her phone, made a call, and asked whoever she called what had happened at the University Club.

She listened for a while, asked a couple of questions, hung up and said, "They say Heath's been crying like a baby. Said he essentially admitted everything to the responders, but said she deliberately provoked him by accusing him of being a murderer, in front of his friends. He called a lawyer, but the man I spoke to doesn't know if the lawyer has shown up yet."

Daisy Jones called Virgil.

"No comment, Daisy. That's the best I can do," Virgil said, without bothering to say hello.

"You can't 'no comment' me," Jones said. "Not after you blew me off this morning. Margaret Cooper told the Heart/Twin Cities board this afternoon that you believe Noah Heath killed Bob Dahl and Doreen Pollard, and that's what touched him off."

"What? What the hell are you talking about?" Virgil asked.

"You're a cop and you don't know? Noah Heath tried to strangle Margaret Cooper at a Heart/Twin Cities board meeting at the University Club, and she's at Regions with a concussion and I guess, you know, whatever happens when you're almost strangled. And her face got cut up bad."

"Really? Holy shit. When's this going up?" Virgil asked.

"Ten o'clock."

"That's really something, Daisy. I've got no comment until I find out what's going on. Thanks for letting us know." He punched her off and ignored her call-back.

Lucas: "Somebody called her. She's always had good contacts in St. Paul."

■ ■ ■ ■

A while later, Weather called Lucas. "Okay. She's done, she's still asleep. I'll talk to her when she wakes up — don't call her until tomorrow."

"I'll go see her in the morning," Lucas said. "How's she gonna look?"

"She'll have two scars that'll look like thin white hairs on her cheek. Even without makeup, you'd have to get six inches from her to see them. With makeup . . . very light makeup . . . they'll be invisible."

"You're good," Virgil called.

"Indeed," said Weather. "You guys are indirectly responsible for this. Who should I send the bill to?"

Melton called. "I'm sitting here at Regions. She's asleep. Weather's still around. Maggie called me before the board meeting and told me about your lunch. I just hope our suspect doesn't show up. Maybe you ought to drive over and hide in the house. Then you could shoot him."

Lucas said nothing for a moment, then, "If I did that, how would I get in?"

"If you go to the basketball net, the pole that holds it up? It's on a concrete pad. At the back right corner of the pad, as you look at it, if you poke around you'll find a thing that looks like a rock. It isn't. It's made out of plastic and there's a key inside. It fits all the doors. If you go in and turn on the lights, he'll think she's home."

"What about the baby?'

"Fatima and Chelsea are at my place. I told Fatima a little about what was happening . . . and she's okay with moving over to Edina."

"I'll think about it," Lucas said. "You take care of yourself. Jesus. Heath tried to strangle her. And he cut her."

"He is crazy. A crazy man," Melton said. "As I understand it, if the board members hadn't dragged him away, she'd be dead."

There was still light in the sky when Virgil and Lucas drove out of Muller's driveway, then drove a quick loop around the neighborhood to confuse a watcher, if there was one, then went back and stopped in front of Cooper's house.

Virgil got out and walked through the opening in the hedge to the basketball net and found the key to the house. He continued to the back door, let himself in, and started turning on lights. When the lights came on, Lucas drove around the block

450

again and back into Muller's driveway. He went in the back door and up to the stakeout room with Muller.

"That boy's going to search her house, isn't he?" Muller said. "Just to see if anyone missed anything."

"Of course not," Lucas said. "I think your dipsy-do, or whatever you call it . . ."

"Picky-Arc . . ."

". . . has made you a little paranoid about cops."

"No, it's made me *really* paranoid about cops. I do admire their ability to lie with an absolutely straight face, even in court, and even when everybody knows they're lying," Muller said, smiling at Lucas.

"It is part of the skill set," Lucas admitted. "Wouldn't be so necessary if we weren't up to our asses in nitpicking lawyers."

"You may be right," Muller said. "I used to be one of those, by the way. A nitpicking lawyer."

While waiting for the killer to show up, Virgil ate one of the chicken wraps and probed gently around the house, looking for cameras, among other things, but not seeing any. He eventually made his way up the stairs, wandered around the home office without touching anything, and poked his

451

head into the boys' rooms. He didn't know which was which, since they were mostly identical in furnishings, but both had framed photos on the walls, of the boys doing sports.

In their first interview with Cooper, she'd mentioned that Alex hadn't been much of an athlete, but enjoyed the sports that he did play, especially basketball, and he admired athletes. He had season tickets to the Vikings and Wild. He was also a decent golfer, she said, but he was more of a team-sports enthusiast.

She'd said, with a smile, that he was worried that his nonathletic genes would doom the kids to a life of spectating. Or worse, that they'd follow in his golfing footsteps.

"Fortunately, they got my genes. They were going to be good at basketball. And probably golf, as far as that goes. I wouldn't let them play football; your life becomes somewhat limited with repeated head trauma."

Virgil was back downstairs, in the kitchen, waiting for Lucas to call, or for a noise at the back door, when he had a thought. He went back upstairs, looked at the photos, then pulled his shirt sleeve over his hand so he could open closets without leaving fingerprints. In one of the boys' closets, he found a gym bag. Then he sat down on a bed and called Lucas.

"You got something?"

"Maybe, but not somebody breaking in," Virgil said.

"Then what?"

"Remember that Russo and Durey were planning to check gyms where the boys might have been taking basketball lessons?"

"And swimming. Yeah. They came up dry. Read the reports . . ."

"I have," Virgil said. "I'm up in one of the boys' rooms. There are photographs of the boys playing basketball, but one of their rooms has a picture of the two of them facing off, wearing helmets and boxing gloves. It looks like they're in a boxing gym. I can see a heavy bag in the background. Then I looked in a closet, and I found a gym bag with a tee-shirt, shorts, a boxing helmet, mouth guard, and a cup."

"Maggie didn't say anything at all about a boxing gym," Lucas said.

"Which you think she might have, since these pictures are so recent," Virgil said.

"Sonofagun."

"Yes."

"We'll get on that tomorrow," Lucas said. "We gotta stay here, though, until midnight,

453

anyway. You can start turning off the lights at ten."

"I'll poke around a little and see if I can find out which gym, and who might work there."

"Do that. Ms. Muller thought you might be searching the place, but I told her that was ridiculous, and man, if you're tempted to, just don't do it. *Just don't do it.* After the fiasco with the search warrant, we've got to play this absolutely straight."

"She's sitting right next to you."

"Yes. But take care: this guy is a gunslinger and I don't want my partner re-shot," Lucas said.

Lucas rang off and Muller, sipping at a cup of tea, said, "Yes, I am sitting right next to you."

Lucas hadn't been using the speaker on the phone. Muller was either clairvoyant, he decided, or had exceptionally good hearing.

Nobody showed up. Virgil turned off the lights at ten o'clock, and at midnight locked the door and Lucas picked him up.

"I got the gym," Virgil said. "The Silver Star over on West Seventh."

"Tomorrow morning, we'll be on it like a hot sweat," Lucas said. "It's like Sherlock

454

Holmes: Cooper is the dog who didn't bark. This is something."

They would have had Hess that night except for the intervention of a woman named Megan Ryan.

Hess had worked out a plan: he'd go to the Silver Star but instead of hanging around as he usually did, he'd leave early and run straight to Cooper's house. This time, he'd go in: he'd climb the bluff, go around to the back door, kick it if he had to. He'd try to take her alive, if he could, to find out where she'd put the flash drives; then he'd kill her. He didn't need the computers, but he had to have the drives.

He had the gun in the car. He'd gotten rid of the Covid mask and replaced it with a ski mask. Had to be done.

If he could move fast enough, he'd go back to the gym and hang out until the last of the boys were gone. Nobody tracked him there, but he'd make a point of staying late, maybe going over to the adult side to work out with the kettle bells. The place closed at ten, and if he was there to close it, it'd be all the alibi he'd need.

As a gig worker, Hess had three jobs. The first was in the morning with the pre-work crew; his second job caught the lunch crowd. He went home at midafternoon, ate, took a nap, and a little before six o'clock, headed for the Silver Star.

He'd noticed driving home that he was low on gas, so on the way out to the Silver Star, he pulled into a BP gas station. He paid with a credit card at the pump, pumped ten gallons, got back in his car and pulled away from the pump just as Megan Ryan in her Jeep cut across the parking lot, moving fast, toward the BP convenience store.

Hess hit her. Nothing more than a fender bender, his left front fender with the left rear fender on her Jeep, but Ryan tumbled out of her vehicle as though she'd been hit by a meteor and began screaming at him. "I love my Jeep! I do! I've had my Jeep for six years, and now you've wrecked it . . ."

Hess kept backing away from her. He would have smacked her in the face if there hadn't been so many witnesses around, but there were a lot of witnesses, and most of them were on his side, because of the way she'd rocketed into the BP lot.

She was talking about her back hurting and one of the guys at another pump said, "I'd call the cops if I were you. Make sure they know what happened."

With Ryan still screaming at him, he got a piece of paper and a pen from his car and wrote down the license plates of everyone at the pumps, and then called the cops.

Fifteen minutes later, they were telling their stories to the police. The guy who suggested that he call the cops testified that Ryan had entered the parking lot at high speed and was at fault. She started to cry, and the cops took Hess aside and said, "Listen, this is all on private property and she doesn't seem hurt and you say you're not, so it's pretty much up to your insurance companies . . ."

Both cars were drivable, but the whole situation ate up an hour. He was late to the job, angry about his car, sapped by the screaming, and at the end of the training session, he went home and went to bed.

He'd worked too long, spent too much emotional energy in the arguments with Ryan, to murder anyone.

Tomorrow.

25

Lucas wanted to drive, so the next morning he backed out of his garage and Virgil parked his Tahoe inside, out of the snow.

The snow wasn't a big deal, more like a heavy flurry, but the weather had turned colder. Before getting into Lucas's Cayenne, Virgil unzipped his equipment bag and took out the lighter of his two Patagonia parkas, and cross-country ski gloves, and pulled them on.

Lucas, in the Cayenne, had dressed for the cold. "Maybe this'll be like an old-timey winter," Lucas said, as Virgil got in the passenger seat.

"You mean like when the chicken house got buried by fifteen-foot drifts, your best friend got his tongue stuck to the school flagpole, and children got lost and froze to death after stepping off the school bus and they couldn't see the house thirty feet away?"

"No, I mean like between 1982 and 1990. Six of those years had at least one day when it was colder than minus 30 in Minneapolis, and between 1980 and 2000, every year had at least one day colder than minus 24," Lucas said.

"Ooo, you're the weather boy, now."

"No, I've been a couch potato since we got shot, and you gotta do something on the couch," Lucas said. "I spent some time looking up the weather."

"I didn't mind the cold so much," Virgil said, after a while as he looked at the newly white landscape. "That's why we got parkas and mittens. What I didn't like was working out on the prairie, the fucking ground blizzards. You could look straight up and see blue sky and little puffy clouds, but from ground level to six feet up, you could see exactly jack shit. You'd wind up plastered with ice crystals and dirt."

"That's bad," Lucas agreed. "I've been in a couple, out in the Red River Valley. I've been here through enough winters that October makes me think of Key West."

They'd decided to stop and see Cooper, who was still at Regions Hospital. Lucas had talked to Weather, who was unconcerned about the repairs to Cooper's face: she'd be fine, Weather said. The cuts had been deep but clean and hadn't damaged any critical nerves and only one serious blood vessel, which she'd repaired.

Virgil had spoken to Durey that morning, who told him that the renewed search of Heath's house had turned up nothing on the murders of either Hinton or Pollard. The examination of both his office and home computers was ongoing.

"Some emails were recently erased, and they might be able to recover those, but that's uncertain. Thieves don't usually go out of their way to document the thefts," Virgil said. "If we can't get him to say something, to step on his dick, we could have a problem getting him to trial."

"Got him for the attack on Maggie," Lucas said.

"Yeah, but . . . his lawyers are already putting up the 'fighting words' defense. They claim that Cooper unreasonably provoked him, knowing that he was already under severe stress. They say he didn't hurt her, the cuts on her face were accidental, caused by a breaking water glass which, they say, Maggie pulled down on top of herself. So . . ."

"Yeah."

The snow was coming down a bit harder when Lucas and Virgil got to the hospital.

They parked, went inside, tracked down Cooper's room, and found her sitting up in bed with Melton in a visitor's chair, rocking Chelsea. When they saw Lucas and Virgil come in, Melton stood up, picked up a towel, tossed it over Virgil's shoulder, and handed him the baby. "She needs to be burped."

Virgil took the baby and began patting her on the back as Lucas moved over to Cooper's bed and said, "Weather says your face will be fine."

"I know. We talked last night and she called me already this morning. I'm still not . . ." She reached up and touched the bandages covering her cheek, and her eyes seemed to kick back in their sockets, crazy eyes, and they trembled there and quickly came down and refocused. "I'm not sure about it. I once cut my wrist with a piece of broken glass, way back when I was a kid, and I still can see a scar."

"Probably not fixed by the best plastic surgeon in the business," Lucas said. "I'm . . . uh, let me show you something."

He took off his parka, a sweater, and his button-front shirt. He was wearing a tee-shirt under all that, and he pulled down the neckline so she could see the scar where the surgeons had gone in to fix his broken arm.

461

"That was done by an orthopedic surgeon. They use suture material that Weather calls 'ropes.' Still, my scar is this little white line." He pulled the neck of the shirt back up. "To find your scars, a person would have to use a microscope."

"That makes me happier, I guess," Cooper said. "I appreciate the striptease."

"He used to be one of those groundhog guys," Virgil said.

"Chipmunks," Melton said.

"Yeah, that's it."

The baby burped and Melton said, "There we go," and the faint odor of vomit dispersed around Virgil. And, she asked, "What are you guys doing today? Any leads?"

"After we talked to you last night, we staked out Maggie's house, and nothing happened, except I froze my feet," Lucas said.

Cooper: "Maybe he won't come at all."

"I think he will," Lucas said. "You deliberately baited the trap, and when he thinks it over, he'll know that he has to take another shot at you."

"I hope," Cooper said. "I'm not going to let you guys back in my house. If you wait outside, I think there's a good chance he'll see you. If he sees you first, he'll never come back."

"Tell us who he is," Virgil said.

"Nope."

"Heath was released last night," Virgil said.

"That sonofabitch," Cooper snarled. "I have to settle with him, too. I just . . ." She touched her face, and the crazy eyes were back. She refocused and said, "Stay away from my house."

"Is she nuts?" Virgil asked.

"The thought had crossed my mind," Lucas said, as he turned onto West Seventh Street. "She seemed to go back and forth between focus and out-of-focus. Might be a concussion, I guess. But . . . I dunno."

They spotted the Silver Star and found a parking place. The gym was in a redbrick building with inset panels of glass blocks that would bring in exterior light, but without allowing passersby to actually see inside.

The front door was windowless, with a full-length steel plate; an unlighted sign in the shape of a silver star hung above the door, and over the sidewalk.

They pushed through the door and walked down a short hallway into a room the size of a basketball court, without the finish of a basketball court: concrete floor, exposed beams, bright white fluorescent lights overhead. Two men were working out in a full-sized elevated boxing ring; a woman was punching at a swinging target in a second ring. There were racks for weights, several speed bags, a line of black heavy bags, hanging like oversized blood sausages, with two more men and a woman punching at them. The place smelled of sweat and something else, something medicinal, that wasn't alcohol; more like all-purpose cleaner.

The back wall showed two doors, one with a sign that said "Men," the other, "Ladies," apparently going to locker rooms.

To the left was a desk and a man sat behind it paging through a copy of *Guitarist* magazine; he had the battered face of somebody who'd lost a lot of fights, but was wearing a pink golf shirt and a turquoise pinky ring. He looked up when they came in, put the magazine aside, and said, "Can I help you, officers?"

Made Virgil smile. "Yes. We'd like to ask you about your employees."

Lucas: "Specifically, about the coaches in the children's evening program."

"Why?"

"That would be between us and them," Lucas said.

"Well, then, I got just the guy for you," the man said. His shirt had a machine embroidered tag that said "Rudy" in sky-blue script. He reached under the desk and came up with a handheld microphone and said, "Wiz, please come to the front desk."

And to Lucas and Virgil, "I think he's back in the Ladies . . ."

A moment later, a chunky man came through the door that said "Ladies" with a wet mop. He leaned the mop against the side of the door and walked over to the desk. Like the desk man, he was wearing a pink golf shirt, and also shorts and boxing shoes. To Rudy he said, "We got cops?"

"We got cops," Rudy said. "They want to talk about the kids' program."

"What do you want to know?" His golf shirt had a blue tag that said "The Wiz."

"Step over in the corner where we can talk privately," Virgil said. As they walked over, Lucas asked, "What's your real name?"

"Buddy Corbin."

"Buddy's a nickname?" Virgil asked.

"Nope. The Wiz is a nickname, Buddy is the name on my birth certificate. It's actually Buddy Jr. My old man was named Buddy, too."

As they got to the corner, a tall woman in a sleeveless tee-shirt, perhaps to show off her full-sleeve tats and biceps muscle, walked over to a rack of speed bags. She began hitting one of them, working into a rhythm that Virgil recognized as the bass line in Queen's "Another One Bites the Dust."

Lucas said to Corbin, "We have a couple of delicate questions for you. We don't want you repeating them. If you do, we'll make life difficult for you, because you could be warning off a criminal. A serious criminal. We're not trying to be mean, we're trying to be informational."

"Kind of a mean way of doing it," Buddy said. "What's going on?"

"Who-all works with the kids in the boxing program?" Virgil asked. "Specifically, the ten-to-twelve group?"

"Well, there are four of us," Buddy said. "There's me, there's Roger Smith, there's Don Hess, and Carol-Ann Lee."

"We're interested in a white man, six feet or so. Not too heavy."

Corbin tilted his head, and said, "Don Hess. What'd he do?"

"We're not sure he did anything," Lucas said. "This is all preliminary. Why isn't it Roger Smith?"

"You said white. Roger isn't, he's black. He's six-four, and big. Don looks more like a high school basketball player." Pause. "What do you think he did?"

466

"Have you ever noticed an . . . interest in the boys?"

Corbin took a step back, looked around as if they might have been overheard, stopping to check the woman on the speed bag: "Oh, Jesus, no. We wouldn't, we couldn't . . . if anybody said something like that, we'd get our asses sued off. Jesus."

Virgil: "So Mr. Hess is all right?"

Another pause, and then Corbin said, "I gotta think so."

"That's not exactly a ringing endorsement," Lucas said.

Corbin looked toward the front desk; the desk man was watching them. He shrugged and said, "I believe he's okay, I believe he's fine. That's all I got to say about that."

"What time are the boys' classes?" Lucas asked.

"They start at six-thirty, that's when the kids arrive, the class starts ten or fifteen minutes later, goes on to eight o'clock. They're out on the street by eight-fifteen or eight-thirty at the latest. Their folks pick them up."

He continued to edge away. Lucas said, "Don't talk to anyone about us. Don't talk to Rudy. If you do, and if Hess turns out to be a pederast, you'll be in court with him. We'll put you in prison until you're a very old man."

"I won't talk to nobody," Corbin said. "But I gotta say something to the boss," and his eyes clicked toward the desk.

"Tell him what I just told you — that if you talk, you go to prison," Lucas said. "And if we trace the talk back to him, he goes with you. Best for everybody if you keep your mouth shut. Tell him that."

Corbin nodded. "Okay. Okay. I can do that."

They let him go. Virgil said to Lucas, "Don Hess."

"Could be."

Virgil glanced toward the woman on the speed bag, who'd lost her rhythm and was looking at them. She mouthed, silently, "Outside," pulled off one of her gloves, glanced toward the desk, where Corbin was talking to the desk man, held up five fingers, then did it again, and mouthed, "Ten minutes."

Virgil nodded and he and Lucas started toward the door.

They didn't have to wait ten minutes, but did have to wait eight until the woman appeared at the front door and looked both ways. Lucas opened the door of the Cayenne, so she'd see it up the street. She hur-

468

ried toward them, wearing a puffy jacket and carrying a duffel, and he popped the door to the back seat to let her in.

She settled in, said, "Hi, I'm Georgia Hooper," and, "I'm sorry, I don't want the guys to see me talking to you. I heard what you and The Wiz were talking about."

"Why do they call him The Wiz?" Virgil asked. "Like the Wizard of Oz?"

She laughed, and said, "No, that's not what I heard. What I heard is that there's only one urinal in the men's room and when he has to go, he has to go, so he heads out back by the dumpster and takes a whiz. They called him 'the whiz' for a while and then it got changed to 'The Wiz' and he kinda . . . stuck with it."

"Nice story," Virgil said. "So, what's up?"

"It's about Don Hess. You were asking about him around boys. I got a boy in middle school and I wouldn't let him alone around Don. There's something about him."

"Just a feeling?" Lucas asked, looking at her in the rearview mirror.

"You know . . . do you have a pencil and a notebook?"

Virgil: "Yes."

"Write this down. There was this boy named Kerry Blackburn . . ." She spelled both the first and last names. "He was with

469

the older boys when I'd see him, the sixteen-to-seventeen group. I'd see Don around him, and there was something between them. Kerry kinda seemed willing to hang out and box, but later on he kinda shied away from Don in a funny way. I thought something might have happened . . . But what do I know?"

"You might know something useful. How old is Kerry now?" Lucas asked.

"Mmm, he must be twenty? He stopped coming to fight club — that's what we call the Silver Star, among us — a couple of years ago. He got accepted to college over in River Falls. Somebody told me he lives over there now, maybe in a dormitory."

"Okay. Will Hess be working tonight?" Virgil asked.

"He works every night but Friday, when it's a girls' class."

"He doesn't work with women? How about The Wiz?"

She shook her head: "The girls work with a woman named Cheryl. I'm a bartender, I work evenings so I don't know her much. I think . . . Cheryl Payton?"

She had nothing else. They thanked her and asked her not to discuss their conversation with anyone else. She said she wouldn't. "I'd like to know if anything happens,

470

though."

"We'll call you, if we can — if anything works out," Virgil said.

She checked the street, hopped out of the car and went on her way, her duffel bag on her shoulder.

Virgil got on his phone, with Lucas watching, to work the phones at the University of Wisconsin-River Falls. The university was a few miles east of the Minnesota border and was popular with Twin Cities residents because of tuition reciprocity agreements between the two states.

Virgil identified himself as a member of Minnesota's BCA, which got him further into the bureaucracy. After assuring several bureaucrats that Kerry Blackburn was not suspected of any crime, he was told that Blackburn was enrolled in Data Science and Predictive Analysis. He was currently living at the George R. Field South Fork Suites residence hall.

Lucas said, "Tsk. They have suites now. I had a top bunk bed above a guy who ate nothing but cheese."

"You'll have to tell me about that some other time, like when we're old," Virgil said. "River Falls is a half hour from here. Crank up this piece of shit and let's go."

They went.

Rather than trying to locate Blackburn on campus, they took a shot at finding him at the residence hall, reasoning that even if he wasn't there, somebody else who lived in the suite might know where he'd be.

The dorm was a modern four-story reddish brick apartment building with a massive parking lot across the street. Lucas put a U.S. Marshal's card on the dashboard, and they crossed the street, encountered more bureaucrats, or perhaps bureaucrats-in-training, and eventually made their way to Blackburn's co-ed suite.

They knocked, and the door was opened by a young woman who didn't want to tell them that Blackburn was asleep in his room, but eventually did.

"Is he in trouble?" she asked, looking troubled.

"No. Not at all. Not in any way. He may have some information we need, and he may not even know he has it." Virgil put his hand over his heart. "I swear to God."

She went to get Blackburn, while Lucas and Virgil stood in the doorway, looking around. Blackburn came out a minute later, a slender, thin-faced man with brown bed hair sticking out in all directions. He wore narrow blue-rimmed glasses, a tee-shirt, and sweatpants. He was barefoot, and did not look like a boxer, although his nose may have been broken sometime in the past. The woman tagged along behind him, still looking troubled.

Blackburn: "Have I done something?"

"Not as far as we know," Virgil said. "But we think you might have some information that we need. It's sort of secret, so . . . could you take a walk?"

Blackburn looked at the woman, shrugged, and said, "Sure, I guess. Let me put some shoes on and get my coat."

Outside, they took a sidewalk that stretched along the front of a couple of block-long residence halls.

Lucas: "We are inquiring about a man that you know in the Twin Cities. At the Silver Star. Do you remember Don Hess?"

Blackburn stopped walking and said, "Oh . . . shit."

"So you know him," Virgil said.

"Yeah, I know him," Blackburn said.

"Did he make a sexual pass at you, while you were working out at the Silver Star?"

"Has he done something?"

"We don't know, but we think it's a pos-

473

sibility. And we think it might be bad."

"Messing with kids?"

"Did he mess with you?"

"No, but he was going that way," Black-burn said. "He was pushing me. I was embarrassed, I didn't want to have anything to do with it. With him. I mean, we were friendly when I first started working out. Then it got weird."

"How weird?"

"You know, he'd touch me, pat me, tell me I was doing good. I knew I wasn't doing *that* good. I was basically there because my father wanted me to go."

"You didn't like it. The boxing," Virgil said.

"Actually, after a while, I did like it," Blackburn said. "I wasn't bad at it, either, I have fast hands. I didn't like getting hit in the face, though, even with the marshmal-lows we were wearing. You know, you read the Internet, and it says you'll wind up mentally impaired. Or get a detached retina. That worried me. I really like working on the speed bags, that's almost like a video game, but feels more real."

"How old were you when he was trying to make friends?" Lucas asked.

"I started there when I was sixteen, left at the end of the summer when I came here. I kinda blew him off maybe when I was seventeen."

"Did he have anything to do with younger kids?"

"I wasn't in a younger kids' class. So I don't know," Blackburn said. "But Don was weird. Is weird, I guess, or you wouldn't be here. Another thing. He had this green duffel bag, pretty big one, you know? One day I was in the locker room and Don was taking a shower . . ."

"He took showers with you?"

"Yeah, but you know, nothing happened. Too many people around, maybe. I wouldn't have wanted to be in there with him, alone," Blackburn said. "Anyway, I got out of the shower first and my bag was near his, sitting on a bench facing the lockers, and I saw this . . . sparkle. This reflection. Nobody was around so I looked, and he had a camera in there. It was pointed inside the bag, not out of it, so . . . I don't know if he was taking pictures."

"You know about cameras?" Virgil asked.

"Not that much, but this wasn't a little snapshot thing," Blackburn said. "Wasn't a big huge one, either. Middle-sized. We had a guy there who sometimes made videos of our boxing matches, so we could see ourselves, what we were doing wrong. It was

475

that kind of camera. The kind that can take videos along with snapshots."

Lucas rubbed his face: "Ah, boy."

"I didn't take any more showers after that," Blackburn said. "Are you going to arrest him?"

"We can't talk about it, much," Lucas said. "You don't know of any other relationships he had with the boys in the boxing classes?"

"No, I tried to stay away from him," Blackburn said. "I didn't know of anything. Maybe . . . I didn't want to know. I didn't want to wind up telling my dad that he put me in a class with a pederast. So I stayed to myself. Did the boxing and got out."

They told him not to talk about the interview "because it's a serious ongoing investigation and we don't want word leaking out."

"I won't tell a soul," he said. "It's embarrassing. I wouldn't want the guys in the suite to know."

In the car, Virgil made some notes about the interview, with the time and date, and then asked, "What do we do with Hess? Stake him out?"

Lucas nodded, started the car. "Maggie thinks he'll come after her. If we get a look

476

at him, then tag him to her house . . . he has to make a move before we grab him."

"He might still have that gun," Virgil said.

"That one, or another one, he wouldn't be going in there with a hammer, like Heath."

"What are we going to do about Heath?"

"Maybe nothing? Let the other guys do something with him."

26

Something had broken in Margaret Cooper.

The break hadn't come at the moment Heath attacked her, but sometime afterward, perhaps during the ambulance ride to Regions Hospital, or the wait in X-ray.

The ball of anger was still there, in her gut, but not so tightly wound: the anger was confused, diffused. She still saw her son's blue eyeball on the floor next to his shattered head, now pressed against her own face as she imagined it to be — the bandages covered her cheek, and she hadn't yet seen the wound — mutilated by the broken glass.

Weather had told her she could fix the face, and she apparently had tried: the doctors all seemed pleased by the result, which Cooper had not yet seen, but only imagined. But doctors were also satisfied if a cancer patient got an extra meaningless two weeks of semi-life before dying, so they were not to be trusted, were not even entirely relevant.

She'd been told that she could check out of the hospital in the morning; Melton was there with Chelsea, and Cooper tried to be interested in them and what Melton had to say, but she kept drifting away, back to the eyeball and the ruined face.

She'd asked Melton, "How ugly is it?"

Melton, trying to be cheerful: "It's not ugly. At all. I'm told that when you're healed, you won't even need makeup, and since you use makeup anyway, you're just fine. These are like shaving cuts. They're not bad."

Cooper had turned her face away: she didn't believe it. Shaving cuts? No.

And she worried: Am I too self-centered? Why am I thinking about cuts on my cheek, when my husband and sons are dead?

She thought about Hess and Heath, arrogant, vicious killers. In what seemed to her to be the cold honesty of her post-attack introspection, she distilled what legal knowledge she'd gotten from Alex, in his role as a judge in criminal cases, and she asked herself, if arrested, would Hess and Heath be convicted of murder, given what was known about them?

She didn't think so. They could get Hess,

479

if they could find a reason to get the police inside his house. But how could they do that? What if he found the hidden computers and flash drives before then? The downside possibilities piled up in her mind; the upside possibilities didn't even occur to her.

The world was a bleak, gray place without hope.

Virgil and Lucas had trooped in, a dusting of snow on their shoulders, and Davenport had shown her his shoulder scar, which in fact was quite visible. She tried to be appreciative, but she could feel her mind drifting again. She didn't want them around, any of them, Lucas, Virgil, Melton, Chelsea.

Soon enough, they left, and she fell back on her pillow, not to sleep, or to relax, but to recall.

The nurses told her she should be on her way home by ten o'clock, but she wasn't. Weather showed up at eleven o'clock, gave her a list of instructions and got her phone number, so her assistant could text the same instructions to her phone.

"You were very lucky, if this had to happen at all," Weather said. "The cuts were clean, there was a gland that I was worried about, but the cuts didn't reach it. You might have a bit of numbness for a while, but that will go away. You didn't lose any major facial nerves. So: go home, take it very easy. Watch television, read. No jerky motions. Take the painkillers: we don't want you taking aspirin or ibuprofen. Do not work out . . ."

And so on.

While Weather approved her discharge, Cooper needed another approval, from an emergency room physician who had evaluated her for possible spinal damage. Melton came back by herself, the baby left with Fatima, to wait for her release. The ER doc didn't show up until almost one o'clock — "Because doctors' time is more precious than anyone else's," Melton said — and took two minutes to sign her out.

A nurse put her in a wheelchair, which she hadn't needed, and rolled her out to the car, and Melton drove her home. Fatima was there with the baby, Melton was attentive, but Cooper smiled and drifted past them, climbed the stairs to her bedroom. Melton puffed up a couple of pillows and scurried around making annoying noises, and Cooper finally told her she'd like to be alone to sleep.

Melton wasn't sure she should be alone, but Cooper took a painkiller and then asked Melton to leave. When the other woman was gone, she sank back into the pillows and . . .

She recalled it all, in widescreen with a billion color combinations, the bodies on the Persian carpet, the attack by Heath, all over again, all mixed up, over and over . . .

The jail was horrifying; not the conditions, the fact that he'd been in it. Heath was released hours after what he considered to be a self-defense fight with Margaret Cooper, rather than an attack on her. His two attorneys, who'd begun asking him for payment, had gone to the county attorney to challenge any charges against him, and had gotten a conditional release without bail.

As the assistant county attorney had seen it, there was a question about whether Margaret Cooper had simply gotten to her feet before shouting at Heath, or had lurched toward him, thereby initiating the fight, or had even attacked Heath. The broken glass that had cut her could creditably be excused as an accident intended by neither party, and the fall to the floor might have been the result of the two becoming tangled up.

And the assistant county attorney had used his ability to hold Heath for a bail hearing the next day, to get him to sign a waiver of any intent to sue for false arrest. Heath signed and was released: the jail was not a happy place for a man of his stature.

He was prepared on leaving to hide his face from reporters and TV cameras, but there weren't any. They either hadn't realized that he was being released, or, worse, he simply wasn't a big enough deal.

The attorneys, who he now considered to be little better than greedy scum, had given him a bill that detailed sixteen hours of work on his behalf, including travel time to his house, to the federal magistrate's court, to his house again, and to the jail.

The bill was for $3,200. They pressed him for a check, reminded him without any subtlety at all that he would likely need them again, and he'd given them the money.

At home, he'd fallen into a fugue similar to Cooper's, full of imagined pasts and futures, with an emphasis on disaster, rather than more pleasant outcomes. What could he do about an investigation into the charities? He was now off the board of Heart/Twin Cities, and when he'd asked the attorneys about the legality of his dismissal, they'd suggested that they were the wrong attorneys to ask — he needed someone with more involvement in the operations of tax-free foundations.

In other words, he might need the help of additional greedy scum. Of course, if he were indicted for problems with the charities, they'd be happy to help at that point. If he paid up front.

Lying on his bed, miserable, the pasts and futures flicking through his exhausted mind, he could think of one thing he could do: flee. Sell the house, sell everything, and get down to Antigua. If he were that far away, and the charges against him were confusing enough, if the evidence wasn't totally convincing, would St. Paul or the state of Minnesota come after him? They let killers walk free all the time . . .

Heath rolled over, face-down in the pillows, briefly — very briefly — considered suicide before rejecting the idea, and began to weep. That went on for a few minutes, then he pulled himself together, wiped his eyes on the pillowcase, and went down to the kitchen to poke around in the cupboard.

Sea-salt crinkle potato chips? Excellent.

Maybe stream a little porn.

Get his mind off things.

27

Sandy found two Donald Hesses in Minneapolis: one was fifty-eight and the other was twenty-eight. The younger didn't show up as a junior, and the two didn't look much alike, so they might not be related.

Sandy maintained a dozen Facebook accounts, went out looking for the right Donald Hess and found him: found a hundred photos taken over at least four or five years. The most recent showed him in boxing togs and posed like a blond Nazi fighter from the World War II era, including a flattop haircut brushed up and held hedge-like with a shiny hair cream.

He lived on Field Avenue, not far off West Seventh Street, a five-minute drive from the Silver Star.

Sandy said, "I looked up the time of sunset. It's like five minutes after six, but it doesn't get dark for a while after that. If he's going after Cooper, and he wants it dark, I think it'd be after the boxing class."

"See if you can find Facebook pages for a Carol-Ann Lee and Roger Smith," Virgil said, checking the names in his notebook. The Wiz had mentioned that they worked with Hess in the boxing classes. "Probably from St. Paul or close by."

There were lots of Carol Lees, including several in Minnesota, most of whom were clustered around the Twin Cities, and hundreds of Roger Smiths, so they gave up on Smith. There were only two Carol-Ann Lees in Minnesota, and only one posed in boxing gear. Sandy downloaded an image of her driver's license.

"Why would you talk to her?" Sandy asked. "You know Hess is the one."

"We're pretty sure, but not positive," Lucas said. "We also think the killer could well be going after Cooper tonight. If we're watching Hess and it turns out to be somebody else, we could have a tragedy. Better to know as much as we can about him."

"Ah. Okay. But — every person you talk to is another one who might warn Hess."

"That's why threats are so useful," Virgil said.

Sandy was working her way through Lee's Facebook page. "Says here . . ." she tapped the screen, ". . . she works at the Wabasha

Credit Union on Wabasha Street."

Lucas looked at Virgil: "What do you think?"

"Sure. Let's talk to her."

The Wabasha Credit Union was ten minutes away. When they got there, they were told by the manager that Lee was visiting her retired parents in The Villages, in Florida. With that dead end, they scouted Hess's house, where they saw no sign of life, and decided that a stakeout of the house would almost certainly give them away.

"Why don't we go to your house and get Ellen to make us some sandwiches," Virgil suggested. "Something healthier than the crap we've been eating."

"Good idea," Lucas said. "We had ribs last night and there are leftovers. Sparerib sandwiches with a light drizzle of sparerib gravy. Home fries with ketchup. Couple Dos Equis."

"Exactly what I had in mind," Virgil said. "Health food."

They did that. Weather got home ten minutes after they did, ate a sandwich with them, told Lucas that her tire alert had come on, on the way home, and he needed to increase the pressure in all four tires.

Right then.

Lucas had an electric tire inflator and he and Virgil spent fifteen minutes doing that and discussing the inaccuracy of inflator pressure gauges. At five-thirty, driving into another snow flurry, they left for the boxing club, leaving behind a satisfied, but not overwhelmingly grateful, Weather.

West Seventh was one of the oldest streets of St. Paul, connecting the downtown area to Fort Snelling, the site of the earliest American settlement in Minnesota. The street was a jumble of low redbrick buildings and new tall glassy structures. Because of the proximity of the Xcel Energy Center, home of the Minnesota Wild hockey team and host to music concerts, the street was dotted with restaurants and bars that gradually thinned out the farther west it went.

The Silver Star was just outside the entertainment area; while parking was easier there than farther east, closer to the Xcel Center, Lucas and Virgil, traveling separately, took a while to find spaces that would allow them to see the front of the boxing gym.

Once parked, they hooked up by phone, and both had binoculars that would let them see people coming and going from the gym. Ellen, the housekeeper, had offered them diminutive Halloween sacks of Fritos before they left, and they'd both helped themselves to four bags, along with Diet Cokes — the idea being not to eat anything that would make a toilet necessary.

Virgil was eating Fritos and watching the snow fall when he spotted Hess drive past. He called Lucas, and mumbled through a mouthful of corn chips, "Here he comes — silver Subaru." Lucas watched as Hess turned a corner a half block from the gym. He hopped out of his Cayenne and hustled a block down to the corner, then around the corner, and saw Hess parking the car in a space down the side street. Hess got out of the car with a duffel, and without looking toward Lucas, walked around the corner and went inside the gym.

"The problem," Lucas told Virgil on the phone, "is that he might walk to Maggie's place. If we're back here watching the car, and he goes out the front, we could miss him. I think you should come down here, and I'll stay where I am on the street."

Virgil agreed, though if Hess should go to the corner and then turn toward Lucas, rather than away, Lucas would have to make an illegal and noticeable U-turn on the busy street to get behind him. Virgil, on the other hand, would have to wait until he was around the corner before he could turn on his lights and follow, and if Hess made another quick turn, it was possible that neither one of them would see him.

"I think we needed another guy to do this," Virgil said.

"Nah. We good."

The next two hours dragged by. The temperature was falling like a rock, and they had to turn the car engines on and off to stay comfortable. The snow got heavier, then quit for a while, and came back for another round.

At ten minutes to eight, earlier than they'd expected, Hess walked out the gym's front door without his duffel, and started jogging away from Lucas, down West Seventh.

"Shit, he's on foot! He's wearing a sweat suit with a hoodie, he hasn't put the hood up yet, he's bareheaded . . ." Lucas called. "I'll try to get ahead of him. He's running, he's jogging."

Virgil pulled out of his parking space. "What do you want me to do?"

"Can't go too slow, he'll spot us. I'll go by and try to get around the block, and come back, maybe you can switch in and track him for a while . . . Christ, it's dark back here . . ."

"Where are you . . ."

"He turned off Seventh, I don't know what street this is. It's that corner by the Day by Day Café, he's running down that street toward I-35 . . ."

"I'm coming."

"I had to go past him. We're coming to the end of the street. Ah, goddamnit. There's a sidewalk here going off to the south, but there's no street, I can't follow him, he's running south . . ."

"I'm looking at my nav system," Virgil said. "I'll try to get ahead of him . . . Let me see . . ."

"Hurry!"

"He's gotta come out at St. Clair Avenue," Virgil called. "I'll park on one of the streets there, maybe I can follow him on foot . . ."

"What, in a parka? If you run in a parka, he'll see you . . ."

"I think he'll go across I-35 at St. Clair and then follow the I-35 exit backwards until he's under Crocus Circle, and then climb the bluff," Virgil said. "You should go right up to the house and hide, I'll blow past him if he gets on the bridge and I'll have to go around a block or two, but I can get on the opposite end of the Circle from you. We should have him between us."

"Do that. Check where he's going before

you make your move . . ."

"If I can," Virgil said. "I'm going past the Day by Day . . ."

"I'm lost back here," Lucas shouted. "The streets aren't where they're supposed to be. I can see Grand but I can't . . . Fuck it, I'm taking the sidewalk."

Lucas bounced over a curb up onto a sidewalk, brushed past a couple of trees, drove a block on the sidewalk to Grand Avenue, bumped over another curb onto Grand Avenue, which would take him most of the way to the Circle. "I'm on Grand. I'm good, if nobody calls the cops on me," he shouted at the cell phone.

"I'm at Webster, I don't think he could have gotten here yet," Virgil shouted back. "I'm gonna hide."

Webster was a short, quiet street, with on-street parking. Virgil pulled to the side of Webster and launched himself out of the truck and ran across the street. His view of the bridge that Hess would have to cross was blocked by a tree, so he ran a half block to the tree and stood behind it, waiting.

Not for long. Hess ran out of the sidewalk he'd taken and onto the bridge over I-35.

Virgil had his phone in his hand and called, "He's crossing the bridge. He's crossing the bridge. He's five minutes from

492

Maggie's, no more."

"I'm almost there. I'll be in old lady Muller's front yard by the streetlight. If he comes up the bluff, I should see him."

"I'm coming," Virgil said. He backed the truck into St. Clair Avenue and accelerated, not too hard, toward the bridge that Hess was crossing. He followed and watched as Hess turned down what the city called Pleasant Avenue, but which served as a very long exit from the parkway.

Hess was running easily — *he works in a gym, what did I expect?* Virgil thought — and was only four hundred yards or so from the point where he'd turn up the bluff. If Virgil followed the network of roads around to Crocus Circle, he'd have to drive more than a mile, because of the odd geometry of the area.

Or, he could turn the wrong way, down the exit, behind Hess, to where another street intersected with Pleasant. Because his truck was a cop car, he had a switch that could turn off all the lights; he did that and turned down the wrong way on Pleasant Avenue. There were no cars coming up, and he coasted downhill. He could still see Hess running a hundred yards ahead of him, but Hess never looked back. Virgil made the turn on the intersecting street, hit the lights and accelerated up the bluff.

In a little more than a minute, he was turning into the Circle. "I'm here," he said on the phone. "He's probably on the bluff by now, or close. I'll be right down by the last streetlight. Don't shoot the bush by the streetlight."

"You're good. I saw you go in," Lucas said.

28

Hess had gone barehanded to the Silver Star's front desk and asked, "Have you seen The Wiz?"

"Isn't he with the kids?"

"Not right now. Maybe he's taking a whiz."

The deskman shrugged and Hess casually pushed through the front door to the sidewalk, as though going out for a breath of air. As soon as the door closed, he started running. Hess ran three miles every other day. Cooper's house was about eight-tenths of a mile away, so to get there and back, he'd be running only a mile and a half.

Routine.

He got off West Seventh Street as quickly as he could, following a pre-planned route through the darker, older neighborhoods north of the street. He followed Goodrich Avenue to the end, then swerved left onto a sidewalk that paralleled I-35. Snow was drifting down around him and he pulled up the hood on his hoodie and stepped up the pace.

A simple plan: run, kill, run.

The boxing-class kids were with The Wiz — Hess had said he was off to the bathroom. The run to Cooper's house would take around eight minutes. Once there, he would go straight in, no hesitation this time. Kick that garage door if it was locked, kick the door to the interior. Confront Cooper, get the flash drives, kill, and leave, running. Down the bluff, back the way he came, across West Seventh, then behind the club, and in the back entrance to the kids' locker room.

Talk to The Wiz, talk to the kids, get his duffel bag, talk to the guys at the front desk, then out to the car and home.

Maybe not a perfect alibi, if he ever needed one, but a good one.

He came to the end of the sidewalk, crossed the bridge over I-35, big gouts of breath-steam now coming from his mouth, his heart beating hard from exercise, cold, and the stress. He turned down Pleasant Avenue until he was directly below Crocus Circle. He stepped off the street and into the brush below the bluff, caught his breath, watched and listened, then began climbing.

He stopped again, with his head below the crest of the bluff, and listened again. Heard the breeze that was pushing the snow, and nothing more. Ahead of him, to his right, he could see the streetlight at the end of the street.

He climbed the last few feet to the top, right to the edge of the brush, ten feet from the street he'd have to cross, and he stopped again, to catch his breath, and to listen.

The front door across the street slammed and Margaret Cooper ran toward him screaming something he didn't understand.

Cooper and Melton had been sniping at each other: Cooper was flapping around the house like a crippled bat. She didn't know why Hess hadn't come the night before, was worried that he'd not come back at all. But if he did, she thought, tonight was the best guess.

Melton wanted to talk with Lucas and Virgil, tell them what they knew — without the break-in at Hess's house — and see if they could find a pretext for a search. "If anyone kills Hess, it should be Lucas. He's willing to do it, and if Hess resists, he *will* do it," she argued.

Cooper was adamant and increasingly angry. "Don Hess is *mine.* I don't want

Davenport or Flowers anywhere near him. Not until he's dead. Then they *will* search his house, and they *will* find the computers and flash drives."

"This is so dangerous. For you," Melton said, turning away. Her eyes flooded with tears.

"If you don't want to stick by me, you can go home," Cooper said.

Melton was shocked. "Go home? I've been with you all the way through this. I helped you buy an illegal gun, for God's sakes. I helped you break into a house. I could go to jail . . ."

Cooper held up her hands. "Okay. Okay. I don't want you to leave. But I want Hess."

They had a quick dinner of tomato soup and rice; carried the baby up to their observation window, and put her in a bassinette, and let her sleep. Cooper had the revolver in her hands, turning the cylinder, checking and rechecking it.

After a while, Melton asked, "If you do this, if you get Hess, then what?"

"Well, after they search his house, I don't think anyone would indict me for —"

"That's not what I meant," Melton interrupted. "What are you going to do with your life? Just go back to the U? After this, you'll be a little controversial."

"I haven't thought through all of that," Cooper said. "I've got all the money in the world. Maybe . . . I could set up a Sand Foundation, support the arts or something. I don't know, Ann. Maybe I'll get out of the Twin Cities. Buy a house in Los Angeles, or maybe a place in New York. I don't know. I didn't expect to be a widow before I was forty. I don't know what I'm going to do."

Melton picked up her night-vision scope. "Is there . . . ?"

"Where?"

"Ten yards left of the streetlight, in Mrs. Muller's yard. I thought I saw . . ."

"I see it. I see *him,*" Cooper said.

Melton: "Is that . . ."

Cooper: "Yes! Goddamnit, that's Lucas. I'm going out there."

"Wait! Just wait!"

Cooper was already moving, gun in hand, running out of the room and down the stairs, Melton trailing. Cooper scooped up a puffy jacket at the door, pulled it on, and said, "Watch the baby."

"Maggie, this is crazy."

"Crazy." Cooper turned on her. "That's right. I'm crazy. I *am* crazy."

She yanked the door open and launched

herself across the porch and down the steps and she screamed "Hey! Hey!" running toward Davenport, who was standing at the end of the block, next to an oak tree.

Lucas thought, *Ah, shit.*

Hess, thirty yards away, thought, *No!*

She was coming for him, Hess thought, and she had a gun. How she'd seen him, he didn't know, but he lifted his pistol and fired four fast shots and Cooper went down.

Lucas, startled, pivoted toward the spot where he'd seen the muzzle flashes and fired a tight spread across the bushes, missed, and heard the shooter thrashing through the bushes, heading slantwise down the hill.

He punched the Favorites tab on his phone and Virgil answered instantly: "What the hell happened?"

"Maggie's shot! He's coming your way, man, I think he's heading back across the slope."

Hess stumbled as he fired, his heel catching on a root, and he fell backwards. He saw Cooper falling as he fell, and then there were more gunshots and close, not from Cooper. Confused, he got to his hands and knees, dropped the pistol, picked it up, and he began half-crawling, half-falling across the slope down the way he'd come. A tree branch ripped across his forehead and he put up a hand to protect his eyes and continued crablike across the slope.

Virgil moved down the slope with his shotgun, couldn't see through the snow and the foliage, and he continued slipping down the slope while listening for Hess coming toward him.

Lucas turned on his iPhone flashlight and when Cooper tried to sit up he pushed her back down and asked, "Where are you hit?"

"I don't know, I . . . my leg hurts."

She was wearing black jeans and he couldn't see a wound but ran his hand down her leg and it came back wet and red in the flash. He probed, found the wound. Melton had come out on the porch and screamed, "What happened? What happened?"

"Maggie's been hit," Lucas shouted back. "Bring a towel, quick, quick!"

Melton ducked back inside the house and Lucas said to Cooper, "This might hurt," and he pushed the tip of his finger through the bullet hole in her jeans and ripped the hole wider, then put his index fingers from both hands in the bigger hole and ripped the hole wide.

The wound was on the outside of her leg,

which was good, because it wouldn't have impacted her femoral artery.

"Gonna be okay," he said to Cooper, who was now lying flat. He turned his phone over and called 9-1-1, interrupted the operator who was starting through her "Is this an emergency?" routine and he shouted, "U.S. Marshal Lucas Davenport. We have a woman shot at . . ." He looked at Cooper. "What's your street address?" She told him and he repeated it to the operator. "We need an ambulance and some cop cars, the shooter is being pursued on foot along I-35 by a BCA agent."

The operator started to ask another question and Lucas shouted, "Just get the ambulances here, I'm going in pursuit."

He clicked off as Melton ran up with a towel and he said, "She was shot in the leg, I've ripped open her pant leg, the slug went all the way through, you need to put pressure on both sides and hold it there, hard. An ambulance should be on the way but call 9-1-1 to make sure it is, I was pretty abrupt . . ."

"What are you . . ."

"I'm going after Hess. I'm hoping Virgil will slow him down."

Muller, the old lady from the Victorian house, hurried up and said, "I'm talking to

502

9-1-1 . . ."

"Get them here," Lucas said, and he ran down the street and at the same time called Virgil.

"Where are you?" Virgil asked, quietly.

"Up on top, on the street. Where should I come down?"

"I can hear him. He's behind and below me, trying to get down to the street. You should get up to the bush where I was and come straight down the bluff. He has to break out in the open. I'll see if I can reach him with the shotgun."

"I'm coming," Lucas said. "Leave your phone on."

At the end of the street, Lucas went over the side, crashing through the brush, not trying for subtlety, using the flashlight on his phone to dodge trees and branches, barely keeping his balance as he went. As he got close to the street, he shouted "Phone" and Virgil was there in his ear and said, "You're above me, go farther to your right. You're close, I'm at the street."

Virgil broke out into the street and looking farther right, saw Hess running hard up Pleasant Avenue toward the bridge over I-35. Virgil lifted the shotgun but a car came across the bridge and slowed, and Hess ran right toward it, and as Lucas broke out onto the street Virgil started running and called back to Lucas, "Car in background."

They saw Hess run onto the bridge and they were forty yards back, running uphill, and Hess was gaining on them. At the bridge over I-35, Hess was about to get off the far end, and Virgil stopped, took aim and fired a shot.

Hess stumbled, recovered, and hobbled toward the sidewalk that ran along the parkway.

"Slowed him down," Virgil called to Lucas. They ran on through the thickening snow flurry and Lucas shouted, "Take it easy. This is like last year, the dark and the cold. Like last year."

Virgil didn't reply, but ran on, the shotgun at port arms, ready to go. They could hear sirens on the other side of the parkway; the ambulance and the cops were on the way, if not already at Cooper's.

Lucas still had the flashlight on and at the end of the sidewalk, shouted, "Blood."

Virgil could see it; not red, but black on the snow in the phone's LED light, like somebody had been dripping oil from a leaky can. They moved slower, Virgil now with the shotgun at his shoulder, Lucas a step behind, scanning the brush on both sides of the sidewalk.

They moved past a jog in the concrete, and saw Hess up ahead, fifty yards, and they closed on him. Hess had the gun by his side and was hobbling, hurt. He looked back over his shoulder and quit. Virgil shouted, "Gun on the ground, gun on the ground . . ."

Hess turned and shouted, "Fuck you," and in one quick motion, threw the pistol at Virgil's head. Both Virgil and Lucas nearly pulled their triggers, but as the gun flew past them, Hess sank to the ground and began to cry.

Lucas got on his phone again, called 9-1-1 and said, "Marshal Davenport. We have a wounded man on the ground near the end of the St. Clair Avenue bridge where the sidewalk runs along I-35. We're about fifty yards up the sidewalk. We need more cops and an ambulance."

Neither Virgil nor Lucas had handcuffs, and they had to wait for a St. Paul squad car. Hess was cuffed and loaded into the ambulance. Another squad car came, and Virgil pointed out to the sergeant where he'd fired his shotgun and shucked out the shell, and the blood trail along the sidewalk.

A third car gave them a lift back to Cooper's. Cooper was on the way to the hospital, Melton following with the baby. Virgil called the emergency room and emphasized that their two wounded patients needed to be kept securely separate.

While he was doing that, Lucas was showing the responding cops the area where Hess had been when he fired the shot that hit Cooper. With the light of two powerful Maglites probing the hillside, they marked two shells, then a third.

Lucas thought there had been four or five shots, but getting down on his hands and knees, looking at the shells, he came to his feet with a grin and said to Virgil, "Same shells. Same gun, I bet. We got the motherfucker."

"You gonna have dreams about this?" Virgil asked. "The cold, the snow, chasing the guy through the trees?"

"I don't think so. This was good. This was fine, didn't even notice my leg," Lucas said. He was ebullient. "What a fuckin' trip, huh? Cooper will be okay . . . probably . . . and we got the Sand killer. Now the question is, do we call Russo and Durey, or Daisy Jones?"

Virgil: "When did Russo and Durey ever put us on TV?"

"My man," Lucas said.

29

The crime scene crew needed specifics about the shootings and the locations. Lucas and Virgil traced Hess's approach, Hess's shots, Lucas's shots, and Hess's flight down the hillside. Three of Lucas's shells and four of Hess's were located and bagged. Virgil's shotgun shell was photographed, measured from marked locations, and bagged. Hess's Glock and Cooper's revolver were photographed and bagged, with the notation that Cooper's gun hadn't been fired.

That took two hours in what had stopped being a flurry and had become a snowstorm.

Russo arrived, shoulders hunched against the snow, and said, "It would have been nice to know what you assholes were doing, but . . . good job. Wish I'd been here. It feels like somebody took a boulder off my chest."

Durey wasn't quite as effusive, but was

pleased.

Not as pleased as Daisy Jones, who broke the story over the heads of the other stations like a big gooey egg. She had numerous details, but never said exactly where she got them. Extensive contacts within the St. Paul Police Department was what she implied. The anchor on the rival WCCO quoted her on the air, while managing to suggest that Jones might not be entirely reliable.

When Virgil and Lucas were released from the scene, they drove to Regions Hospital, where Cooper had been treated for the leg wound and taken to a private room. The docs said she'd hurt for a while, but a moderate amount of physical therapy would see her fully repaired.

They were allowed to see her, in her room. Melton sat in a corner, with the baby, and smiled quickly, but Cooper didn't: "You didn't kill him!" she screeched. "You let him go!"

"We don't execute people," Virgil said. "I shot him, they're still taking pellets out of his legs, and he quit. He threw his gun at us."

"I don't give a shit about that," Cooper snarled. "You had a chance to kill him and you didn't. He's going to get away with it!

He murdered my family and you let him get away with it!"

"That's not how . . ." Lucas began.

One of her arms was wired into a bag of saline, but with the other, she pointed at the door: "Get out of here. I don't want to see you. I thought you were my friends. Get out."

Walking down the hall, Virgil said, "She's a mess."

The next morning, Hess had a public defender who told him not to talk to anyone, about anything. A search warrant from a state judge got the BCA's crime scene crew into Hess's house, and it didn't take long to notice that the cold air return register had been repeatedly taken off and screwed back on. Inside, the crew found three laptops and three flash drives, all conveniently carrying Hess's fingerprints.

Hess, through his attorney, claimed that he didn't know how the computers and flash drives got in the cold air return. He suggested that Cooper had broken into his house and planted them there, but couldn't — wouldn't — explain how his fingerprints got on everything. Cooper said she had no idea where Hess lived. The videos on the flash drives, along with the fingerprints, hanged him.

The gun hanged him again, in case being hanged once wasn't enough. Everything about it matched the Sand murder weapon. He was charged with three first-degree murders as well as the production and possession of child pornography. Some videos of the children in the locker room were traced to his iPhone through a tiny, nearly invisible flaw on the phone's lens. More were traced, through metadata, to a Sony video camera apparently hidden in his duffel bag, with a cutout at one end so only the lens would be visible from the outside.

St. Paul cops began tracking down his young victims and found some. They never found images of the Sand boys.

A week after the shooting, Cooper still wouldn't talk to Virgil, because she'd decided that Virgil was the one who could have taken the shot but didn't. She did take a call from Lucas.

"Hess has no defense," Lucas said. "He'll get life without parole. With a reasonable life expectancy, he could spend forty or fifty years locked in a pen. I personally would rather be dead."

"He *should* be dead, really dead," she said. "These criminals understand one thing: if you murder people, you die. That's clear. Specific. A lot of these thugs think spending time in prison is like a badge of honor."

Lucas: "You could talk to the U.S. Attorney. If the feds took the trial, he could get the death penalty. Probably would. You could go watch him die."

"Go away," she said, and she hung up.

There would be no reconciliation; not soon, anyway.

Durey called her and said, "We have no evidentiary use for your revolver. I can have somebody drop it off at your place."

"Keep it. Or throw it away," she told him. "I have no use for it anymore. You're keeping Hess nice and safe, aren't you?"

Melton stayed with Cooper for three days after she got out of the hospital, and then Cooper asked her to leave.

"But why?" Melton asked. "We're a team, we pulled this off . . ."

"We didn't pull off anything, Ann. Hess got away from us. But basically . . . I want some very quiet time. I don't want people talking to me. I have to get my mind straight . . . I love you, dear, but . . . I really need some space."

"You're going to take care of Chelsea on your own?"

511

"I can do that," Cooper said. "I'll have Fatima when I need her."

Melton had brought a suitcase full of clothes to Cooper's house, so after more talk, she repacked the case and went back to Edina. The first day she was gone, she called Cooper four times, and finally Cooper said, "Could we agree to talk every couple of days? I just want to sit. And sleep. And try to work out what has happened to me."

So they stopped talking.

The next day, Cooper was sitting in the family room with Chelsea, turned on the television, and saw Noah Heath on *Jonesing for News*.

"How long have you known me?" Heath demanded of Jones. "These lies, these speculations . . ."

He broke down and began to weep real tears. Jones may have rolled her eyes, but she dug under the set and handed him a Kleenex. He thanked her, wiping his eyes.

"You're saying that what we have heard — that there might have been irregularities with the charities, that you may know . . . something . . . about the murders of Doreen Pollard and Darrell Hinton, none of that is true."

"Not true! Not true! I poured my *life* into

those charities. And my *own* money. I gave more than *anyone.* There was very unethical police investigation that led to a search warrant that turned up nothing! Nothing! But the real problem was that these allegations were spread by a woman who, indeed, did suffer a tragedy and perhaps was . . . disoriented by the tragedy. She was the person who got me removed from the board of Heart/Twin Cities. My charity!"

"That was the situation when you were arrested . . ."

"I was released! Almost immediately! Never prosecuted! All the witnesses knew that she was the one who attacked *me.* Frankly, we are not done with that. I plan to pursue civil damages . . ."

He went on for a while. Cooper listened with interest and calm, at one point shaking her head: "Liar."

That night, she spent time thinking about Heath, and everything he represented. And in her mind, quoted herself, from the last time she'd spoken to Davenport: *"He should be dead . . . These criminals understand one thing: if you murder people, you die. That's clear. Specific. A lot of these thugs think spending time in prison is like a badge of honor."*

She wasn't quite asleep when the dreams

513

came, like bad actors edging onstage, Alex and Blaine and Arthur and Heath, all mixed up, and she began running in bed, her knees churning, and Chelsea began to cry and she woke up . . . she sat hunched over the edge of her bed and didn't sleep. Feared the sleep.

She finally got up, wandered into the bathroom, and looked at her ruined face. Everyone who saw it, Melton, the doctors, even Fatima, said it looked fine. Better every day. But it didn't. Her face was ruined, she'd never act again. She couldn't bear to look at herself . . .

She was sick, but . . .

Then she cured herself.

The cure came to her as she sat watching Chelsea in her crib waving her hands and feet and gurgling and pooping, like a baby prodded to follow a movie script.

And the light went on.

She sat at the breakfast table each morning for the next two weeks and wrote a script, complete with the necessary characters and plot points. When she was done with it, and satisfied, and well rehearsed, she called Melton.

They agreed to meet at a café in Minneapolis for lunch. She left Chelsea with Fatima and drove over, mouthing her lines and mentally rehearsing her actions. Her smile was professionally perfect when she saw Melton scrunched in a far corner of the café.

And she gave the other woman an ever-broader smile as she walked between tables to Melton's booth. There, she leaned over and gave Melton a lingering kiss on the lips, noted without rancor by the other patrons of the restaurant, the audience.

"You look different. Like something happened," Melton said.

Cooper agreed. "I turned a corner," she said, right on script. "I've been talking to Tom, and we're going to meet tomorrow and hit some tennis balls. I've asked the U to give me the next quarter off, and they've agreed. I'm going to run out to LA, to Malibu, to look at a house."

Cooper didn't give a rat's ass about the tennis practice or the time off.

Melton reached across the table and gripped her wrist: "This is wonderful. How's your leg? You said you were still limping last week."

"Ah, it's fine. Probably have an odd scar that you'd see in a bathing suit. I mean, it couldn't be anything but a bullet wound. Maybe I'll have Weather look at it. I know she does scar revisions."

"I bet she can fix it so nobody would ever know . . ."

They talked for an hour, Melton getting more excited as they ate the meal.

Finally Cooper said, "Listen, I know you have to work, you're a working lawyer with a big practice. Do you think you could get away to Malibu with me? Look at this house. We could run out a week from Friday, stay the weekend, and be back on Monday . . . Go first class all the way."

They talked about schedules and favored airlines and Melton took out her computer and they looked up the listing for the Malibu house, and Melton *ooh'd* and *aah'd* and talked about learning to surf . . .

The talk about real estate pinged at the back of Cooper's damaged mind.

Heath claimed she'd ruined him. Both Lucas and Virgil were positive that he'd murdered his employees, but as far as she could tell from Daisy Jones's interview, he seemed much more concerned about his reputation as it involved the charities than the question of whether he'd committed murder.

On the way home, she drove past his Summit Avenue mansion; nothing moving. No "For Sale" sign. Maybe he was going to try to gut it out in the Cities.

Then at home, she'd had a cup of coffee with Fatima and helped feed the baby, though Fatima, she had to admit, was better with Chelsea than she was. When they were done with that, she went up to her office and called up the Zillow real estate site . . . and there it was.

Heath's house was for sale for $1.4 million. He was getting ready to skip. She thought about it, got her phone, and called Virgil.

Virgil wasn't polite: "Yes?"

"Virgil, I'm sorry," she said, injecting a note of regret into her well-trained voice.

There was a moment of silence, but Virgil came back with a softer tone. "It's been rough," he said. "You're allowed the anger."

"Well," she said. Then, "I saw Noah Heath on the Daisy Jones show. He seems to think everything is okay."

"Not okay, people are digging. There's not much to go on. We've got that dirt from his shovel, but there's a question of whether we're going to be allowed to use it. When we searched his house, we never found that rain hoodie that the man in the van was wearing at the airport . . . So . . ."

"He's going to get away with murder."

"There's a question of what would be worse for a guy like him — going to jail, or

517

just being generally despised as a murderer and swindler of charities," Virgil said. "Heath lived for his status in the community."

"I suppose," she said. Then she laughed and said, "I called you because I thought you'd be a little more forgiving about my . . . attitude . . . than Lucas. I'm going to have these bullet wound scars on my leg. Do you think if I called Weather and talked to her about that, that Lucas would, you know, object or discourage her?"

Cooper didn't give a rat's ass about the scars on her leg.

"No. You know, Lucas might have killed Hess if it had been him, by himself. He knows that I wouldn't go along with it. He's a hard case. He's like you. He thinks Hess should be dead," Virgil said. "But he wouldn't discourage Weather at all. Give him a call. I believe he'd be happy to hear from you."

That evening, she called Lucas, and talked to him about Hess and Heath, and about the freedom brought by resignation, about letting the law have its way.

The new Cooper didn't give a rat's ass about the law.

After talking to Lucas, she spoke with Weather. Weather would be happy to look at her leg. Cooper told her, "I'm thinking of buying a place in Malibu. I'm going out a week from Friday . . ."

Cooper and Melton stayed at an inn on the Malibu beach, an excellent but slightly rustic hotel. They didn't swim, the days were too cold and the water colder yet. They did see young girls in bikinis making Tik-Tok dance videos . . . and they got drunk on a bottle of wine each night and laughed together. Building the relationship.

Cooper didn't give a rat's ass about the relationship.

They spent an hour looking at the Malibu place, which was nice, at a ridiculous price. The Realtor had looked her up on the Internet and was aware of what had happened to her family, and also of Sand's net worth, now Cooper's.

"Prices *are* ridiculous," the Realtor said, "But there's no better investment than a California beach . . ."

The house, Cooper told the Realtor, was not exactly what she wanted; she could wait. But please stay in touch . . .

Cooper didn't give a rat's ass about a California beach.

Back in St. Paul, the weather was cold and clear. Fatima made dinner, and then went home, leaving Chelsea with Cooper. Cooper took her upstairs, to the office, put her securely on Alex's treasured full leather club couch, went to the desk, dug through the file cabinet, and there behind the last of the files, took out the silenced pistol she'd gotten from Henry James Carter.

Melton and the cops, Virgil and Lucas, Tom Burston, all believed she was coming back. Hess was in jail. Heath's ramblings easy to ignore: he was finished in St. Paul, a fate, Lucas told her, worse than death for a man like Heath.

But she was not back.

She was *not.*

She looked at the pistol, handled it, jacked a shell in the chamber. Picked up Chelsea: "C'mon baby."

Noah Heath had a sack of caramel corn and he intended to eat all of it, sitting in front of the television. He had lots of worries: the investigations, the sale of the house — no firm bites, yet — a conversation that the board of the Town and Country Club had asked to have with him.

He'd put them off, but he couldn't delay forever. They would ask him to resign.

So he was worried. He called up Fox News to see what was going on in the world, marveled at the news reader's presence: she was so beautiful, he thought, she might have come from a different planet.

He was still marveling and crunching when the doorbell rang. He looked at his watch: seven o'clock. Dark outside. He wasn't expecting anyone.

He turned on the porch light and looked out through a small window inset in the door. A thin figure, back turned, holding what looked like a bundle of some sort. A delivery?

He opened the door and the person turned and smiled at him. If he weren't punished, he would get away with murder.

And Noah Heath snarled, "You! What the fuck do y—"

Cooper pulled the door closed. She could see or hear no alarms, just the calm, cold, November night. Far up the avenue, somebody had already put up Christmas lights, winking red, blue, and green into the night.

She said, "C'mon, baby. Let's go home."

ABOUT THE AUTHOR

John Sandford is the pseudonym for the Pulitzer Prize-winning journalist John Camp. He is the author of thirty-one Prey novels; four Kidd novels; twelve Virgil Flowers novels; three YA novels coauthored with his wife, Michele Cook; and three other books.

The employees of Thorndike Press hope you have enjoyed this Large Print book. All our Thorndike Large Print titles are designed for easy reading, and all our books are made to last. Other Thorndike Press Large Print books are available at your library, through selected bookstores, or directly from us.

For information about titles, please call:
  (800) 223-1244

or visit our website at:
  gale.com/thorndike